Praise for

Dream On, Ramona Riley

"Ashley Herring Blake writes sweet, sexy romances with a supporting cast of queer found family like no one else. In *Dream On, Ramona Riley,* I was so invested in Ramona and Dylan rediscovering the fireworks they'd felt with each other even as far back as an early teenage encounter. Set in a *Schitt's Creek*–esque small town filled with homey diners and gossip and secret places, this book is such a breath of fresh air. I can't wait to spend more time in Clover Lake!"

—Alicia Thompson, *USA Today* bestselling author of *Never Been Shipped*

"Another winning sweet, sexy, sapphic small-town romance from Ashley Herring Blake. As always, Blake gives readers two complicated but lovable heroines to root for and fall in love with—as they fall in love with each other. I ate up the behind-the-scenes moviemaking that descended upon Clover Lake, the family drama swirling throughout the narrative, and of course the beautiful—and sexy!—love story between Dylan and Ramona."

—Amy Spalding, author of *On Her Terms* and *For Her Consideration*

"A lovely romance about finding the person who makes you want better for yourself. Dylan's and Ramona's respective heartaches are fully captured on the page, and yet the story still felt as cozy and comforting (and, occasionally, scorching hot) as a cup of tea in a small-town café."

—Rachel Runya Katz, author of *Isn't It Obvious*

"Blake enchants with this sapphic second-chance romance. . . . The ensuing relationship is equal parts sensual and sincere, and the exploration of ambition, aspiration, and resilient bonds adds heart. This is a winner."

—*Publishers Weekly* (starred review)

"This contemporary fake-dating romance is multilayered, with plenty of deep emotion, revealing backstories, humor, and steamy scenes that scorch the pages. Blake's fans will be over the moon at this series launch, while newcomers will find a new favorite author to follow."

—*Library Journal* (starred review)

"The book is steamy while also being a sweet and sensitive look at the complex feelings of the characters, exploring how difficult it can be to trust others when you don't trust yourself. It's a fantastic start to Herring Blake's Clover Lake queer rom-com series."

—*Booklist* (starred review)

Berkley Titles by Ashley Herring Blake

Delilah Green Doesn't Care
Astrid Parker Doesn't Fail
Iris Kelly Doesn't Date
Make the Season Bright
Dream On, Ramona Riley
Get Over It, April Evans

Get Over It, April Evans

ASHLEY HERRING BLAKE

Berkley Romance
New York

BERKLEY ROMANCE
Published by Berkley
An imprint of Penguin Random House LLC
1745 Broadway, New York, NY 10019
penguinrandomhouse.com

Book design by Alison Cnockaert

Library of Congress Cataloging-in-Publication Data

Names: Blake, Ashley Herring author
Title: Get over it, April Evans / Ashley Herring Blake.
Description: First edition. | New York : Berkley Romance, 2026.
Identifiers: LCCN 2025023615 (print) | LCCN 2025023616 (ebook) |
ISBN 9780593816011 trade paperback | ISBN 9780593816028 ebook
Subjects: LCGFT: Fiction | Romance fiction | Lesbian fiction | Novels
Classification: LCC PS3602.L3413 G48 2026 (print) | LCC PS3602.L3413 (ebook)
LC record available at https://lccn.loc.gov/2025023615
LC ebook record available at https://lccn.loc.gov/2025023616

First Edition: February 2026

Printed in the United States of America
1st Printing

The authorized representative in the EU for product safety and compliance is Penguin Random House Ireland, Morrison Chambers, 32 Nassau Street, Dublin D02 YH68, Ireland, https://eu-contact.penguin.ie.

For everyone who's ever been made to feel
like they are too much and not enough all at once.

You're perfect.

Author's Note

While *Get Over It, April Evans* is a joyful romance, please be aware that this story contains discussions of religious trauma, discussions of homophobia, discussions of gaslighting by an ex, mentions of parental neglect and indifference, mentions of family estrangement, and one mention of parental death in a car accident. There are also consensual and explicit sex scenes, and a scene at a BDSM play party, which includes some light impact play. Please take care of yourself while reading this story, and always.

Get Over It, April Evans

Chapter One

APRIL EVANS KNEW she was prone to astrological panic.

She'd always put a lot of stock in the stars, knew when some planet's position was messing with everyone's communication skills, and had three different zodiac-themed tattoos. Still, she'd like to think *panic* was the wrong word, despite what her parents would say about it. She was simply dealing with at least twenty complicated feelings at any given time, just like any triple Scorpio.

But right now, as she stood in her own driveway and handed her house keys over to a divorced MILF with shiny brown hair named Trudy while her two kids poked their fingers through the holes of April's cat carriers, April definitely felt a sense of astrological doom.

"So garbage day is on Monday," she said to Trudy, even though these sorts of details were posted on the refrigerator. "And if you have any trouble with that hallway bathroom faucet, just shoot me a text."

"Perfect," Trudy said, tucking the keys into her linen shorts. "I know the kids and I are going to love summering here. Your house is adorable. So eclectic!"

April smiled without her teeth, her eyes gazing up at her

admittedly adorable mint-green bungalow. She'd bought it nearly eight years ago, the first year her tattoo shop made a profit, and now she was a landlord, renting it out to a Clover Lake summer person for the next three months because she could no longer afford her mortgage.

She looked at her houseplants on the front porch, which Trudy had promised to water, but had a sinking feeling in her gut they'd all be dried out and brown by August.

Just like her life.

Okay, fine, that was dramatic, but in her defense, her horoscope for the last month had been nothing but darkness and gloom, words like *change* and *risk* and *decisions* constantly floating before her eyes. She shivered, thinking of Madame Andromeda's declaration about her life just this very morning.

> Lately, you've been feeling small and overlooked. For a Scorpio, this is unfamiliar territory. So this week, try to view challenges as bright new opportunities to grow—there is always something beautiful hiding in the unexpected.

She was fucking tired of *unexpected*. And while she was a devout believer in Andromeda's clairvoyant insights, this proclamation was simply a sugarcoated way of saying, *Buckle up, bitch.*

And she'd really, really rather not.

"Mommy, can't we keep the kitties?" one of Trudy's kids asked. The smaller one—named Coltrane or Copeland or something else that sounded like a jazz musician's last name—pressed their face against the carrier's door. Bianca del Kitty, April's grouchy lynx point Siamese cat she'd had for seven years and who was named for one of April's favorite drag queens, hissed, while Bob the Drag Cat, her beloved orange dumb-dumb and the namesake of another incredible queen, lounged in his own carrier like he was at a spa.

"I don't think so, honey," Trudy said, but then lifted her eyebrows at April. "Any chance you need a couple of cat sitters for the summer?" She placed a hand on top of each of her children's heads. "They'd take good care of them."

April pressed a hand to her chest, appalled. This woman had taken her house—granted, April had freely offered it to her—but she would not take her fucking cats.

They were literally all she had at this point.

Two cats, one broken-down business, and a partridge in a pear tree.

In reality, she knew she had a lot more than that, like disapproving parents and a failed engagement and a best friend who lived three thousand miles away and hadn't responded to her last four texts. And let's not forget a love life that made her want to drill a hole through her skull. Add *uncertain financial future* to the list, and she was a veritable cornucopia of success.

"I'm good, thanks," she said as calmly as she could, then said a quick goodbye before she could add *victim of catnapping* to her list of accolades. She grabbed both carrier handles and hauled them to her ten-year-old turquoise MINI Cooper, which was already stuffed to overflowing. She didn't look at her house as she backed out of the driveway, nor did she mentally acknowledge the lump rising in her throat. And she definitely didn't glance at Wonderlust Ink as she drove through downtown, her tattoo shop, which she'd only just closed four weeks ago.

Permanently.

She'd been fighting against the decision for over a year. Just six months ago, she'd let Mac go—her only employee, who was now working at a fancy shop in Concord—but that had hardly fixed April's financial woes. A small town like Clover Lake had only so many regular clients, and the summer crowd was no longer keeping her in the black. She'd lived in the red for the last two years, but when she started struggling to pay for high-quality ink and other crucial supplies, she knew it was time to throw in the proverbial towel.

So, about a month ago, she'd referred her regulars to Mac, flipped the sign to CLOSED on her shop door, and proceeded to spend the next week on her couch eating jalapeño Cheetos and trying to will Paris and Rory from *Gilmore Girls* to kiss.

Needless to say, they never smashed, and April had to face the reality of her situation, which was how she ended up renting out her home, packing her bags for the summer, and taking a job teaching art classes at Cloverwild, the ritzy new resort opening in just a few days on the north shore. The position came with room and board—a tiny lakeside cabin complete with a cabinmate—and the owner, Mia Gallagher, had asked absolutely zero questions about April's suddenly wide-open summer schedule and need for housing when she'd applied.

April hadn't exactly told anyone about closing her business. Not her parents; not her best friend, Ramona. Only Bianca and Bob knew her secrets, and they weren't talking. In Clover Lake, it was only a matter of time before the news broke, but she'd like to maintain her dignity as long as possible.

She pulled into a parking spot in front of Clover Moon Café, then stepped out into the warm June sunshine. The New Hampshire weather wouldn't get truly hot until July, so she cracked the windows, promised Bianca and Bob she'd only be a second, then ducked into the café for some coffee. She'd already enjoyed one cup this morning in her quaint kitchen, soaking up the way the pale sunlight streamed through her vintage-style windows for the last time, but she needed another hit to get through this day.

She stepped inside, the bell over the door dinging, and took in the familiar vibe of Clover Moon, all rustic wood, navy and green accents, and mismatched chairs. She slid onto a barstool and smiled at the owner, Owen—a bald man in his late forties covered in tattoos, a lot of which April had done herself.

"Usual latte, please," April said. "Oat milk if you've got it."

"I've got it," he said, wiping down the counter in front of her. "Triple?"

"Do I look like a woman who wants a small amount of caffeine right now?" April asked, pointing at the bags under her eyes.

Owen pressed his mouth together. "I'm going to shut my mouth and get to work on a quad shot oat milk latte."

"Good man," April said, then rested her elbows on the counter. Behind her the café buzzed with activity from the usual clientele—Violet Chalmers sipping on a mocha latte spiked with a few dribbles of Baileys that she kept in her purse; Duke Hansard and his brother Jake with their daily helping of sausage links wrapped in buttermilk pancakes, then smothered in strawberry syrup; Logan and Natalie Adler fighting about what to name their soon-to-be-born twins. Personally, April liked Natalie's most recent favorites, Maple and Oak.

"Hey, darling, how are those cutie patootie cats of yours?" Penny Hampton asked, popping up next to April like an annoying neighbor in a sitcom.

April startled but managed a smile. "They're little demons."

Penny laughed, clicking her long russet-colored nails on the plastic menu in front of her. "Good company, I imagine."

April said nothing, not sure how to take that. Plus, the last thing she wanted was to show up as some story in Penny's gossip blog, *Penny for Your Thoughts*.

"Any juicy news from Ramona lately?" Penny asked, eyeing April over the tops of her tortoiseshell reading glasses. Her hair was copper red—just like a penny—and April was pretty sure she was wearing bright green contact lenses, which were new.

"Not lately, no," April said, widening her eyes at Owen to hurry it up. He just smirked at her, steaming milk happily.

When people started plying April for Hollywood news, it was time to get the hell out of Dodge. Mostly because she had no idea what Ramona was up to these days. At least, not the details. A few months ago, in a desperate attempt to feel more connected and informed about what her best friend might be doing around LA, she'd set up a Google alert for Ramona's name. So far, she'd only gotten one alert, informing her that Ramona and Dylan had attended some charity function last month. Other than that useless bit of information, she knew Ramona was immersed in a historical romance for Netflix with her boss, Noelle Yang. She knew Dylan, Ramona's movie star girlfriend, was just about to wrap filming a biopic in which she played Marlene Dietrich, which she'd been working on for over a year. But specifics? Those details were spotty at best, like bad cell reception on the south end of the lake.

She glanced at her phone, eyes drifting over her and Ramona's last text interaction. Several blue bubbles sent from April, asking Ramona if she thought getting a tattoo of an actual scorpion was a little too on the nose. And underneath the last text—the last text with no response from Ramona—were the words Read 8:41 PM.

That was two days ago.

April really didn't want to use the L-word—*lonely*—but ever since Ramona had moved to LA to work as a costume designer nearly two years ago, the word haunted her like Miss Havisham's ghost. Ramona was crushing it as Noelle Yang's assistant, taking on more and more responsibility with each project. It was everything Ramona had ever wanted, everything she deserved after giving up her whole life when she was nineteen to help raise her little sister, Olive, after her father's debilitating car accident, and she certainly didn't need her small potatoes BFF whining about loneliness and a struggling business.

Still, over the last few months, her texts with Ramona had been sporadic at best, and she couldn't remember when they'd last Face-Timed. She did know, however, that they hadn't seen each other in person since this past November, when Ramona and Dylan had come back to Clover Lake for Thanksgiving with Dylan's rock icon parents, Jack Monroe and Carrie Page. Even then, their time was taken up with Ramona's family and April hadn't wanted to impose.

Her own Thanksgiving was a quiet affair with Dr. and Dr. Evans, sipping red wine around her mother's immaculate table while trying to deal with her father's insistence that she invest Wonderlust's profits—that was a laugh—in the stock market, and her mother's constant hints about *settling down*. April didn't think Jacqueline Evans, a Capricorn sun with a Virgo rising, would appreciate April's long-term plans of becoming a cat lady, or how she'd recently decided to give up dating altogether, because what the hell was the point, so instead she'd sipped her drink and gotten a little too tipsy, which had only invited further disapproval from her parents.

Then, after walking home in a red-wine haze because her dad hadn't wanted to drive in the inch of snow that had fallen the night before, she'd promptly opened up her favorite dating app looking for something fresh and intriguing, only to be met with the same boring people asking the same boring questions.

Casual dating had been her bread and butter for the last three years, after her engagement had imploded in spectacular fashion, but it all felt so tiresome to her—the first dates that she never had any interest in turning into a second, getting naked in front of someone new, the whole song and dance afterward, when all she wanted was to go home and sleep in her own bed.

She wasn't really interested in anyone she dated and hadn't been since Elena. No matter how she tried to open her mind to possibilities, no one stimulated her imagination or affections, no one made her stomach flutter with that first-crush feeling or caused her heart to feel like it was going to bust right through her rib cage. No one made her smile uncontrollably or wake up in the morning marveling at how fucking lucky she was.

Lately, the only thing she woke up to was a hair ball vomited up by one of her cats at the foot of her bed.

But even if some Taylor or Scott or Lydia *had* inspired such feelings, April had been there, done that, and consequently been crushed into oblivion when the only person she'd ever fallen madly in love with left her after three years together for a twenty-two-year-old artist named Daphne Love.

Daphne *Love*, for crying out loud.

She'd rather not relive that experience, thanks, no matter what Ramona, her mother, or the entire town of Clover Lake thought about it.

"Ah, well," Penny said now, shoving her glasses back up on her nose. "We've got enough going on with this fancy new resort opening this weekend."

April hmm'd politely, dug her debit card from her bag and tossed it on the counter. Owen whipped it away, then set her latte in front of her. She gulped at it greedily, burning her tongue a bit.

"I hear it's to be quite the gaudy affair," Penny said, leaning closer to April and whispering. Loudly. Penny didn't really do quiet.

April nodded as Owen handed back her card and receipt. Cloverwild was a luxury resort and was indeed rumored to be extravagant. April had no idea if *gaudy* was an accurate description as she hadn't seen it yet, but when a vacation spot's entire purpose was to bring in tourists with a lot of money, it was bound to be pretty high-end.

"It's not gaudy," Owen said. "It's Mia. She's a classy broad."

"Ah, yes," April said, tucking her card away again. "Just what every classy broad wants to be called."

Owen laughed. "I've seen the main lodge," he said, setting a glass of water in front of Penny. "It's gorgeous. Should bring in a lot of good business."

"There's a fine line between gorgeous and gaudy," Penny said, pointing her straw at him before sliding it into her drink and turning to face April again. "Your car outside has a lot of stuff in it. Heading out of town?"

April sighed. No way around it, really—sooner or later people would notice there were vacationers in her house and she wasn't frequenting the city square quite as much.

Goddamn small towns.

"Actually, *Penny*," she said, voice probably a bit too saturated with attitude, "I'm headed to Cloverwild myself. Going to teach an art class there this summer."

Penny's brows shot up. "And you're *living* there? Why in god's name would you do that?"

April gave her a toothless smile.

"Although, maybe you'll meet a nice hot thing while you're there," Penny said, her voice dripping with meaning. "It's been, what? Three years?"

April's smile dropped away. "Not you too," she said.

Penny presented her palms in surrender but proceeded to surrender absolutely nothing. "I'm just saying. Elena what's-her-name was always too big for her britches. And Ramona's got her true love now, living her dream. It's your turn, isn't it?"

She smiled beatifically at April, who refused to show any emotion whatsoever on her face. Absolutely not.

"And on that horrifying note," April said, taking her coffee and tucking her phone into her pocket. She hopped off the stool while Penny tutted, Owen cracking up behind the counter. "Have a lovely day, everyone."

She walked to her car and opened the door, but as she slid inside, the lid from her coffee cup popped off, and half of the heavenly brew spilled down her favorite Paramore T-shirt. She fell into her seat, Bianca hissing as the searing liquid soaked through the cotton to April's skin.

"Fucking figures," she said, then started the engine and drove toward Cloverwild and all of her bright new opportunities.

OWEN HAD BEEN right—Cloverwild was gorgeous.

The lodge itself was a huge two-story craftsman facing the lake, with a large patio area built over the water that contained a firepit and several Adirondack chairs. Cabins dotted the property in the distance, along with a pier and a dock where canoes and kayaks bobbed in the lake. Carrying both Bianca and Bob, who were growing quite restless by this point, in their carriers, April walked up the white-and-gray pebbled path to the wraparound front porch, which was filled with cushioned furniture, rocking chairs, and tiny rustic tables the color of maple syrup. A string of lights circled the porch, already lit and dancing softly in the early-afternoon breeze.

She climbed the stairs and set the cat carriers behind a chair, hoping they'd stay quiet while she checked in with Mia and got her cabin key. She hadn't exactly cleared housing her cats with Mia, but she had no other options at this point.

"Be right back, babies," she said.

Bob mewled pathetically, and Bianca simply glared at her through the slats in the carrier, her ice-blue eyes disdainful.

"Yes, yes, I know, I'm a mess," she said, straightening and catching sight of her warped reflection in the wavy glass set into the large oak door. She tucked the front of her coffee-soaked shirt into her faded black jeans, hoping it hid most of the stain. Her hair fell just shy of her shoulders, and her most recent color experiment—purple and teal streaks through her natural dark—was starting to grow out a little, giving her locks a faded iridescent look she loved. Her makeup was on point—winged liner and dark red lips—despite the slight shadows under her eyes.

She took a breath, the scent of espresso wafting around her as she did so, then pushed the door open.

Inside the lodge's lobby, it was just as immaculate. Rustic wooden beams crossed the twenty-foot ceilings; squashy couches were arranged by a stone fireplace, their buttery brown leather accented with plaid-patterned pillows in navy and hunter green and burgundy for a bit of color. An enormous wagon wheel chandelier cast a warm amber light throughout the room, in addition to the watery glow of a single stained-glass lamp on the oak reception desk by the staircase. It was simple and decadent all at once.

The space was busy, full of preparations for opening day, which would kick off with a party tomorrow evening. People hurried about, carrying luxury sheets and towels to guest rooms upstairs, as well as outside to the larger guest cabins near the lake and the smaller staff cabins around back toward the woods. Others filled rustic shelves with colorful books and knickknacks, carried racks of clear glasses to the bar, straightened paintings on the walls.

She even spotted two people walking by in light pink leotards and leggings, sheer skirts around their waists, hair in tight buns at the napes of their necks. April remembered hearing Cloverwild would have dance instructors à la Patrick Swayze in *Dirty Dancing*, as well as gourmet meals served in a huge dining room complete with a shiny dance floor, waterskiing, guided midnight hikes to Moon Lovers Trail, spa treatments, watercolor classes, and pottery. You name it, Cloverwild was probably offering it.

For the right price.

April spotted Mia Gallagher behind the front desk, her phone cradled between her ear and shoulder while she tapped away on her iPad. Mia was in her midforties and had brown skin and long dark-and-silver braids. Her family's grocery store—which had started as a stall at the Clover Lake farmer's market back in the 1940s and was now a statewide chain, soon to go national if the rumors were to be believed—had given her the means to invest in prime lakefront real estate and open a resort like Cloverwild.

"Hey there," Mia said as April approached the desk, taking her phone off her ear and tossing it—a bit violently, if you asked April—onto the desk. "Good to see you."

"Everything okay?" April asked as Mia took a slug from the largest coffee cup April had ever seen. It was like a Big Gulp from 7-Eleven.

"Ask me tomorrow," Mia said. "No, wait, ask me next month. Maybe even September. Hell, ask me in five years."

"That good, huh?" April asked. She knew opening a new business was hard as shit—she couldn't imagine getting one of this scale off the ground.

Closing a business, however . . .

April shook her head, ignoring the sudden spike of panic and sadness in her gut.

Mia seesawed her hand in the air. "Big picture is fine. Little tiny details that make me question my existence on earth? That's a different story."

April laughed. Mia was funny. Always had been. She had a dry sense of humor April appreciated, and as one of the first out-and-proud lesbians April had ever met, Mia was a bit of an icon in April's mind, a touchstone for all the baby queers in Clover Lake.

"Let me grab your key," Mia said. "Your cabinmate hasn't checked in yet."

"No worries," April said. "More time to get settled." She'd

known from the jump that she'd have a cabinmate, who was also her co-teacher for the art classes. April was ready for the distraction, and excited to plan a fun and unique curriculum.

"Oh, hey, a guest mentioned you the other day," Mia said as she riffled through a stack of papers with key cards clipped to the corners. "When they called to check their reservation."

"Really?" April asked. "Who?"

"Nicola something. Let me see . . ." Mia moved over to the computer and clicked around. "Reece. Nicola Reece. Apparently she works at some fancy museum in London."

"And she's staying in Clover Lake?" April said.

Mia laughed. "Right? But I guess she came to town a few summers ago with her partner and loved it. She said you did a tattoo for her."

April frowned, trying to recall the name, but her mind was blank. She did a million tattoos a year, and she remembered most of them, but she'd always been a visual learner. A name wasn't going to do much for her. "I'm better with faces. And the tattoo itself. Did she say what it was?"

"No, but she's taking all your art classes, so I'm sure you'll see her then," Mia said as she went back to searching for April's information. "Ah, here we go."

She handed April a dark green card with Cloverwild's logo etched on it in gold—the resort name and a canoe stretched underneath the length of the word—along with a few sheets of paper. "That's your itinerary, your cabinmate's information, your class schedule and rosters, things like that. There's a map of the property on the back. It's all online too, but some people like a physical copy."

April tucked the key into her pocket, then thanked Mia before heading for the door and her contraband cats, scanning the top paper as she went.

Her eyes snagged on a set of letters.

A name.

She froze, slowly turning back toward the desk.

"Hey, Mia?"

"Yeah, hon?" Mia asked, shuffling through another stack of papers.

"Is this right?" April's heart had sped up, then left its designated place in her body, catapulting around like a pinball.

"Is what right?"

"This name." April blinked at the two words. "My . . ."

Her cabinmate.

Her co-teacher.

A name she definitely knew, no face required.

"It's all correct, whatever it is," Mia said, who understandably didn't have time for whatever meltdown April was currently experiencing. "Checked it myself this morning. Excuse me." She frowned down at her phone, then hurried off toward the kitchen.

April barely noticed any of that though. Barely heard Mia's answer. She stood in the middle of the room, fingers trembling on the papers, her vision blurring as she stared down at the name of the very person who had ruined her life three years ago.

Chapter Two

DAPHNE LOVE HADN'T washed her hair in over two weeks.

Granted, her blond curls were naturally coarse and dry, requiring no more than a weekly wash day with some deep conditioning and high-quality gel, but by this point, she was far beyond the freedoms afforded by her hair type.

She sat up on Vivian's tufted sky-blue couch and pushed off the mustard-colored fleece blanket she'd been sleeping under for the last month. Her back screamed at her. Vivian's sofa was definitely an aesthetic choice, the stylish tufts making Daphne's body feel about two decades older than her twenty-five years, but it wasn't as though she had room to complain.

"Oh, good, you're awake," Vivian said, glancing up from where she sat at the bar in her tiny kitchen. She wore leggings and a wide-necked sweatshirt, revealing one smooth dark brown shoulder, and her long twists were piled on top of her head and secured with a mint-green headband. She tapped on her phone and sipped her usual matcha latte—Daphne could smell the grassy aroma from here.

"I'm not sure *awake* is quite accurate," Daphne said, rubbing the sleep from her eyes. The morning sun streaming through the windows in Vivan's one-bedroom Boston apartment was so bright it made her teeth ache.

Vivian sighed.

Vivian had been sighing a lot for the last month, not that Daphne could blame her. Daphne had been crashing on her couch since the end of April—something neither of them planned or wanted—and Vivian had put up with oceans of Daphne tears, at least a dozen pints of ice cream, days of staring into the void, and twelve-hour sleep cycles on the aforementioned couch, which was located in the middle of the small living room.

Needless to say, Daphne had worn out her welcome.

"I've got to get going pretty soon," Vivian said, sliding off the stool and then hand-washing her mug in the sink. "So should you. Clover Lake is only a little over an hour away, but my aunt doesn't appreciate lateness."

Daphne nodded.

"Are you excited?" Vivian asked, shutting off the water and drying her mug with a pink towel.

Daphne forced a smile. "Absolutely."

Vivian sighed. "Have you packed?"

Daphne nodded again, a bobblehead doll stuck to a car's dashboard, before stopping abruptly. "Well, mostly."

Vivian released her third sigh in the last ten minutes, then stepped over Daphne's giant teal suitcase, which was one of the only things she owned other than her clothes and a few books. It was a nice suitcase too. Elena had bought it for her about a year ago, though she'd never really had a chance to use it yet.

She sent both hands through her hair. Or she tried, but her fingers tangled in the myriad knots scattered throughout her curls. She grabbed a hair tie from the coffee table, secured her locks into a messy bun on top of her head.

Took a deep breath.

She had to get it together.

Had to.

Vivian was beyond sick of her, she knew. Until a month ago, she'd only spoken to her college roommate sporadically since they'd graduated Boston University three years ago. They'd been close during their shared time in the fine arts department—Vivian studying modern dance, Daphne visual art with a concentration in painting—but had drifted apart after they graduated. Daphne wished she could say it was simply a natural progression of their relationship, a product of a transition in both of their lives. Vivian got a job with a professional dance company in Boston, while Daphne . . .

Well, what *had* Daphne done, exactly?

She'd fallen in love.

That was it, the extent of her foray into adulthood. She packed up her heart, tied it all up with a silk bow, and gave it freely to Elena Watson. Sure, she had a part-time job at the renowned art museum where she'd interned her senior year (and met Elena), and she'd produced a lot of paintings in the last three years (mediocre, and which were probably tossed in the recycling bin outside of Elena's penthouse apartment the second Daphne moved out), but mostly, Daphne had been a girlfriend.

And she'd been a *great* girlfriend.

She made dinner.

She ran errands.

She dusted and made their bed every morning.

She made sure Elena's kitchen was always stocked with her expensive espresso and her favorite oat milk.

She was *there* for Elena.

Every gallery event, every art-world party, every quiet night snuggled on the couch together watching indie films Daphne secretly found depressing. Their sex life was incredible—at least in Daphne's limited experience—and Elena had always held her close afterward, whispering how much she loved her.

Three years of domestic bliss, and then . . .

Daphne pressed the heels of her hands to her eyes until color exploded behind her lids.

She'd been expecting a proposal.

That was the worst part.

Elena had taken her to Bistro du Midi, a fancy French place they'd only ever been to on birthdays or anniversaries, and the restaurant served the most decadent chocolate soufflé—it was so good, Daphne had dreams about it. So on a cool evening near the end of April, when Elena came home and took Daphne in her arms, kissing her passionately and whispering "Let me take you out" against her mouth, Daphne had felt a zing of anticipation.

She'd smiled, pulled back so she could look at her girlfriend, so beautiful and elegant with her long dark hair and pale skin, her nearly black eyes, and a beauty mark right above the left side of her top lip, like that supermodel from the nineties whose name Daphne could never remember.

Her future wife.

And she thought, *Wow, I'm so lucky.*

Twenty-nine days later, she was waking up with chiropractic problems and questionable hygiene, three hundred bucks and some change left in her checking account, and exactly one friend, whom she hadn't spoken to in six months before she called Vivian begging for her couch.

She'd had nowhere else to go. Contacting her own family was out of the question, and Vivian was the only person she knew who wasn't inside Elena's art-world bubble—literally every one of Daphne's "friends" from the last few years was Elena's friends, and they'd clearly chosen her in the split.

And why shouldn't they?

Daphne was twenty-five, unemployed, inexperienced, and was starting to suspect she'd been the equivalent of a trophy wife for the last three years.

She'd spent the first few years of college in a kind of bubble too. After high school, she'd left her small Tennessee town with a full scholarship for tuition, but that hadn't covered room and board, textbooks, supplies, toothpaste, face cleanser, and new underwear when the pairs she'd had since she was sixteen grew too thin and worn to be considered practical, so she'd waited tables at a middling Boston restaurant at least twenty hours a week. When she wasn't in class or serving medium-rare steaks, she focused on her art, trying to produce good work. Sometimes, she managed to hang out with Vivian's friends, watching their community with wonder, trying to figure out what kind of queer she wanted to be. She'd known she was a lesbian from age nine, then spent the next nine years hiding it from her preacher father and rigid mother. Finally letting herself out was terrifying, and while she went on a few dates here and there in college, she always managed to get in her own way when it came to sex, or even making out.

And then she met Elena Watson, the curator at the Museum of Fine Arts, where Daphne had landed a coveted senior-year internship.

The rest, as they say, was very depressing history.

The only glimmer of light in all this gloom was her summer job. Vivian's aunt Mia lived in a small town in New Hampshire, close to where Vivian had grown up, and she was opening a lake resort this summer.

Tomorrow, in fact.

By some miracle, Vivian had managed to convince her very generous aunt to hire Daphne to teach art classes. Daphne had no idea why Mia agreed. She hadn't even talked to Daphne, really, but Daphne suspected it had something to do with Vivian's desperation to get Daphne out of her hair, and the fact that there was another art instructor on staff as well, a local person Mia knew and trusted, and with whom Daphne would also share a cabin.

All of which was very, very fair.

On top of that, Mia had emailed Daphne a few days ago to see if it was okay to share her digital portfolio—which Mia *had* at least requested before hiring her—with a guest named Nicola Reece, who had asked about the art instructors' work.

A curator at a museum in London, no less.

While this information had sparked a bit of interest in Daphne—curators had the power to make or break careers in the art world, after all—she was also quite tired of, well, curators and their power to make or break careers in the art world. Elena had made it very clear over the course of their doomed relationship that Daphne's career would not be made.

Regardless, as Daphne stretched her arms into the air, she tried to drum up a little excitement for her summer ahead. She'd googled Cloverwild and it was beautiful, every photo featuring a sparkling sapphire lake and bright green trees, a veritable paradise. She could almost smell the fresh air already, and she knew she needed to get out of Boston. So while the job didn't pay all that much, she at least had a roof over her head, and three whole months to figure out what to do with her sad, single, solitary life.

"You almost ready?" Vivian asked, coming out of her room with her dance bag slung over one shoulder. "If you want me to drop you at the train station, we need to leave now. I've got rehearsal in an hour."

"What?" Daphne asked, then realized she'd been sitting on the couch staring out the window for the last twenty minutes, still in her sleeping tank and shorts, hair still a rat's nest on top of her head. "Crap. Yeah. Ten minutes!"

She shot up—a move that made her dizzy—and ran for the bathroom for the fastest shower of her life, which with the time constraint now meant she would not be utilizing shampoo and conditioner.

"Ten minutes!" she yelled again.

And right before she closed the door, she heard Vivian sigh.

DAPHNE COULDN'T GET into her cabin. The door unlocked just fine with her key card, but when she tried to push it open, she was met with resistance.

And this—this dark green wooden door that would only open a few inches while she stood on the log cabin's porch between two red Adirondack chairs—was the final straw. After an hour-long ride in a train car that smelled like Doritos, all she wanted was to lie down and stare at the ceiling.

But no, she was well and truly doomed.

Never mind her useless college degree, lack of financial security or professional prospects—this recalcitrant door was the real proof that she couldn't function as a human being. As she stood there, her flowing tears turning into audible sobs, she knew she was being ridiculous, but that was the thing about final straws: They rarely made any sense whatsoever.

She let out a grunt of frustration and slammed the side of her fist against the door.

"What the hell?" a voice said from inside.

Daphne heard footsteps, then rushed to wipe under her eyes, which were puffy, dark-circled messes anyway.

"Why is this door open?" the same voice said, closer now. "I thought I—" The person cut themself off, then Daphne heard what sounded like a very heavy bag or box being dragged across the floor, followed by a . . . meow?

"I know, Bianca, calm the hell down," the person said, and Daphne was fully confused now.

The door drifted open effortlessly, revealing a petite woman with lavender tips in her dark hair, perfect winged eyeliner, ripped black jeans, and black boots that that could probably blow a hole in a wall after one solid kick. Colorful tattoos spiraled down both of her arms, and she smelled faintly of coffee.

"Hi," Daphne said, then cleared her throat when her words came out a bit tear-logged. "Sorry, I couldn't get the door open."

The woman pursed her mouth, then looked Daphne up and down. From the way her jaw tightened and her nostrils flared a little, her gaze was more scrutiny than friendly observation.

"I'm Daphne," Daphne said.

The woman continued to stare at her, eyes slightly narrowed now.

"Daphne Love?" Daphne tried again. "Your roommate? And, um, teaching partner?"

The woman's throat bobbed as she swallowed. "Right. I'm April Evans."

"It's lovely to meet you," Daphne said.

"Is it?" April said.

Daphne opened her mouth but closed it again without saying anything. The woman didn't move, remaining in the doorway with her eyebrows lifted and her breathing a bit heavy for a casual meeting.

"April Evans?" April said again, her inflection rising on the end this time like she was asking a question. "From Clover Lake?"

Daphne wasn't sure what the right answer was here. She'd never been the most socially capable person, spending most of her childhood either hiding her true feelings about almost everything or denying them if they happened to slip into the light. Vivian had been her only solid friend in college, and even that, it seemed, she was continuously screwing up.

Then Elena . . .

She shook her head. Couldn't think about Elena right now, absolutely not. She focused, tried to figure out how this tiny, beautiful woman wanted her to respond.

She settled on something simple.

"Yes," she said.

April tilted her head. "Yes? That's it?"

Daphne blinked, and . . . oh no . . . please, no . . . she felt tears starting to swell up her throat. She swallowed repeatedly, shoving them back down again until she felt steady enough to talk.

"I'm . . . I'm sure Mia told me your name," she said carefully. "I'm sorry if I forgot."

April blinked, clearly unsatisfied. She looked a little pale, and her jaw was still like a vise. Daphne could hear her teeth grinding.

"Right. Whatever," April said, then opened the door all the way. "Come in, I guess."

"Thank you," Daphne said, stepping into the cabin. She still felt a little shaky—a newborn deer on spindly legs—but at least she was inside now, at her home for the summer.

The space was small but airy, a single room with knotted pine floors, walls, and ceiling. Two full-size beds sat on opposite sides of the room, a large dark green dresser in between. The linens were white and crisp, with green plaid blankets folded at the foot of each mattress. A large picture window to the right of the beds filled the room with bright light. There was a small closet to the left, along with a bathroom, and Daphne could see a white porcelain bowl sink and tub shower with a green-and-navy plaid curtain.

She also saw a complete and total mess.

Everywhere.

The room was lovely, but Daphne was having a hard time focusing on those details because both beds were covered in clothes, the bathroom light was on and the counter was already littered with toiletries, and she could barely see the pine floor because there were boots and scarves and black jeans and tees literally everywhere. It was as though someone had stuffed the entire contents of their suitcase into a T-shirt cannon and started firing at random.

Daphne stood frozen in the doorway, her own large suitcase next to her, blinking at the mess.

"Yeah, sorry," April said, snatching a pile of shirts off one of the beds and stuffing them into the bottom dresser drawer. "I had a lot of shit to unpack, and it helps me organize it if I can see it all."

Daphne let her shoulders relax. She wasn't exactly a messy person—she liked things in their place, particularly after years of living with Elena—but she understood the harrowing unpacking process.

Which was exactly why she never quite made it that far at Vivan's.

"No worries," she said, pulling her suitcase behind her and heading for the now-cleared bed. She plopped down, exhaling as she did so, before looking around and wondering what to do first. She'd been hoping April hadn't arrived yet so she'd have a bit of time to simply stare at the ceiling fan, but that wasn't in the cards. The last thing she needed right now was for her grumpy roommate to develop some kind of personal issue with her.

And clearly, they were already off to a strange start.

She glanced up to find April staring at her, brows lowered in what could only be described as a glower, and a black bathing suit covered in tiny constellations in her hands.

A very, *very* strange start.

Daphne cleared her throat, then turned her suitcase over on its side so she could get it unzipped.

But then she heard it again—a meow.

She straightened, her eyes wide.

"Shit," April said. She tossed the bathing suit on her bed and headed toward not one but two pet carriers by the door. "I really need to let them out. Do you mind?"

Daphne could only blink as April—who didn't seem to need an answer from her anyway—proceeded to unlatch the wire doors, releasing two cats, who stepped out of their cages like royalty.

"Bianca del Kitty," April said, motioning to a regal white-and-gray cat with blue eyes, then pointing to an orange feline, green eyes glowing. "And that's Bob the Drag Cat. I've got their litter box in my car. I hope you're not allergic, because I have nowhere else for them to go right now."

Daphne had never had house pets before. Elena hated cats, and Daphne's family in Tennessee had raised chickens, which required too much care and maintenance to add a dog or cat to the mix.

"Well, are you?" April asked.

The orange cat, Bob, wandered over to Daphne and rubbed itself on her legs, nosing at a loose string on her cuffed jeans.

"Am I what?" Daphne asked, looking down at the feline.

"Allergic," April said, impatience tightening her voice.

"No," Daphne said. "No, I'm—"

Bob mewed, looking up at Daphne with liquid eyes before leaping into her lap.

"Oh," she said, lifting her hands into the air to give the beast some room. The cat kneaded Daphne's legs, turning in circles a few times, rubbing its face on Daphne's belly.

April scoffed, then mumbled something that sounded like *traitor* under her breath. Daphne couldn't be sure, and she couldn't slow down her emotions long enough to figure it out, because Bob settled in her lap then. It tucked its paws underneath its furry body and started purring, happy as can be.

Daphne suddenly realized it had been a full month since anyone had touched her, hugged her, patted her on the shoulder, anything. Suddenly, this tiny animal's body—its weight and its heat—was all too much, a shock of affection Daphne hadn't even known she needed.

And then, because this day truly couldn't get any worse, she promptly burst into tears.

Chapter Three

OH, FUCKING HELL.

April watched as Daphne started crying with her precious baby Bob in her lap, for god's sake. She had no clue what to do or say. Clearly, the woman had issues.

Well, join the fucking club.

"I'm sorry," Daphne said, wiping her eyes, but then Bob, aka Lucifer, snuggled even closer to the woman, rubbing his head on her stomach and even peering up at Daphne as if to inquire after her well-being.

And all this pulled a fresh wave of tears from Daphne's infernally pretty eyes.

She was pretty all over, really, if a little worse for wear today with her too-loose jeans and heather-gray T-shirt with what looked like Cheeto-crumb stains swiped over the middle. Still, April could tell she was gorgeous—green eyes and silky curls the color of spun gold, lithe limbs, and a surprisingly curvy ass.

Not that April didn't know all of this already—well, everything but the ass part, which she was determined to ignore—as she'd spent the better part of the first month after Elena left her three years ago poring over her ex's Instagram, which of course led her to Daphne's profile.

An art student—painting, as far as April could tell.

Young.

Beautiful.

Sweet.

Southern.

A country apple plucked fresh from the tree.

The exact opposite of April in every way, who painted her nails black and didn't even own a lipstick shade lighter than crimson.

Then again, she supposed that was the point.

Daphne had now pulled Bob closer and pressed her face into his orange fur, taking such deep breaths April wondered if she was going to inhale a hair ball. One thing she knew for sure—she needed a fucking minute. She left Daphne and Bob to their canoodling and hightailed it for the bathroom, where she closed herself inside and pressed her back against the door.

"Fuck," she said on an exhale, all the adrenaline of seeing Daphne in the flesh settling now, leaving her trembling and out of breath.

She had no idea what seeing the woman the love of her life had left her for would be like—turned out, it wasn't pleasant, particularly when said woman looked a little bit haunted and then started sobbing uncontrollably because of a cat. April wondered briefly what was wrong, then squeezed her eyes closed, because no.

She couldn't go there.

Wouldn't.

Of course, April was mature enough—her parents might have a different opinion there, but whatever—to understand that when infidelity occurred, the person your partner cheated with wasn't fully at fault. Your *partner* was the asshole, a fact April absolutely did not contest. Still, the other party in this case had to have known Elena had a partner, a *fiancée*, and still Daphne had dated Elena.

Then again . . .

April rubbed her tired eyes, replaying the last fifteen minutes in her brain. When April had opened the door, Daphne's expression was completely blank, and it remained so when April said her own name—*twice*. Daphne very obviously didn't know who April was, not even a glimmer of recognition flickering in her eyes. She had never heard April's name, never seen her picture via Instagram or anywhere else. To Daphne Love, an infamous person in April's mind, the person she'd measured herself against for that first year, April Evans hadn't even existed until this very moment. At the very least, Elena had never told Daphne her name, never told her about her life in Clover Lake with April.

Either that, or Daphne was the greatest actress in the world. Still, April didn't think that woman snuggling Bob in the next room could fake a sneeze right now, much less something this huge.

April let the truth of it all settle, and god, it was heavy. All these facts, this evidence. It had been three years, and April had moved on—went weeks without even thinking about Elena sometimes—but now, knowing that her own name wasn't even worth telling . . .

She slid down to the floor, plunked her head against the door as the box of memories she'd shoved into a corner of her mind tipped over, spilling its contents everywhere.

April and Elena had met in Boston six years ago, when April was twenty-seven and Elena was thirty. April had been in town for a workshop with a well-known tattoo artist at the time, and on her last evening there, she'd wandered into a lesbian bar called Pearl, which should've been her first clue it wasn't exactly her kind of place. The second the door closed behind her, a proverbial record scratch echoed through the air as every single person inside stopped what they were doing and turned to look at April.

The bar was, in a word, immaculate. The space was dim, lit by an ornate chandelier and a few sconces set into the periwinkle walls. The bar itself was dark mahogany, with padded stools covered in a rich lavender velvet. Everything, in fact, was some shade of purple, but it was elegantly done with decadent aubergine tufted settees, chairs painted in a stormy lavender-gray, and gold accents warming up the space.

Oh, it was a lesbian bar, all right.

A power lesbian bar.

A *rich* lesbian bar.

Every person inside was dressed to kill with their dark suits and sharply cut bobs. Some wore ties, some wore little black dresses that left very little to the imagination, but everyone was *styled*. They were tailored and intentional and chic.

And April had on her black leather jacket, a Nico T-shirt with a hole near the hem, torn gray jeans, and a pair of white high-top sneakers.

Still, once she came through the door, she couldn't possibly leave. She refused. A bunch of snobs in a bar were not going to dictate to her where she belonged, goddammit. So she smiled beatifically at all the eyes on her, then walked toward the bar as calmly as she could and ordered a Manhattan. She still felt everyone's gaze on her, but she ignored them, even though her heart was threatening to beat right out of her chest.

"You're a long way from home," a voice said.

April glanced to her right as a woman slid into the space next to her.

A *gorgeous* woman.

Long dark hair, smooth pale skin, a beauty mark on the left side of her full lips. Eyes so dark, April knew if she fell inside them, she'd probably never find her way out. She wore one of those little black dresses, skintight, the V-shaped neckline plunging to below her sternum.

"I think I'm right where I need to be," April said, tipping her glass at the woman before taking a slurping sip.

The woman lifted a perfect eyebrow, but then smiled widely, showing off her very white, very straight teeth.

"Refreshing," she said, lifting her own glass toward April, a deep red wine. "A rebel."

"No," April said, slipping the dark cherry between her teeth and chomping down. "Just don't give a shit."

The woman laughed, then introduced herself as Elena Watson. April replied in kind, and soon, she was lost. Because Elena was funny. And interesting. A bit stuck-up, sure, but she was easy to talk to, sharing details about growing up in Virginia, coming out when she was twelve by writing a letter to her parents and mailing a copy to both of their places of business.

"My penmanship was impeccable," she'd said, laughing.

"And how did they take it?" April asked.

"Oh, I'm very convincing," Elena said, winking.

April found herself revealing things about her own parents too, how Drs. Preston and Jacqueline Evans, general practitioners with enough earth in their star charts to pull a mountain from the sea, had rarely understood anything their only daughter did or said or dreamed about. April was a water sign, a triple Scorpio at that, and she'd fallen in love with magic and the stars at a young age precisely because her parents . . . well, hadn't quite fallen in love with her.

She remembered suspecting this fact as young as five, when her mother told her they'd have a *quiet night at home* for April's birthday, instead of the Rainbow Brite party April had asked for. A party was too messy. Too wild. Too . . . *April.* A formative memory, and one of her first. But that was also the birthday that her grandmother Harriet sent her a picture book about the zodiac, then read it to her that night over the phone and every night for weeks until April had the entire thing memorized.

Her parents disapproved, of course, but April found something in the stars she'd never experienced with her parents—a sense of purpose.

A destiny.

Preston and Jacqueline had tried to have a baby for years before they got pregnant with April. They'd had miscarriages and failed rounds of IVF, until they finally stopped trying. Gave up hope.

And then, two months later, the strip turned pink on a pregnancy test.

April had always loved this story, or at least the *idea* of it—but whenever her parents told it, there was no awe in their voices, just clinical facts, followed by a glance in April's direction that could only be described as nonchalant. April's existence might be a miracle, but she could never shake the feeling that her parents, after so much failure and heartbreak and waiting, were a bit underwhelmed with the kid they finally got.

"That must've been hard," Elena finally said, her fingertips brushing the top of April's hand.

April could only nod, because it was true, and because hearing this stranger confirm it was so validating, she felt close to tears. She couldn't believe she was sharing these sorts of details with Elena. April hadn't felt this entranced by a person in years.

No, that wasn't right. She'd *never* felt this entranced by another person. Ever.

Of course, April had dated people. Mostly boys, until she realized she was attracted to all genders and came out as pansexual her junior year of high school, mainly with the help of Leigh Reynolds, a friend (with benefits) she often hooked up with even to this day whenever they rolled back into town. In college she dated girls and people of other genders. She'd even dated a few of them for a long time, calling some of them partners or boyfriends or girlfriends. Never anything life-changing though.

She'd never felt that *thing.*

But she felt it with Elena.

"I'm a Taurus," Elena had said after April shared about her parents, leaning close and whispering with that husky voice of hers. "Is that compatible with a Scorpio?"

April had grinned. "Actually, yes. Perfectly compatible."

"Well, thank god for that," Elena said. Then they left together, walking the streets of Boston slowly, the chilly October air perfect for just such a stroll. And when Elena took her hand at a crosswalk, then didn't let go as they reached the next block, April's heart did something funny in her chest.

Grew, or shifted, or simply beat with a stronger rhythm. She didn't know, but she loved it. Felt addicted already.

They went on a ghost tour in a carriage, shrieking and clinging to each other the entire time, and when midnight came around, Elena asked April to come back to her apartment.

Yes was the only possible answer, and they had sex all night in Elena's huge bed, silk sheets cool under their skin. April felt drunk afterward, even though the effects of her Manhattan had long worn off. Still, she half expected Elena to bid her farewell in the morning, say she had a great time, then turn her eyes to the morning paper as she sipped espresso, a signal for April to see herself out.

But none of that happened.

Elena seemed just as intoxicated as April, and April ended up staying in Boston for the rest of the week, even though her workshop was long over. Mac, her employee at Wonderlust, handled things at the shop, and Ramona kept texting and asking if April was ever going to come home.

And April . . . well, she didn't know.

Eventually, though, reality set in. Elena had to work—she was a curator at the Museum of Fine Arts—and April knew she needed to face whatever the hell the two of them were doing.

So she asked.

And Elena said she loved April.

Just like that, said so easily, offered so freely. The only person who had ever said those words to April like that was Ramona. Not even her own parents said it that often. And right then, April knew.

She'd found her person.

Her match.

The person who loved *her*, every part of her, and happened to know exactly how to make her scream in bed.

Things moved fast after that—she and Elena dated long-distance for a few months, but they both hated it, so they soon worked out a bi-city arrangement where they spent a week or so at a time in Clover Lake or Boston. The commute was only a little over an hour, and both were willing to make it for the sake of sleeping in the same bed and waking up together. Elena wasn't exactly a small-town gal, but she seemed to enjoy her time in Clover Lake, even helped April with things around her shop, and April always loved how much Elena was willing to do—her commute, living with April's two cats, eating fried eggs every Saturday at Clover Moon with Ramona—to be with April.

This went on for two years until, one evening in Boston, Elena suggested they take a ghost tour again—the same one, in fact, they'd taken the night they met, except this one was exclusive, a carriage through haunted Boston just for April and Elena. Then, under a full moon near the most notorious cemetery in the city, Elena slipped a black diamond ring onto April's finger.

April cried.

She never cried, but she cried right then. Before Elena, she truly believed she'd never find someone who loved all of her quirks and interests, the fact that she still dressed in an elaborate costume every Halloween even if there was no party to attend. But here was this lovely, elegant, accomplished woman who wanted to marry her.

A few months later, however, things started to shift. Elena started working longer hours, coming home later in the evening. Then she started begging off the weeks they were supposed to spend in Clover Lake, insisting April go on ahead without her, that she'd join her in a few days. The days stretched into weeks, though, and soon it had been months since Elena had even stepped foot in New Hampshire. April grew irritated and sarcastic around her fiancée, which always sparked Elena's own temper, and things between them bent and stretched, growing more tense by the day, until Elena finally broke up with her, over the phone no less, the words slipping out of her mouth so easily like oil over silk—*I've met someone else.*

Now, three years later, April groaned and knocked her head against the door, pushing back the memories. She couldn't believe this was happening. She'd moved beyond this, didn't need this, but here was Daphne Love in the flesh, who didn't even know April's fucking name.

But surely, *surely*, Daphne had known Elena was with someone when they'd met, even if she'd never learned April's name. April had even bought Elena her own ring after they'd gotten engaged. Granted, it wasn't much, as she didn't want Elena's help paying for it. But Elena wore the small geo-cut emerald set in a matte gold band on a very important finger. It wasn't as though April and Elena were just messing around—they were *engaged*.

No, Daphne had to have known.

And she'd gone and fucked Elena anyway.

A knock sounded on the door, reverberating against April's head.

"April?" Daphne called. "Are you okay in there?"

April exhaled heavily and stood up, checking her reflection in the mirror. She sniffed, rolled her shoulders back.

"I'm fucking great," she said, then swung open the door before she slid past a befuddled Daphne Love holding Bob in her arms and went to finish unpacking.

Chapter Four

APRIL EVANS WAS terrifying.

That was all there was to it.

While Daphne unpacked, April banged around the room, slamming drawers and the closet door and stomping over the rough hardwood in her big black boots. Daphne had no idea what had gotten her so irritated—maybe the fact that April's cat liked her?—but Daphne simply kept her head down and organized her own clothes and possessions as best she could.

"We should head to the studio," April said as she zipped her last suitcase closed—she had two—and slid it under her bed. "See what we're dealing with there."

"You haven't seen it?" Daphne asked. She slipped her favorite sundress on a hanger—kelly green with thin straps; she'd worn it on her last real date with Elena. She remembered because Elena loved to slowly undo the buttons in the front, one by one, until—

Daphne hung the dress in the closet, a sudden knot in her throat. She surveyed her other clothes, and every single garment seemed attached to some memory with Elena. If she had the money, she'd burn everything, buy a whole new wardrobe.

"No, I haven't," April said curtly.

Daphne turned to look at her. "I just wondered since you were local."

"I've been busy."

Daphne said nothing to that. Said nothing as April grabbed her silver laptop and an iPad from the little desk by the window and tucked them both into her dark blue canvas bag, the fabric covered with white and yellow stars and moons. Daphne said nothing as she slipped her sketchbook into her own bag—her iPad had died a year ago, and she'd been using Elena's ever since, because of course she had—and followed April out the door. Said nothing as they walked the gravel path to the main lodge. And she said nothing when April opened the side door, then nearly let it close on Daphne before she'd walked into the building. Luckily, she seemed to have expended all her tears with Bob, so she didn't cry, which at this point, she'd take as a win.

Clearly, she needed tougher skin if she was going to work with April all summer, and she'd already established herself as *that girl who cries*. To be fair, if she'd been in April's shoes and a woman she'd just met started sobbing into her cat's fur, Daphne would be a bit put off as well. Still, she'd at least *ask* the poor soul what was wrong, or if there was anything she could do to help, but maybe April wasn't a very warm person.

Fine.

Neither was half the art world in Boston. Daphne could deal with this. She *had* to deal with this.

She straightened her posture as they walked down a hallway that hugged the edge of the lodge, huge windows letting in the June sunlight all along their right side. The floors were a lovely honey-colored wood, the walls adorned with paintings and sketches of the lake, all done in different styles and colors.

"Here it is," April said, consulting the map Daphne had also received from Mia when she arrived, then stopping in front of a wooden door.

"What gave it away?" Daphne said, smiling as she pointed to the intentionally rustic wooden sign next to the door that read ART STUDIO.

April just stared at her, and Daphne cleared her throat, cheeks burning red. Clearly, April Evans was not a jokester.

Noted.

Inside, the studio was lovely. A dream, really.

"This is gorgeous," Daphne said, taking in the space.

April said nothing. She simply walked to the front of the room, where there was a projector screen affixed to the wall with an instructor's easel set on either side, and took her iPad out of her bag.

Daphne made a slower journey. Two walls were nothing but windows, and the natural light streaming into the room shed beautiful hues onto the fifteen or so stools and student easels, already set up with blank 8x10 canvases. Near the front in one corner, there was a sink and a table covered in different paints and brushes, as well as cabinets above that Daphne assumed were filled with supplies. There was also a tan leather love seat in another corner, two green velvet throw pillows perched primly on the cushions.

Daphne's fingers tingled. She hadn't painted anything in a month—she had no way to do so anymore, as she'd used Elena's spare room as her light-filled studio, paints and canvases and brushes just a click away on the internet via Elena's AmEx. Granted, it wasn't as though anything she'd produced over the last three years was all that inspiring anyway. Elena was never very moved, always tilting her head at a new piece, mouth only just pursed. Her brows didn't lower or lift, her expression rarely changing much past a simple observation that she was looking at a canvas with some paint on it.

Boredom.

That's what her expression communicated. Of course, she

never said as much, always encouraging Daphne to dig deeper, but she didn't *not* say it either. Elena's reactions built up in Daphne, that apathy toward her own work, like cholesterol in the arteries, a slow hardening. Elena was an honest-to-god curator of art—it was difficult to feel passionate about her own pieces when they seemed to inspire nothing more than a metaphorical yawn.

But right now, walking into this beautiful space—a space Elena had never been in, never touched—Daphne felt something long dead inside her flutter, as though shocked by a defibrillator. She walked to the table full of acrylic paints, drifting her fingers over the array of colors. Vibrant images danced in her mind. Nothing concrete, just dreamlike flashes, but even that felt monumental after the last month, which replayed in dull black-and-white in her memory.

"Are you here to work or daydream?"

April's curt voice slugged through her thoughts. Daphne glanced up, but April wasn't looking at her at all. Instead, she tapped on her laptop, which she'd already connected to project on the screen.

Daphne wasn't prone to anger or temper, and growing up the way she had, she was an expert at stuffing her emotions down so deep one would need a bulldozer to unloose them. Right now, however, her chest warmed with irritation. Whatever April's problem was with her, she was positive she didn't deserve it.

She lifted her chin, then walked over to the desk and sat down before taking out her sketchbook and pen, slapping them onto her lap in a show of annoyance.

April didn't even react, stoically tapping around on her iPad. "So we have three classes—illustration, watercolors, and acrylics."

Daphne nodded, scribbling into her sketchbook. "What's your medium?"

"Illustration. You?"

"Painting—acrylics and oils—but I have experience with illustration as well. I sketch out all my pieces beforehand."

"And I have experience with paints," April said. "I went to RISD."

Daphne fought an eye roll. In her experience, people who went to Rhode Island School of Design seemed very keen on announcing that they *went to RISD* at every possible opportunity.

"I went to Boston University," Daphne said.

"Oh, I know," April said, her voice laced with a now-familiar disdain. "And interned at the Museum of Fine Arts."

Daphne frowned. "How did you know that?"

April just stared at her. "Really?"

"What?" Daphne asked, lifting her arms and letting them drop. "Why is that such a ridiculous question?"

April sighed again.

Daphne was getting very tired of people sighing in her presence. *Because* of her presence. "You know what?" she said, holding up a hand. "Never mind. Let's just talk about the classes."

"Good idea," April said.

"Brilliant."

"Great."

"Wonderful."

"Excellent," Daphne said, her voice a bit louder.

"Superb," April said, nearly yelling.

Daphne felt her nostrils flare.

"I can keep going," April said.

"You like the last word, I take it," Daphne said.

"I'm a Scorpio," April said. "I *love* the last word."

"Then take it."

"I did."

Daphne groaned out loud, and she swore to god, she caught the ghost of a smug smile on April's mouth. It was going to be a very, very long summer.

Chapter Five

APRIL WASN'T SURE how she was going to make it through this summer with *Daphne fucking Love* as her cabinmate and colleague, but she did know that this champagne was helping.

The next evening, the Cloverwild lobby was packed, the opening party in full swing. Guests from all over the country filled the room wearing their summer best—halter dresses baring shoulders and backs, myriad variations of Nantucket Reds, hair freshly highlighted and blown out. The front doors were thrown open, guests coming and going between the lodge and the stone walkway that led to the firepit, boathouse, and lake. Canoes were available for twilit rides through the water.

It was quite the event, laughter and jazz music floating through the room like bubbles.

April stood alone near the expansive windows in the Cloverwild lobby, dressed in wide-legged dark green pants, heeled boots, and a short-sleeve mesh black top that revealed her black bra and tattoos underneath. She sipped on her second glass of champagne and wondered how long she was required to stay.

Then again, the only thing waiting for her in her cabin was a doe-eyed Tennessean and traitorous cats.

She and Daphne had spent most of today in the art studio, putting together slide presentations for their upcoming classes. April was loath to admit that Daphne knew her stuff and was even excited to dabble in watercolors herself. Still, April couldn't seem to put away her scorpion's tail when it came to Daphne.

April sighed and took another bubbly gulp of her drink, finishing it off and setting the empty glass on a nearby table. She was just about to seek out another when her phone buzzed in her back pocket.

Ramona.

"Hey," April said after scrambling to slide her finger over her screen. She'd texted Ramona yesterday about Daphne's presence in Clover Lake, the cosmic insanity of it all, but hadn't heard back yet. At the sound of Ramona's voice now, April's chest felt lighter, airier.

"Apes, hey, sorry," Ramona said. "I just remembered you're at the Cloverwild party."

"It's boring as fuck," April said, leaning her hip against the window. "Did you just get home from work?"

"Yeah, thank god. But we're leaving for this movie premiere in twenty minutes."

"Fancy," April said.

Ramona laughed. "We're exhausted."

April nodded even though Ramona couldn't see her. Always the royal *we* these days. April remembered when she and Ramona were the *we*. Of course, she was happy for her best friend—wouldn't want Ramona to have any less than everything she wanted—but she was learning that being happy for her friend sometimes came with loneliness for herself.

And she hated it.

"Did you see my texts?" she asked.

"Oh, I . . ." Ramona trailed off, and April imagined her pulling back to check her phone. There was a pause, then a softly uttered "Holy shit."

"Yeah," April said.

"Wait, wait. Your teaching partner is Daphne Love."

"In the flesh."

"*The* Daphne Love?"

"The one and only." April snagged one of the bite-sized appetizers from a tray the servers carried through the room, a crab cake topped with Old Bay mayo, and popped it in her mouth. "And she's a mess," she said around the food.

"I bet she's terrified of you," Ramona said. "How did she react?"

April swallowed. "She didn't."

"She . . . didn't?"

"No clue who I am."

Ramona blew out a breath so strong it buzzed in April's ear. "Apes."

"It's fine," April said, but her throat thickened, the knowledge that Elena hadn't even bothered to tell Daphne about her hitting all over again. "Anyway, how are you?"

"Wait, Apes," Ramona said softly.

Too softly.

She thought she wanted that—Ramona's tenderness and caring, her empathy—but suddenly, her gentle, *oh honey* kind of tone was making April feel the opposite of comforted.

She felt exposed.

Silly and strange and alone.

"This is a big deal," Ramona said.

April didn't say anything. She couldn't. Ramona didn't know just how big of a deal everything was in her life right now. April hadn't been very forthcoming about Wonderlust, about her mortgage struggles, renting out her house. And she definitely hadn't told Ramona about *living* at Cloverwild with Daphne. Ramona thought she'd simply taken a fun summer job and that Mac was handling things at the shop. The truth was embarrassing, for one—April Evans, business entrepreneur and failure. Of course, she'd tell Ramona everything eventually, but on the phone while her heart felt like a tender piece of meat stuck in her chest at a ritzy party was not the moment.

"I'll live," April said, wanting to shut down the conversation as soon as possible. "Plus, I think you're right. She seems terrified of me."

Ramona exhaled. "You're not being very nice, are you?"

April felt herself flinch. "Should I be?"

"Well . . . I don't know. I'm just saying, you don't know her situation. Are her and Elena even together?"

"Of course they are."

"Then why is she at Cloverwild? Why is she a mess, as you say?"

Goddamn Libras. April's head swam with all Ramona's balanced logic. She loved her best friend. Would lie down on a train track for her. But sometimes, she swore to the goddess, she simply wanted Ramona to lose her shit along with her.

"I don't know, and I don't care," April said. "Whose side are you on?"

"Yours," Ramona said. "Always yours. I just think . . . she's one of us. She's queer, she's an artist."

"So was *Elena*."

"I know, but she's not Elena. And it's been three years. There's no need to hate her so vehemently without knowing all the facts first."

"And if I get the *facts*, am I allowed to hate her then, Mom?"

Silence on the other end.

April closed her eyes. "I'm sorry."

"It's okay," Ramona said. "I know this is hard."

"I said I'll live."

"No, I mean . . ." Ramona trailed off for a second. "I miss you, Apes."

April's eyes stung, her throat achy and tight. "I miss you too."

In the background, April heard Dylan say something.

"Listen," Ramona said, sighing. "I—"

"You've got to go," April said.

"Yeah. I'm sorry."

"Don't apologize. You've got a life. So do I."

This last part was a stretch; April's *life* was practically in shambles, but she didn't want Ramona to worry.

"Have fun at the premiere," she said, and then ended the call once Ramona said a far-too-gentle goodbye. April dropped her phone into her pocket, the party spinning all around her, everyone so beautiful and smiling. She turned to face the large window, the lake's wide swath outside, and her shoulders relaxed. She'd always loved the water, loved the simple sight of it, its constancy and easy beauty.

"April?"

April glanced to her side, where a woman had stepped up next to her. She was in her midforties and beautiful, with dark brown skin and dark curls that spiraled past her shoulders. She wore a white keyhole cocktail dress that fell past her knees, her bare arms glowing under the amber lights. She held two sparkling glasses of champagne.

"I thought that was you," she said, a London accent curling around her words as she held out one of the glasses.

April tilted her head, but recognition came almost immediately—a hot August day four years ago, a sketch of weeds and wildflowers surrounding a rough wooden door opening into a dark space.

"Nicola," she said, taking the proffered glass and then flicking her eyes to Nicola's left thigh, where April had inked the piece onto her skin, even though it was now covered by her dress. "The wild unknown."

"You remember?" Nicola said. "I'm impressed."

April laughed. "Don't give me too much credit. I mostly just remember my work."

Nicola nodded. "Which means you put a lot of care into it. I like that. I remember that. Your shop was quite an experience. I've never forgotten it."

April smiled but felt a pang of loss along with the flare of pride in her chest. "I'm sorry to say I had to close it."

She said it quickly—the first time she'd uttered those words out loud.

Nicola's expression fell.

April nodded and took a sip of champagne. She wasn't sure what else to say, but she braced for the inevitable *what's next* question. A terrifying, soul-sucking inquiry.

"I'm very sorry to hear that," Nicola said, "but the timing might be fortuitous."

April narrowed her eyes. "How so?"

"I'm at Cloverwild off and on during the summer while my husband finishes writing his dissertation," Nicola said, taking a delicate sip of her own drink. "I was hoping to get a chance to talk to you in person tonight. And here you are."

April lifted her brows, waiting for the *why* of it all.

Nicola pursed her mouth, smiling at April, and April got the distinct feeling that she was intentionally building drama.

"I'm putting together an exhibition at the Devon."

April's eyes widened. "The Devon."

Nicola's smile spread like the Cheshire cat's. "The Devon."

A good reason for all the drama, then. The Devon was a world-renowned museum in London. It housed a regular collection of art by now-famous contemporary artists as well as showcasing new talent on the regular, mostly from marginalized artists. It was known for art that pushed boundaries, challenged systems of power, spun well-known stories in a different light. April remembered learning about the Devon at RISD during her modern art class, as well as experiencing intense jealousy when a classmate had landed a fellowship there after graduation.

Everyone who even moderately dabbled in visual art had heard of the Devon.

"You're a curator at the Devon?" April asked.

"I am."

"Now I'm the one who's impressed," April said.

Nicola didn't deny the clout that came along with her position, which April sort of loved about her. She simply continued to smile—no teeth, small mouthed—and took another sip of her champagne.

"I'm looking for one more artist," she said after swallowing.

"For what?"

"I have an exhibition that's going to run for three weeks in October called *Evolution*," Nicola went on. "Full transparency, it's the first of its kind I've ever curated completely independently, so I have a lot riding on this."

April could only stare at her, because honestly, she couldn't think why Nicola would be telling her any of this, or why any of this meant *fortuitous timing*.

Unless . . .

"I thought of you," Nicola said.

April's whole body froze. "Me."

"You," Nicola said. "Like I said, I've never forgotten my experience with you. When my husband suggested we spend the summer in Clover Lake, it felt like a sign."

"A sign," April echoed.

"You believe in those, right?" Nicola asked. "If I remember correctly. The stars and such."

April opened her mouth but closed it again. Her brain felt suddenly fuzzy, packed to the brim with ideas and what-ifs.

And doubts. A lot of doubts.

"But I'm a tattoo artist," April finally said. "I'm not—"

"You're an illustrator. Correct?"

April swallowed hard. "Yes. But . . ." She trailed off, unsure of how to finish that sentence. She *was* an illustrator. She was an artist. And she was a damn good one. Once upon a time, she knew that. It wasn't that she thought tattooing was a lesser art—it certainly wasn't—but somewhere along the line, between struggling to keep her shop open for the last two years and feeling perpetually stuck, she might have forgotten exactly who she was. Just a little.

"I am," she said firmly.

Nicola nodded once. "Good. Do you think you could put some pieces together over the next several weeks? I'd love to see what you come up with. Of course, I can't promise a place in the exhibition, but I can promise serious consideration."

April blinked at her. "In the . . . in *your* . . . at the Devon?"

Nicola smiled beatifically. "See you in class, April."

April continued to gawp at her as she wandered off, sliding her hand through the arm of a tall Black man in an impeccable gray suit, who handed her a fresh glass of champagne. They ambled into the crowd and disappeared, but April still couldn't pull her eyes away.

Couldn't breathe.

She finally managed to blink, the room and the party's noise coming back into focus.

The Devon.

The *Devon*.

One of the most prestigious contemporary art museums in the world, and she might . . .

Nicola was . . .

It was possible that . . .

April wiped a hand down her face as the last ten minutes settled into her blood. She needed air. She needed air and a good pinch on the arm, and—

No.

What she really needed was a great idea.

APRIL WALKED QUICKLY through the front doors and outside. She immediately breathed a little easier, the cool evening air a balm to her overheated skin. The sun had just set, a lavender twilight glow quickly darkening to a comforting black. The sky was cloudless, the moon a shining crescent. A few guests were about, drinks in their hands.

April headed toward the pier, her mind ablaze. Lanterns lit the path from the firepit on the stone patio toward the water, making everything glow gold. The path blossomed out onto a larger rectangular area bordered by a wire-and-wood barrier keeping people safe from toppling into the water. A few small blue chairs were set around the space, but right now, the pier was empty.

April reached the edge and pressed herself against the barrier, leaning over a bit to stare down into the deep green water growing darker by the second as evening faded into night.

She tried to catch her breath, but it kept coming faster. Ramona, Nicola, Elena, Daphne, the Devon—it all swirled in the center of her chest, wild and untamed. Maybe a tumble into the lake would shock her into thinking straight. Normally, she'd consider it. She'd always been up for lake shenanigans as a kid—as a teen, as an adult, the wilder the better as long as she was safe—but she was at her place of business, potential art class guests milling about. Standing on the railing in her fancy outfit and cannonballing into Clover Lake was probably not the greatest idea.

So she simply dreamed.

Seemed about all she was capable of these days.

Except . . .

The Devon.

It was real. *Right there.* Not just a dream, but actually possible. Honestly, showing her work in a museum's exhibition was never even something she'd fantasized about. In college, she'd studied a lot of different styles and mediums for illustration, enjoyed the museums and galleries she'd visited for classes, but she could never quite picture herself in one—her work, her creations on the wall.

Then again, she'd always planned to come back to Clover Lake after college. She loved her town, and Ramona had moved back after her first year. April didn't regret any of that, her time with Ramona and Olive, her time with Wonderlust. But she was curious about what else was out there. A normal dream, she supposed, but now . . . now she had to do more than dream about what she wanted.

She had to actually figure it out.

"April?"

Her head shot up, eyes landing on Daphne Love.

She groaned inwardly.

"Look, I'm sorry, but I'm really not in the mood," she said. She knew her tone was harsher than Daphne deserved, but her brain could not take one more thing right now. She wanted to simply stand here, look out at the water, and dream.

Still, Daphne flinched slightly, her nostrils flaring a little. She wore a backless gray dress with a halter neck, the material thin and silky and hugging her thighs. Her hair was in a knot at the back of her neck, the sides brushed slick and straight against her head, an elegant part down the middle.

She wasn't beautiful at all. Nope. Not one damn bit.

April looked away, eyes back on the water.

"I saw you walk down here," Daphne said evenly. "You looked like you had a lot on your mind."

April said nothing. Just stared out at the water.

"And *I* am a decent human being," Daphne went on, "so I check on people when they seem overwhelmed."

Oh, that was fucking rich.

"*You* are a decent human being?" April asked. She turned to face Daphne, one elbow leaning on the railing.

Daphne's jaw went tight, arms rigid at her sides. And fine, yes, April had to admit it—the *less* decent human being side of her was getting a very small kick out of seeing this woman get angry. It was much better than all the tears, that was for damn sure.

"Listen," April said, tilting her head. "I realize you're probably used to batting those baby greens at whoever the fuck and getting anything your little country heart desires, but that's not going to fly with me."

Daphne's face went red then, and her eyes widened, the whites nearly fluorescent in the dim evening light. Her hands were closed fists, her mouth nothing but a tight bud. She looked so akin to a cartoon character with steam coming out of her ears, April wanted to laugh, but she was pretty sure that would be a touch over the line.

April knew she was being a dick.

But for the life of her, she couldn't figure out how to *not* be one when it came to Daphne, and honestly didn't care to put forth the effort.

"That's it," Daphne said, bouncing on her feet a little, a tiny volcano about to blow.

"What's it?" April asked, feigning boredom.

"You," Daphne said, waving her hand between them. "This toxic, *I'm a big bad Goth bitch* vibe you've got going on."

April smiled like . . . well, like a big bad Goth bitch. "I'm going to get that on my tombstone."

Daphne grunted in frustration, and April did laugh then, which only made Daphne's lovely face deepen into a darker shade of crimson.

"I'm going to head in," April said, pushing her arm off the railing and starting to turn back toward the lodge. "Feel free to stay out of the cabin until I'm asleep."

"Oh no you don't," Daphne said, then hooked her arm through April's, stopping her from moving.

April flicked her gaze down to where their elbows linked, then back up to Daphne's face. "What are you doing?"

"We're going to settle this," Daphne said.

"Settle what?"

"Whatever your problem is with me." Daphne started pulling her toward the wooden stairs that led down to the dock.

"Are you going to throw me into the lake?" April asked, letting Daphne tug her along. Honestly, she was curious if this Tennessee waif had it in her.

"If only," Daphne said as they stepped off the last stair and onto the dock. Several canoes bobbed in the water, and Daphne approached the closest one, a deep green vessel with a bright yellow paddle. She released April, then motioned toward the boat. "Get in."

April lifted her brows. "Get in? Just like that? You could be planning to murder me."

"You'd deserve it."

April flinched. "*I'd* deserve it?"

"Have you been here for the way you've treated me the last two days?" Daphne's voice was nearly a screech. "For no reason."

"I have reasons," April said. "Many."

Daphne literally stomped her foot. If April wasn't such a

dizzying mix of frustrated and intrigued right now, she'd smile and comment on how cute it was.

But no. Goddammit, Daphne Love was anything but *cute*.

"Get *in*," Daphne said. "We figure this out now, because I've had the worst spring of my life, I need this job, and I cannot spend the summer terrified my partner is casting spells to bring about my demise while I sleep."

"You said I was Goth, not a witch."

Daphne just pointed to the boat.

April blew out a breath, too tired to fight her on this anymore. And she had a point—they did have to work together. April understood that she was still in a bit of shock from meeting Daphne, a person she'd never expected to lay eyes on in real life.

Ever.

But this was the reality of the situation, and maybe a bit of exposure therapy would help her lower that scorpion stinger a little.

Plus, she had the Devon to think about now, and it was just too fucking exhausting feeling poised to attack all the time.

"Fine," she said, holding on to the post next to the boat, and stepping into the canoe. "But you're paddling."

Daphne made a noise behind her, but April was too busy scrambling to sit down on the bench on one end, wobbling as she did so, to pay her much mind. Daphne, for her part, glided into the canoe as though she'd lived on one half her life. She untied the vessel, then picked up the yellow paddle and closed her fingers around the T-grip, using the blade to push them away from the dock.

"Done much canoein' in yer day down South?" April said, putting on an admittedly horrible Southern accent.

"As a matter of fact, yes," Daphne said calmly, except she sounded more like Emily Gilmore at the moment. April did hear the hint of a Southern twang in her voice at times, though, cutting off final consonants and using a few elongated vowels here and there.

"Have you?" Daphne asked. "Didn't you grow up here?"

April lifted a brow. "And who told you that?"

Daphne sighed. "Why is every inquiry into your life taken as a knife in your back?"

April had no answer for her, really. At least, not one she wanted to get into at this moment. So she simply sighed dramatically, lifting her shoulders with the inhalation and jutting out her chin on the exhale.

Daphne dug the paddle into the water, moving them quickly away from the dock. Cloverwild grew smaller and smaller, and Clover Lake spread out before them, trees nothing but dark shapes against the blue-black sky.

"Yes, I grew up here," April said finally. "Since I was nine. And I love the water. I just have horrible balance."

Daphne smirked. "Was that so hard?"

"Excruciating."

"Well, I'm about to ask you another question, so brace yourself."

April grimaced. "I'd rather discuss the mating habits of brook trout."

"Brook trout?"

"The official freshwater fish of New Hampshire."

"Of course," Daphne said. "I'm fascinated by their mating patterns."

"As are we all."

Daphne cracked a smile, and April very nearly mirrored her expression, but stopped herself just in time. She didn't want to smile at Daphne Love. And she definitely didn't want to answer any of her questions. They fell silent, and Daphne sliced through the water one more time before setting the paddle across her lap. They drifted lazily in the darkness.

April tilted her head toward the dark sky packed with stars, hoping they could just stay like this—quiet, getting used to each other's presence without having to deal with anything real. That was all she really needed. Simple adjustment. A settling in.

Of course, Daphne had other plans.

"So what exactly is your problem with me?" she asked.

April kept her gaze on the sky, eyes searching for constellations. She could always spot Orion, the Big and Little Dippers, Cassiopeia. Others were a little trickier, but she loved the hunt. She wondered how long she could simply ignore the question, looking for Virgo and Hydra, but then something Daphne said on the dock floated back to her.

"Why have you had the worst spring of your life?" April asked, head still tilted to the heavens.

Daphne was quiet for a second. April spotted what she thought was the crab in the sky—Cancer.

"That's how you're going to play this?" Daphne finally asked. "Answering a question with a question?"

April looked at her now. "Tit for tat. And you answer first. Those are my terms."

Daphne pursed her mouth. "Can't we start with something easier, then?"

"Like what? Your favorite color?"

"Perfect," Daphne said. "It's gray. What's yours?"

April gave her a look. "Gray. Your favorite color is . . . *gray*."

"Even my favorite color annoys you?" Daphne asked.

"It doesn't annoy me. I'm surprised, that's all. I figured someone like you would pick lavender or baby blue or, like, fuchsia."

"Someone like me?"

April sighed.

"Would you *please* stop doing that?" Daphne asked, teeth obviously gritted.

"Doing what?"

Daphne just pressed her eyes closed, shook her head, and took a deep breath. "I like gray because it's soft and calm, like a cloudy day. A blanket pulled over the world. And I like the possibilities of it—it's not black, it's not white, just a million shades in between."

April felt something in the center of her chest loosen. Daphne's green eyes were big and liquid, and she looked at April as though waiting for her to offer back some sort of poetry about colors.

April cleared her throat, straightened her shoulders, then motioned toward her pants. "I like black." And that was true, she did . . . but black wasn't her favorite color. Not by a long shot.

Daphne pressed her lips together, nodded. "Got it."

"Why did you have the worst spring of your life?" April asked again, barely letting a beat pass. She understood the absurdity here—she didn't want to share her favorite color, for goddess's sake, but she wanted to know all about Daphne's pain.

Maybe she *was* a terrible human being.

Daphne dipped the paddle back into the water. For a few seconds, April didn't think she was going to answer and they'd be back to square one talking about long walks on the beach or favorite ice cream flavors.

But then Daphne inhaled. The tiniest sound, the simplest motion, but the air dragged slowly into her lungs, as though fighting its way in against Daphne's will, and April felt it.

A shift.

A *knowing.*

A familiarity.

"I thought I was going to get engaged," Daphne finally said. "And instead . . ."

Her voice was quiet, but steady. April, however, felt her insides disintegrating. Daphne hesitated, then kept hesitating, her throat working in a swallow. April wanted to scream at her to go on, but somehow a softer side of her prevailed.

"Instead what?" she whispered. Even though she knew. Maybe Ramona was right about Daphne and Elena, and maybe April had known she was right the whole time, ever since Daphne showed up on the cabin's porch teary and stressed.

Daphne smiled, but it was sad, resigned. "Instead, I got my heart broken."

April let the truth settle between them. She waited to feel some kind of relief. Maybe even a little glee. She wasn't proud, but there it was, her grudge-holding heart reaching for a tiny bit of smug satisfaction.

But she didn't feel any of that.

She just felt an old ache, familiar and lonely.

"Elena," Daphne said. "That's her name."

April just looked at Daphne, still digging for any clue that Daphne knew who she was. But there was nothing. Only a heartbroken woman sitting across from her.

"She's older than me," Daphne went on. "Eleven years. We met when I was a senior in college and I interned at the Museum of Fine Arts."

April stayed silent.

"I know, right?" Daphne said, shaking her head and laughing a little. "Such a cliché. The young intern and her hot, single power-lesbian supervisor."

That described Elena all right. Everything except . . .

"So she was single when you met her?" April asked.

Daphne frowned. "Of course she was."

"You're sure?" April asked.

Daphne blinked rapidly, clearly taken aback. "Yes. I'm sure. God, can you imagine? Why would you even ask me that?"

April opened her mouth, but nothing came out. She could tell Daphne the truth. Just get it off her chest, clear the air, explain why she'd been such an asshole since they'd met. But goddammit, she didn't want to feel like this again—the ex, the woman scorned, the one who was left. And if she told Daphne the everything right now, that was who she'd be. All summer. Every art class. Every time she walked into the cabin to find Daphne reading or snuggling with Bob, that's *all* she would be.

Elena's ex.

And that's not who she was anymore.

So she offered Daphne a scrap, the tiniest crumb of truth.

"I get it," April finally said. "I had a fiancée."

Daphne sniffed. "You did?"

"Once upon a time. She was . . . well, she was lovely. Until she wasn't."

Daphne's lips pressed flat. "I'm so sorry."

April shrugged. "It was a long time ago. I got over it, and so will you."

Daphne's eyes welled again. "What was her name?"

April sent her gaze skyward again. She could *feel* Daphne's silence though. She waited for it to pass—she could wait anyone out, never had to say a word. April was content to hold her secrets close, always had been. She waited and she waited, but the quiet between them just grew thicker. April looked for more shapes in the stars, looked for herself, though she knew Scorpius was in the southern sky.

"You do that a lot," Daphne said.

April didn't look at her. "Do what?"

"Look at the stars."

April's gaze drifted over the heavens. "I guess I do."

"Why?" Daphne had turned them around and started paddling again, the canoe slicing through water and air toward Cloverwild.

And for a split second, wildly, April wanted to tell her. Tell her something real. Something true. She wanted to tell her about the loneliness of her childhood, all about her parents' desire for a child and the child they actually got. She wanted to tell her about her grandmother teaching her about astrology, about going to the library and devouring everything she could find about star charts and signs. How it all made April feel like she had a reason.

Like *she* was a reason, as opposed to a random amalgam of cells her parents would've altered if they could.

But then April heard laughter from Cloverwild's dock, and April remembered who Daphne was, who *she* was, how she hadn't told these stories to anyone since the night she'd fallen in love with Elena Watson.

And that was the way she'd rather keep it.

"No reason," she said, eyes locked on the dock, on her freedom from this conversation. She still had no clue how she was going to get through this summer with Daphne, but she was an adult. She'd acted like an asshole, yes, but she could figure out how to move past all of this.

She'd done it before with no help from Daphne Love or Elena Watson.

She'd fucking do it again.

April took a deep breath, nodding to herself, but noticed Daphne had stopped paddling again, about twenty feet from the dock. Daphne watched her with an expression April couldn't really parse. Eyes softly narrowed, but mouth taut—curiosity and suspicion all at once.

"What?" April asked.

"You suck at tit for tat," Daphne said.

April laughed lightly. "Maybe I do."

"Why did you ask me if Elena was single when I met her?"

April's spine went rigid. "I was—"

"Because that's not exactly a normal question to ask someone who just went through a breakup."

April cleared her throat, looked down at her lap now. "I was curious. That's all."

But Daphne shook her head, sadness spilling into her expression now. "I don't think so."

"Goddamn water signs," April said under her breath.

"She cheated on you, didn't she?" Daphne asked softly. "Your ex."

And it felt like taking a bullet. The shock of Daphne's assessment. Yes, it had been three years. April felt no pain for Elena herself, but she still felt the heartache of the act—the heartache and betrayal, how disposable it had made her feel.

"Yes," April said curtly. "She did, okay? She dumped me like a piece of trash three years ago. Now can you row us back to the dock?"

Daphne didn't start paddling though. She simply stared at April with a devastated look on her face. And dammit, for all of Daphne's emotional transparency, April couldn't tell if it was pity, empathy, or some clairvoyant *knowing*.

"What was her name?" Daphne asked again.

"Fuck," April said quietly, then looked down at her lap, picked at her chipping black nail polish. And she knew she couldn't do it—couldn't lie to Daphne, no matter how much easier this would be if she did. Blissful ignorance and all that.

And maybe part of her wanted the truth out there, the air fully cleared. Maybe a smaller part of her wanted Daphne to know—wanted her to understand exactly how and why and when and who.

Maybe, really, she just wanted to exist in this sordid history, because ever since yesterday when it became clear that Elena had never once mentioned April's name to Daphne—April, who Elena had asked to marry her once upon a time—April felt like she was disappearing.

She thought about her parents, about Ramona, about her complete lack of other adult friends. She'd been disappearing for a while now. Maybe her whole life, one tiny millimeter at a time. And goddammit, she was tired of it. She didn't want to be Elena's ex, no. But she had to be something, didn't she?

Someone.

So she sent a hand through her hair and met Daphne's probing gaze. "Her name was Elena."

Chapter Six

DAPHNE FELT HERSELF go still, but it took a second for her brain to catch up with what her body was already processing.

"Her name is . . ." She trailed off, because the name April said couldn't be right. Or it was just a massively ironic coincidence. "Elena."

April nodded, her eyes a little glassy.

Daphne took a breath. "Elena—"

"Elena Watson," April said. "Yes, that Elena Watson. *Your* Elena Watson."

Daphne blinked rapidly. "Wait . . . what are you saying?"

April blew out a breath. "You really didn't know?"

Daphne tried to swallow but couldn't. "Know what?"

April just stared at her.

Daphne felt her world shrinking.

Or expanding.

Exploding.

She dumped me like a piece of trash three years ago.

"Wait," Daphne said again, as though asking the truth to back off and hang on a second would actually work.

Three years ago.

"How . . ." Daphne said, but didn't know how to finish the sentence. How to finish any sentence. "Why . . . when . . ."

"Three years ago," April said. "I'd met her three years before that in Boston. We lived together here and in the city. She asked me to marry her. We were happy, and then—"

"Wait, wait, wait," Daphne said, holding up a shaking hand. "You're talking so fast."

April stopped, but only for a second. Her voice was soft, but her words felt like bombs detonating. "You really didn't know that she—"

"No, no, I didn't know anything," Daphne said, then pressed her hands to her ears. She was sure she looked ridiculous, like a little kid, but she couldn't help it. The universe was flying, spinning, and she just needed a second to breathe, to think.

April gave it to her.

They sat silently while Daphne tried to understand the meaning of letters, syllables, words.

Three years ago.

That could mean any time in the year she'd met Elena. It didn't necessarily mean it all overlapped, that Elena had—

She met April's eyes again, so dark, like pools of ink rimmed in black liner, and she knew it all matched up perfectly. The puzzle pieces of the last two days locked into place, creating the full picture—April's immediate animosity toward her upon meeting, her sharp tones that bordered on mean.

Angry.

Hurt.

"You knew who I was this whole time," Daphne said. It wasn't a question. "That's why you've been so awful."

April fiddled with the crescent moon ring on her middle finger, one of the several silver rings she wore.

"I was surprised," April said. "I never expected to meet you in person, and then I couldn't believe that Elena never . . ." She trailed off. Daphne could've sworn her lower lip wobbled a little, but in the next second, April's jaw was steel and iron. "That you didn't know."

"I didn't," Daphne said. "I swear."

April released a loud breath. "Yeah. I can see that now."

Daphne didn't know what to do. What to feel. What to say or think or be.

Elena had cheated on someone.

With her.

Elena had cheated on her fiancée, the woman sitting across from Daphne right now in this canoe, with *her.*

She stood up suddenly, the paddle thumping into the bottom of the boat. The canoe pitching wildly.

"Whoa, hey," April said, gripping the sides.

"I need to get off this boat," Daphne said. Her airway was closing. Her heart felt too large in her chest. "I can't breathe."

"Okay, okay, just sit down," April said, leaning over for the paddle. "I'll get us back."

Daphne nodded, but she couldn't get her legs to bend. She felt locked, frozen, couldn't get her brain and body to connect. She looked down at her sandaled feet, the skirt of her dress fluttering in the breeze. She started to ease down, but she lost her balance and tilted too far to the left.

"Shit, Daphne," April said, reaching out for her.

Daphne's arms, however, were too busy flailing. She wasn't even sure how it all happened, but one second she was pinwheeling, and the next she was in the lake.

It was freezing.

And wet.

And completely humiliating.

Daphne had barely come up to the surface, still sputtering

water, the mineral scent of the lake clinging to her hair and skin, when she heard another splash.

She yelped, eyes still closed as something came close, brushed against her back.

"Oh my god!" she yelled, imagining some lake creature ready to devour her.

"Daphne, stop!"

April's voice, close and panicked.

Daphne forced herself to slow down long enough to see April in the water next to her, April's arm around her waist.

"What are you doing?" Daphne asked, legs frantically treading water.

"What am *I* doing?" April asked. "You're drowning."

"I am not! I'm just—"

But she wasn't sure what she was doing. She was in the lake fully clothed, a mere twenty feet or so from the dock, with her ex's ex-fiancée floating next to her looking like a drowned rat, mascara streaming down her cheeks.

"Why did you jump in here?" Daphne asked.

"I didn't know if you could swim," April said, wiping the water out of her eyes. "And you were in shock. It's deep in this part of the lake."

"You're an idiot," Daphne said, but she started laughing.

"Me?" April said, splashing her. "You're the one who fell in a lake."

Daphne laughed harder, which was not very conducive to keeping herself afloat.

"God, don't drown now," April said, tugging her toward the canoe. Her arm was tight around Daphne's waist, her face close as she directed them both.

It was no small feat getting back into the canoe without tipping the whole thing over. It took a few tries, Cloverwild guests observing from the dock with glasses of champagne as though watching a show.

Finally, they managed to spill onto the boat's floor like slippery eels, lying next to each other and breathing hard, their limbs entangled and soaked to the skin.

Daphne looked up at the sky, stars spread over the dark like glitter. For a second, she understood why April loved them so much. They made her feel small and big at the same time. Inconsequential, just a cluster of cells riding around on a rock in the middle of space. But also, a point of life in the middle of all that chaos.

A *being.*

"Show me something," she said, waving her hand at the sky.

"What?" April said.

"A constellation. A star. Anything."

April was quiet for a moment but then lifted her hand and pointed. "You see that line right there?" She traced the sky, dragging her finger down and to the side. "Then how it forks, like an upside-down V?"

Daphne squinted, following April's fingers as they outlined the shape again, stars forming what sort of looked like a broom.

"I see it," Daphne said.

"That's the crab."

"The crab?"

"Cancer," April said, turning to look at Daphne. "You."

Daphne met her gaze. "Me?"

"At least, that's your moon sign," April said.

Daphne's mouth dropped open a little. "How did you know that?"

April smiled softly. "I have a knack. I'm still working on your sun and rising."

"I could just tell you."

"Nah," April said, sitting up and carefully moving herself to the bow seat. She picked up the paddle and started rowing them back to the dock. "I like figuring it out."

Daphne said nothing as the boat moved through the water. She stayed prone at the bottom, her soaked dress growing cold on her skin, watching as the crab blurred across the sky.

"You know, Elena is why I even know anything about my signs," she said, eyes still on the stars. April stayed silent, the paddle pulling through the water the only sound. "Did she learn all of that from you?"

April sighed. "Probably."

"My family wasn't into astrology at all." She laughed, a sort of exhausted giddiness filling her chest. "Actually, that's an understatement. They thought it was *evil.* Divination. The Devil with a capital D."

"Jesus."

"Exactly."

April huffed a tiny laugh, which somehow worked to settle the swirling feelings around Daphne's heart.

"So you grew up Christian?" April asked.

"Also an understatement," Daphne said, eyes blurring on the pinpricks of light now. "My dad was the pastor of the Baptist church in our town."

"What town was that?"

"Crestwater, Tennessee."

"How did you end up in Boston?"

Daphne released a breath and squeezed her eyes closed, Elena and April and the last three years washing over her like a wave in a storm. And then she started talking. Because talking was the only way to quiet her thoughts, and maybe, just maybe, if she laid everything out for April, she'd figure out how she got here too, how she ended up in this canoe with the person whose heart she unknowingly helped break.

"I was fifteen when my mom found my sketchbook," she said.

April sucked in a breath but said nothing as she paddled them closer to shore, so Daphne kept talking.

It had been ten years, but the day she walked into her room to find her mom sitting on her bed, her posture impossibly straight, flipping through the pages slowly, methodically, still felt viscerally recent. Pages that held drawings and journal entries of all of Daphne's secrets. Secrets she had to tell someone, some*thing*, and the god her parents worshipped wasn't listening. She didn't even have a best friend to trust, to whisper to, because all her friends went to her family's church, and they all loved church, felt right at home lifting their hands and singing in the choir, while Daphne just felt invisible.

"This isn't who we raised you to be," her mother had said then. "This isn't what a daughter of God should be."

And that was it—two sentences that broke Daphne's heart in two, the truth of what her parents thought about her after so many years of fearing exactly that.

That she was wrong.

That she was only lovable if she fell in line, fit a certain mold.

And so she tried. She tried and tried and tried, for the next two years. Her mother took the sketchbook, and Daphne didn't start a new one. She painted, but only innocuous images like flowers and cats, oceans she'd never seen and cityscapes she wasn't sure even existed. She went to church, and she prayed and prayed and prayed. She didn't look twice at cute girls, and she even stopped talking to Gabe, her only other gay friend at school, whose parents supported him and loved him and championed him.

She fell in line.

She stuffed herself into a mold.

And she withered and dried, like a butterfly caught in a net, then pinned down for display.

"Daphne," April said when Daphne paused. "That's . . . that's awful. I'm sorry."

Daphne just shrugged. "Homophobia in a small town is nothing new, I know. Clover Lake is pretty small."

April sighed. "It is. Though I definitely didn't have Baptist parents and a whole conservative church community watching my every move. Still, I was one of three out queer kids in my high school. We stuck together, to say the least. Sounds like you didn't have even that."

"No," Daphne said.

April nodded. "How did you . . . well . . ."

"Escape?"

April laughed a little. "That sounds like a horrible word for it, but yeah."

"It is horrible," Daphne said. "But that's exactly what it was. I had an art teacher at school. Ms. Hale. She wore bright skirts and red lipstick and no ring on her left hand, a total aberration in Crestwater. My senior year, she convinced me to join her advanced painting class, and that changed everything."

Over the next few months, Daphne slowly came back to life, painting an entire body of work during her time in Ms. Hale's class. She painted girls and rainbows. She painted drag queens and queer identity flags and self-portraits. She painted everything in her heart, everything her family said was wrong, everything she'd been keeping inside since she'd lost her sketchbook.

Lost *herself.*

When the time came to think about life after graduation, applying for colleges, and the future, Daphne worked with Ms. Hale to apply to the best art schools in the country.

She didn't tell her parents.

As far as they knew, she'd only applied to the state school in the next town, an option that would let her stay at home while she studied to be a teacher.

When she got into Boston University and Savannah College of Art and Design and UCLA and Bard, it felt like a dream, something she wasn't sure would ever be real. But then Boston offered her a full scholarship, and she knew that was it.

Her lifeline.

Her chance.

And she took it.

The whole process felt gauzy and bright at the same time. How she kept Boston a secret for months; how she sat through her graduation with a serene smile on her face, her mom snapping photos and waving from the school auditorium's audience; how she never said a thing about her plans until the night before, when her mother walked into her room without knocking to find her packing.

How she told her mother she was leaving.

How her mother simply turned around and walked out of the room.

How her older sister, Amelia, had watched her pack from the hallway, her eyes red and watery, and never said a word.

How her father told her calmly that if she left like this, she would not be welcomed back.

How *quiet* it all was.

How final.

"And that's how I ended up in Boston," Daphne said. She felt the boat hit the dock, but April didn't move. Neither did she.

"Do you talk to your family at all?" April asked.

Daphne's throat went thick, just like it always did when she thought about her parents and Amelia. "No," she said, and left it at that.

She hadn't meant to leave and cut off all communication. But her father's declaration paved the way for silence, and when months passed of her new life in Boston—a timid life, sure, but one filled with art and other people just like her—without any contact from her family, she let it happen.

She let the line break.

She missed her family—her sister especially; memories of when they were tiny girls making mud pies near the creek, fairy hunting in the woods, felt like a physical pain sometimes. But what she missed most was a family that loved her.

Loved *her.*

Not some image of her they'd created.

She sat up in the canoe, her skin cold and pebbling with goose bumps. She glanced at April, who was shivering, hair wet and slicked against her head, her makeup a mess.

"God," April said, laughing a little. "Do I look as bad as you do right now?"

Daphne scoffed but couldn't keep from smiling too. "How dare you."

April smiled back. It was small, maybe a little sad, a little wary still, but it was there.

"Thank you for telling me," Daphne said as April stood to tie the canoe to the dock. "About Elena."

April's shoulders went a little tight, and she looked out toward the water. "Thank *you,*" she said quietly.

And that was the end of it as they secured the canoe, then climbed onto the dock and walked toward the lodge side by side, garnering curious looks from the guests as they went.

DAPHNE COULDN'T SLEEP.

After they'd gotten back to their cabin, she'd stood under the hot spray of the shower for half an hour, warming her skin and bones and blood. She'd washed her hair, finally, and even taken care to slide some gel through her curls. She'd brushed her teeth, gone through all the motions of getting ready for bed, all the while trying to slow down her brain.

Trying not to stare at April.

Trying not to wonder about April and Elena.

Trying not to ask questions.

But she had so many, most of which she wasn't even sure April could answer.

Or *would* answer.

April hadn't said much since they'd returned to their cabin. She let Daphne shower first, then stayed in the bathroom so long during her own turn, Daphne nearly knocked on the door to check on her. Daphne had no idea how to act, so she'd lain in bed with Bob curled up by her side, staring at the ceiling fan going around and around.

Now, a couple hours later, the cabin dark and quiet, nothing but the sound of cicadas and April's deep breathing, Daphne tried to keep her eyes closed, go through the lyrics of her favorite songs. She even resorted to counting sheep, watching fluffy white animals jump over fences in her head.

Finally, she sat up, drawing a soft mew from Bob as she grabbed her phone off her nightstand and tapped the screen. Then she stared down at the name of the only person she wanted to talk to right now.

Elena.

It was two in the morning. Elena wouldn't be awake anyway. In fact, Daphne knew her phone would be in sleep mode. And besides the impracticalities of a middle-of-the-night call, Daphne really, really shouldn't.

She knew that.

God, she *knew* that. She already felt pathetic. Stupid and silly and naive and young—how could she not have known? How was she *the other woman* and didn't even know? Talking to Elena right now would only make her feel more ridiculous, because Elena always had an explanation for everything, which just made her want to talk to Elena even more.

Because maybe there *was* an explanation.

She shook her head, then opened her nightstand drawer and threw her phone inside. It clattered loudly, startling Bob so much he jumped off the bed. Daphne froze, waiting for April to wake up too, but she simply murmured something that sounded weirdly like "None of your business, Penny," then rolled over.

Before she could scramble for her phone again, Daphne threw off her covers, grabbed her bag, and slid on her shoes, then stepped out the door and into the cool night.

~

SHE ENDED UP in the art studio.

She sat at the desk and clicked through the slides featuring tomorrow's class plan on the computer, but she couldn't focus, her mind whirling fast in every direction. She hadn't felt this way in a long time. This unsettled and helpless. This desperate for something. Anything. She didn't even know what. Maybe it was because she'd just told her entire story to April, but she felt exposed and alone, just like she had when she was fifteen and her mom found her sketchbook.

Like she was still letting someone else define the kind of life she was going to live.

She looked around at all the blank canvases waiting for stories to fill them, then stood up abruptly and went to the back cabinet, flinging it open. It was full of extra supplies—paints and brushes and charcoal and watercolors, as well as a few larger canvases for instructor modeling. She grabbed one—a huge 24x30—carried it up to the front of the room, and set it on the instructor easel.

After that, she didn't think. She simply *did*, followed the spark in her stomach and let it lead the way. She gathered paints and brushes and pencils, a palette and a palette knife, cups of water, an apron. She tied her still-damp hair back, picked up a pencil, and started sketching on the canvas. She never erased, never stepped back to think. She felt like she was seventeen, standing in Ms. Hale's classroom and sketching out two girls kissing for the first time, driven by pure fury and fear and hope.

Except in this image, there was only one girl.

And Daphne drew and drew until the girl took shape. After that, she mixed paints, color and texture and shading bringing the girl to life.

Bringing her back from the dead.

Chapter Seven

APRIL WOKE UP to furious meowing.

Bianca had staked her claim on the small navy love seat in one corner of the cabin, her blue eyes slitted in annoyance, because Bob was sitting on Daphne's bed and making a horrible racket.

"Bob, shut it," April said. Early morning light streamed in through windows, casting a lavender glow throughout the room. April pulled the covers over her head and rolled over, but Bob continued his protest.

April sat up in a huff, glaring at her cat.

Which was exactly when she noticed Daphne's bed was empty.

She grabbed her phone from where it was charging on the nightstand and checked the time.

7:09 a.m.

Far too early to be up and at 'em, in her opinion. They didn't have a class until two. She rubbed her face, while Bob continued to meow his own concern, everything that had happened the evening before washing over her. Honestly, Daphne had reacted better to their Elena connection than April thought she would. She was stunned, sure. She was upset, absolutely. But she was calm. She hadn't even really cried, which was honestly a true shocker.

And then, god, with everything Daphne had shared about her family and how she grew up, how she was completely estranged from her parents . . . it was a lot. April didn't particularly vibe with her parents, that was no secret, but total alienation? That was hard to imagine.

But Daphne was an adult.

She knew herself better than April did.

She knew what she needed, how to take care of herself.

April flopped back down into bed, closed her eyes, and tried to go back to sleep, an effort that lasted exactly fifteen seconds before she threw the covers back and got up. She went to the front door, flung it open, and walked out onto the small porch.

The morning was gorgeous—a cloudless lavender-blue sky brightening by the second, a cool breeze drifting in from the cerulean lake, the trees tall and green around her.

But no sign of April's cabinmate.

She closed the door, poured the cats some dry food. She washed her face, brushed her teeth, put on her makeup. She got dressed in a pair of black jeans and a black racerback tank top. She made coffee in the tiny pot on the desk. All the while, Bob mewed for the love of his life, and Daphne refused to appear.

Finally, April texted her a very casual Where the hell are you, then determined not to think about the woman again until it was absolutely necessary.

Unfortunately, by the time nine thirty rolled around, April knew thinking about Daphne was absolutely necessary. She'd spent most of the past two hours on the porch, trying to drum up some ideas for the Devon—her mind either a complete blank or filled with all the wrong things—but Daphne should've arrived by now, back from whatever errand she'd been running or walk she'd been taking. At the very least, she should've answered April's text. April didn't want to feel it—*concern*—but she felt partially responsible for whatever bender Daphne might have catapulted herself into. She stood up from the porch chair and tapped around on her phone before pressing the device to her ear.

She walked inside and heard a faint buzzing sound coming from Daphne's side of the room. She hurried to the nightstand and ripped open the drawer, pulling out Daphne's vibrating phone.

"Fucking hell," she said, trying to stay calm. They were in the woods. There was a very large, very deep lake not a hundred feet away. Daphne didn't know the area. She was a heartbroken disaster. And she didn't have her phone.

"Fucking *hell*," April said again, grabbing her bag and stuffing Daphne's phone inside before she stormed out the door.

APRIL WOULD NOT panic.

She would *not*.

She opted for the lodge first, mostly because she couldn't drag a lake by herself, had no idea where to start in the woods, and refused to give in to the growing sense of astrological doom. She was living and working with her cheating ex's ex, for fuck's sake, and was now searching the wide world for the woman to make sure she was still breathing. She'd had enough astrological interference for the time being, thanks very much. Surely—*surely*—the universe was done with her for right now.

The main lodge was bustling at this time of morning—breakfast dishes clinking in the dining room, guests walking around with towels over their shoulders and beach bags hanging from their arms—and the whole space smelled like rich espresso and bacon. April hurried down the hall toward the art studio, hoping Daphne had just gotten up absurdly early to prepare for their class.

Inside the studio, however, the light was off, and it was quiet.

April stood in the doorway for only a second before walking toward the front of the room, looking for any sign of her cabinmate.

And she found it.

Many signs in the form of a complete and total mess. Daphne—well, April assumed it was Daphne—had pulled a table over to an instructor's easel, then proceeded to use every color of paint in creation. Brushes of all different sizes littered the tabletop, though some were sticking out of murky glasses of water; at least five white plastic palettes smeared with paints were stacked up like pizza boxes; and there were various rags and paper towels crumpled up all over the place.

"What the fu—"

But April cut herself off when she caught sight of the easel. Or rather, what was on the easel.

A painting of a young girl.

Standing in a field of wildflowers, purples and pinks and yellows and oranges flourishing around her, so lush they might swallow her whole. The sky was clear, only a few clouds marring the pristine swirls of various shades of blue, a white farmhouse in the distance. The girl had on a plain white dress, and her blond curls were wild and unruly, as though she was shaking her head vigorously. She looked about nine or ten years old.

It was a standard image. Almost boring, even—a country girl picking flowers.

But her face.

Her face was a blur, as though the paint wasn't quite dry and someone swiped a hand through her features. April wasn't sure what it meant, but it made her feel something.

Something big.

"Holy shit," April whispered, taking a step closer, nearly pressing her nose to the canvas. The textures were incredible, the brushstrokes almost circular. The juxtaposition of the serene landscape with the girl right out of a horror story in the middle of it all . . . well, it was striking.

"Oh, god, I fell asleep."

April yelped at the voice, clutching at her chest and whirling toward the sound in the back of the room. Daphne sat up from the love seat in the back corner, her hair a wild mess, and squinted into the sunlit room.

"Jesus," April said.

"Nope, just me." Daphne rubbed her face.

"Have you been here all night?"

Daphne stood up and stretched. "I think so? I don't know. What time is it?"

"Nearly ten."

"At night?"

April just glanced pointedly toward the sunlight streaming in through the windows.

"Right," Daphne said, straightening the T-shirt she'd worn to bed the evening before.

"Is this yours?" April asked, motioning toward the painting.

Daphne froze, her mouth dropping open a little. She walked toward the front of the room, eyes never leaving the canvas. She stopped next to April, pressed her folded hands to her mouth.

"Is it?" April asked again.

Daphne nodded, gaze still locked on the blurry girl.

"It's incredible," April said.

"Really?" Daphne asked, dropping her hands.

"Are you serious?" April asked. "Do you see this thing?"

"I see it." Daphne still stared at the painting as though for the first time.

"Is she you?" April asked.

Daphne sighed. "It hurts to look at her, so I think she might be."

"What do you mean?" April asked.

Daphne shrugged, her eyes a little glassy. "She's like a bruise that's not quite healed. Or maybe it's already healed, but you still remember that achy press."

April stared at her. Of course, she knew art reflected human experience, pain, joy, everything. But somehow, Daphne's explanation was like poetry.

"Is that what art is like for you?" Daphne asked.

April frowned, the simple question like a sudden electric shock. She took Daphne's phone out of her bag, handed it back to her just for something to do with her hands. "My art is ink and needles and working off someone else's vision."

Daphne's eyes scanned the flowering tree curling over April's collarbones, the vibrant bloom of wisteria and irises on her inner forearm. "You're a tattoo artist?"

April nodded, her eyes on the blurry-faced girl in the painting. She was proud of her work. People trusted her with their bodies, and she took that seriously. She already missed her clients, missed the collaboration, but as she looked at Daphne's painting, she knew she wanted more too. Not even *more*, necessarily, because she loved tattooing, just . . . different. She wanted to create something she loved so much that it made her feel drunk. She hadn't felt that in a long time. To be taken over by something inside her that didn't even make sense except on the page. She wanted to create something for the Devon that changed her, altered her entire world. And she wanted Nicola to feel that too, feel it so much she had no choice but to put April in her show.

"Will you design a tattoo for me?" Daphne asked.

April lifted her brows. "Are you serious?"

"Yeah, I'm serious," Daphne said. "Surprise me."

"Surprise you?" April laughed. "With a tattoo."

"Just the design. Then we'll go from there."

"You don't strike me as someone who has many tattoos."

Daphne frowned. "I don't have any."

"Exactly. You really want to mar that soft baby skin?"

Daphne's frown stayed in place as she turned back toward her painting, but her eyes were suddenly distant and sad.

April felt a pinch of guilt. "Look, I didn't mean—"

"It's fine," Daphne said. "I know I'm . . ." But she trailed off, shrugging and shaking her head.

April sighed, the silence between them thick and heavy. She wanted to thin it out, change it somehow. Offer Daphne something real.

"I *was* a tattoo artist," she finally said. "I owned a tattoo shop. Wonderlust. Opened it when I was twenty-three, with some financial help from my parents. And a few weeks ago, I closed it for good."

Daphne blinked at her. "You mean . . ."

April nodded. "Couldn't do it. Even ten years in."

Daphne let that settle between them for a second, and April was grateful for the beat of space.

"I'm sorry," Daphne said.

"I haven't even told my best friend yet," April said, picking at her nail polish.

"Why not?"

April shrugged, stuffed her hands into her pockets. "She lives across the country right now. She's busy. She's . . . I don't know. We're barely talking these days."

"That all sounds really hard." Daphne shifted next to her, shoulder just an inch from April's own. "But I don't think any of that means you're not still a tattoo artist. Or any kind of artist you want to be."

Something in April's chest went tight—honestly, she wasn't sure what the hell she wanted to be. Who she was right now at this moment in time. She felt adrift and angry about being adrift, and she had no place to direct her anger, no one to share it with.

No one but Daphne fucking Love.

She nearly laughed at the irony of the whole thing. She motioned toward the painting again. "This is really good. You should do more. Like a series."

"More?" Daphne said. "This one nearly killed me."

"Maybe," April said, "that was the whole point."

Chapter Eight

THEIR FIRST CLASS was a moderate success.

Daphne took the lead, as this class was paint focused, but she was sleep-deprived and overly caffeinated from the large coffee April had fetched her while she cleaned up from her nighttime painting spree, and she kept tripping over her words for the first ten minutes, hands shaking as she clicked through their slides. She eventually found her footing, reverting to her teaching experience in college when she was a TA in the foundation program for first-years, but she felt distracted the entire session.

April.

Elena.

April and Elena.

Her painting, which now sat behind the desk, her younger self's blurry features facing the wall. The night before felt like a fever dream, as though someone else had inhabited Daphne's body, using her hand to splash paint on a canvas. But Daphne knew exactly who that girl in the painting was.

Knew it was *her.*

Unseen, lost, unformed.

And she knew she wanted to paint more, create more, tell more of her story, just like April said, even if it killed her.

Maybe that was the whole point.

April's words reverberated through her skull, terror inducing and exciting all at once. By the time class was over, she just wanted a break from all the *knowing.*

"Will you get a drink with me?" she asked April as they packed up from the class. "It's five o'clock somewhere, right?" She laughed nervously.

April gave her a look. "It's six o'clock here."

Daphne pointed a finger gun at April. "Right."

"Are you okay?"

"Fine," Daphne said, but her voice was high-pitched. She cleared her throat. "Fine."

April continued to frown at her, unbelieving.

"Please?" Daphne said as she dried off the last of the brushes. "Just one drink."

April sighed as she tucked her iPad into her bag, along with her sketchbook. "I guess I don't really have anything else to do."

"A high compliment," Daphne said, "but I'll take it."

April laughed. "Sorry, I just meant . . ." But she trailed off, shaking her head as she swung her bag over her shoulder, then met Daphne's gaze. "One drink."

"Thank you," Daphne said, then turned to grab her things to head out, but one of their students remained in the back of the classroom leaning against the counter, tapping at her phone. Nicola, Daphne believed her name was. She was beautiful, with smooth brown skin and curly hair. Right now, she was dressed in a plain white tee tucked into a pair of navy shorts, but Daphne could absolutely picture her in a pencil skirt and high heels.

"Excellent first class, you two," she said in an elegant British accent. She pushed off the counter and tucked her phone into her Prada handbag, walking toward them.

"Nicola, hi," April said.

"You did a good job too," Daphne said brightly, remembering the messy apple Nicola had painted.

Nicola laughed. "I didn't, but I'm not a painter, so I'm okay with that. Just here to learn and observe, but I did want to meet you officially." She offered a long-fingered hand to Daphne. "I really enjoyed your portfolio."

"Her portfolio?" April asked as Daphne shook Nicola's hand.

"My portfolio?" Daphne echoed, but then remembered Mia had emailed her the week before she came to Cloverwild, asking if she could give the portfolio Mia had on file to a guest.

A curator.

At the time, Daphne hadn't given it a second thought. *Curator* could mean a hundred different things in terms of style and place and mediums. Most likely, it also meant arrogance and snobbery, to be honest, but Daphne knew she was a little biased after so many years with Elena.

"That's right," Nicola said. "Alluring stuff. I especially liked those three pieces featuring that dark-haired woman as the subject. Set in the gallery? I could really feel the longing of the viewer."

Daphne felt her cheeks go red at the mention of the pieces she'd done of Elena as part of her senior project. April shifted next to Daphne, cleared her throat.

"I don't know about that," Daphne said quietly. "All of those pieces were from three years ago. Some even older than that."

Nicola nodded. "Which means you've grown. That's exactly what I'm looking for."

Daphne frowned. "Looking for?"

"I'm a curator at the Devon," Nicola said.

Daphne's mouth dropped open—the *Devon*—but Nicola pressed on, explaining about a fall exhibition called *Evolution*, how she was looking for one more artist, didn't matter what medium as long it *moved* her, and how she'd love to see what Daphne might have to offer.

Daphne could only blink at her, dumbfounded. She never imagined, not in a million years, that *this* was behind Mia's email.

The Devon.

"I'm desperate for something transformative, something that will leave me absolutely shattered," Nicola said. She gestured toward April. "April is in the mix too."

Daphne felt like she kept getting slapped—not so much the pain or cruelty of it, but the shock, one loud crack after another. Her portfolio, a curator, the Devon, April. She turned and met April's eyes briefly, then looked away, her breath shallow.

"Nothing wrong with a little healthy competition, right?" Nicola said, glancing between them, brows lifted. "Is that okay?"

"Of course," April said. She smiled, but her voice was tense, her eyes mirthless.

Daphne simply gawped and blinked.

"I'll need to make my decision by August first," Nicola said. "Can you have something ready to show me by then?"

"Absolutely," April said.

"Wonderful," Nicola said. "We'll have ourselves a little exhibition of our own."

Daphne could only bob her head—*yes, yes, yes.*

"We'll see you next class," April said.

Nicola's smile was like the Cheshire cat's. "Yes, you will," she said, her long brown legs carrying her toward the door. Daphne hadn't uttered a word after Nicola flung *the Devon* into the atmosphere, and still she could only stare as the woman left.

"Did I just hallucinate?" she finally asked, her voice raspy.

Next to her, April released a long sigh. "Nope."

"Oh my god," Daphne said as it all settled. "Oh my *god.*" She turned and grinned at April, grabbed her upper arms. "The Devon. The *Devon*. I used to get their quarterly catalogue as a kid, and I would study it under my covers with a flashlight like it was my Bible. I still remember certain paintings. Certain artists. Audrey St. John got her start there. Amal Rutland. Valeria Ramos. Do you know what this could mean?"

April pulled free, her expression grim. "Yeah, I think I do."

Daphne frowned, confused, but then . . .

Oh, but *then.*

Daphne stared at April, and April stared back, her expression somehow both cool and charged all at once.

"You want it," Daphne said. It wasn't a question.

"Of course I want it."

Daphne licked her lower lip and nodded. "Okay. Right. This is . . . We can . . ."

But she wasn't exactly sure what it was or what they could do right now. *May the best artist win* felt a little trite, but that was essentially the situation. If Nicola chose her, Daphne's whole life would change. Artists who showed at the Devon didn't fade into obscurity. Artists who showed at the Devon went on to be working artists. Meaning, they sold their work, they were guest lecturers and artists-in-residence in prestigious art programs, they were sought-after and lauded and emulated.

Even Elena salivated over the Devon and had tried to collaborate with them more than once, to no avail.

If Daphne could get into the Devon . . . she could do anything. Go anywhere. *Be* anyone.

"You know what I think?" Daphne asked, hitching her bag over her shoulder.

"I'm on pins and needles," April said drolly.

"I think we should get that drink now."

April blew out a breath and nodded. "Yeah. I think that's a damn good idea."

~

DAPHNE FELT DIZZY as the two of them walked in silence down the hall and through Cloverwild's lobby. The bar was situated just off the dining room, all shiny lacquered wood, glowing bottles in every color on the backlit wall, and tan leather stools with bentwood seats and oak legs.

Daphne slid onto a stool with a sigh. She hadn't been to a bar—or a restaurant, a grocery store, the post office, or any place outside of Vivian's apartment—in over a month.

"This is nice," she said as April sat next to her.

"It's decent," April said, checking her phone, then tucking it away again.

"Has your best friend texted?" Daphne asked brightly.

April side-eyed her. "What?"

"Earlier today. You said you and your best friend weren't talking very much."

"Do you remember everything I say?"

Daphne smiled beatifically. "I'm observant and have a memory like an elephant."

April shook her head. "I guess I'll have to be careful with my words from now on."

"Don't be ridiculous—tell me everything."

April laughed. "So you're also a gossip?"

"Horribly so," Daphne said. "After keeping secrets my entire life, I'm hungry for other people's drama."

"You and Penny Hampton would be two peas in a pod," April said.

"Who?"

"Town gossip. Kind of like Miss Patty and Babette."

"Who?" Daphne repeated, laughing a little.

April leaned her elbows on the bar and clasped her hands together, like she was about to pray. "Please tell me you've seen *Gilmore Girls.*"

Daphne grinned. "I haven't seen anything." She pointed her thumb to her chest. "Suffocating religious upbringing, remember?"

April blinked at her as though she was a rare exhibit in a zoo.

"Well, hey there."

Daphne's head swung toward the silky voice behind the bar. Cloverwild's bartender pressed her palms to the glossy bar top, cerulean eyes glittering. Her skin was pale and smooth, and she had a silver name tag pinned to her black button-up that read SASHA, SHE/HER. Her white-blond hair was short on the sides and tall and messy on top, and she flashed a crooked smile that Daphne was pretty sure could disintegrate cotton.

"Oh," Daphne said, sitting up a little straighter. "Wow, hi."

Sasha grinned, that smile emanating from her over Daphne and April like some sort of sexy radiation. "What can I get you?"

"You've got to be kidding me," April said under her breath as she looked at the cocktail menu printed on thick recycled paper.

"Something wrong?" Daphne asked.

"Fuckbois abound," April said quietly.

"I'm sorry?" Daphne asked.

"Never mind," April said, then louder, to Sasha, "I'll have a pink lady."

Sasha nodded once. "Coming right up. And you?" She slid her gaze to Daphne, who felt her cheeks warm inexplicably.

"Dirty gin martini," she said.

Sasha lifted her pale brows, then slid her gaze down Daphne's torso once before settling on her eyes again. "Unexpected."

"What's that?" Daphne asked.

Sasha flipped a navy towel over her shoulder, then started pulling glasses and bottles to make their drinks. "If I had to guess, I would've flipped your orders." She chin-nodded at April. "Dirty martini"—then did the same toward Daphne—"pink lady."

"Well, you guessed wrong, didn't you?" April said.

Daphne was a bit relieved to see April's sass wasn't only reserved for her.

Sasha laughed. "I love a surprise."

"Oh, I bet you do," April said, shaking her head.

Sasha stirred Daphne's martini, then poured it into a glass before spearing two olives to finish it off. She set the drink in front of Daphne, then got to work on April's cocktail, shaking the mixture before pouring a very pink, frothy liquid into a champagne glass. Daphne had to admit, she also hadn't expected a tiny Goth like April to sip on something quite so vibrant. She laughed as April rolled her eyes back as she drank, moaning with pleasure.

"Wow, maybe we *should* switch," Daphne said.

"Over my dead body," April said, clutching the pink lady to her chest.

Daphne smiled, happy to see April relax a little. "To fresh starts," she said, taking a deep breath and holding up her glass.

April hesitated for a second, her eyes dark and deep, but finally she tipped her head and clinked her glass against Daphne's. Daphne drank, loving the salty tang of her martini. She'd never been a huge drinker, despite years of repression, but right now, she felt like draining her glass of every drop.

In fact, that's exactly what she did.

"Well, damn," Sasha said. "Another?"

"Please," Daphne said, popping both olives into her mouth at once. Sasha, she noticed, followed the motion with her eyes.

"What's your name?" Sasha asked, taking the empty glass.

"Really?" April said.

Sasha frowned as she started making Daphne's second round. "Something wrong with asking your names?"

April tipped her head back and laughed. "That's all you're after? A name?"

Sasha shrugged. "It's a start. And you are?"

April shook her head, but she was smiling. "April. And no."

"No?" Sasha asked. "Just like that?"

"Just like that."

"Can't even give me a chance?" Sasha asked.

"I know your type."

"Well, I don't," Daphne said, eyes bouncing between them like a ping-pong ball. "What is happening right now?"

"Your friend," Sasha said, setting Daphne's martini in front of her, then resting her elbows on the bar and steepling her fingers, "is turning me down."

Friend.

Daphne rolled the word around in her brain, tried to focus on the matter at hand. "She is?"

"I am," April said. "And so are you if you know what's good for you."

"I think we've established I definitely don't know what's good for me," Daphne said.

April sipped her drink. "Let's not add insult to injury, then."

Sasha presented her palms. "Fine, fine. I get it. Just looking for some summer fun, that's all."

"And we look like fun?" Daphne asked. She still wasn't completely sure what was going on—was Sasha asking April out, or

Daphne? Or both of them? Maybe neither, but her face heated again anyway. To be fair, she blushed when someone smiled at her on the subway, so that wasn't saying much.

"You sure do . . ." Sasha trailed off, expression expectant as she waited for her name.

"Daphne," she said, then very nearly giggled at the way Sasha smiled at her. It wasn't that she was turned on or even tempted—Sasha was just *charming*, and Daphne had never fared very well around hot and charming people, as her recent history testified.

"Daphne," Sasha said, then winked. "Lovely name."

"Oh my god," April said.

Daphne did giggle then, covering her tomato-hued face with her napkin, which made both Sasha and April laugh out loud.

"I'm sorry," Daphne said. "I'm so new at this."

"New?" Sasha asked. "Are you a baby gay?"

"Um, sort of?" Daphne said. "I just got out of something serious, and before that . . ."

"Before that?" Sasha asked.

Daphne slurped at her martini and glanced at April, who simply lifted her brows. "Before that, I grew up in a fundamentalist Christian family with my preacher father and Sunday school–teaching mother, both of whom believed, along with most of my town, that being queer was a one-way ticket to hell. I'd never so much as held a girl's hand before college, where I kissed exactly three people and couldn't move past first base until I fell in love with someone I suspect might actually be evil."

Daphne's face grew even hotter, and she grabbed her martini again, taking a big, salty gulp.

"Well, shit," Sasha said.

"Exactly that," April said, though her voice was softer than Sasha's. Daphne glanced at her, but the eye contact with her ex's ex at that moment was a bit too much, so she stared down at the olives floating in her foggy drink.

"So . . . you've slept with . . ." Sasha started, a baffled expression on her face.

"One person, yes," Daphne said, eyes still on her glass.

Sasha nodded, her mouth pursed. "That's . . . that's . . . wow."

"Spoken like a true fuckboi," April said. "She doesn't have to have notches on her bedpost to have a fulfilling queer experience. Ace people exist. So do monogamous people who fell in love with their person when they were, like, seventeen."

"No, yeah, I know," Sasha said. "Just couldn't be me."

"I refer you, again, to my fuckboi comment," April said.

Sasha laughed as she wiped down the bar. "No argument here."

April rolled her eyes, but Daphne barely heard their interaction, her mind whirring. She knew April was right, but at the same time, she didn't feel like she'd had a fulfilling queer experience at all. Or even a fulfilling *life* experience. No wonder Elena's reactions to her art were always lackluster—she hadn't lived enough to produce anything earth-shattering.

She hadn't produced anything worthy of the Devon.

"It's not just about sex," she said, finally looking up. "It's about my whole life. I feel so . . . young."

"You are young," April said.

Daphne laughed mirthlessly, met April's eyes. "Young *and* naive, right?"

April let out a breath. "I didn't mean it like that."

Daphne shook her head. "No, but I am. Elena said so all the time too."

"Fuck Elena," April said, spitting out the name like it tasted terrible.

"Who's Elena?" Sasha asked.

"No one," April said, but Daphne wanted to say it. Say something, at least. There was power in words, she knew, power in speaking things out loud, and maybe if she said everything to this hot bartender, it would make more sense. She could leave April out of it.

"She's my ex," Daphne said. "And I just found out she cheated on someone with me. She was engaged when we met three years ago."

"Well, shit," Sasha said again, and took out a shot glass and a bottle of tequila. "Next round is on me. Sounds like you need it."

"Make that two," April said, holding up two fingers.

"It's more than Elena though," Daphne said, still unsettled. If anything, saying it all out loud made her more desperate to do something. Be something, anything other than this version of herself. "I had a boring college experience, too scared and unsure to really try anything, followed by a too-serious relationship that ended in literal disaster. I have no career, no money. No best friend. I've never had a one-night stand. I can't even say a curse word without blushing. I've never stayed out all night and gotten so drunk I puked the next morning."

"I wouldn't recommend that last one," Sasha said, pouring the shots.

"Point is," Daphne said, "I want to *do* something."

"Like have an actual one-night stand?" Sasha asked, adopting a wide-eyed, innocent expression. "Because I have a few ideas for that."

Daphne, predictably, blushed again.

"Okay, slow down," April said, holding up her hands. "Zero to a hundred and fifty is probably not the best plan here."

"So you'll help me?" Daphne asked.

"Wait, what?" April said, brows lifting. "Me?"

Daphne couldn't stop herself from smiling. For the first time in a month—no, longer than that. For the first time in multiple months, maybe a year, even, she felt excited about something. The Devon, and now this.

This was what she needed.

Something *fun*. Something sexy and wild and maybe even a little dangerous. And perhaps it was silly or juvenile, but as she sat at this bar with two fierce and gorgeous queer people, she realized just how little she'd lived the kind of life she wanted.

The kind of life she'd left home for.

And April and Sasha were the perfect people to help her.

"Yes, you," she said, then looked between them. "Both of you."

"Oh, I'm in," Sasha said, rubbing her hands together. "What tattoo are we all getting?"

"Right?" Daphne said. "I *need* a tattoo. I'm long overdue, and yes, I do want to mar this soft baby skin."

Sasha laughed. "Okay, well, let's mar away."

"Wait," April said again, shaking her head. "I don't—"

"Please," Daphne said. She reached out and took April's hand before thinking twice about it. April glanced down at their fingers, and Daphne let go. "Please," she said again, quieter this time. "You're the only person I really know here."

"You don't know me at all," April said softly. Her eyes searched Daphne's, the brown so dark, pupil and iris blurred together. "And what you *do* know is a clusterfuck."

Daphne pressed her lips together.

"You know it's true," April said.

"That's not all you are though," Daphne said, and April's eyes widened, her mouth parting just a little. Daphne swore her lower lip trembled a little too, but the next second April had looked away, her jaw steeled. "And I need a cluster . . . whatever right now."

"First order of business," Sasha said, "you need to use the word *fuck*."

Daphne cracked a smile but stayed focused on April. "Please."

April looked at the ceiling as though trying to see the stars again.

"Your cat already loves me," Daphne added.

"Bob's a traitor."

"*Bob* is an excellent judge of character."

April blew out a long breath. "This is a few too many bright new opportunities to grow if you ask me."

"What?" Daphne asked.

"Nothing." April knocked back the rest of her pink lady, then slammed the glass down onto the bar. "Fine. I'm in."

Daphne felt like someone had set off a sparkler in her stomach. She squirmed on her stool, clapping quietly. "Okay, so what do we do first?"

"First?" April asked. "As in tonight? Aren't you exhausted?"

"No time like the present," Sasha said. "I'm off at eleven."

"I have to do something now," Daphne said, sliding off her barstool and bouncing around on the balls of her feet. "If I don't, I'll lose my nerve."

"After two martinis, I don't think it's the time to go cliff diving," April said.

Daphne stopped moving and paled. "Cliff diving? People actually do that? It's so dangerous."

"A true adventurer, this one," Sasha said.

"One step at a time," April said, taking Daphne's arms and guiding her back onto the stool.

"Maybe I should make a list," Daphne said, taking out her phone. She opened her Notes app, but then just blinked at the cursor.

"You don't need a list," Sasha said. "You just need to feel it."

April gave Sasha a look. "My best friend lives by a list. Lists can help organize emotion."

"Sounds horrible."

April cracked a smile. "You're an Aquarius rising," she said to Sasha, tilting her head. "Am I right?"

Sasha lifted a brow, but she just grinned.

"Oh, I'm right," April said.

Sasha turned her attention back to Daphne. "What do you *want* to do?"

Daphne's shoulders dropped a little. There was so much, though to her, it all sounded either too immature or too wild. But she wanted to be brave—that was the whole point here—and maybe that started with verbalizing desires.

"I want to change my hair," she said.

"Slow down, rebel," Sasha said, winking.

Daphne laughed, but she didn't feel embarrassed. Sasha's teasing tone was sweet and supportive somehow, so she typed her idea into her app and kept going.

"I want to go skinny-dipping," she said. "I want to kiss someone I barely know, and I want to get high, and I really do want to get a tattoo. I want to make out at the top of a Ferris wheel like in all those gay teen movies, and I want to have—"

She cut herself off, cleared her throat.

Sasha leaned closer. "Go on."

Daphne laughed nervously, glanced at April for a split second, meeting her dark eyes, which glinted with curiosity. She wasn't sure why she looked April's way—April was such a force, such a strange person in her life. A surprise, that was for sure, but Daphne felt a pull toward her she couldn't explain.

She looked away, focused on Sasha.

"I want to have a fling."

Sasha's brows lifted.

"Easy, tiger," April said.

"Hey, I'm a helper, not a lover, in this whole adventure," Sasha said, presenting her palms. "But I think we can definitely help you achieve those goals."

"Yeah?" Daphne said. Her cheeks were on fire.

"Yeah," Sasha said. "Teenage and young adult rebellion, here we come."

"Are we going to TP our history teacher's front yard too?" April asked.

Daphne gasped. "Oh my god, I've never done that."

"I was kidding," April said, but she was smiling. God, she really was gorgeous. Dark and brooding and a little scary, but gorgeous. Daphne stared at her for a second, while April fiddled with her full tequila glass, those lavender and teal streaks through her hair catching the dim bar lighting.

"I'm ready now," Daphne said, sliding off her stool again.

"I don't think we can gather that much toilet paper in time," Sasha said. "Mia would surely notice."

Daphne laughed. "No. I want to dye my hair. Tonight, before I can talk myself out of any of this. Are you with me?"

She looked at April again. Her stomach swooped with nerves or excitement or exhaustion, she wasn't sure—maybe all three. Maybe everything. April watched her, then lifted her shot glass into the air.

"I'm with you," April said.

Daphne smiled, and they clinked glasses before tossing the liquor down their throats. It burned all the way down, and Daphne loved it—a wild and queer baptism by fire.

DAPHNE AND APRIL shared one more shot of tequila before they headed outside into the warm summer evening. Since Sasha had to work until eleven, she couldn't join in the hair dye extravaganza, but they all exchanged numbers for future Wildling Events, as Sasha called them.

Daphne's head was gloriously fuzzy, the world blurry, like everything was underwater. She might be drunk.

She was definitely tipsy.

But it felt good, her whole body like rubber, her mind, her heart.

"I've got a ton of hair dye in my trunk," April said, heading toward the parking lot behind the lodge. She popped her car's trunk, then started rooting around while Daphne leaned against the cool back door. "You sure you're up for this?"

"I'm sure," Daphne said, her words only slightly slurred. She knew she should feel tired, but she only felt exhilarated, adrenaline and tequila cocktailing together in her blood. She not only wanted to be wild, she *felt* wild.

And she never wanted to feel anything else.

Never wanted to feel weak or scared or stupid again.

Never wanted to feel like a hungry kid begging for crumbs.

She took her phone out of her back pocket, stared at the blank screen for a second. No notifications. No texts or missed calls. But in this moment, that didn't feel like a bad thing—it felt like freedom. Like a new start.

But if she was really going to start over, she had to finish something first. She needed closure, needed to be seen and heard. So even though her head was fuzzy, and somewhere in the very back of her mind there was a tiny, reasonable voice telling her to slow down, put her phone away, she unlocked it anyway.

She tapped on Elena's name in her text app.

Then she thumbed two tiny, devastating words into the message box.

April Evans.

"Purple or turquoise?" April said, emerging from her trunk,

her eyes a bit glassy too. She held up two bottles of hair dye, shaking them in Daphne's direction.

Daphne hesitated, but only for a moment.

"Purple," she said, then hit send, catapulting her text message into the ether.

Chapter Nine

SASHA MUST HAVE slipped twice the amount of alcohol into April's drink. Either that, or she'd hit her head and just didn't remember. Maybe the lake was poisoned, and jumping into the water after Daphne last night had caused toxins to soak into her pores. Some bodily malady was the only explanation for agreeing to help Daphne wild up her life. Daphne, who was not only *Daphne Love*, but was now April's competition for the Devon exhibition.

Still, as soon as April's acquiescence flowed out of her mouth, Daphne's face had illuminated like the Bristol Family Farm's holiday light display, and there was no way to take it all back. Not with Daphne looking like April had just saved her puppy from becoming roadkill.

The tequila certainly hadn't helped matters, that was for sure, not that tequila ever did.

And now, as April pulled a chair from their small breakfast table into the bathroom and set it up in front of the sink, her last bottle of lavender hair dye ready and waiting, she couldn't help but feel a little nervous.

"Okay, I'm ready," Daphne said, appearing in the bathroom doorway.

April glanced up, her nerves cresting even more, because Daphne didn't have on a shirt. Granted, she had on a very staid sports bra—a sweat-wicking material in a cerulean blue—but still. There was suddenly a lot of skin in April's vision, and it didn't really matter that the skin belonged to Daphne Love. It was still skin, and it was very smooth and soft-looking, and it swelled over small boobs, dipping into a subtle cleavage and—

April shook her head, squeezing her eyes closed. Damn tequila. Never led to anything good.

"I need some water," she said, sliding past Daphne and into the main room, grabbing her water bottle and tossing half its contents down her throat. She was suddenly very aware that the entire process of dyeing someone's hair was pretty intimate, someone else's armpit or boobs or face was usually *very* close . . .

"April?" Daphne called from the bathroom.

"Yeah," April said, swallowing a few more gulps. "All good." She capped the bottle, then walked back to the bathroom. Daphne was already sitting in the chair, her hair loose and a bit frizzy around her bare shoulders.

A client, April thought as she walked to the sink and snapped on a pair of the black latex gloves she used at her shop. *Daphne is just like a client.*

"You ready?" she asked.

Daphne nodded, her cheeks still a bit pink from the alcohol. April wrapped a towel around Daphne's shoulders and secured it with a hair clip at the base of her throat. She picked up the jar of coconut oil she used when dyeing her own hair, started applying it around Daphne's hairline.

Daphne's eyes fluttered closed.

April tried to breathe normally.

Her stomach was a riot of nerves, which was simply ridiculous. She thought of her cats, of tattoo ink, the Providence River

Pedestrian Bridge near RISD. Anything but the relaxed sighs coming out of Daphne's mouth.

April squirted the dye into the large mixing bowl she'd also stashed in her car, then started working it through Daphne's dry hair with a dye brush.

"You have a nice touch," Daphne said. Her voice was muzzy, sleepy, and April knew it was the alcohol, but the entire vibe here was making her hands shake.

She needed a distraction.

"What kind of tattoo do you want?" April asked.

Daphne's opened her eyes, and she seemed momentarily startled by how close April was. Her gaze flicked down to April's chest—which, yes, it was impossible for April to *not* press her boobs against Daphne's shoulder.

April cleared her throat, focused on Daphne's hair.

"I want you to design one for me," Daphne finally said. "I told you that."

An image blew into April's mind, like the wind pushing a storm over the lake—wildflowers and light, the hues almost like watercolors over Daphne's pale skin.

"Tattoos are personal things," April said, shaking her head. "I can't choose one for you."

"What do yours mean, then?"

April laughed lightly. "Which one?"

"All of them."

April was quiet for a second. She had over twenty tattoos right now, spiraling down both arms, over her chest, a few on her thighs, one right between her breasts.

"What's this one mean?" Daphne asked when April remained silent. She reached out, her fingertips lightly grazing the flowering tree on April's right upper arm, which curled over her shoulder and down toward her collarbone. She had a mirror image on her left arm, but of a barren tree in winter.

April shivered, and Daphne pulled away.

"It means change," April said, and the word felt heavy on her tongue. "Seasons, life, death."

"'A time to be born, and a time to die,'" Daphne said.

April paused in her work. "Did you just quote the Bible at me?"

Daphne winced, then tapped her temple. "Some parts are stuck in there like a bad song."

"I don't know," April said. "I've always liked that bit—a time for everything."

"It's from Ecclesiastes, which is a wisdom book," Daphne said. "'A time to weep and a time to laugh, a time to mourn and a time to dance.'"

April nodded, smoothing a thick swirl of lavender through the blond. "Basically what these tattoos mean."

"What else do you have?" Daphne asked.

"I have a few astrology tattoos. Three, actually." She held up her arm, showing off one of them on her left forearm, a simple gray-and-black sketch of a woman with short dark hair and a scorpion's tail, kneeling in the grass and holding a blazing sun between her hands.

"She looks like you," Daphne said, and April smiled.

"I guess that was the point," April said. "She was my first tattoo. Got her the second I turned eighteen."

"Did you always want to be a tattoo artist?"

April frowned, watching Daphne's hair grow more and more lavender. She loved tattooing—loved designing them, placing art on people's bodies in a way that became part of them forever. But looking back on her childhood, high school, college, she wasn't sure she'd ever wanted to be one thing or another.

She'd just wanted to create, and as the only child of two parents who didn't really understand the inclination, she wasn't sure she'd ever felt the safety to explore. Then in college, she had a curriculum, a path she had to follow.

"I don't really know," she said, suddenly wanting to tell Daphne the truth. "After RISD, I moved back home because I wasn't sure what I wanted to do exactly. I started working at a tattoo shop in Concord to pay my bills, but then I liked it. I started apprenticing with the owner and eventually got my license. Opening my own shop just felt like the natural next step. Ramona helped me set up Wonderlust and now here I am."

"Ramona's your best friend?"

April nodded. "Ramona Riley."

"Wait . . ." Daphne said. "Ramona Riley? Why is that name familiar?"

April laughed. "Probably because she's dating Dylan Monroe. Quite famously dating her, in fact."

"Oh my god, that's right."

"Yep. That rom-com Dylan was in last year was filmed here in Clover Lake."

"Now that, I have seen," Daphne said. "It's so good. And Ramona grew up here too?"

April nodded. "Her mom left when she was young. She pretty much raised her younger sister, and I . . ." April trailed off, remembering how after graduation, a few of her RISD friends were going on a road trip across the country, and something about the idea made her feel as though she was made of light. Not just a road trip, but the possibility of it all—being twenty-two, the whole world laid out before her. But she came home to Clover Lake instead.

She thought about that first year back at home, Ramona working at Clover Moon, nine-year-old Olive playing softball and learning long division, and April was involved in all of it. She'd been by Ramona's side the whole way, through all of Olive's growth spurts and teenage twists and turns. April had felt needed, felt at home with the Rileys. Always had. But looking back on the last ten years, it suddenly felt as though April mostly gave advice Ramona rarely followed, received with a laugh and an eye roll, a joke about April becoming a childless cat lady, or how she needed to try and date someone seriously again.

It's been a year, Apes.

It's been two years, Apes.

It's been three years, Apes.

April always waved Ramona's concern away, and Ramona never pressed it too hard. Not like April, who knew she pressed too hard on everything. The funny best friend in a rom-com with all the right quips and quirks.

And then Dylan showed up, Ramona fell in love and met Noelle Yang, and there was no one left in Clover Lake to push April to date or get another cat or give her any kind of comfort after closing her business.

No one but Penny fucking Hampton.

"April?" Daphne said softly. "You okay?"

April shook her head, unsure of how long she'd been frozen, her gloved hands stained purple and tangled in Daphne's hair.

"Sorry," she said quietly. She blinked, felt her breath go shallow in her chest. Everything felt tight. Fuck, she was about to have a panic attack right there, her hands covered in hair dye like she was a teenager again and wanted to freak out her parents.

So she focused on that.

Breathed in and out and started talking.

"The first time I dyed my hair," she said slowly, letting the oxygen back into her lungs, "I was sixteen and shoplifted a bottle of blue hair dye from Gallagher's Grocery."

Her hands started working again, thumbs massaging the color through Daphne's tresses.

"Were you a little rebel growing up?" Daphne said.

April laughed. "I went and confessed a week later, gave the cashier a twenty-dollar bill. So, a wannabe rebel, maybe. Soft-core. I thought bright blue hair would get a reaction out of my parents."

"Did it?"

April went quiet. She'd started the story for something to focus on, forgetting the ending. "Barely a blink," she said.

She raked the lavender down to the ends of Daphne's hair, then used a brush to comb everything through evenly. Daphne was quiet for a second, but she didn't frown in confusion. She didn't ask for more details or anything else about April's parents. She just nodded, her eyes soft and knowing; April had to look away.

"Sit up," April said, and Daphne did. April twisted her hair into a knot, then clipped it on top of her head before pulling a plastic cap over the swirls of purple. "Thirty minutes."

Daphne nodded, standing and moving away from the sink so April could clean up. "Thank you," she said.

"No problem," April said, but Daphne didn't move, didn't head into the living room, didn't leave April with her whirling thoughts.

"I think you're really brave," Daphne finally said.

April glanced up, catching Daphne's gaze in the mirror. "Brave."

The word sounded like gobbledygook. If April was anything—moving back to her hometown after college, opening a business mostly on her parents' financial support, which she was sure stemmed mostly from their desire to get her out of their hair—it wasn't brave.

It was the opposite.

But Daphne nodded, and despite the cap on her head making her look like a purple mushroom, her expression was lovely and genuine.

A knot tangled in April's throat as she stripped off her gloves, threw them in the trash. "I guess I'll have to take your word for it."

Daphne tilted her head. "What, you don't trust me?"

"I don't know yet," April said, turning on the water and scrubbing dots of purple from her wrists. Because despite Daphne's innocence regarding Elena's betrayal, trust no longer came easily for April Evans.

"What are you going to do for the Devon?" Daphne asked.

April laughed, a quick, somewhat panicked burst from her mouth. "God, I have no idea. Are you going to use your new painting?"

"I think so," Daphne said quietly. "I think you're right. I should do more with it. More paintings. I *can* do more."

"You should. It's incredible." She pressed her palms to the cool porcelain of the sink, eyeing Daphne in the mirror. "I guess we're really doing this."

Daphne tilted her head. "The Devon?"

April could only laugh mirthlessly. "The Devon."

They both went quiet for a beat. April stared at the purple streaks in the sink.

"I really want it," Daphne finally said.

"Me too," April said, her voice almost a whisper. She didn't say that she needed it. She didn't say that she *had* to show in the Devon, because what else did she have in her life if she didn't? She didn't say she was scared and exhilarated at the same time, that she'd felt more alive in the last few days than she had in months.

Years, even.

She didn't say any of that, because she knew that Daphne felt the same.

"By the way," April said, wiping down the sink and glancing at Daphne in the mirror. "You're a July Leo."

Daphne's mouth dropped open, and April laughed.

"July twenty-ninth," Daphne said. "How did you figure that out so fast?"

April shrugged. "I thought you were a water sign at first, like your moon, but then . . . I don't know. What you've been through, leaving home." She focused on getting all the purple out of the sink, her throat suddenly a little thick, thinking of Daphne Love running away from the only family she'd ever known.

Running away, but *toward* herself.

"And all these wild things you want to do now," April said. "As a late July baby, you're also pretty close to the border between a Cancer and Leo sun. A watery Leo if ever I've seen one."

Daphne smiled and shook her head, her cheeks reddening. "And my rising?"

"Oh, I'll get it," April said, meeting her eyes in the mirror again and winking. "Don't you worry."

Chapter Ten

FOR THE NEXT week, Daphne got so many compliments on her lavender-hued hair, she wondered why she'd never dyed it sooner. It was wild, how different her hair color could make her feel, but she *did* feel different somehow.

She wasn't sure what kind of different quite yet. After all, she couldn't stop checking her phone, and she cursed chasing a gin martini with shots of tequila last week, which was the only explanation for why she would've sent April's name to her ex. The text sat in her messages like a brick in her stomach, Delivered underneath those two tiny yet huge words, because of course Elena had turned off her read receipts for Daphne.

Either that, or she'd deleted her number altogether.

Or she'd read it, hadn't cared.

Daphne squeezed her eyes closed, forcing her brain to stop. She really needed to stop thinking so much about Elena.

About the lying, the cheating, the—

"Stop," she said out loud, even though she was alone in the art studio.

She stood before the painting she'd been working on and took a deep breath. It was early afternoon, and she and April had an illustration class in about an hour, so it was the perfect time for Daphne to work on her own piece for the Devon. April was . . . well, she didn't know where April was, and that was probably for the best.

For the last few days, they hadn't spoken again about the Devon. April hadn't asked her any more questions about her painting or plans for any future pieces, and Daphne hadn't asked April about her own ideas.

Though she was dying to know.

Daphne had only seen April's art on her Instagram, which was mostly shots of people's arms and legs and torsos covered in ink. It was all beautiful, and she loved April's style, but she'd never seen anything on paper or any other medium, a medium that could hang in the Devon, and she was beyond curious.

Hang in the Devon.

Her eyes roamed over her own painting, trying to picture it in the Devon. She'd never been there, of course—she'd never been anywhere; despite the few times Elena had gone to London for work, she had begged off taking Daphne, claiming she'd be too busy to keep her entertained—but she'd studied the museum enough online over the course of her life to be able to picture it clear as day.

Goose bumps erupted along her arms, thinking about how she might fit into that place.

Even the opportunity felt unreal and dreamlike.

The girl in this painting would never have believed it, that was for sure. Daphne tilted her head, trying to find the girl's expression even under the blurry mess she'd intentionally painted.

Unseen.

That was what Daphne had named the painting. It was done—the flowers were bright and full of motion, as though swaying in the breeze; the sky was packed with different shades of blue, deeply saturated and textured; the farmhouse in the background a fortress of white, the outline of a woman watching the girl in the field from the porch.

But the girl.

Her colors were less vibrant. Her blond curls were nearly gray, the white of her dress washed-out and dingy. And, of course, her face, a smeared slash of peach with a bit of green and pink right where her eyes and mouth should be.

Daphne stood staring at the girl, knowing the painting was finished, but still feeling unsettled.

She closed her eyes, saw the rustic sanctuary of the smaller chapel that stood on her church's property. It was old, built in the late 1800s as the church's first gathering place. When the congregation expanded over the decades and electricity and running water became available, a new sanctuary was built, which eventually became the bright white space the church used today. But the little chapel, all rough wood floors and bench-style pews, remained as a history marker.

Daphne saw it now, saw herself as a slightly older girl standing in the aisle, that rugged wooden cross looming above her in the pulpit, and—

"Daphne?"

A voice yanked Daphne from her thoughts. She flipped her eyes open to see Nicola standing behind her wearing another cute pair of shorts and a black sleeveless blouse.

"Oh. Hi," Daphne said. She folded her arms but then let them drop as the motion didn't feel too friendly. But then she didn't know what to do with her hands, so she tucked them behind her back. Cleared her throat.

Predictably, her cheeks went red and hot.

Nicola smiled kindly.

"Can I help you?" Daphne finally managed to ask.

"I didn't want to bother you," Nicola said, then tapped the sketchbook in her hands, the one the resort provided for the art students. "I was hoping to use April's model to work on that bird drawing we started a few days ago. I cannot get the feet right. They look like desiccated worms."

Daphne laughed as she walked to the back closet and took out the sketch of a bird in flight that April had modeled during their first illustration class. It was a goldfinch, its feet curled up to its body, wings spread as though taking off or landing. The shading was exquisite, and Daphne herself had learned a lot about working with pencil from the lesson.

She brought the thick paper to the front of the room to clip to April's easel, but when she got there, Daphne found Nicola staring at her painting. She stopped short, her heart leaping into her throat as Nicola's eyes roamed the canvas.

She wasn't supposed to see this yet.

No one was, but certainly not Nicola Reece, who, after an extensive deep dive on the internet last week, Daphne had discovered was not only a curator at the Devon, but the youngest chief curator in the museum's history, as well as the first Black woman to hold the position.

Daphne froze, waiting for the investigation to end, ready to play off whatever comment Nicola might have, but Nicola continued to stare, her brows lowered in thought, eyes a bit narrowed as she leaned closer, within inches of the paint.

Finally, Nicola straightened and turned to face Daphne. "Tragic," she said, her eyes locked on Daphne's before moving toward the painting again.

Daphne waited for more, for anything, really, because *tragic* could not be all Nicola had to say about this painting that felt like Daphne's own beating heart on a canvas.

But the other woman said nothing else. She studied the painting for a few more seconds, her fingers on her chin, before she walked toward the chair and easel she utilized during class.

Daphne grabbed the sides of her canvas to move it to the back of the room to fully dry, facing away from any more analysis.

"Is there more?" Nicola asked when Daphne came back to the front of the room. The woman's sketchbook was propped on her lap, and she wasn't even looking at Daphne, instead scrutinizing April's bird drawing.

Daphne paused, saw that preteen girl in the chapel again, her hair a little longer, her body developing in ways that made her feel excited and ashamed all at once. She'd never quite understood her body's place in the kind of church she'd grown up in—God's temple, a man's property, an evil temptation. She remembered feeling confused and even scared, terrified when she saw that first red streak in her underwear when she was twelve.

"I think so," she said quietly.

Nicola's smile was brief, her eyes now on her own sketch pad. "It's probably best to know."

Daphne swallowed thickly, all that bravery vanishing like fog under the late-morning sun. Her throat ached, and suddenly, this entire thing—the Devon, her painting, her ideas—felt ridiculous.

Because Daphne rarely *knew* anything.

Daphne nodded, even though Nicola wasn't looking at her, and was about to excuse herself to possibly go cry in the bathroom, when her phone buzzed in her back pocket. She fished it out of her jean shorts, then blinked at the name flashing across the screen.

Elena.

Daphne's vision swam, the letters rearranging themselves as she stared at the phone. Elena loved a cold call, had hardly ever texted when they were together.

And of course, Daphne always answered.

So when her finger slid across the screen, picking up the call, it didn't feel wrong. Didn't feel strange or unwise. It simply felt like what Daphne had always done.

She pressed the phone to her ear, muscle memory taking over, but didn't say anything. Everything felt suddenly dreamlike—Elena wasn't actually on the other end after over a month of silence, Daphne hadn't actually answered the call.

But then—

"Daphne?"

Elena's alto voice, a bit of a Sophia Bush husk to it, a tone that had always made Daphne's insides melt just a little.

And right now was no exception.

She sank down onto one of the student stools, her legs suddenly rubbery.

"You all right, love?" Nicola asked, pencil hovering in the air.

Daphne nodded, a reflex, but the truth was she had no idea. She knew she should hang up. Throw her phone in the lake, even. But then Elena said her name again—soft and familiar—and Daphne could barely think, much less take action on anything.

"Daphne, I can hear you breathing," Elena said. "Are you going to talk to me?"

Daphne cleared her throat. "Hi. H-hello."

"There she is," Elena said.

"Here I am," Daphne said, getting to her feet. She suddenly couldn't stay still, couldn't sit and talk to Elena at the same time. She walked out of the studio and into the hallway, one hand pulling at the ends of her lavender hair.

"How are you?" Elena asked.

Daphne leaned against the interior wall and faced the row of windows on the other side. The lake sparkled like a sapphire in the distance, speckled with dots of color from swimmers and boats and sails. She wasn't sure how to answer Elena—truthfully, at this moment, she felt as though her skin were melting off her bones. Her heart was pounding like she was in full fight-or-flight mode, and she was sweating.

But "Fine" was what came out of her mouth, because she certainly wasn't going to share any of that with Elena.

Daphne closed her eyes, remembering the text she'd sent Elena last week. That must be why she was calling. To explain. To apologize. To say anything about April. Literally anything.

"Where are you?" Elena asked. "Still in Boston?"

"No, I'm . . . I'm in a town called Clover Lake for the summer."

Elena was silent on the other end for a beat. "I see."

Daphne wanted to ask if she knew it—because of course Elena knew it. She wanted to scream at her. Wanted to ask why, wanted to demand they stop with these pleasantries and just *talk*, but Daphne couldn't get any of that to come out of her mouth either.

"Why are you calling me?" she finally asked.

"Why did you answer?" Elena said back.

Classic Elena.

And classic Daphne to have no rebuttal.

"I was worried about you," Elena said when Daphne said nothing. "I care about you, Daph."

Daphne shook her head, even though Elena couldn't see her, more a way to dislodge Elena's words than anything else, try to keep them from soaking into her bones.

Like you cared about April?

There it was—right there on the tip of her tongue. *The* question. But she couldn't say it. It was clear she couldn't say anything about anything when it came to Elena Watson. The years they spent together, all of Daphne's firsts with Elena, had her in a chokehold, freezing up every emotion.

And she hated herself for it.

But she couldn't seem to get out from under it.

"I've got to go," she said.

"Daphne, wait, I—"

But Daphne ended the call, tapping the red button so hard, she nearly sprained her finger. She was breathing hard, her eyes immediately filling with tears. She stared at her phone for a good thirty seconds.

"As far as vehement hang-ups go, I'd give that one an eight out of ten."

Daphne startled at the voice to her left, dropping her phone in the process. It clattered loudly onto the hardwood floor.

Sasha bent down to pick it up, flipping it around in her hand and inspecting the screen before offering it back to Daphne.

"No harm done," she said. She was dressed in black jeans and a plain white tee, her platinum hair tall and swoopy.

"Thanks," Daphne said, tucking her phone into her pocket.

"So," Sasha said, making a clicking sound with her tongue.

Daphne could only laugh. It wasn't necessarily a pleasant sound, but it was better than breaking down into tears. Maybe she was growing, but the small feeling in the center of her chest indicated otherwise.

"So," she said, wiping her eyes.

"That sounded intense."

"You have no idea," Daphne said, letting her head thunk against the wall and closing her eyes.

"Do you want to tell me about it?" Sasha asked. She leaned against the wall as well, one ankle crossed over the other.

And god, Daphne actually did. Of course, she'd told Vivian all about the breakup when it had happened, and April clearly knew, but there was no one Daphne could really talk to about April herself.

The confusing, mysterious, bruise-like conundrum who was April Evans.

So she slid down the wall until she was sitting, then crossed her legs. Sasha sat too, resting her forearms on her knees.

"Remember my ex who cheated on someone with me?" Daphne said.

Sasha lifted a single devastating brow. "I do."

"That someone was April." Daphne went on to explain the particulars of the last week and a half, including Nicola Reece and how Daphne and April were pretty much competing against each other for the chance of a lifetime.

Sasha steepled her fingers. "Wait. So April is . . ."

"Yeah."

"And Elena was—"

"Oh, yeah."

"And you never knew she was—"

"Nope."

"And now the Devon," Sasha said.

"I could not make this stuff up," Daphne said.

"Fucking hell," Sasha said, sending a hand through her hair. "I mean, *fuck*."

Daphne laughed—a true laugh this time. It felt good to have someone completely unrelated to the mess that was her life verify that it was, indeed, a mess.

"What's with all the fucks?"

Both Sasha and Daphne swung their heads toward the new voice—April Evans herself walking down the hall. Sasha got to her feet.

"Okay, that's it," she said, putting her hands on her hips.

"What's it?" April asked. "Am I in trouble?"

"More like in desperate need of some fun," Sasha said as Daphne stood as well. "I mean, look at you two. The hair is hot, Daphne, but seriously?"

"You think my hair is hot?" Daphne asked, fingers playing with the ends.

Sasha rolled her eyes. "Tonight. Dance studio."

"Are we learning the foxtrot?" April asked.

"We're going to a party," Sasha said. "Some of the dance instructors are throwing it, and they know how to have a good time."

Daphne's eyes lit up. "Oh my god, really? That sounds perfect. I've never been to a party before."

Both Sasha and April gave her a look.

"Never?" April asked.

"Well, not one that didn't involve a cocktail dress and tiny hors d'oeuvres and violin music. But I guess, if you go way back, I went to a lot of VBS parties."

"VBS?" Sasha asked.

"Vacation Bible School," Daphne said. "We'd make paper doll Bible characters and drink a *lot* of Hawaiian Punch."

Sasha and April blinked at her.

"This is more dire than I thought," Sasha said, turning to April. "And you? What was your biggest party ever?"

April narrowed her eyes. "This is Daphne's wild adventure, not mine."

"Yeah, but you need something," Sasha said, flicking her gaze up and down April's form. "Not sure what it is yet, but Jesus."

"What is that supposed to mean?" April asked.

Sasha just flailed her arms between April and Daphne. "Need I say more?"

April lifted her eyes to the ceiling. "Fuck my life."

"Exactly," Sasha said, clapping her hands together. "Now meet me in the dance studio at nine o'clock tonight or I will hunt you down."

And with that, she strode off in her white sneakers, hands in her pockets and whistling some tuneless song.

"She knows, doesn't she?" April asked when Sasha was out of sight.

Daphne winced. "She sort of caught me right after—"

She cut herself off, closing her eyes and inhaling through her nose as she looked down at the floor. Somehow, she didn't want to admit that she'd answered Elena's call.

Couldn't.

Not to April Evans.

She sighed before glancing back at April. "I'm sorry. I'm pathetic."

April frowned, but her eyes were gentle. "You're not pathetic."

Softly.

Almost sweetly.

They stared at each other for a few seconds. Daphne felt her heartbeat everywhere as April's dark eyes searched her own.

"Ready for class?" Daphne finally asked, even though she still couldn't pull her gaze away.

"Yeah," April said, her voice nearly a whisper.

For a second, neither of them moved. And when April eventually looked away, hitching her bag higher onto her shoulder and heading into the studio, Daphne felt dizzy and breathless. She wasn't sure if it was because of talking to Elena or the party or something else altogether.

Or maybe, it was because of some*one* else altogether.

Chapter Eleven

APRIL COULDN'T BELIEVE she'd let Sasha talk her into this.

The dance studio was crowded and loud, music blaring, people laughing, which wasn't exactly the kind of environment April wanted right now. She felt antsy, nervous, and couldn't figure out what she needed to calm her down.

Normally, she'd call Ramona.

Actually, no. Normally, Ramona would be here with her.

The two of them had barely talked over the last week. They'd texted here and there, and Ramona had asked more about Daphne, but April hadn't offered much. She knew she did this—retreated when she felt hurt, self-isolated until she was ready to talk. And Ramona knew this about her. She also knew she was being childish—in fact, Ramona had texted several times today asking April to call her—but April just couldn't seem to work herself out of this funk that had settled over her since she'd gotten to Cloverwild.

Since Daphne.

But no, she knew that was a lie. As much as she hated to admit it, April Evans had been in a funk for much longer than that. Daphne Love was just the complicated icing on the cake.

She sighed, leaned against a wall with her red Solo cup full of . . . she wasn't even sure. It was light purple and smelled like pine needles and soap. Tasted like that too. She set the cup down after one sip and folded her arms, her eyes finding Daphne of their own accord, who was walking around with Sasha. Daphne wore a red halter-style sundress printed with cherry blossoms, the waist cinched and the skirt flaring a little to her knees. The excitement in the room increased, cheers swelling as more people joined in the fray.

Suddenly, Daphne's eyes flicked to April's as she and Sasha started dancing as well. April felt something pinch in her stomach, though she didn't know what or why, so she looked away, down, anywhere else.

She fiddled with the silver rings on five out of ten fingers, letting her mind wander. It had been over a week since Nicola had invited April to try for the Devon—a week exactly since she'd also extended the opportunity to Daphne—and April still had no ideas. Nothing concrete at least, just color and blurry images, a *feeling* rather than any way to express it visually. She'd started a new sketchbook just for this project, and was at least thirty pages in with nothing but crap filling every one of them. It had been so long since she'd created her own art, rather than working off a client's vision for their tattoo, that she wasn't sure she even knew how to come up with original ideas anymore.

"Your girl is doing well," Sasha said, appearing next to April, a slight sheen of sweat dotting her brow.

April straightened as she realized she'd been watching Daphne dance, her lavender hair glowing in the dim lighting, the mirrors catching her reflection like a prism. She was laughing, her eyes glittering at her dance partners as she held their shoulders and twirled around them.

"She's not my girl," April said.

Sasha laughed softly. "And yet, you knew exactly who I was talking about."

April glared at her, but Sasha's gaze was on the dancers.

"You're not dancing anymore?" April asked.

Sasha side-eyed her. "I will if you will."

April lifted a brow. "Is that a dare?"

"It's one hundred percent a dare."

April laughed and pushed off from the wall. "Oh, I am in." She never turned down a dare—at least, she never had before, and dammit, she wasn't going to start now. Because at this moment, *this* was what she wanted—her old self back.

A song by a popular queer artist started up, the beat fun and sensual. April headed into the group of dancers, Sasha laughing behind her. She lifted her arms in the air and let out a whoop as she pushed farther into the crowd, others closing around her like a force field. It had been a long time since she'd gone out dancing like this, felt the press of other bodies. Since deleting all of her dating apps, she simply hadn't had the motivation, but now, god, she wondered why she'd ever given this up.

The adrenaline.

The anonymity.

She grinned at the people dancing around her, most of them with another person, arms slung around necks, barely any space between their bodies. Her eyes met a man's—broad shoulders and dark skin, a dimpled grin that would make anyone swoon. She reached out and pulled him close. His arms went immediately around her waist, hips pressed just where she wanted them. She looped her hands around his neck and he drew her even closer, one leg sliding between hers. She laughed as he twirled her around the other couples—a few had even throupled up, and the pheromones were thick and heady.

This was exactly what she needed.

The man lifted her arms from around his neck and spun her into someone else, another man with gingery hair and biceps the size of her thighs. The new man dipped her, then turned her around so her ass was right against his hips, both of their lower halves swirling in ways that would've marked a movie as PG-13.

At the very least.

She loved it. Every minute of it, a new face every time she turned, encircled by arms she'd never felt before. She laughed as she danced with a woman in a twirly dress who was clearly a dance instructor, leading April effortlessly in some kind of salsa-like moves before disappearing, a tall person with box braids taking April in their arms next.

On and on it went, a revolving door of dance partners, each of them fun and sexy and nameless.

Until they weren't so nameless at all.

A person April vaguely recognized from the resort's waitstaff spun her back toward the center, and she fell directly into the arms of Daphne Love.

April's hands went to Daphne's shoulders, more to keep from bowling Daphne over than anything. But Daphne's fingers pressed into her waist, soft and tentative. They stared at each other for a second, Daphne's green eyes glowing. She was breathing heavily, a gleam of sweat on her chest from spinning through the crowd too, her cheeks flushed and that full mouth parted slightly.

April needed to pull away. Needed to laugh and twirl Daphne to the next dancer, but she didn't want to.

She couldn't explain it or understand. She waited for Daphne to move away as well, but Daphne didn't do that either. Daphne stayed exactly where she was, still gripping April's waist while others swirled around them in a blur of color.

April didn't want to laugh and find another anonymous partner.

She wanted to loop her arms around Daphne's neck, so that's what she did.

She wanted to press a little closer, so that's what she did.

She wanted to move her hips against Daphne's, so that's what she did.

For a split second only, she felt Daphne sort of freeze up, and April nearly pulled away, but then Daphne's arms tightened around her, pulled her even closer, and April gave herself over to it all—how Daphne smelled like smoky vanilla mixed with a little acrylic paint, the way her eyes grew darker as they moved, their legs slotted together like puzzle pieces, Daphne's thigh pressing to her center, that sundress a tantalizing flare of cotton around them.

April's whole body flushed warm.

They danced like that, completely entwined, faces close, breathing each other's air. They didn't say anything, and April barely noticed anyone else around them. She felt dizzy and light, as though she'd been filled with sparkling water. She tipped her head back, throat exposed, and felt the barest brush of Daphne—her lips, her nose, April wasn't sure—against her skin. She closed her eyes, let herself get lost.

Somewhere in the back of her mind, she knew this moment would feel different in her memory, once the music's rhythm and the room's energy didn't feel part of her blood and bones.

But right now, she didn't care.

Time seemed to stop, and the only thing that mattered was music and skin, the caress of Daphne's hair and the way April couldn't tell where her body ended and Daphne's began. She was a heady drug, this person in her arms, and April didn't want to wean off too soon.

But then the music changed. Still upbeat and fast, but less sultry. The shift forced April's eyes open, and before she knew it, she was whisked away from Daphne, someone else pulling her into their arms. It felt like a scene from a movie, everything slowing down while April and Daphne drifted farther apart, their eyes locked on each other's, the space between them growing wider.

"Hey, there," the person who had pulled April away said in her ear, a white man with nerdy-sexy glasses and messy black hair who suddenly felt all wrong. April forced her gaze away from Daphne. The loss of contact was like a broken twig, an almost audible snap in April's ears. She shook her head, tried to clear the gauzy feeling throughout her body, and hooked her arms around her new partner's neck.

She wanted to get lost again. Wanted nameless faces, that beautiful anonymous nothing, but as the music played on, as she continued to twine her body with others, she kept seeing a green-eyed gaze in her mind, and fuck if she couldn't look away.

Chapter Twelve

DAPHNE'S HAND OUTSTRETCHED toward April, their eyes still pinned on each other's, like Daphne was some damsel in a movie whose true love had just ridden off into battle.

It took her a good three seconds to lower her arm, even longer to realize she was standing frozen in the middle of a tightly packed crowd trying to dance. Shoulders jostled her in different directions, and by the time April finally cut the connection, snapping her gaze away and toward her new dance partner, Daphne was having a hard time getting a full breath.

"Sorry," other dancers said as they continued to bump into her.

She glanced around, everyone partnered up while she stood like a deer in the proverbial headlights. She tried to push her way out of the crowd, but just as she was about to break free of the group, her feet tangled with someone else's, and she went down.

Hard.

And visibly.

The crowd went silent, a collective gasp rising into the air like a dust cloud. She'd caught herself on her hands, but before that, the offending foot had turned on its side, sending a bloom of pain around her ankle. It hadn't hurt all that much, but the attention, the spectacle of it all, made blood rush into her cheeks. She scrambled to her feet, limping as fast as she could toward the studio door, her ankle screaming at her more and more as she went.

In the hallway, it was about twenty degrees cooler. She closed the door behind her, then pressed her back to the heavy wood. She looked down at her sandaled foot, which definitely looked a little puffy, and when she tried to rotate it in a circle, she hissed in pain.

Before she could figure out how to deal with it, however, she was sent catapulting forward as someone in the studio shoved the door open. She managed to stay on her feet this time, but her ankle was not happy. She stumbled and pinwheeled, a real elegant show, she was sure.

"Shit, I'm sorry," April said, appearing at her side and grabbing her elbow. "Are you okay?"

April's touch was like fire. Goose bumps broke out along Daphne's skin, but she tried not to react, focusing instead on her swollen ankle. "I'm fine."

"Yeah, you look just peachy," April said, leading Daphne to one of the wooden benches lining the hallway.

Daphne plopped down, sighing when she got her weight off her ankle. April peered down at her, an uncertain expression on her face.

"I saw you fall. Just wanted to come check on you," she said.

Daphne nodded, couldn't look at her. Her whole body felt hot, a little sweaty, and she wasn't sure if it was pain endorphins rushing to her rescue, or something else. Something she probably needed to forget but also couldn't seem to stop thinking about—legs entwined, April's scent as she pressed close, like pears and lemons, with something a little spicy just underneath. Chili or peppers, Daphne wasn't sure, but whatever it was had addled her thoughts, made her feel drunk.

She'd love to blame that awful poison-purple concoction they were serving in the studio, but she'd only been able to stomach a couple of sips. She could blame the day itself, her painting and Elena's call, getting caught up in dancing, in strangers' attention, which she'd never really experienced so closely before, but no. She'd danced with at least five or so other people before April, just as close, just as . . . well, *dirty,* and they hadn't reduced her to a trembling mess. She'd laughed and tipped her head back and grinned and felt nothing but pure freedom and joy, a wildness to her body and heart. She could certainly blame the situation, the tight, fraught cord between her and April making everything feel more intense, and maybe there was some validity to that.

But that didn't explain why she was so . . .

She was . . .

God, she was *turned on.*

There. She could admit it. Had no idea what to do about it, but there was no other way to explain the dull throb between her legs right now.

She shook her head, sucked in a lungful of air.

"I'm okay," she managed to say, but then couldn't hold back a wince as she rolled her ankle to test it.

April squatted down to inspect Daphne's ankle. Her touch was gentle, fingers light as they held her foot. "Looks a little swollen," she said quietly, glancing up at Daphne. "Maybe a bruise forming. We can get some ice in the cabin."

Daphne nodded, swallowed hard.

"You think you can make it back there?" April asked, standing up.

"Yeah," Daphne said. She stood, relying on her good foot, but she wobbled, and April grabbed her elbow again to steady her. Then she took Daphne's arm and slung it around her shoulder, hooking her own arm around Daphne's waist.

Daphne got a whiff of pear and spice again, and her knees

nearly buckled. Somehow, though, she managed to hold herself upright as April led her toward the exterior door at the end of the hall.

OUTSIDE, THE WEATHER was humid and heavy, the lake a dark swath to their right. Daphne couldn't say the air was fresh, necessarily, but it was different, the breeze swirling April's scent away from her, clearing her head.

But then April's fingers would tighten around her, and she'd remember the way her nose grazed that spot right above the dip in April's collarbones, and her thoughts would muddle all over again.

She squeezed her eyes shut, trying to block it all out, but she quickly realized that was not a wise move while hobbling along the cobblestone path toward the staff cabins, so she stared down at her feet. She opened her mouth a hundred times to say something—anything—to April, but nothing ever came out.

And then, a rumble of thunder.

"You've got to be kidding me," April said as the first drops of rain started falling, plinking onto Daphne's bare arm.

Very suddenly, the sky opened up, as though someone from above had dumped a bucket full of water onto the earth. Daphne was soaked in seconds, and lightning crackled across the sky, flashing an eerie purple-white as April tried to move them along faster.

"This seems excessive," Daphne said, her teeth chattering.

April laughed at that, and then Daphne laughed because she'd made April laugh—an air-light, bright sound through the dark—and then they were both cracking up as they pulled themselves through the deluge and toward the cabin lights sparkling ahead of them.

They stumbled up the porch steps, Daphne's stomach muscles aching from laughing just as much as her ankle at this point. April managed to tap her card against the reader, and they fell through the door, spilling onto the floor in a splay of arms and legs. Daphne wasn't sure if her ankle was still attached anymore, much less how injured it was.

They were both drenched, making a mess on the hardwood, but still they laughed in the middle of their darkened cabin, the door wide open, the storm raging just outside.

And Daphne couldn't remember the last time she'd felt this free.

This . . . happy.

It was such a small, silly thing—rushing through an ill-timed rainstorm with her moody cabinmate—but somehow, it felt big.

It felt like a *moment*.

A few minutes later, the laughter faded, and Daphne waited for April's expression to shutter, for her to sigh, clear her throat, and go back to being the April that Daphne expected—perfectly nice at this point in their relationship, sure, but reserved. Cautious.

And April did sigh. She did clear her throat as she stared up at the ceiling, her fingers laced over her stomach. But then she turned on her side, wet hair slicked back, and propped herself up on her elbow, head resting in her hand.

She didn't say anything at first.

She just looked at Daphne, and Daphne looked back, her breathing suddenly shallow and quick. They stayed like that for what felt like hours, April's eyes dark as she studied Daphne's face. Daphne expected to start squirming, or maybe even start laughing again, but for once, she found she didn't mind the scrutiny. Didn't mind studying April right back, finally allowing herself to really *look* after days and days of forcing her gaze away.

And now that she could, she saw that April was like a painting—intricate and layered and lovely. Fathomless eyes, smooth skin and round cheeks, a thin top lip over a fuller bottom one, both curving into barely noticeable dimples at the corners. A work of art, really, and Daphne felt as though she could look forever and still not have her fill, still not truly capture the whole picture.

Daphne wondered what April saw when she looked at her.

April's gaze slid down to Daphne's mouth, then back up, and Daphne's stomach fluttered.

No, not fluttered.

Swelled and then crested and crashed, like a tsunami just offshore.

She wasn't sure what to say or do, but she wanted . . . she *wanted*, and she didn't know what to do with that feeling. It was wild and reckless and possibly just plain stupid, but she couldn't seem to get the feeling to calm down either, like an involuntary response—fight, flight, or freeze.

But this was April. And that fact—the two of them, existing together at all—already felt like stepping into a minefield, tiptoeing through danger.

"Thanks for helping me back to the cabin," Daphne said.

April shrugged. "It's what friends do."

"Are we friends?" Daphne asked, smiling.

April laughed. "I think that's at least partially accurate."

"I'm glad," Daphne said. "I haven't got many of those."

"No?"

Daphne shook her head. "I had a best friend in college. Vivian. But I've . . ." She trailed off, a knot in her throat.

"You've what?" April asked.

She was inches away, and her question sounded so earnest, Daphne felt herself relax. She blew out a long breath.

"I've been a bad friend." Daphne sighed, looking toward the ceiling. "Vivian was my roommate all four years of college and one of the first queer friends I ever had. We never dated or anything, but she really helped me navigate . . . I don't know. The *world*. It was overwhelming. So much freedom after so little. I was a mess for a while. Most of my first year, really, and Vivian was there for all of it. She helped me ask out the girl I was crushing on sophomore year, and she was there after I couldn't relax enough to let the same girl under my shirt and preemptively broke up with her."

"Ouch," April said.

Daphne smiled. "Yeah."

"And now?" April said.

"I don't know. After I met Elena—"

"The Devil herself, yes, go on," April said.

Daphne grinned. "The actual Devil? Seems a bit hyperbolic."

"Potayto, potahto."

"A Disney villain, maybe," Daphne said.

"I'm shocked you were allowed to watch Disney."

"Oh, I wasn't," Daphne said, laughing. "I saw all the movies I missed as a kid in college with Vivian. Elena has some strong Cruella vibes. Or Maleficent. Similar cheekbones."

"Bite your tongue. I adore Maleficent," April said.

"You adore the sorceress who wanted to kill a baby princess?"

April groaned. "Well, when you put it like that, it sounds awful."

"How is Maleficent *not* awful?"

April popped back up on her elbow. "All the Disney villainesses are fed to us from the quintessential male gaze. Twist it just a little, and they're women who have been forgotten, mocked, and berated. They're badasses who go after what they want."

"Okay," Daphne said slowly. "They go after what they want. Admirable for sure." She nodded vigorously, then stopped and pointed a finger in the air. "By . . . killing baby princesses?"

April shrugged. "Two sides to every story. After all, the spindle that Aurora—the most boring heroine, by the way—was enchanted to be pricked by only sent her to sleep. Didn't kill her."

"Oh, great merciful Maleficent," Daphne said, then frowned.

"Plus, I thought that was the fairies who altered the spell so she wouldn't die."

"So we've been told," April said. "I think we need to watch the Angelina Jolie movie posthaste."

Daphne smiled, something bubbly and light filling her chest. "Deal."

April smiled back but then grew serious again. "So what happened with Vivian?"

"Oh, she was totally obsessed with Ursula, now that I think about it."

April smiled softly but said nothing.

"I disappeared on Vivian," Daphne said, sighing. "After—"

"Beelzebub."

Daphne huffed a small laugh. "After Beelzebub. I let her take over everything and I lost Vivian in the process. Lost myself. Lost everything that was Daphne Love."

The words sounded dramatic, but they felt true. They *were* true. April's eyes searched hers, and Daphne couldn't look away. She felt locked on to April's face, entranced as though under a spell.

"Better find her, then," April said softly, and Daphne nodded, still locked, still enchanted.

A swath of orange suddenly blocked Daphne's vision. She gasped, which resulted in Bob the Drag Cat's fur in her mouth and eyes and nose.

"Bob, ugh, oh my god," she said, turning her head away and sputtering.

April laughed, then sat up, plucking Bob from next to Daphne and kissing the top of his head before setting him on her other side. Whatever spell had been tangling between them was broken, the atmosphere immediately thinner, lighter. Bianca let out a mew from near the open front door, her tail perked in curiosity.

"Bianca, don't you dare," April said, nearly leaping on top of the cat to keep her from going outside. She stood, the ball of white-and-gray fur in her arms—hissing, no less—and kicked the door closed before setting down the recalcitrant beast.

Daphne still lay on the floor, plucking fur from her lips.

April peered down at her, an amused expression on her face.

"Not so thrilled with being the favorite now, are we?" she said, hands on her hips.

"Oh, shut up," Daphne said, but she laughed.

April held out a hand. "Let's get that ankle iced, yeah?"

Daphne nodded, then slid her fingers into April's cool palm and stood up before hobbling over to the sofa.

HOURS LATER, DAPHNE lay in bed, her foot resting on several pillows after a long icing session on the couch while she and April very pointedly didn't look at each other and watched *Maleficent* on April's laptop. April had wrapped Daphne's foot using a bandage from the cabin's first aid kit, then handed her two ibuprofen and a glass of water.

April had been gentle and careful and hadn't said much, but then again, neither had Daphne. April's fingers were featherlight, but electric, as though each one had tiny bolts of lightning flickering at the tips, producing in Daphne shock, comfort, and something else she didn't want to attach a word to all at the same time.

It had been a confusing evening, to say the least.

And now, with the rain plinking soothingly on the cabin's tin roof and Bob curled up at her side, she couldn't seem to stop thinking.

Thinking and remembering.

Thinking and remembering and, even worse than both of those brain functions, *imagining*.

That dance with April—it kept going further in her brain, the scene continuing. As if the reality of those three or four itty-bitty minutes wasn't tortuous enough, her imagination added more color, more texture, more scents.

And she had always had a very, very good imagination.

Daphne's eyes fluttered closed, music swelling in her mind. The other dancers around them faded away, leaving Daphne and April alone in the studio, the lights dim. Their bodies pressed together, legs tangled, hips grinding desperately. Daphne drifted her fingers down April's neck, dancing over the delicate skin, and April tipped her head back, lips parted. Daphne wanted her mouth on April's exposed throat, wanted to breathe in that pear scent.

Daphne was a little taller than April, and she directed them toward the nearest wall, moving with the music, hands roaming until April's back hit the wall. April laughed, but nothing was funny to Daphne, who immediately hooked one of April's legs around her own hip, cutting off April's laugh with a gasp. Daphne's other hand slid under her tank top, fingers bumping over her ribs while she pressed her mouth to April's neck. April arched into her, and Daphne had never felt so ravenous, so desperate. She tilted April's chin up and kissed her, tugging on her bottom lip, licking into her mouth, the hand holding April's leg sliding up her thigh to her ass now. They pressed closer, their hips as one, moving, rutting, and god, Daphne wanted to make April co—

Daphne's eyes flipped open.

She was breathing heavily, the rain and the dark of their cabin coming back into focus. Her mouth was dry, and she felt dizzy. She swiped a hand over her forehead—damp from sweat—and glanced at April, who was turned on her side facing Daphne, her breathing deep and regular.

Daphne gulped at the air, trying to get her body to come back to earth. She was wet between her legs, her clit throbbing from her daydream.

Which was . . . no.

Just *no.*

She hadn't had sex in over a month. Maybe closer to six weeks, as Elena hadn't seemed to have the time in the last few days before their breakup. And Daphne liked sex. She loved it, actually. Elena had always been good in bed, and god, she was really good at cunnilingus. She was good with a strap-on too. Good with her fingers. Good with—

Daphne squeezed her eyes closed, but then April bloomed in the darkness there, her head thrown back while Daphne unbuttoned her jeans and dipped her hand—

"Fuck," Daphne whispered quietly. It was true, she didn't swear much, but sex always brought it out of her. And right now, she was horny. That was it. She was just horny, and it had been a while, and she hadn't even gotten herself off since the breakup because she honestly hadn't had the energy.

But now, her libido was screaming, and loudly.

She turned on her side—jostling Bob so that he hopped off the bed—and tried to ignore the insistent pulse between her legs.

She'd sleep it off.

But every time she closed her eyes, she was back in that dance studio, the scene against the wall going on . . . and on . . . and on . . .

Finally, she threw the covers back and got out of bed. Carefully, of course, keeping the weight off her wrapped foot as she made her way to the bathroom. She closed herself inside, turned on the light and the fan, then braced her hands on the sink. She turned on the faucet, splashed her face. She brushed her teeth again. She gulped a cup of water.

And still, she felt April's fingers lifting the hem of her dress, moving closer to her center.

Daphne knew orgasms were normal bodily functions for people who wanted them, and she liked to think she was long over the shame associated with self-pleasure that had been ingrained in her growing up.

And April was hot.

That was just a fact. Didn't have to mean anything at all, and right now, Daphne needed to come. She needed it so badly a whimper escaped her throat as she pressed her back against the wall for leverage, then slid her hand inside her sleep shorts, wasting no time before touching herself over her underwear.

"Oh my god," she whispered, eyes fluttering closed as she leaned her head against the wall. She was soaked, right through the cotton, and she almost couldn't believe how good it felt to press her fingers against her pussy, massaging and rubbing, gently at first, working herself up.

Soon she needed more though, so she dipped inside her underwear, glided her fingers up from her entrance to her clit, spreading her wetness. A moan slipped out of her throat, and she clapped her free hand over her mouth as she rubbed harder, finally sliding two fingers inside herself and pressing her palm to her clit. The angle would be better lying down, but she couldn't do this in the same room where April slept. Plus, she needed this now, right here, needed to come more than she needed air, needed to fuck herself until she broke.

She felt her cunt clenching around her fingers, felt her thighs start to tremble. And god, she couldn't help it, she had a flash of April's face between her legs, tongue swirling over her clit, humming into her pussy, and that did it. Daphne came hard, weeks of buildup slamming over her entire body. Her knees nearly buckled, her weak ankle barely able to hold her up, but she managed it, grabbing the sink for support while she came on her own fingers, gasping as quietly as she could.

Daphne waited until her body stopped shuddering, the waves still radiating down her legs. She took her hand out of her shorts, then moved to sit on the closed toilet lid while she caught her breath.

She smiled, laughed almost, as she thought about what had just happened. It had felt good, of course, and she didn't feel ashamed at all. It had taken her years in college—with a lot of talking with Vivian, actually—to not feel an instant wash of shame after touching herself. She'd worked hard to leave the purity culture of her youth behind. So, no, she didn't feel ashamed.

But she felt . . . something. A bit of postorgasmic euphoria, sure, but underneath all that, there was something else. Something light and free and happy.

She felt like herself.

Maybe a self she'd never met before—dirty dancing and letting her body feel what it needed to feel. Laughing with the last person she ever thought she'd meet in real life, much less feel some sort of camaraderie with.

She liked this Daphne. It was a glimpse, a moment that might vanish at any second, but for now, even with a sprained ankle and an uncertain future, she felt a tiny sliver of hope that she might actually, really, truly find her—the Daphne Love she'd lost all those years ago.

Chapter Thirteen

> Today, prepare for calls to adventure and embracing the unexpected. Your evolution requires packing away the stories that weigh you down and following less toxic narratives for your life. Your boldness will transform you.

A couple of mornings later, April sat at a table by the window in Cloverwild's dining room and read Madame Andromeda's daily assertions for Scorpio on her phone. She forced herself not to glare at words like *evolution* and *transform*. Trigger words, as of late, but today, they hit a little different.

Daphne fucking Love.

April couldn't stop thinking about her.

The dance.

The ankle.

The way they'd talked while lying on the cabin floor, like they were two teenagers at summer camp, the sentences flowing so easily between them, the laughter.

The *dance.*

Somehow, practically dry humping with Elena's ex wasn't

exactly what she thought Madame Andromeda meant by embracing the unexpected.

Then again . . .

April squeezed her eyes closed. Absolutely fucking not. She sipped her coffee, then took out her sketchbook and flipped to a new page. Her mind worked—or tried to, clawing at ideas like fingers grabbing at the empty air.

And then . . . there.

An image, clear as day, though it wasn't anything she could use for the Devon. No, this was for pale skin, randomly freckled and smooth.

Soft baby skin.

She smiled, just a little, then flipped her pencil over her knuckles once and started sketching, the dining room fading behind her. It all took shape quickly, the sketch of what she'd eventually fill with warm colors for the wildflowers, the faintest flame flickering against the glass of a lantern. Her fingers moving as though separate from her, driven on by some force she didn't understand. She loved it when this happened, when art and creation and beauty took on its own life. Not because she wasn't the artist, or because she hadn't worked hard to create it, but because what she'd made felt inevitable.

It *was*, and she was simply the vessel through which it came into being.

She nearly had the entire outline before she slowed down or looked up, the dining room filling with guests as the clock ticked closer to lunch. She hadn't meant to sit here this long, but she knew Daphne was painting in the studio, and it didn't seem right to hover while she created her masterpiece for the Devon.

Either that, or April felt suddenly shy around Daphne, but that would be ridiculous, wouldn't it?

"Hey, I need you both to try this," Sasha said, appearing at April's table with a plate in her hands.

April blinked up at her. "Both who?"

Sasha tilted her head toward something behind April. "Daphne's on her way over here."

April's stomach undulated, but she squashed the feeling down.

"What's that?" Sasha asked, setting the plate on the table as she sat across from April and nodded toward her sketch pad. "Looks interesting."

April slapped the book closed. "Too early to tell."

"You are a moody little mystery, aren't you, Evans?"

April laughed, rubbed at the graphite staining the side of her left hand. "Not the first time I've heard that."

"Shocking," Sasha said.

"Heard what?" Daphne asked, pulling out the chair next to Sasha. She still hobbled a bit on her ankle, but as far as April could tell, it was better. Just a mild sprain.

Today, Daphne's hair was pulled up into a messy bun on top of her head, lavender tendrils curling around her face. She wore a plain white tee and loose light-wash jeans, paint smeared on both as well as her arms and fingers. A slash of green streaked across her cheek, and April felt an irrational swell of affection.

It was paint. On her face.

Get a fucking grip, April Evans.

Daphne met April's gaze, though, and her cheeks immediately went a little pink. April had quickly learned that Daphne blushed if someone so much as complimented her shoes, but, unless April was imagining it, her cheeks seemed to be flaming a lot more around April over the last couple of days.

She was probably imagining it.

"That April is an enigma Goth," Sasha said.

Daphne frowned. "Is that a thing?"

"I just made it a thing," Sasha said.

April laughed. "I'll put it on my website." She leaned forward, finally taking full notice of the plate Sasha had set down in the middle of the table. "Oh, hello."

"That smells amazing," Daphne said. "What is it?"

"Oh, yeah, right," Sasha said, sitting on the edge of her seat as though she'd forgotten her own dish. "My buddy is the sous chef, and she lets me use the kitchen here and there between meal prep, just playing around."

"You cook?" Daphne asked.

"A hundred percent," Sasha said. "I spent the summer as a dishwasher in a Michelin-starred kitchen in Paris last year. I learned how to make a mean chocolate soufflé."

"Bartending, cooking, dishwashing," April said. "What the hell do you actually *do*?"

Sasha's eyes went a little dark, her jovial expression faltering for a split second. "This and that."

April's brows lifted, and she pressed her hand to her chest before gesturing toward Sasha. "Enigma Goth, meet Enigma Butch."

Sasha laughed. "I'll take that title very gladly."

April shook her head. Sasha baffled her more and more each time she hung out with her. Still, she had to admit whatever Sasha had just placed on the table smelled incredible. It looked like a pizza, but not like any pizza she'd ever known. It was purple, for one thing, with a sweet and savory scent all at once. Sasha plucked a triangle from the dish and set it onto an empty plate for Daphne, then another for April.

"I'm starving," Daphne said, digging in immediately. Her eyes rolled back in her head. "Oh my god, Sasha."

"Right?" Sasha said. "Blackberry ricotta pizza. I think it's perfect for summer."

April took a bite too, inhaling the aromatics from the basil as she did so. Tang exploded on her tongue from the berries, and the cheese added a decadence and luxury to the whole thing. The crust was incredible—thin, but still chewy, dusted with semolina.

"Fucking amazing," April said with her mouth full.

"Yeah?" Sasha said, her eyes wide and hopeful. "I got the inspiration from when I was in Italy last fall."

"You've been to Italy too?" Daphne said after swallowing another bite.

"I've been all over," Sasha said, taking a bite of her own slice. "For the last couple of years, I've just been traveling around, seeing the sights, working odd jobs."

"This and that," April said, taking another bite.

"Exactly," Sasha said.

"Where's your family?" Daphne asked.

And there it was again, that dimming in Sasha's expression. She cleared her throat, shifting on her seat. "I grew up in LA."

"LA, really?" Daphne said. "That's exciting. Are your parents involved in movies or something like that?"

Sasha's smile was small. "Yeah," she said. "Something like that."

Silence fell over the table, and April got the distinct impression that Sasha wouldn't exactly welcome any more questions. She glanced at Daphne, who widened her own eyes with meaning.

"Do you have a favorite city?" April asked, desperate to change the subject.

Sasha brightened. "So hard to choose. Prague. This little town in Montana you can't even find on a map. Bangkok is spectacular."

"I've never been anywhere," Daphne said, sighing. "Tennessee. Boston. Now Clover Lake."

"I haven't either," April said, a sort of longing tightening in her chest. New York City, a little town in Maine where her parents liked to hole up in a cabin every July, Boston. She was thirty-three and she'd never even left the East Coast.

"I highly recommend expanding your literal horizons," Sasha said. "I'm taking off across the country at the end of the summer myself."

"You are?" April asked, pausing with her pizza slice inches from her mouth.

Sasha nodded. "Heading west for a month or so before I head out of the country again. I'm planning on visiting some sites I've never seen, like the Wave in Arizona and Carlsbad Caverns."

"So you're an outdoor queer," April said.

Sasha laughed. "I appreciate the natural world."

"That sounds incredible," Daphne said as she took another bite.

"It does," April said, her voice taking on a dreamy tone. She cleared her throat, then looked up to find Sasha watching her.

"Hey," Sasha said, leaning forward, "you're both more than welcome to—"

But she cut herself off when the dining room went oddly quiet, and the heads of almost every single guest turned toward the wide double doorway that led into the lobby.

"What's going on?" Daphne said before ripping off the end of her crust with her teeth.

"No idea," April said, but she got up and headed toward the lobby, just in case Mia needed help with anything. She wove around other people bottlenecking, but the crowd didn't thin as she left the dining room. A bevy of guests congregated around the reception desk. They formed a sort of circle, but April couldn't see who was at the center.

"I'm such a big fan," said Grace Latimer, an octogenarian hippie April recognized from her and Daphne's watercolor class.

April picked up her pace but then froze when she saw the familiar luggage sitting off to the side—two huge suitcases, mint green with ruby-red cherries printed all over them.

"Okay, everyone, let's give Ms. Monroe some room," Mia said, coming out from behind the desk. "She's here to relax, after all."

The crowd parted a bit, and there was Dylan Monroe, brown hair longer than the last time April had seen her, ice-green eyes sparkling, and dressed in wide-legged jeans and a cropped T-shirt that featured a picture of a tabby cat wearing heart-shaped glasses, the word *Lover* printed underneath.

"Thanks, Mia," she said. "And thanks, everyone, I'm so excited to be back in Clover Lake." She waved, but then clearly stepped away from the group. The guests disbanded, chattering as they went.

April could only stare as she saw Ramona standing at the desk, her back to April as she seemed to be signing a receipt. She wore a black-and-white blouse covered in starlings and tucked into a pair of high-waisted jeans, which hugged her thick thighs.

"Mona?" April finally managed to say.

Ramona turned and her eyes found April's, a smile spreading over her freckled face. "There she is!" She jogged toward April and scooped her into a hug, lifting her off the ground a little. April's arms felt dead at her sides.

"What are you doing here?" April asked when Ramona put her down. Dylan walked over to join them, and she and April hugged too.

"We both have a break for the rest of the summer, can you believe it?" Ramona said.

April smiled without her teeth, because no, she couldn't believe it. She didn't know anything about either of their work lives lately, only that Dylan was filming that Marlene Dietrich biopic, and Ramona was . . . she didn't even know, honestly. Designing costumes as a costume designer.

"That's great," April said.

"We thought we'd get some R & R at Cloverwild," Dylan said. "Of course, we have our house in town, but we wanted to get the full treatment."

"You're staying here?" April asked.

Ramona grinned and held up a key card. "Just for the weekend. Lucky cabin thirteen!"

April grinned too. God, she'd missed Ramona so much.

"Are you surprised?" Ramona asked. "I wanted to surprise you."

"Totally surprised," April said, pulling Ramona into a hug again. She breathed in her best friend of almost twenty-five years and felt herself relax.

"Can you come to our cabin with us?" Ramona asked, pulling back to look at her.

"I have a one o'clock class," she said. "But I can—"

"Oh, can I sit in on it?" Ramona said quickly. "I'm dying to see you in action. You don't mind, do you, babe?"

Dylan waved a hand, then grabbed both suitcases by their handles. "I'm so butch, I'll take care of both of these."

"So butch, you needed a sleeping seat on our flight," Ramona said.

Dylan shrugged. "So I'm a tired butch."

Ramona laughed. "Speaking of nonbutch queers—"

"I am offended," Dylan said, but she kissed Ramona on the cheek, then sauntered off, pulling the eyes of everyone in the lobby as she went.

"I can't wait to meet Daphne," Ramona said, not missing a beat. "How's everything going with you two?"

April opened her mouth but closed it again. She had no idea how to answer that question. It had been over a week since Ramona and April had spoken on the phone, and Ramona had advised April to give Daphne the benefit of the doubt.

Which April most definitely had not done and then realized she most definitely should have.

April hated when she was wrong.

But what she hated even more was this feeling of embarrassment around Ramona about being wrong, about her entire life right now. They didn't get embarrassed around each other. Never had. They'd seen each other through the most humiliating moments in life, including the time April had peed her pants a little from laughing so hard the first time Ramona pulled out Llama Face on the way back from a field trip to Bristol Farm. April had been terrified of the llamas—they looked fucking freaky, plain and simple—and Ramona had impersonated a llama by hooking her fingers under her lips and pulling them out as far as they'd go, sticking out her tongue, and making the funniest sound April had ever heard.

There was also the time Ramona had her wisdom teeth taken out when they were seventeen and was so doped up on painkillers she pretty much recited a romantic ode to Gillian Anderson. Which, yes, everyone of every gender was in love with Gillian Anderson, but Ramona spun a truly epic tale of marriage and kids and a big farmhouse in Scotland where they raised baby goats and made their own soap, and April had recorded every moment of it on her phone.

She still had the recording, in fact.

So this strange shyness April felt right now was weird. It was weird and uncomfortable, and April had no idea how to make it go away.

"Uh," April said brilliantly. "It's going okay."

"Is she still with Elena?" Ramona asked, lowering her voice and stepping closer to April. "Does she know who you are? How's teaching with her?"

April's head spun. She sent a hand through her hair as she tried to think which question to answer first.

"Teaching is fine," she said. Simplest to most complicated, she decided. "And . . . yeah, she knows—"

"Oh my god, is that her?" Ramona said, cutting April off and grabbing her arm, gaze focused over April's shoulder.

April turned to see Daphne and Sasha leaving the dining room and heading straight for them. She braced herself, body locking up at the prospect of Daphne Love's impending collision with Ramona.

"That's her," April said softly.

"She's so pretty," Ramona said just as quietly, then louder as Daphne reached them—not only louder, but to Daphne herself. "You're so pretty."

Daphne's eyes widened, her hands in her pockets as she looked around for whoever Ramona might be talking to.

"Me?" she finally asked.

"You," Ramona said, then stuck out her hand. "Hi, I'm Ramona."

Daphne smiled broadly, lighting up as she took Ramona's hand. "You're April's best friend! I'm Daphne."

"Oh, I know," Ramona said, laughing lightly, and April truly wished the earth's maw would open and swallow her into hell.

"And this is Sasha," April said, clearing her throat.

"Hey there," Sasha said to Ramona, tapping her forehead with one finger, suave as ever. "You staying here?"

"She's taken," April said before Ramona could respond, then clapped her hands together. "And now that everyone's met everyone, I'm going to give Ramona a tour before our class."

"You both can come if you'd like," Ramona said.

"No, they can't," April said, hooking an arm around Ramona's waist and pulling her toward the back of the lodge. This entire dynamic was just weird. She needed a minute to think, and she couldn't think with Daphne around, looking doe-eyed and cute with that paint still smeared across her cheek, grinning at Ramona like they were best friends too. And Sasha, affectionately, was nothing but trouble.

"What's the rush?" Ramona said as April whisked her away from Tweedledee and Tweedledum.

"Oh, hey, April," Daphne called to their backs. April froze and turned to look at her. "Is your laptop in our cabin? I didn't see it in the studio."

April blinked, her stomach sinking. But dammit, yes, the laptop was in their cabin, and they needed it for class as April had been working on new slides last night.

"Yeah. Can you grab it?" she asked.

Daphne nodded, and then April was off again, hurtling Ramona toward the back patio so fast, Ramona nearly tripped on her own feet.

"I thought we were going on a tour?" Ramona said as April pushed open one of the back French doors and they spilled out onto the expansive deck.

"Tour is boring," April said, walking them to the railing that overlooked the woods and sucking in a lungful of warm June air. "We eat in the dining room, swim in the lake, et cetera."

Ramona leaned her forearms on the wooden railing. She was quiet, and for a second, April hoped Ramona's attention hadn't snagged on certain pronouns Daphne had used, that she hadn't paid close enough attention to realize that—

"What did Daphne mean by *our* cabin?" Ramona asked.

April closed her eyes for a beat, then focused on the green of the forest. Between the trees, near Moon Lovers Trail, she could see some resort employees setting up tables and chairs for Mia's summer solstice party tonight. April had been looking forward to the soiree, complete with a bonfire in the woods under the full moon, flower crowns, special cocktails, and tarot readings.

"Apes?" Ramona pressed.

April sighed. "Daphne said that because we're cabinmates."

Ramona let that settle for a second. "What do you mean, you're cabinmates? As in . . . you're staying here?"

April knew there was no way around it, no way to spin it that wasn't outright deceit. Plus, she'd never lied to Ramona. Not so blatantly at least. *Withheld*, absolutely. It often took April a while to sift through her own emotions before she understood how to put them into words, and that was true even with Ramona. She was a riot of feelings, and that didn't always translate well to spoken language.

But right now, the truth was clear and simple.

"I rented out my house for the summer," she said.

"You what?"

"And I closed Wonderlust Ink."

"You . . . you *what*?"

Ramona had turned to face her, but April kept her eyes on the trees, the way the leaves flickered from green to silver in the breeze.

"April, what the hell?"

"I closed Wonderlust Ink," April said again.

"Yes, I heard you the first time. That's not what I meant by *what the hell*."

"It'd been struggling for a while." April shrugged. "It was time."

"It was . . . it was *time*?" Ramona asked. "Why didn't you tell me?"

"I just did."

"That's not what I mean, and you know it."

April turned to face her now. "And when would I have done that?" Her tone was sharper than she'd intended, and Ramona flinched.

"Apes."

"No, really, Mona," April said. "When should I have told you? At Thanksgiving when I was pretty sure that's where the shop was headed, and you were with your family and Dylan's family, and I saw you *once* when we met for brunch at Clover Moon, and the whole town couldn't calm the hell down over seeing you and Dylan again?"

Ramona's shoulders lowered, her frown deepening.

"Or maybe during all those FaceTime dates we scheduled," April said. "Except, oh, wait, you canceled most of them. Or, I guess, I could've told you over text, but call me sensitive, I'm not a huge fan of telling my best friend about major life decisions only to have it remain unread for forty-eight hours, which is probably why I also haven't told you that I have an opportunity to show my work in the Devon. Because I just wasn't sure if you had the time."

Her voice cracked a little on the last word, and she hated herself for it. Silence filtered between them while she looked out at the woods, swallowed around her thickening throat.

"April," Ramona said softly.

But April didn't want pity or excuses or even rational explanations. Because her best friend was here. Ramona had come home for *her,* and April was infuriated that she couldn't simply be happy about that. That there was all this baggage between them now, when they'd never, ever had secrets or distance between them since the day they met in the fourth grade on the playground at Clover Lake Elementary School.

So April opened it all up. Every secret. She told Ramona how it felt closing the shop, how she'd been in the red for nearly two years, and how her parents still didn't know. She told Ramona about meeting Daphne, and the canoe ride, and how Daphne had no idea Elena had cheated. She told her about meeting Sasha and dyeing Daphne's hair and how the curator from the Devon was an old client who had all but thrown April and Daphne into a competition for their very lives.

"And I *have* to win that spot," April said, her chest tightening more and more with every word. "I'm thirty-three, and I don't know what the hell I'm doing, and I'll be damned if Daphne Love, no matter how innocently, is going to take something else from me. I can't—"

"Okay, okay," Ramona said, pulling April into her arms and holding her tight. "Just breathe."

April did, resting her chin on Ramona's shoulder and kind of collapsing, arms loose around Ramona's waist. She felt suddenly exhausted, but also lighter. She tightened her embrace and exhaled heavily.

"Anything else?" Ramona asked, rubbing April's back.

"I may have dirty danced with my ex's ex," April said nonchalantly.

Ramona pulled back, but just enough to look April in the eye. "I'm sorry, what now?"

April laughed, because god, it *was* funny, and explained about the dancing, followed by Daphne hurting her ankle and their trek back to the cabin in the rain.

"And then I wrapped her ankle, and we watched *Maleficent*," April said, wiping at her smudged mascara.

Ramona's brows could not possibly get any higher. "Are you telling me you engaged in lesbian wound tending?"

"Well, of the two of us, she's the only lesbian, so—"

"Lesbian *wound* tending, Apes," Ramona said.

April dropped her head into her hands. "God, okay, yes, I know." She took a breath, remembering the feel of Daphne's delicate skin under her fingers, the way she'd gasped a little when April had shifted her foot in a certain manner, the way—

Good goddess on earth, stop.

She lifted her head. "Look, someone had to take care of her. It doesn't mean anything."

"Famous last words."

April shook her head, because the entire thing was ridiculous. "Tell me about you. Quickly, before I say something else that lands me in an Iris Kelly rom-com."

"Oh, have you read her latest? God, I love the enemies-to-lovers trope."

"Mona."

Ramona laughed, but then folded her arms, a sad expression settling on her face. "Your shop. Your *house*."

April closed her eyes and took a deep breath before opening them again. "Not right now. Please. We can dig deeper into every humiliating detail later, but please, *please*, tell me something about you. Anything."

Ramona's cheeks went a little pink and she looked down at her hands, tangling her fingers together. Her nails were painted a sparkly teal. A professional job, if April had to guess. Ramona could thread a needle in under two seconds, but she'd always been shit with nail polish.

"Well, actually, I wanted to come home for a lot of reasons," Ramona said, lifting her gaze to April's. "And one of them is that I wanted to . . ."

She searched April's eyes for so long, April started to squirm. "You wanted to what?"

Ramona opened her mouth. Closed it again.

"Mona," April said. "You're scaring me. Is your dad okay? Olive?"

"No, no," Ramona said, grabbing both of April's hands. "They're fine. Everyone's fine. Olive's coming home from Vanderbilt next week, in fact."

April lit up. "So that's why you're home, then. I'm always playing second fiddle." It was true, but it was a good truth—April adored Ramona's little sister, Olive, and she couldn't wait to see her.

Ramona laughed, but her eyes were still a bit hooded, a million thoughts behind them. "Olive is one reason, yes. But, honey, I—"

"Okay, well, that's a great reason," April said as her phone buzzed in her back pocket. She fished it out and glanced at Daphne's text, asking where she was. "Shit, I'm going to be late."

"Then let's go," Ramona said quickly, hooking her arm through April's and heading back inside. "You've got to work, I know. I want to hear more about the Devon though. Do you have an idea yet?"

April swallowed, dread washing over her. "Not a one."

Ramona smiled softly. "You'll get there. You will. You're extraordinary."

April nodded, but honestly, she had her doubts, because Daphne's work was truly extraordinary, and April hadn't thought of herself in the same terms in a long time.

But Ramona did.

She looked at her best friend for a second, the most familiar face in her life. Despite her hurt feelings the last few months, despite the way she still felt tender, as though her heart was covered in a healing bruise, she'd missed Ramona so much. "I'm glad you're here, Llama Face."

Ramona smiled, but her eyes got a little shiny, which she covered quickly by pausing in the middle of the hallway and hugging April tight.

"I probably have time to deeply analyze your horoscope for the week," April said.

Ramona laughed, then pushed April away. "Save it for a rainy day. We're having dinner with my dad, but maybe we can meet up at Clover Moon later tonight?"

"You got it, Llama," April said, grinning as they started walking again. And for a second—if she ignored that royal *we*—it felt like old times. For a brief, lovely moment, while April tried to slap Ramona's butt and Ramona dodged her, laughing and squealing like they were teenagers again as they went into the art studio, it felt as if the last two years had never even happened.

Chapter Fourteen

"DEATH?"

Daphne stood in the middle of the woods in a sky-blue cotton dress that flowed to her knees, spaghetti straps hooked over her shoulders, and stared down at the tarot card in her hand. "I got *Death*?"

April laughed and tapped the card's image—roses blooming around a skull. "It's a good card."

Daphne scoffed, her stomach tightening. "It's *Death*."

"Which means imminent doom and peril?" Sasha asked as she plucked her own card from the table at the entrance to Moon Lovers Trail, where the solstice bonfire was taking place. Every guest who came to the party got to pick a tarot card, all Major Arcana, according to April, whatever that meant.

"Which means transformation," April said. "Change and revolution." She wore soft flowing pants and a loose cropped top. The outfit was a set—black silk with creamy yellow stars, moons, and galaxies swirling over the material. The top was off the shoulder and sported a deep V-neck that showed off the flowering tree on her right upper arm and the barren tree on her left, both of which curled down toward her collarbones.

Daphne shook her head, then forced her gaze to Sasha. "What did you get?"

"The Tower," Sasha said, frowning at the card. "Sounds innocuous, but people are falling out of a building on fire, so I'm thinking bad."

"Imminent doom and peril," April said, chuckling. "Everything's falling apart."

"Oh, this is yours, then," Sasha said, offering the card to April, who laughed and flipped her off.

Daphne laughed too, her eyes following April as she picked a card of her own. Since Ramona had shown up earlier in the day, April seemed happier. She and Ramona had arrived a little late to their afternoon art class, but April had been smiling, and that was something Daphne hadn't seen much since they'd met. She had a beautiful smile. Subtle and secretive and sort of sly, but also—

Daphne squeezed her eyes closed, and when she opened them, she made sure she wasn't staring at April's mouth, intoxicating smile notwithstanding, and instead focused on the lovely night. The moon was bright and full, spreading silver over the trees and the forest floor. Ahead, Mia had set up lanterns along the trail that wandered deeper into the woods, the amber glow leading guests to the bonfire. Daphne could hear laughter and music. It all felt somewhat magical, as though she might find anything in those woods.

"The Hanged One," April said, staring down at her card. Daphne peered closer at the image, which featured a person wrapped in ropes and hanging upside down.

"Kinky," Sasha said, and Daphne laughed.

"It means I'm in limbo. Dangling in the unknown," April said, then scoffed. "Figures."

"Dangling in the unknown can be exciting," Sasha said.

April just glowered at her card before tucking it into her pants' waistband. "Yes, we all know you're footloose and fancy-free and live in a renovated Airstream trailer."

"Oh, god, I wish," Sasha said. "Those things are amazing. But I've got a 2015 Subaru Outback—"

"Of course you do," April said.

"—and I don't think ole Gertie could handle pulling an Airstream."

"Gertie?" Daphne asked.

"My car," Sasha said as the three of them started along the path and toward the bonfire. "For Gertrude Stein."

"The OG butch," April said.

"Exactly," Sasha said, grinning. "She said 'One must dare to be happy.' I read that in high school and never forgot it."

"I love that," Daphne said as the trees opened into a large clearing. A huge fire roared in the center, a triangle of flames licking into the night sky. Log benches surrounded the blaze, where people sat and drank spiked apple cider. To the side of the fire, underneath a huge oak tree, a small trio performed folky music. Mia sat at a nearby table covered in flowers.

"Come make your flower crowns," she called as she handed a bunch of daisies to Ms. Caldwell, a woman in her seventies and one of Daphne and April's students who had a penchant for turning every subject of her drawings into something slightly risqué. Apples became boobs, birds somehow turned into thighs or butts.

"Yes, do," Ms. Caldwell called, her short silver hair spiked up with gel. "I'm hoping these daisies will catch a fairy's eye and they'll drag me off into the woods for a magical orgy."

Mia sighed loudly, pressing her fingertips to her forehead.

Sasha snorted a laugh. "Oh my god, I love her."

"Up to your old tricks, I see, Ms. Caldwell," April said, hands on her hips.

"At my age, dear, all I've got is tricks," Ms. Caldwell said, waving her daisies at them before wandering off along the trail.

"I'll have what she's having," Sasha said as the three of them approached the table.

"Me too," Daphne said, laughing. Suddenly the idea of it all—fairies and flowers and dancing—made Daphne feel giddy. She wanted to be more like Ms. Caldwell, it was true. Up for anything, carefree, and wild.

She took a deep breath, forgot about her tarot card of Death, and wove a crown of lavender and sunflowers, the dreamy purple and bright yellow fitting her mood perfectly. Sasha's crown was pure eucalyptus, and April had chosen peonies, the voluminous blooms heavy but somehow perfect on her petite frame.

Topped with her crown, Daphne moved toward the dancers, who were now engaged in a sort of group routine. Her ankle still smarted a little, but she needed to move, to tilt her head toward the open sky. She loved dancing, despite the confusing memories of the other night. She pulled Sasha and April with her, and they all linked hands and joined the circle, laughing as they followed a woman across from them, lifting their hands in unison, stumbling over a turn, but smiling all the while. The music was magnetic, simple and full of possibilities all at once.

"You look like a wood nymph," April said to Daphne as everyone in the circle hopped left and then right.

"And what's that look like?" Daphne asked, slightly out of breath.

April looked her up and down, her own crown falling over her left eye a little, and Daphne's stomach undulated like a stormy sea. Since the night of the dance party, every time she was around April, her body reacted without her permission. Daphne's thoughts would start whirling like a printing press, spitting out sheet after sheet filled with the details of their dance, of lying on the floor talking, of the way Daphne had touched herself while imagining how April's mouth might feel on her—

"Daphne?" April said.

Daphne blinked the night back into focus, realizing that she'd stopped dancing for a second and was messing up the circle. She quickly fell back into the movements. "Sorry, what?" she asked.

"I said I imagine that a wood nymph looks just like you—flowing dress, flowing hair, sandals made out of tree bark or something," April said.

"Don't forget beautiful and unassuming," Sasha said from Daphne's other side. Her flower crown perched on top of her head at a mischievous angle, reminding Daphne of Puck from *A Midsummer Night's Dream*.

"How could I ever forget?" April said, laughing.

Daphne nearly stumbled again but managed to correct herself before landing in a heap on the forest floor.

"She thinks you're beautiful," Sasha whispered theatrically out of one side of her mouth.

"Shh," Daphne hissed, but Sasha just grinned. Puck, indeed.

After the revelry, people dispersed for drinks and snacks, but Daphne didn't want to sit. If she sat, she'd *think*, and wasn't this party all about the opposite? Feeling and doing. She grabbed three cups of cider and offered two of them to April and Sasha.

"We should go on Moon Lovers Trail," Daphne said, sipping on the potent brew. She coughed a little.

"Aren't we on it?" Sasha asked.

"Not quite," April said. "But we definitely do not need to go on Moon Lovers Trail."

"Why not?" Sasha asked, eyeing April. "Scared?"

"Scared?" April asked. "Of what? It's not haunted."

"It's haunted by true love, the way I hear it," Sasha said.

April rolled her eyes. "You're ridiculous."

"Am I?" Sasha asked, grinning.

"Wait, what?" Daphne asked. "I thought it was just a nice trail."

"Oh, it's *very* nice," Sasha said, smirking. "Plus, you can't get much wilder than kissing on Moon Lovers. Right, Daph?"

"Kissing?" Daphne said, her stomach fluttering.

"Kissing who?" April asked.

Sasha just laughed and started walking across the clearing to where the trail continued into the woods. "Let's go."

"I swear to god, she makes me dizzy," April said, then groaned and grabbed one of the tiny solar-powered torches sitting in a basket by the drinks table. "You can't go in the dark!"

Daphne hurried to follow, her drink sloshing onto her wrist as she went.

"What is Sasha talking about?" she asked as they dived into the thickening woods, the trail a thin line along the floor.

April sighed. "Moon Lovers Trail. It's a local legend. They say any couple who walks its path under a full moon will fall in love and live happily ever after or some shit."

Daphne smiled at April's explanation, which was somehow romantic and cynical all at once. "Do you know anyone who has?"

April was silent for a second as they walked. Sasha was a few feet ahead of them and started singing the song "Moon River."

"Wow, she really can't sing," April said.

"I heard that," Sasha said. "Now answer Daphne's question."

"So bossy," April said.

"I'm a power top," Sasha said.

"I'm shocked," April said, and Sasha resumed her singing.

"So?" Daphne asked.

"Fine, yes, I know some people. Owen, the guy who owns

Clover Moon Café. He took his high school sweetheart on the trail when they were, like, seventeen, and they've been married for eight hundred years. And Ramona and Dylan."

"Really?" Daphne said. "That's really cute. Who else?"

"It doesn't matter," April said. "It's a silly legend."

"I thought you loved stuff like that," Daphne said as they came to another, smaller clearing. This one was quiet and peaceful, the bonfire far enough away now that the only sounds were the cicadas chirping in the brush.

"Stuff like what?" April asked.

Daphne arched her arm in a semicircle, indicating the sky, the woods, the soft golden glow from the torch mixing with the moon's silver. "Like this. Stars and fate and legends."

"Not this legend," April said curtly.

Daphne frowned at her, but only for a second before the unspoken truth all but slapped her in the face.

Elena.

April had brought Elena here.

"Okay," Sasha said, setting her cup on the ground and rubbing her hands together. "So what do we think?"

"About what?" April asked.

"Falling in love," Sasha said.

Both April and Daphne stared at her.

"I'm kidding, take a breath," Sasha said. "Just a little light kissing among friends."

"Kissing," April said.

"Kissing?" Daphne asked.

"You two act like you've never heard the word before," Sasha said. "Yes, *kissing*. K-i-s-s-i-n-g."

Daphne waited for April to protest, but instead, she simply set the torch on the forest floor, then took a sip of her drink, her expression impassive.

"Kissing," Daphne said again.

"The beloved pastime," Sasha said, then folded her arms. "You said you wanted more queer experiences, and you can't get more queer than making out with your friends."

"It's true," April said.

"Have you ever kissed Ramona?" Daphne asked.

"No," April said slowly, lifting her chin in thought. "Though I think she's one of the few friends I've never kissed before. She and I were too much like sisters from the moment we met. But I've kissed every roommate I ever had, and a lot of people I met at college. A few strangers in bars."

Daphne's cheeks warmed again, as she thought of April kissing so many different people. She imagined her floating through a party at college, smiling, hooking her fingers into collars and under dress straps.

Daphne swallowed, looked at Sasha. "And you?"

Sasha grinned, all Puck. "Who haven't I kissed, honey?"

April rolled her eyes but laughed.

Daphne's heart thumped so vehemently in her chest, she was sure the other two could hear it. She *had* said she wanted to kiss people she hardly knew. And this was the perfect setting—the moon, the stars, the trees. It was intoxicating, and she didn't want to lose the feeling. Didn't want to say no, didn't want the night to end. The last person she had kissed was, of course, Elena. She'd love for that to not be the case, but this . . . this was . . .

She glanced at April only to find April looking right back at her. Neither of them looked away. Daphne wasn't sure what her stomach was doing—roiling or fluttering or rebelling against the spiked cider—but she felt nauseous and excited and nervous all at once.

"It's up to you," April said. "We can just keep walking, enjoy the trail and the moon."

"You're fine with this?" Daphne asked her.

April tilted her head. "With you and Sasha kissing? Why wouldn't I be?"

Daphne's mouth dropped open. "Oh, I . . ." She trailed off. She'd thought . . . well. Didn't matter now, did it? But when she glanced at Sasha, she lifted a brow at her as though she knew exactly what Daphne had been thinking.

"This is your wild rumpus," Sasha said, that mischievous glint in her eyes sparkling in the moonlight. "You're in charge."

The words settled around her like a strange sort of hug. *In charge.* She'd never been in charge of anything before.

She could kiss Sasha. It would be fun, and Sasha was safe and sweet—if a bit randy—and Daphne could experience kissing someone new, someone she had no intention of dating. As she stood there in the middle of Moon Lovers Trail, she realized she really did want to kiss Sasha.

But she wanted to kiss April too.

She had no intention of dating April Evans. Of course not. The entire idea was preposterous—the two of them existing together at all, right here in this New Hampshire forest, was preposterous. It was ridiculous and wild and *funny.* If she really thought about it, removed her heart from Elena's betrayal, she and April were a Shakespearean comedy.

And that was exactly what she needed right now. Every interaction with April had felt heavy and loaded from the jump, and her thoughts of late hadn't helped matters. She needed to lighten things up. Needed to laugh about how they'd danced together, how they'd ended up in the same cabin, the cosmic twist of it all.

She wanted to be *friends* with April. Wanted to think about kissing her the same way Daphne thought about kissing Sasha—fun, silly, free.

"Okay," she said a little too loudly, her blood pumping quickly and forcing out her words. "I'm in."

"Really?" Sasha asked.

"On one condition," Daphne said.

"And what's that?" April asked, sipping casually at her drink.

"We all kiss," Daphne said.

April frowned. "We all . . ."

"Kiss, yes," Daphne said.

"As in all three of us," April said.

Sasha covered her mouth with one hand as though holding in a laugh.

"All three of us," Daphne said, her eyes locked on April's flummoxed expression. "It's just kissing. Right?"

"Right," April said slowly, but she didn't look convinced.

"I dare you," Sasha said.

"Oh, fuck you," April said, but she laughed.

"In that case, I double-dog dare you," Sasha said.

"Sasha," April said, her tone a warning.

"Shall I skip the triple dare and go straight for the coup de grâce?" Sasha asked.

"What's actually in this cider?" April asked, looking down into her cup. "Did I take a drug-induced tumble into *A Christmas Story*?"

"If the kiss fits," Sasha said.

"That doesn't even make sense," April said.

"I triple-dog dare you," Daphne said.

April froze, a smirk on her face. "Et tu?"

Daphne laughed, but she felt as though her entire body was braced for a storm—a leaf thirsty for some much-needed rain.

"Fine," April said, setting her cup on the ground. "Fine, fine, you want some kissing? I'll show you some kissing."

She stretched her arms above her head, causing her top to rise even higher and showing off more smooth inked skin. She rolled her shoulders back, knocked her head from side to side as though readying herself for a boxing match. Then she walked up to Sasha, hooked her hand around her neck, and pulled her closer.

"Don't you dare grab my ass," April said.

"I wouldn't dream of it," Sasha said a second before their lips touched.

Her hands went to April's waist, and April's fingers curled into her hair. They kissed almost chastely at first but soon opened their mouths to each other. Daphne watched, fascinated, as though she were observing two characters in a movie, and when the two of them broke apart, she clapped.

"Thank you, thank you," Sasha said, dipping into a low bow.

April just laughed and pressed two fingers against her lower lip. "You're up, wildling."

Daphne nodded, but her heart was everywhere—fingertips, toes, her throat. Everywhere except where it should be. But she wanted this. She could do this. She could be casual and fun and wild.

So she walked right up to Sasha and grabbed her by the waist, pressing her mouth against her a little too vehemently. Her teeth bumped against Sasha's lower lip, and she gasped.

"Oh, god, sorry," Daphne said, her face hot.

"No worries, love," Sasha said, then chucked her under the chin to lift Daphne's mouth toward her again. Their lips met and it took Daphne a second to register she was kissing someone new, someone who wasn't Elena, her whole body freezing for a second. But then Sasha smiled against her mouth and Daphne laughed, relaxing into the kiss. Their tongues touched, and it was nice. Sexy, even. Daphne could tell Sasha was a great kisser, and had she been less aware of April's presence nearby, she probably could've kissed her for even longer.

Kissed, and maybe done even more.

But April *was* there, and Daphne *was* aware of her, and unfortunately, so was her body.

She pulled away from Sasha, and her eyes went immediately to April, who had been watching them with an expression Daphne couldn't parse.

"Okay, yes, fine," Sasha said, then pushed at Daphne's hip to angle her toward April even more. "Pucker up."

April didn't react to Sasha's teasing. Her eyes were locked on Daphne's, her mouth slightly parted, and Daphne couldn't get her breath. Couldn't think straight, couldn't think about anything, really, except April Evans standing in the moonlight.

It's just a kiss, she thought.

She took a step toward April.

And then another.

They were so close now. Close enough that Daphne's hair brushed April's cheek. For a moment, she froze. April would have to make the first move. Daphne couldn't possibly initiate this moment any more than she already had, but her body had other plans. Daphne felt her own hands cradle April's face, fingertips sliding against her skin and into her hair, palms soft on her cheeks. She tilted April's head up to meet her gaze. April's eyes were fathomless, like the deepest parts of the lake on the darkest night, and Daphne felt it.

The moment she fell.

There was a sensation of tumbling and snapping into place all at the same time. April's fingers curled into the cotton at Daphne's hips and pulled her closer. She pushed up onto her toes and captured Daphne's mouth with hers.

Daphne let out a small gasp before she sank her fingers deeper into April's hair, then trailed them down her neck to her collarbones. Her fingertips danced along April's skin as she opened her mouth a little more, Daphne's teeth tugging gently at April's lower lip right before their tongues finally touched.

April made her own sound, hands sliding around Daphne's waist, then up her torso to feel every rib under the dress. And god, Daphne wanted April's touch under that fabric. She wanted April to lift the skirt's hem, drift her fingers up Daphne's thighs to her hips, the dip at her waist, her belly button. The space between her legs throbbed, and she could tell she was getting wet. Daphne felt suddenly feral, wanted to lay April down right here on the forest floor and explore.

Every freckle.

Every goose bump.

Every muscle covering every bone.

April's hand went to Daphne's throat. Gentle, her fingers barely applying any pressure while she licked deeper into Daphne's mouth, her tongue gliding along her teeth before her mouth closed around Daphne's top lip. The combination of everything was almost too much—no, it *was* too much, and Daphne moaned.

She *moaned*, and it was loud and needy and perfect, but the sound of it jolted her back to the woods.

Back to Moon Lovers Trail.

Back to Sasha standing ten feet away with her eyes popping out of their sockets and one hand resting on her chin.

Daphne pulled away.

They were all silent for a second.

April cleared her throat, adjusted the neck of her off-the-shoulder top, which had slipped halfway down her arm. Daphne stood staring at her for a second, her lips bee-stung and pink. April met her gaze once, then looked away.

Daphne took another step back, creating space. Good god, what had they done?

"Well!" Sasha said loudly, folding her arms and nodding. "That was . . . yeah, that was something. You are full of surprises, Daphne Love."

"What do you mean?" Daphne asked, adjusting her dress's straps, both of which had gone a little cattywampus.

Sasha laughed. "I just . . . I don't know, I didn't expect *that*." She waved her hands at Daphne and April. "But even with me . . . you're a damn good kisser."

Daphne's posture went straight. "Did you not think I would be?"

Sasha and April locked eyes and then started laughing. They seemed to try and hold it in at first, but then they gave in, really putting their whole bodies into it. April bent forward, her hands on her knees.

Daphne put her hands on her hips. "I am offended."

But somehow, she wasn't, really. She laughed too, because it *was* all so unexpected, so unlike anything she'd ever experienced before. And it was intense. So intense that if she didn't laugh right now, she'd tumble down a rabbit hole of lust and questions and cares.

And right now, she just wanted to be happy.

April straightened up suddenly, still laughing a little as she dug her phone out of her pocket. Sasha and Daphne collected themselves as April tapped at her screen.

"Ramona wants us to meet her and Dylan for some pie in town," April said.

"God yeah," Sasha said.

Daphne nodded, meeting April's gaze. They felt frozen for a

second, teetering on the very edge of that rabbit hole. But then April broke the spell, clapping her hands three times.

"All right, let's go," she said, picking up her cup and the torch, then started along the trail that would lead them back to Cloverwild without another glance at Daphne. Daphne took a deep, shaky breath and followed.

Chapter Fifteen

CLOVER MOON CAFÉ was packed.

It usually was during the summer, even at ten thirty at night, so April wasn't surprised to find the dining room filled with both locals and summer people, all of them desperate for chocolate malts and the café's famous honey whiskey pie.

April had driven the three of them into town, focusing on the hilly roads, her hands dutifully clutching the steering wheel at ten and two, trying not to think about Daphne's exposed thigh *right there* in the passenger seat, her dress hiked up just above her knee.

April needed pie.

She needed pie and chocolate, and she needed to freak out with her best friend, though how exactly she was going to do all of that with Dylan, Sasha, and the object of her freak-out surrounding them, she wasn't sure. She'd figure it out. Steal away into the bathroom. Something.

Because Sasha was right—whatever April had expected from their kissing adventure in the woods, it certainly hadn't been *that*.

The sounds Daphne had made.

Her soft mouth, the way she'd held April's face.

April's hand on Daphne's delicate throat.

Fuck, she *really* needed pie.

Once inside, April wove through the crowded tables to reach Dylan and Ramona's corner booth near the back, Sasha and Daphne trailing behind her.

"You need to do it sooner rather than later, babe," Dylan was saying as they approached. Her back was to April, and she had her arm slung around Ramona's shoulders. "Before it leaks. You know how these things go. Best-laid plans."

Ramona leaned into her. "I know. But it wasn't the right time earlier, and I—" She froze as her gaze shifted and landed on April. "Hey! You're here!"

Her voice was too bright, her smile wide and showing off all her teeth.

"I am," April said, plopping down on the other side of the booth, then scooting all the way toward the wall. "What are these best-laid plans?"

Ramona opened her mouth, but then focused on April's companions. "Daphne. Sasha. Hi."

"Hi," Daphne said, waving as she slid in next to April, followed by Sasha, creating a tight squeeze in the booth. The aforementioned bare thigh pressed against the thin fabric covering April's own leg. She held her breath for a second, picked up the menu she knew by heart just to focus on something else.

Daphne shifted, her woodsy vanilla scent wafting over April. She nearly passed out right there.

Sugar. She needed sugar.

She cleared her throat as Ramona introduced Sasha and Daphne to Dylan, glad when neither of them fawned or preened in front of the star. Daphne was especially cute, her cheeks going predictably pink and her shoulders curling inward a little, a shyness that April somehow wanted to protect.

"I need pie," April announced, flipping the plastic menu in

front of her face again. "And a shake. Preferably with peanut butter and Oreos. Oh, and dark sour cherries."

"That sounds disgusting," Sasha said.

"That sounds like magic," Daphne said, her eyes bright as she scanned the menu herself.

Ramona widened her eyes at April—she also thought April's favorite combo for a shake was revolting—a small smile on her lips. Most likely, Ramona knew something was up, and April felt a wash of relief in Ramona's presence.

At her best friend's ability to just *know*.

It had felt like so long since anyone just knew anything about April, and while she was trying to get used to a more private and insular life, she'd missed this so much—eyebrows lifted, mouths pursed, feet tapping feet under the table. This nonverbal language she and Ramona had been speaking for nearly twenty-five years.

"I need the bathroom," April said abruptly. She couldn't wait any longer. She needed to tell Ramona now—she might burst if she didn't, or dissolve right there, Daphne's warm thigh creating a giddy feeling in the center of her chest, growing every second. "Ramona, come with me?"

"Oh," Ramona said, glancing at Dylan. "Actually, can we order first?"

April frowned but nodded. Of course, she didn't want to be rude. Didn't want to hold up the table if they were hungry. Plus, if she ordered now, her desserts might be ready by the time she got back.

She'd text Ramona.

Probably easier to type it all out anyway, then she and Ramona wouldn't have to waste time with facts. They could go straight to *holy shit*.

She got her phone out of her pocket and tapped on her messages while Sasha and Dylan talked about the science of making pie crust. April's fingers hovered over her text thread with Ramona.

She'd just started to tap out the naked truth about the kiss when a notification for her email popped into view. She heard a few dings around the dining room at the same time, but didn't register why until she tapped on the notification—more to clear it than anything—and found herself looking at a Google alert for Ramona. She hadn't received one of these in several weeks, had mostly forgotten that she'd even set one to begin with.

The alert included a single link to a *PopSugar* article. April tapped on the link, and her browser bloomed to life, along with an innocuous headline about Dylan heading east for the summer. But as April scanned the short article, posted just minutes ago according to the byline, everything in her froze.

> After wrapping work on the Marlene Dietrich biopic that's already garnering Oscar buzz in postproduction, Dylan Monroe and her partner, Ramona Riley, set their sights east, back to where it all began. They'll be summering in Clover Lake, New Hampshire, where the couple originally met as adorable preteens, then again seventeen years later while Dylan filmed the romantic comedy *As If You Didn't Know* two years ago, but sources close to the couple say this isn't just a vacation. We might soon be hearing the distant chime of wedding bells in a small, intimate ceremony, purportedly at Dylan and Ramona's private Clover Lake home. Oh, to be a mosquito tangled in Ramona's tulle skirt on that blessed day. #DylonaForever

April blinked. Then refreshed the page, hoping it would change, disappear, literally melt the phone in her hands. Anything but what she was seeing.

"Apes, what is it?" Ramona asked.

April just swallowed, tears already blooming. This wasn't how this was supposed to happen. This news. This moment in Ramona's life. April wasn't supposed to learn about it through a Google alert. Through a fucking celebrity gossip site, no less. And it certainly wasn't supposed to be accompanied by a sudden swell of hurt tangled up with secrets and distance. Of course April knew the engagement was coming. Even welcomed it, because Ramona was happy, and April loved Dylan. The announcement was supposed to be joyous and thunderous and followed by April and Olive dragging Ramona out for florescent-colored shots at Four Leaf, the only bar in Clover Lake, while they ogled the ring and let Ramona wax on about the wedding dress she was going to design.

But this . . . this felt like a punch in the gut.

April swallowed hard, trying to get herself under control before she said anything. The dining room, however, had gone oddly quiet, whispers floating on the air. Patrons looked down at their phones, then shifted their eyes to Ramona and Dylan.

Looked like April wasn't the only one with a Google alert for Clover Lake's favorite daughter.

"What the hell is happening right now?" Dylan asked, looking around while everyone glanced at her. But she had to know. She'd been at this too long not to. She released an annoyed breath. "Ah, shit. Babe."

"What?" Ramona asked, pushing herself up in the booth to look around.

April glanced at Ramona's left hand pressed against the table for leverage, but her ring finger was bare.

"So where is it?" April asked, her voice shaking. She knew she should shut up. Shut up, and get up, because *this wasn't how this was supposed to happen.*

"Where's what?" Ramona asked, settling back into the booth.

"Ramona," Dylan said, staring down at her own phone now.

Finally, Merrit Connolly, a woman in her sixties who had taught both April and Ramona social studies in middle school, broke the spell. She lifted her milkshake into the air, calling out to Ramona and Dylan from her table with her husband, Dale, by the window. "Congratulations, you two!"

A chorus of well-wishes echoed through the room, glasses lifted in cheers. Dylan waved demurely, but Ramona was staring at April, a stricken expression on her face. "Apes."

"Didn't Dylan get you a ring?" April asked. For some reason, that was all she could think about, all she could focus on. This secret ring Ramona had had for who knew how many days already, the ring she wasn't wearing specifically so April wouldn't see it, most likely vintage and beautiful and unique, just like Ramona.

Daphne and Sasha were awkwardly silent, but Daphne set a hand on April's leg, and that single, gentle touch forced air into April's tight lungs. She grabbed Daphne's hand, tangling their fingers together, and Daphne let her hold on as tight as she needed.

Because Ramona was getting married.

Married.

To the love of her life.

After all Ramona had done, sacrificed, worked for.

And April couldn't ruin that now.

So she took a deep breath, kept hold of Daphne's hand. "Let me see it," she said to her best friend. Her words came out wobbly, a little watery, but she said them. She said them with a smile, with her eyes shining and her heart beating regularly—if a bit quickly—in her chest.

Ramona watched her for a second, wary.

Dylan curled her arms around Ramona's shoulders and nudged her. "Show her," she said softly, then pressed a kiss to Ramona's temple.

Goddess, they were sweet.

Dylan was sweet. She'd been a bit of a mess when she and Ramona had gotten together, but as far as April could tell, she was rock solid now. She was good for Ramona. Made Ramona smile.

And that was all that mattered.

Ramona swallowed, then pulled her bag into her lap. It was the same gray canvas bag with red mushrooms printed all over it that Olive had given her years ago. Inexplicably, April latched on to that pattern, familiar and tried-and-true, eyes locked on the illustrated fungus while Ramona sifted through the bag. She pulled out a small rainbow-colored pouch, READ BANNED BOOKS written across the front. After she unzipped it, she plucked a ring from inside, smiling down at it as she slipped it on her finger.

She held out her hand.

April gripped Daphne's palm with one hand, her other trembling only slightly as she held Ramona's fingers.

The ring was lovely, just as April knew it would be. Understated, even. A round jewel sat on a simple gold band surrounded by a half-moon of tiny diamonds. The jewel itself was the color of mint, with darker green swirling inside.

"Is that moss agate?" Daphne asked.

Ramona nodded. "I love how natural and unique it looks."

"It's gorgeous," Sasha said.

"How did it happen?" April finally asked, and Ramona and Dylan proceeded to tell a story about the Griffith Observatory in LA—which was where Dylan had professed her love for Ramona two years ago—and a star-packed sky, not another soul in sight because Dylan had arranged to bring Ramona at midnight, after the observatory had closed to the public.

"It was amazing," Ramona said, leaning into Dylan. "I had no idea what was happening. Even when this one started crying and pulled a ring out of her pocket."

Dylan grinned, her cheeks a little pink. "Best night of my life."

April listened and smiled, her heart in her throat. "When?" she asked, even though it didn't matter. *Shouldn't* matter, at least.

Ramona grew serious, cleared her throat. "Three nights ago."

Daphne's thumb rubbed across April's. She managed a nod, a smile, could feel the corner of the Hanged One card pricking against her stomach. She wasn't the Hanged One right now though. No, this moment wasn't suspended in limbo, wasn't waiting for anything. This felt more like the Wheel of Fortune, destiny spinning onward, with or without April's say or knowledge.

"I wanted to tell you in person," Ramona said quickly. "We don't want a big wedding. Just family and a few friends at the end of the summer. Dylan and I had the time off, and Olive is due home this weekend, so we decided to come home too. I wanted to tell you earlier today at Cloverwild, but . . . it just . . . You were . . ."

She trailed off, and April felt herself nodding again, still a bit numb.

"We told my dad earlier tonight," Ramona went on. "I'm sorry, Apes, I don't know how *PopSugar* got the information."

"How they always get it," Dylan said, but no one asked what that meant. April assumed it was about money and Hollywood insiders or some shit she didn't care about right now.

"It's okay," April said. The right thing to say.

"Honey," Ramona said softly, as though she wasn't buying it, but April needed her to. She needed the way she was holding herself together right now to count, to be worth the effort.

"We should celebrate," she said, an idea occurring to her. "An engagement dinner. Family, friends."

"I can help cook, if you want," Sasha said.

"Yes, perfect," April said, sending a grateful smile toward Sasha.

Under normal circumstances, Sasha and Daphne probably wouldn't come to an intimate engagement dinner, but April knew she wanted them both there, including Sasha's amateur chef skills.

"We can have it at our house," Dylan said. "Right, babe?"

"Of course," Ramona said, but she was still watching April.

"Great," April said brightly, then lifted her glass of water. She still had no milkshake, no pie, no center of gravity. "To the happy couple."

"To Ramona and Dylan," Daphne and Sasha echoed—along with a few nearby patrons—and lifted their water glasses as well.

"It's bad luck to toast with water," Sasha mumbled under her breath, but April ignored her. She ignored the clench in her stomach and the sting behind her eyes, and she lifted her fucking water glass to the happy couple.

Chapter Sixteen

APRIL DIDN'T TALK at all on the drive back to Cloverwild.

None of them did, in fact. Daphne wasn't sure what to say, and the only thing she really wanted to do was hold April's hand again. Even Sasha was mostly quiet in the back seat, offering a few meal suggestions for the engagement dinner—which they'd decided would take place at Dylan and Ramona's lake house in a week's time, as Sasha had that Friday night off and Ramona's sister, Olive, would arrive home earlier that afternoon—to which April simply hummed her acquiescence as she drove.

She didn't talk when they reached the resort, nor did she say anything when Sasha yanked April into her arms for a quick back-slapping hug before heading down the path toward her cabin. April also didn't speak when she and Daphne walked inside their own cabin, when she fed the mewling cats, or when she finally sat on her bed with a sort of lost look in her eyes.

Daphne stood in the middle of the room, trying to figure out what to do.

If she needed to do anything.

April's best friend getting engaged was happy news, obviously, but Daphne knew there was a lot more to what April was feeling than that. Her own mind was spinning from the events of the evening—the hand-holding at the café, how April hadn't let her go until only a few minutes before they were ready to leave.

The kiss in the woods.

A kiss to end all kisses. Which was a dramatic way to remember it, yes. Quite possibly, Daphne's imagination was blowing it into legendary proportions, but she was pretty sure it was the best kiss of her life. But more than all that, she was worried about April. She wanted to make it better, make April laugh or smile or even cry if that was what she needed to do.

And she knew—she just *knew*—that April needed to do *something.*

"Are you okay?" Daphne asked. Such a banal question, but it was the only one she could think of right now.

April looked up at Daphne slowly, but then she smiled. Which was exactly what Daphne had wanted, but this smile was soulless, didn't reach her eyes even a little bit, and showed zero teeth.

"I'm fine," April said, but continued to sit on the bed, fiddling with a loose thread on her moon pants.

"You're sure?"

April looked annoyed now. "You should really believe people when they answer your questions."

"I would if everyone around you hadn't been doing exactly that for a while now."

April frowned. "Should they not?"

Daphne should probably shut up, but she couldn't stop the next words from falling out of her mouth. "Letting you lie about being okay? I don't think so. Not if they care about you."

April stared at her. "And that's you? Someone who cares about me?"

Daphne didn't know what to say to that. April's tone was multilayered, like a fine perfume. Top notes of vitriol and irritation, middle notes blooming with exhaustion, bottom notes tinged with a little sadness and actual wonder. Daphne shuffled in place, unsure of how to proceed, when she had an idea.

She held out her hand. "Come with me."

"What?" April said, flicking her eyes down to Daphne's proffered fingers as though they were on fire. As though she hadn't been clinging to them just an hour earlier, palm sweaty and anxious.

"Just come with me," Daphne said again, as firmly as she could muster. April intimidated her, but right now, Daphne needed to be in charge. "Don't think, don't question, and for god's sake, don't assume I have your worst interests at heart."

April's mouth fell open, and she looked up at Daphne with those dark eyes full of mysteries. A million stories and ideas and dreams, unknown to everyone but her. She inhaled as though she was going to protest again.

"Don't," Daphne said, then pressed her forefinger to her lips, her other hand still reaching for April.

April's eyes narrowed a little, but her mouth lifted in a subtle smile. She slid her palm against Daphne's, let Daphne pull her up from the bed. She let Daphne lead her out of the cabin and back down the cobbled path to the lodge, and she let Daphne keep hold of her hand all the way to the art studio.

Daphne only released her when they got inside and she flipped on the light, then went straight to the supply cabinet. April stood there silently as Daphne pulled out a drop cloth, two hunter-green painter aprons, and two large blank canvases. She spread the cloth onto the floor near the front of the room, then set the canvases up on their instructor easels before handing April an apron and then tying on her own. After that, she collected bottles of nontoxic acrylic paints, squirting them onto the largest palette she could find. Finally, she handed April a thick paintbrush.

April took it, the apron nearly swallowing her small frame, but then stood there holding the tool like a sword she wasn't sure how to wield.

"I'm not a painter," she said.

Daphne ignored this. "When I was a teenager and I was feeling particularly shitty—"

"I think that's the first time I've ever heard you swear," April said.

Daphne laughed. "You're a bad influence."

"You're welcome."

They smiled at each other for a second, the air thick between them. Daphne cleared her throat. "Anyway, when I was feeling particularly shitty about my family or the fact that I had no friends, my art teacher, Ms. Hale, would throw down a drop cloth in the art room and put a canvas on the easel and tell me to paint it."

"Paint it. What's *it*?"

Daphne shrugged and dipped her own brush through a blob of rich paint. "Whatever you need it to be. Usually? I just made a mess, but the product wasn't the point."

She turned to face the canvas, then slapped the brush over the surface, marring the clean white with a slash of deep purple. She didn't rinse the brush before slicing it through some red paint and throwing it at the canvas. Crimson dotted the white like blood on snow, splattering onto the drop cloth and her apron as well, speckling her bare arms and legs. The effect on the canvas was pleasing. Unformed and messy, and that was exactly what it was supposed to be.

After a few moments, April stepped up to her own canvas. She dipped her brush through a blob of green on the palette between them. She stood there for a second, frowning at all that white as though it were a window into another world. Then she started slow, a spread of green in a wobbly arc over the white. But soon she added more color, more textures, creating a riot of swirls and stripes. Daphne went back to focus on her own mess, loving the effect of the multi-hued splatters and drops.

They worked like that for a while, and Daphne lost herself in the random patterns, months and years of pain and anger and fear kaleidoscoping over the canvas.

At some point, she heard April laugh.

She paused, glancing over at April's work, the canvas covered, not in blasts of paint but in slashes. Harsh in some places, but smooth and lyrical in others, layers of color Daphne wouldn't expect from April—lavender and mint and turquoise and cotton-candy pink.

But then, subtly, shades of gray and black.

The dark started gradually in the right bottom corner but then burgeoned and spread into darker, elegant swirls snaking through the pastel.

The effect was striking.

Beautiful and terrifying.

Just like April.

Daphne smiled and watched April laughing quietly at what she'd created, a single tear escaping her eye and rolling down her paint-splattered cheek. Daphne had the sudden urge to wipe it away, but that wasn't what this was.

This was tears set loose.

This was tears *felt*.

April glanced at her, a smile on her face despite the tears, and Daphne smiled back. And soon, the smile turned into more laughter, more tears, an amalgam of emotions mirroring the paint on their canvases.

By the time Daphne slowed down, her canvas a thick explosion of color—speckles and slashes, all done in mostly jewel tones of deep greens and purples and navy, a bit of shocking red here and there—she was breathing hard, her lungs burning for more oxygen.

"Well," April said, her breathing just as labored.

"Well, indeed," Daphne said, her eyes locking with April's.

They stared at each other for a second, then busted out laughing again, because they were both covered in paint. Not just covered—coated. Paint was everywhere, completely layered over their aprons, in their hair, and splattered over their exposed skin, all mixing together into one dark greenish-bluish hue.

"Oh my god," Daphne said, inspecting her own arms.

"We look like swamp creatures," April said, plucking her paint-soaked apron away from her thigh. "It's starting to dry in places already."

"On the bright side, I think we got more paint on our bodies than the drop cloth." Daphne's cheeks flamed at the usually innocuous word—*bodies*—but luckily paint concealed any reddening of her face.

"Easy cleanup, then," April said, glancing down at the lightly speckled cloth.

"Can't say the same for us," Daphne said.

April laughed. "I'm trying to think of the best method here." She wiped her face but only smeared the paint over her skin even more. But then she froze, her eyes snapping to Daphne's. "Actually, I do have an idea."

Daphne lifted her brows. "Oh?"

April grinned. "Well. It's kind of wild."

Daphne grinned back.

Chapter Seventeen

THEY DROVE TOWARD town, the night dark and starry around them.

They'd cleaned up the brushes and paint and palette quickly, leaving their canvases in the art room to dry for now. April had taken the drop cloth, though, spreading it over her car's driver and passenger seats so she and Daphne wouldn't leave paint everywhere, but honestly, she wasn't sure she cared all that much at this point.

She wasn't sure she cared about anything, and it felt good. She wasn't numb, exactly, just blissfully empty. Cleaned out. All her emotions thrown at the canvas, all of her worry and hurt and loneliness.

And she was glad to have done it with Daphne.

Glad to laugh with her as they slung paint, glad to cry, glad to be in this car with her right now, heading toward Mirror Cove. Any emotions she did have left were focused on the woman next to her, paint covered and smiling, the wind from the open window licking through her lavender hair. April wasn't sure what the emotions were, only that they existed.

She pulled into the public beach lot near the cove, threw the car into park. "We're going to have to walk for a second," she said as she unclipped her seat belt. "Is that okay?"

"I go where you go," Daphne said, smiling at her in the dark. April smiled too, but something about those simple words—silly words, even—made her stomach flutter, her heart swelling in her chest.

Her phone buzzed in her bag, but she ignored it as she got out of the car. She knew it was Ramona, but right now, she just couldn't.

She rounded the car and, before she could really think about what she was doing, held out her paint-splattered hand to Daphne. Daphne's eyes widened a little, but she tangled her fingers with April's. This was the third time they'd held hands tonight, and it felt almost natural and easy, even though she knew there was nothing natural and easy about the two of them. They were a rare event, like a super blue blood moon or Halley's Comet, flaring in the sky and then gone.

April led them to the woods in front of the lot, then onto a lesser-walked trail.

"I feel like someone just yelled 'action' on a horror film set," Daphne said as she stumbled next to April, ducking when a branch nearly swiped her across the face.

April laughed. "I said it was a wild idea."

"So I should expect someone with a bloody machete at the end of the trail?"

"Something like that," April said, squeezing Daphne's hand playfully.

Daphne squeezed back, and soon, the trees parted. The lake here was very still and clear, and the moon played hide-and-seek with the clouds, shedding silver onto the water before covering it back over with shadows. The area was deserted, the rocks in the water and along the beach making for a precarious swim, and most summer people didn't even know this cove existed.

But April knew it by heart.

So did Ramona and Dylan, as it was where they'd first met, but before that, before the Hollywood romance captured Clover Lake's hearts and minds, Mirror Cove was April's.

Ramona's and April's, really, a place they'd go as kids to tell secrets, to get away from pressures in their homes, to be seen and understood. She'd never even brought Elena here. Elena hated beaches, claiming that sand was just a beachy word for dirt, and she hated the feel of it between her toes, the way it hid in every nook and cranny.

"Are you ready for a swim?" April asked as she pulled Daphne onto the tiny beach and released her hand.

Daphne's brows lifted. "We don't have bathing suits."

April laughed. "I believe skinny-dipping was on your list, was it not?"

Daphne's eyes grew round. "Skinny-dipping." Her gaze dropped down to April's mouth, and April felt her own face redden. She didn't blush easily, but right now, with the word *skinny-dipping* floating between them, coupled with the *dance* and the *kiss* and all the *hand-holding* of the evening, heat pooled into her cheeks.

And a few other places.

She shook that off, though, and focused on the actual task.

"We need to clean up anyway," she said, but then felt her stomach plummet as Daphne continued to stand there looking uncertain. "Only if you want to, of course."

Daphne shifted her feet in the sand, her mouth slightly parted.

And April felt ridiculous.

Because this *was* ridiculous. A super blue blood moon at all the wrong times, in all the wrong ways, which didn't even make sense, but that was how April suddenly felt. Not embarrassed, necessarily. Just . . . unaligned.

Out of place in the sky.

"Never mind," she said, shaking her head. "This was silly. We can just—"

"No, wait," Daphne said, her hand on April's arm. She squeezed once before letting go and then pulling off her dress in one fell swoop.

All of April's breath left her lungs.

Daphne's hair settled around her bare shoulders, the straps of a yellow—though maybe it was white, as it was hard to tell in the dim light—bralette still arching over her collarbones. And they were lovely collarbones. Elegant and spotted with dried paint, dipping in the middle right where Daphne's throat moved as she swallowed. April had always had a bit of a thing for collarbones, and Daphne's were perfect.

As was everything about her, really. April tried not to stare, she really did, but they'd already kissed, already pressed their bodies together in ways she never did with anyone she wasn't about to sleep with, so now, actually seeing her like this was . . .

It was a super blue blood moon.

And Daphne hovered in the sky, letting April look at her as much as she wanted—the way the cotton of her bralette rounded over her small breasts, the softness of her stomach, the mismatched blue underwear, one side hitched up a little higher on her hip than the other.

April didn't dare move her eyes lower—couldn't, or she might really lose her shit.

And goddess, there were so many reasons not to. For starters, Daphne was eight years younger than April. Secondly, *hugely,* she was Daphne fucking Love. She'd been April's silent ghost for so long now, a haunting. A myth, or even a legend. Anything but flesh and blood.

Thirdly . . . there had to be a third reason, right? And probably a fourth, at the very least. But right now, as they stood in Mirror

Cove together, Daphne was so real, and so beautiful, and so sweet, that all those reasons flew right out of April's head.

"Your turn," Daphne said, tilting her head a little, a tiny smile on her full lips.

April blinked, her stomach now catapulting into her throat, a blush spreading past her cheeks and over her chest. This was her idea, dammit. She'd gotten naked with practical strangers before, she could certainly strip down to her undies.

She shucked her pants down her legs, fighting her feet out of them by stomping in the sand.

Daphne laughed but went silent when April's fingers went to her top. Because they both knew—Daphne *had* to know, right?—that April wasn't wearing a bra. Her top was off the shoulder, nary a strap in sight. Granted, it was dark, but the moon was also pretty damn bright. Her hands trembled a little, but she kept her eyes on Daphne, whose expression was unreadable.

April did it fast.

Whipped the top over her head, let it drop into the sand.

Daphne's mouth parted, eyes dropping down quickly before lifting back up to April's face.

"Beautiful," she said.

And that was it.

That was all she needed to say, really, all April wanted in this moment. She reached out and took Daphne's hand—for the fourth time, no less—and pulled her toward the water.

"Stay close to me to avoid the rocks," she said, and Daphne did, the bare skin of her torso brushing against April's. They splashed into the lake, and Daphne cried out.

"Holy shit, it's cold," she yelled.

"Another swear," April said, laughing and pulling her deeper. The water was up to her thighs now. "I am scandalized, Ms. Love."

"I don't cuss often," Daphne said. Her teeth chattered, and it was pretty fucking cute. "Only when—"

She cut herself off, but April kept moving until they were deep enough that there were no rocks on the bottom and the water covered her bare chest. She let Daphne go and turned to look at her. "Only when what?"

Daphne just smiled, the moon glinting off her teeth.

"Tell me," April said, laughing.

"No," Daphne said, laughing too and splashing April gently.

April lifted her brows. "You do *not* want to get in a water fight with me, Love."

Daphne tilted her head. "I think I do."

April splashed her immediately, aiming the water right below her face to collide with her neck and chest.

Daphne flinched, but laughed, sending a wave of water back toward April. Soon it was nothing but splashes and shrieking as they flicked and slapped and threw water at each other. Finally, April ducked beneath the surface and swam to grab Daphne by the waist and pull her under too. They twisted and spun, limbs tangling in a sort of aquatic wrestling match before they both came up to the surface.

"I think I grabbed your boob," Daphne said, spluttering and wiping at her face. "I'm sorry."

"Oh, I think I would've remembered that," April said, laughing.

Daphne grinned, then swam a little closer, the water up to her chin, her hair dark purple and slicked back, floating around her shoulders. Her gaze was intense, and April sucked in a breath, not sure what was about to happen.

"So who won the battle?" Daphne asked, a teasing lilt to her tone. She was close enough now that April could see the green of her eyes, even in the darkness.

"I think it's a t—"

But April's words were cut off as she was yanked under the water, Daphne's hands silky around her hips before letting her go, there and then gone. April surfaced with her mouth pursed, flicking the water from her eyes dramatically.

"I won," Daphne said smugly.

April just sniffed. "Where did you learn how to fight dirty?"

"I had a bossy older sister in a small town where we called the lake a watering hole. I'm country." She smiled softly, a bit more distance between them now as she trailed her fingers through the water.

"Do you miss them?" April asked. "Your sister and your parents?"

Daphne flinched as though April had sent another wave of water into her face.

"Sorry," April said. "We don't have to talk about it."

"No, no, it's okay," Daphne said, looking up at the sky.

April swam a little closer. She made sure to keep her chest covered, despite the fact that Daphne had already seen everything. Somehow, this didn't feel like a tits out kind of conversation. If Daphne was willing to have it at all. She was still quiet, still gazing at the stars.

"Which one is the crab again?" she asked.

April looked up too, searching for the constellation between the clouds, but she couldn't find it.

"Hidden," she said.

Daphne huffed through her nose. "Figures."

And it took her a second, but then she started to talk. As she did, her eyes weren't on the sky, nor were they on April, but following her own hands through the water.

"I do miss them. A lot," she said. "My mom is beautiful and kind and gentle. She's funny too. So smart and creative. She used to give us watercolor lessons, and she painted the most gorgeous sunsets. They were incredible. I use a lot of her techniques in our class, actually, like how to do the perfect graded wash. I've still never seen anything that equals her work, even in Boston. But her life . . . it's just not one I ever wanted. Not like my sister."

"What's your sister's name?"

"Amelia. She's three years older than me. And I was supposed to follow her example, right? This paragon of what a good Christian girl looked like, going to Sunday school and fantasizing about marrying the town golden boy and making sure I only dreamed good Christian girl dreams."

"When did you realize you didn't want a golden boy?" April asked.

Daphne grinned. "That I wanted a Golden Girl instead?"

"Well, Blanche is very hot," April said, laughing.

Daphne laughed too. "Her name wasn't Blanche, but I was nine when Danielle McCrae grabbed my hand during a tornado drill and held it for, like, five minutes."

"Were you about to throw up?"

"Oh my god, it's amazing I didn't," Daphne said, splashing April again, but lightly this time. "Your turn. How old were you when you realized you were queer?"

"Oh, god, Leigh Reynolds," April said, dropping her face into her hands.

"An embarrassing story?" Daphne asked. "I'm intrigued."

"Not embarrassing so much as long-standing."

Daphne's posture went a little straighter, but April ignored it, kept talking.

"Leigh is nonbinary and helped me realize I was pansexual when I was sixteen. I like all genders, and it really depends on the person for me," April said. "But Leigh was—*is*—a total fuckboi."

"Oh, like Sasha?" Daphne asked.

April laughed. "Exactly like Sasha."

Daphne nodded and looked down, inspecting her wrinkling fingertips. "So . . . do you still see Leigh?"

"Oh, god, no," April said.

And maybe April only imagined it, but she could swear that Daphne's shoulders dropped a little.

"At least, not since last summer," she went on. "I just got tired of the whole scene. And Leigh made it pretty clear they weren't into the vibe anymore when I got a little too snuggly one night."

Daphne widened her eyes. "April Evans? Snuggling?"

"I know, I know, I'm still processing the whole ordeal."

Daphne laughed but then grew serious. "Actually, I don't think it's so hard to imagine."

Somehow, they'd gotten even closer as they talked, the nearly nonexistent current pulling them together. April could see a water droplet on Daphne's bottom lip.

"No?" April asked, her voice a whisper.

"No," Daphne said. She stared at April, eyes soft, her irises flashing from green to black as wispy clouds passed over the silver moon. Unspoken words floated between them, but April understood somehow.

She understood that if she swam a little closer, Daphne wouldn't move away.

And she understood that if she set her hands on Daphne's waist under the water, pulling her closer still, Daphne would let her.

April also understood that when all this happened, and they bumped noses, laughing into the night air, Daphne's lashes fanning beautifully across her cheekbones, she wanted to kiss Daphne.

And Daphne wanted to kiss her.

And maybe it was wild and reckless. Maybe she wanted to experience something new and exciting—kissing a pretty girl while half-naked in a lake—but April didn't care. Because why shouldn't she kiss Daphne Love if that was what she wanted? And why shouldn't Daphne have what she wanted too? Why couldn't they reach out and take it, whatever *it* was at any given moment in their lives, whatever was possible? Seemed to April, they'd both spent a hell of a lot of time not taking anything.

She yanked Daphne even closer, fingers spreading over her torso, thumbs pressing into her bare hips. Daphne gasped a little, smiled a little too, right before their mouths met. The mineral scent of the lake surrounded them, the water rippling as they moved, but April barely noticed any of it.

There was only Daphne.

Daphne and the moon and the stars.

The tang of lake water on Daphne's mouth, the sounds she made as April tugged at her lower lip, then licked into her mouth. Daphne's hands rested on April's shoulders, but soon dipped into her hair, pulling at the roots just a little.

Just enough to make April crazy.

But this was all crazy anyway, and April wanted nothing more than to lean in.

All the way in.

She slid her hands down Daphne's hips, then around her waist to pull her flush against her own body, not a breath of space between them. April slid her mouth down to Daphne's neck, swirling her tongue just under her ear.

Another gasp, and the sound went straight to April's clit. She felt ravenous, almost unhinged. Granted, she hadn't had sex in a while, and she knew how to take care of herself just fine. But this wasn't the anonymous lust she felt when she watched porn or read a superspicy novel and then reached for a favorite toy in her nightstand drawer.

This was Daphne.

This was . . .

Fuck, this was trouble.

Daphne made a sound then—so sweet and provocative at the same time, her fingers sliding to April's face to take her chin in her hands—and April pulled back.

Daphne inhaled sharply at the shock of it, but she didn't protest. She didn't move at all, really, except to look at April, their eyes locked. Then Daphne pressed one more kiss to April's mouth—soft, sweet—before putting a bit more space between them. She kept her arms draped over April's shoulders, however, and April felt her eyes start to sting with how much she liked them there.

And she couldn't.

There was nothing but disaster down that road.

"I think I finally have an idea for the Devon," she said.

Daphne's brows lifted, and, just as April suspected she would, she removed her arms from April's shoulders. April felt the loss immediately. She had a wild urge to grab Daphne's wrists, circle them back around her neck.

"Oh?" Daphne said. She smiled softly, knowingly, as though she could see right through April's chest to every conflicting part of her heart—the want and the denial, the exhilaration and the fear and the uncertainty.

April nodded, but she didn't know what else to say, and Daphne didn't ask. They hadn't made a habit of talking about the Devon, sharing ideas, or asking about each other's progress. April, of course, had seen the first incredible installment of Daphne's series—what April *assumed* was a series—and knew Daphne was hard at work in the studio on more.

But she never asked.

And Daphne didn't either.

It was easier to pretend the Devon was happening to both of

them separately, had nothing to do with the other person at all, than face the reality that they were competing.

Which was probably why April had said what she'd said. Deep down, she knew the Devon would put a stop to everything happening in this lake right now, the ultimate cold shower.

And she was right.

She and Daphne watched each other for a second, everything floating between them like stardust.

"We should probably head back," April said.

For a second, Daphne looked stricken, but she covered it up so quickly, April wondered if she'd imagined it.

"Yeah," Daphne said softly, then started swimming for the shore. "We probably should."

APRIL SAT ON the porch late into the night, her sketchbook open on her lap.

As it turned out, Ramona's engagement news paired with rage painting and topped off with kissing her ex's ex—*again*—was excellent creative fodder. All that angst and turmoil, the lust and the panic and the loneliness. An artist's dream, really.

She shook out her hand, achy from the sketching of the last couple of hours, the side of her palm coated in graphite. She was left-handed, so any work with a pencil—a marker, paints, anything, really—always left her hand and fingers a mess.

Her sketchbook was a mess too. A beautiful, feverish mess, full of smudged pencil and bits of eraser peppering the pages, but she already had five full sketches. They were rough—just outlines of what she'd do in the final medium, which would be pencil and pastels on thick textured paper, but they were there.

They existed.

She flipped back to the first drawing—the Fool. In the sketch, she'd drawn a young version of herself, no tattoos at all—not yet, at least—a beatific smile on her face, her eyes lifted to the sky, while one foot stepped off the edge of a cliff. Behind her, a hand reached out to grab her shirt and hold her back but couldn't quite get to her. Beyond her, a city gleamed. Above her, a sky full of stars sharing space with a blazing sun. In her mind, the colors she planned and the way it all came together in the final product were dreamy and ethereal. Uncanny and wild and strange and even a little silly.

Just like her.

She flipped the page to the Magician, then the High Priestess, followed by the Empress and the Emperor. Each illustration was her, each one depicting classic tarot imagery blended with her own story, her own journey.

She smiled down at her work, her fingers already itching to get started on her final products, which would certainly take some time. Right now, though, she didn't have the materials she needed, and she wanted the full picture first, all twenty-two biographical—*evolutionary*—Major Arcana sketched out and ready.

She sat back in the chair, resting her head against the back. She felt good. She felt empty and full all at once, that blissful, exhausted sensation she got when she created something she truly loved, something that made her feel alive.

Made her feel like she had a purpose.

"Finally," she whispered to herself, her eyes on the sky above. It was fully cloudy now, the stars hidden from view, but she knew they were still there, fixed and steady while the world turned. She knew she should take a break and go to bed—Daphne had been asleep for hours—but she felt anything but tired right now. She felt motivated and driven and inspired, and she never wanted it to end.

She flipped a page, ready to start on the Hierophant, but her pencil hovered over the blank page. She had a plan for this stage, this card about knowledge and external systems, about breaking free from the expected and the orthodox.

But suddenly, she saw a flash in her mind, a vision for the next card in the set. It wasn't her original idea for this card, but she couldn't stop seeing it—a recent memory—and maybe she simply needed to release it, expunge it, before she could move on.

She flipped the page and her pencil started moving before she even made a decision to draw. Soon, she was looking down at Mirror Cove and two people in the lake. One was her, of course, tattoos and bare shoulders, her hair slicked back and her lashes spiked with water. The other person had damp lavender curls and lovely collarbones, her fingers soft on April's face. Their heads were close, a kiss either just about to happen or already experienced. Or both.

April stared at the image.

The Lovers.

She blew out a long breath and ripped the page free from the wire rings, bits of torn paper dangling in the air. She was about to ball it up, toss it in the recycling when she went inside, but instead, she folded it once and slid it inside the folder attached to her sketchbook's back cover.

Then she flipped back to the Hierophant and started to draw.

Chapter Eighteen

DAPHNE JOLTED AWAKE.

It was still dark outside, and April's bed was empty. She stared at the messy covers—April never made her bed—and felt a swell of panic before she spotted April's outline sitting on the porch, the warm amber light next to the front door beaming down on her.

She relaxed, but only slightly, as her phone was having the equivalent of a heart attack on her nightstand. She grabbed it, realizing too late that it was simply vibrating with a phone call, a rare occurrence for the device.

Elena.

Daphne tensed, the name flashing across her screen causing a wild range of emotions. She clicked the side button for some silence, but Elena's name continued its broadcast, right under the numbers *2:08 a.m.*

She frowned, a different kind of panic moving her finger without her permission, and before she knew it, she'd answered the call and had the phone pressed to her ear.

"Elena?" she said. "Are you okay?"

Because surely, *the* Elena Watson, who insisted on seven and a half hours of sleep a night—no more, no less—would not be calling Daphne at two in the morning unless something was gravely wrong.

"There she is," Elena said, her voice smooth and languid, like pulled taffy at a Tennessee state fair.

Daphne's stomach went wobbly. Elena had said those exact words the last time they'd spoken on the phone, as though she'd simply misplaced Daphne and that explained why they'd been apart for the better part of two months. Regardless, Daphne couldn't stop her reaction to Elena's voice, to her words, to the fact that she'd called at all.

"What do you want?" she forced herself to ask.

Elena laughed softly. "Couldn't sleep. Talking to you always helped when I couldn't sleep."

Daphne said nothing, but her throat went a little thick. She remembered many nights when Elena was restless and Daphne would make them cinnamon tea and they'd talk about everything Elena was stressing over. It always worked, and within the hour, Elena would be curled up with her silk sleep mask, breathing deeply, while Daphne tossed and turned from her own disrupted sleep cycle. It was one of those memories Daphne never knew how to view. Was it sweet? Selfish? Was it a warm display of partnership, or evidence of the self-tinted lens through which Elena viewed everything and everyone in her life?

"I can't make your tea anymore, Elena," Daphne said as firmly as she could muster, which wasn't all that firm considering she was trying to be quiet. April was only a wall away, and for some reason she couldn't parse in the moment, she didn't want her cabinmate to know Elena was on the phone.

"Oh, I know," Elena said softly. Daphne heard the sound of rustling fabric, could easily picture Elena in her big bed all alone, the ivory silk sheets cool and clean around her.

They sat in silence for a second, listening to each other breathe while Daphne tried to drum up the courage to say goodbye, or better, simply hang up. But then Elena spoke again.

"How's April?"

Two tiny words, but they felt like a bomb going off, shrapnel flying. Daphne's hand went to her chest, the *boom* making her heart feel off beat, or maybe it stopped beating altogether. Hearing Elena say April's name . . . she wasn't ready for it.

"If we talk about April, we talk about April," Daphne said.

Elena was silent for a second, then Daphne heard her take a deep breath.

"April was special," she finally said. "But she wasn't you."

Daphne blinked into the dim room, the porch light streaming through the windows making everything in the cabin look ghostly and pale.

"That's it?" Daphne said. "That's all you have to say?"

Elena sighed. "What do you want me to say? I fell in love. And both April and I had suspected the incompatibility between us for months."

"So you *cheated* on her? And made me a part of it without my consent?"

"I made a decision," Elena said firmly. "A bad one, I understand that, but at the time, it was the best I could do. Feelings aren't black-and-white, Daphne. It took me some time to figure out how I felt and what I needed to do about it. For both of you."

Daphne shook her head, even though Elena couldn't see her, because it almost sounded logical. It *almost* sounded okay. But this was what Elena did. What she always did. She spun and she wove until Daphne was tangled in the most beautiful web, completely unaware she was even trapped.

That she was prey.

And it was so, so exhausting.

She lay back down in her bed, tucked the covers under her

arms. She watched the ceiling fan spin slowly, wondering why, if she was aware of the crouching black widow in the corner, she still couldn't seem to get out of its path.

"April is incredible," Daphne finally said.

Three words this time, but she felt them land all the same. Not only with Elena, whom Daphne could hear inhale slowly through her nose as though trying to achieve some sort of calm, but with Daphne too.

April *was* incredible. She was smart and strange and beautiful, and Daphne thought she might—

She squeezed her eyes closed, but even that didn't push out the thought, the complicated feelings, the memory of being in April's arms in the lake, soft skin and wet hair and fingers that ached to explore.

Elena was right about one thing—feelings weren't black-and-white. They were a kaleidoscope of color and sensations. Love and hate bleeding together, lust and affection and fear, how right something felt reminding her in the same breath how wrong it could all go.

"I miss you," Elena said softly, as though to prove everything Daphne had been thinking. "I really do."

Daphne's chin trembled, her eyes stinging suddenly. "I miss you too," she said. Because it was true, right or wrong or somewhere in between, the whole kaleidoscopic mess of it all.

Chapter Nineteen

APRIL LAUGHED AS Sasha whirled through Ramona and Dylan's immaculate kitchen in a plain white tee and black jeans, singing "Les Poissons" from *The Little Mermaid*. She dropped chunks of ripe avocado into a blackberry and arugula salad, then glided Disney princess–style toward the stove to stir the sauce for the spicy peanut noodles.

"You know that song is about fish, right?" April asked.

"I've got crab cakes in the oven," Sasha said.

"Still not a fish."

"Shell*fish*."

Sasha finished the chorus even louder, then grinned before tasting the sauce. "This is heaven."

April laughed as she cut cucumbers. "The sauce or the kitchen?"

"Both, obviously."

The space was beautiful, with swirled white-and-gray quartz counters, navy blue cabinets, matte gold fixtures, the largest stove April had ever seen next to a separate double oven, and a white porcelain farmhouse sink the size of April's bathtub. A stainless-steel Sub-Zero refrigerator held the groceries Dylan had insisted on buying for tonight's engagement dinner, and a butler's pantry was fully stocked with all manner of sundries despite the fact that the Riley-Monroes lived in LA eleven months out of the year.

Riley-Monroe.

Or maybe they'd go with Monroe-Riley, or simply keep their names as they were. She knew Dylan and Ramona would never give up their last names entirely—they needed them professionally. She took a sip of the chilled white wine Dylan had poured for them all when they'd arrived before whisking them off on a tour. April oohed and aahed right along with Daphne and Sasha as they walked through the rooms, all painted different colors, all expertly decorated. April had only ever been in this house once, after all, and that was last summer when Dylan and Ramona had come home for a few weeks, right before Dylan started filming for the Marlene Dietrich biopic, and they'd updated a bit since then.

Of course, the house *was* beautiful. Right on the lake, modern yet comfortable, spacious enough to host friends and family for any occasion, full of light and color and style.

But it wasn't familiar. It wasn't *Ramona*, at least not in April's mind. Since arriving at the house, she'd seen Ramona only once, at the end of the tour when they had gone outside to the expansive patio where they'd be dining. Ramona had been setting up the table, had hugged April tight, and then April had promptly followed Sasha into the kitchen, claiming Sasha needed help with the preparations.

"I probably don't," Sasha had said, her voice deadpan, and April had laughed and punched Sasha's shoulder lightly like the kidder she was.

Now, after Sasha did indeed have to take time out of actual preparations to show April and Daphne how to properly cut vegetables, April hadn't seen Ramona again. She knew Olive and Mr. Riley would be arriving soon, and she couldn't wait to see them.

"How long are you going to hide out in my kitchen?" Sasha

asked as she hip-bumped April away from the cutting board and finished slicing the cucumbers in a flurry of motion, the knife nothing but a blur.

"I'm not hiding," April said.

"You're hiding," Daphne said without looking up from her task. She was chopping stalks of green onion with such concentration—brows furrowed, fingers curled in on the produce just like Sasha had shown her—that April felt a ridiculous swell of affection.

"I am *not* hiding," April repeated. "I'm simply . . . I'm just . . ."

"Hiding," Sasha said, stirring the peanut sauce again, then filling a mint-colored Le Creuset Dutch oven with water for the pasta.

"Helping," April said, setting a glass container full of raw noodles next to the pot. "Plus, it's not your kitchen."

"Am I the cook in this kitchen right now?" Sasha asked.

"Yes, Chef," April said.

"Then it's mine."

April groaned but then caught Daphne's eye and smiled. She smiled, and her stomach fluttered a little. She smiled, her stomach fluttered a little, *and* she flashed back to the way Daphne's mouth had tasted in the lake, how her hands had felt in April's hair, how—

"Good god, you two," Sasha said.

April blinked.

Daphne blinked.

And April realized, horrified, they'd been staring at each other like two idiots on Moon Lovers Trail.

"Just fuck already," Sasha said, sipping her own wine.

"Oh my god, wait, what?" Daphne spluttered in one breath, her cheeks going adorably pink.

Except it wasn't adorable at all, dammit.

"Sasha, Jesus," April said calmly, bracing her palms on the counter.

"I'm just saying, you both want to."

"We do not," Daphne said, the knife shaking in her hand.

April lifted a brow at her but said nothing.

"There's nothing wrong with a casual dalliance," Sasha went on, tossing stuff April didn't even recognize into the peanut sauce. "In fact, I found a play party in Concord tomorrow night. You should both come with me. Get *something* out of your systems, at the very least."

"A play party?" Daphne asked. "What's that?"

"Oh my god," April said, dropping her face into her hands.

Predictably, Sasha smirked. "It's a social event in the BDSM or kink community where people hang out, talk, share ideas, and sometimes kiss and have sex. It can be really chill or really intense. Whatever people want to make of it. Someone hosts at their own house, usually, and there are toys and gadgets you can use if you want. It's fun."

"Oh, wow . . . okay," Daphne said, her voice a squeak.

"I think you broke her," April said.

"No, no, I'm . . . I'm into it," Daphne said.

Sasha laughed, but before any of them could discuss it further, the heavy front door opened and closed, followed by a flurry of voices and footsteps through the expansive living room, which opened into the kitchen. Soon, a slew of people came into view with Dylan and Ramona, including Ramona's dad and sister, and Dylan's rock legend parents, Jack Monroe and Carrie Page.

April and Ramona locked eyes, something unspoken traveling between them April couldn't even translate, but thankfully, she didn't have time to focus on it because Olive Riley flung herself into April's arms.

AFTER INTRODUCTIONS WERE made, they took drinks and some crab cakes with a homemade remoulade to the back patio.

Sasha stayed inside to finish cooking, despite April's protests that she take a break.

The sun was just starting to set over the lake, spreading blood orange and crimson and gold over the water. April sat in a turquoise wooden chair around the firepit, and Olive tumbled into her lap. April wrapped her arms around the girl's waist and hugged her close.

"I can't believe how big you've gotten," April said, rubbing her face against Olive's back.

Olive laughed, her light brown hair newly cut short, a very butch-like hard part on the left. She was dressed in baggy shorts and an oversized white tee, and she was the most beautiful thing April had ever seen. She hadn't realized exactly how much she'd missed Olive—missed being part of a family—until this moment.

"I'm the same height I was when I was thirteen," Olive said.

"You're *huge*," April said, still snuggling. Olive even smelled the same, like cotton and worn leather from her softball glove. "Where's Marley?"

Olive sighed. "Still in Nashville. We're working at a softball camp for kids this summer and I only got a few days off to come home and see Ramona."

"More chances to pine," April said. Secretly, though, she was glad Olive's girlfriend had stayed in Tennessee. She loved Marley, who'd been practically attached to Olive's hip since they became best friends in eighth grade, but April wanted Olive to herself.

She wanted everyone to herself, if she was being honest—Ramona, Olive, even Mr. Riley. She wanted a moment where everything felt like it used to. Before Dylan, before Noelle Yang, before LA and film sets in Clover Lake, before Elena.

Just April and her family.

She pressed her forehead against Olive's back. If she closed her eyes, focused on certain voices as they chattered on, she could pretend she was sitting on the beach with Ramona and Olive, Mr. Riley in one of those straw sun hats and that pink Hawaiian-print shirt Olive was always so horrified he insisted on wearing.

"She's pretty," Olive whispered, jolting April out of her happy place.

She lifted her head, her eyes going immediately to Daphne. She didn't have to ask who Olive was talking about—Daphne was the only new person outside right now, and yes, Daphne was very, very pretty. The late-day sun filtered through her lavender hair as she sat in a chair with her legs crossed, making her look almost as though she were glowing underwater. She wore a floral sundress, tiny opalescent buttons trailing down the middle.

April suddenly wanted to unbutton each one. Slowly.

She shook her head while Daphne laughed at something Dylan's mom, Carrie, was saying, the two of them deep in conversation. Still, Daphne's eyes flitted over to April, just once, and April's stomach billowed upward like a deployed parachute.

"She keeps doing that," Olive said.

"Doing what?"

"Looking at you."

"She does not."

"She does too," Olive said, pinching the skin on April's forearm lightly.

"She's looking at *you*."

"Well, I am very cute, but you're full of shit."

"Language!" April said, feigning being appalled.

Olive laughed, then turned to look April in the eyes. "So how are you doing? Really." Her expression was full of concern, even a tinge of pity.

April pressed her mouth flat. "Exactly how much did Ramona tell you?"

"Ramona tells me everything."

April flinched, but she wasn't even sure why. Of course Ramona told Olive everything. She always had since Olive became an adult, and April couldn't even be mad about it. She could, as it happened, feel left out.

"I'm fine," she told Olive, because it was true. Because she needed it to be true, even as her gaze slid to Daphne, even as Daphne's eyes met hers, even as April looked away for the four hundredth time.

"There she goes again," Olive said out of the side of her mouth.

"Oh, shut up," April said, then proceeded to tickle Olive's middle, and she giggled like she was ten years old again.

April was still digging a finger into Olive's ribs when the back door opened and Ramona came outside.

"Look who's here, everyone," she called, her eyes finding April's and widening.

April frowned at the blurry shadows behind Ramona. She hadn't even noticed when Ramona left the gathering to answer the front door, and April couldn't imagine who else—

She froze as her parents stepped onto the patio, the twilit glow making them look almost angelic.

Almost.

They stood stoically together, the Drs. Preston and Jacqueline Evans. April's mother clutched the strap of her black pocketbook—it wasn't a purse or a bag, it was a *pocketbook*—her brown bob cut severely just below her chin. She wore a crisp white blouse tucked into knee-length navy shorts, as though she were attending the summer session of an East Coast private school. Preston wore his usual khaki pants—flat front, to keep up with the times—a starchy light blue dress shirt, and a bow tie. The bow tie was a signature look for her father, something he'd donned every day since his residency at Northwestern, claiming a bow tie was jovial and set patients at ease. April had always found this quirk of her father's strange, as the word *jovial* had never exactly described the Preston Evans she knew.

"Mom, Dad," April said, patting Olive's back to stand so she could get up. "What are you doing here?"

Her mother gave a tight-lipped smile. "Mr. Riley invited us."

"He did," April said, barely a question.

"That he did," Preston said. "I ran into him at Gallagher's yesterday."

"You've all known our Ramona since she was nine years old," said Mr. Riley, who had joined them to shake the Evanses' hands. "I figured you'd want to help us celebrate as well."

"Of course," Jacqueline said, smiling without her teeth. "April hadn't even told us the good news yet."

"I've been busy," April said. A paltry excuse, sure, but the only one she had.

"Well, we're glad to have you," Mr. Riley said, then squeezed April's shoulder meaningfully. He knew almost as well as Ramona that April's relationship with her mom and dad was a bit tense. But he was a parent too, and probably abided by some sort of code April didn't understand.

"Congratulations, you two," Preston said. He handed Ramona a bottle of wine, no doubt something French and expensive. April's parents were wine snobs.

"Thank you so much," Ramona said, taking the bottle and then hugging them both.

Everyone was on their feet now. Mr. Riley introduced April's parents to Jack and Carrie, and then Ramona introduced Daphne while April stood frozen next to the firepit as though watching a play unfold onstage.

She felt suddenly young and useless.

"Sweetheart," her mother said, walking up to her with her mouth pinched.

"Mother," April said politely.

Jacqueline proceeded to take in April's clothes—her usual black jeans, boots, and dark purple racerback tank—even going so far as to reach out and pluck at the material of her top, rubbing it between two fingers.

April rolled her shoulders back, just to remove her mother's claw, and Jacqueline cleared her throat.

"You didn't tell us you were teaching art at Cloverwild this summer," she said.

April sighed. She'd always known it was impossible to keep secrets in this damn town, but she was hoping for a little more time before she had to talk to her parents about her poor life choices.

"I am," she said simply.

"And your shop?" her mother asked as Preston joined them, handing Jacqueline a glass of white wine.

"We passed by there the other weekend," he said before taking a pompous sip—pursing his mouth, making a slurping sound as he rolled the wine on his tongue, which was sort of disgusting, if you asked April. After he swallowed, he tsked. "Closed at two in the afternoon on a Saturday. Not a great business model."

April inhaled deeply through her nose. Slowly, letting her lungs fill completely, while she decided how to play this. She didn't want to ruin Ramona's engagement dinner. Nor did she want to deal with her parents' potential horror at her aimlessness.

But she was also tired. Tired of caring, of not owning what she was doing—or not doing—with her life. She was fucking tired of keeping every thought and feeling inside and hidden until the right time, until the people around her were able to digest them.

"Closed it," she said calmly. Factually. She folded her hands in front of her and forced her chin north a few centimeters. "A few weeks ago."

At first her parents simply blinked at her. Her mother's mouth opened, just a fraction, and her father looked at her as though she were bacteria under a microscope he was trying to identify. Next, they glanced at each other.

April braced herself for their disappointment, for the lecture from her father on how she'd mishandled their investment in her business, the way her mother would somehow work in April's lack of professional demeanor as a reason for failure.

Translation: her tattoos, dyed hair, and overt queerness.

While her parents had never really expressed an opinion one way or another about the fact that April was pansexual—they'd adored Elena, after all—their long-suffering sighs seemed to stem mostly from who April was as a whole person. Queer, straight, dyed hair or mouse brown, April herself inspired baffled expressions and furrowed brows, which only intensified as she got older. Thirty-three and still gallivanting through life like a twenty-year-old without any ambition, passion, or plans.

April held her breath, readying herself for the same fight they'd been having April's entire life.

"Well," Jacqueline said finally before taking a demure sip of her own wine. "I'm very sorry to hear that."

"Shame," Preston said, his frown etching deep lines into the sides of his mouth, then glanced around as though desperate for someone else to talk to. He looked back at his daughter, his expression impassive. "Let us know where you land."

Then he put his arm around Jacqueline's shoulder and led her off to join a raucous discussion going on with Mr. Riley, Jack, and Carrie.

April stood there for a second, feeling as though she was watching her own life unfold on a movie screen, powerless to influence it, completely uninvolved in any choice. Her mother looked back at her once, but then quickly focused again on the adults in her new conversation.

April wasn't sure why she was surprised. Her parents had always hovered between disappointment and disinterest when it came to April, but as it turned out, the way they made her feel never dulled. The pain was still quick and razor-sharp, drawing blood before she even realized the blade had touched her skin.

And dammit, April would not cry.

Not here.

She would fucking not.

"Apes," Ramona said, hurrying toward her. She wore a pink tee that said *Feed the Birds* over a sketch of St. Paul's Cathedral inside a snow globe, tucked into a pleated gray skirt. She looped her arm through April's. "I'm sorry."

"For what," April said, her voice unintentionally deadpan.

"I didn't realize Dad had invited them. He said it happened so fast and it was awkward, and then it slipped his mind until they—"

April untangled her arm from Ramona's, holding up her hand to stop her best friend from talking. Because even though she knew this wasn't Ramona's fault—wasn't even Mr. Riley's fault—she didn't want to hear excuses.

"I need a sec," April said quietly, then turned and headed down the stone steps and along the path leading from the patio to the dock, the lake sparkling a deep purple in front of her. She walked fast, not slowing down until her boots clomped onto the wooden dock. There wasn't a railing, just a flat plane of wood, a canoe bobbing in the water. She sat down, letting her legs dangle over the edge.

Then she breathed.

Or tried to, but her body was still trying to cry, her throat tight and achy, her eyes stinging. She'd just bitten back the worst of it, finally gotten her chest to loosen up a little, when she heard footsteps behind her.

She groaned inwardly. "Mona, I said I needed a minute."

"It's me."

April looked over her shoulder to see Daphne walking down the pier toward the dock, her sundress swinging around her thighs. Honestly, it looked like something a true country girl would wear in the summer—tiny pink, blue, and yellow flowers covering the cotton, the hem teasing above her knee, the fluttery short sleeves showing off her pale arms.

And those damn buttons trailing down the front, like a tiny path leading—

April turned back toward the lake, focused on the water. "Hi," she said. She felt Daphne sit next to her, their shoulders brushing lightly.

"You okay?" Daphne asked.

April watched the water undulate with a stronger-than-normal breeze, morphing from purple to black as the sun disappeared. Solar-powered lights clicked on around the dock, filling the space with a warmer glow.

I'm fine was on the tip of her tongue. She was fine about Ramona's engagement, and she was fine about her shop closing, about Trudy and her brood living in her house, about her parents' lack of care, about the uncertainty of the Devon.

But right now, she didn't want to be fine.

She wanted to be real.

"I don't know," she said.

Daphne took a deep breath, her arm settling heavier against April's as she exhaled.

"Your parents seem . . ." Daphne started, but then stopped, her mouth open, her brow furrowed.

"Like assholes," April said. "Those are the words I believe you're looking for."

Daphne laughed. "I'm sorry."

"Don't be. They are. Not your fault."

"I get it," Daphne said. "Having parents who don't quite get you. When I was eleven, we read this story in school about fairies, and I remember wondering if I was a changeling."

"Really?" April asked.

Daphne nodded, waving her hand at the lake. "The real Daphne Love—the straight, devout, smooth-haired girl her parents really wanted—was out there somewhere, frolicking in the Unseelie Court while the Daphne in Crestwater, Tennessee, wreaked havoc upon her family."

Daphne's glassy eyes were focused on the water, her thoughts far away. Shame flared in April's chest. Here she was sulking at her best friend's lakeside mansion about how Mommy and Daddy didn't love her. They let her go to RISD. They sent her money when her job didn't cover all her expenses. They helped her start up Wonderlust Ink. She'd had everything she'd ever needed, while Daphne literally ran away from home and pulled herself into adulthood all alone.

"I'm sorry," April said. "I shouldn't complain, I know."

Daphne's expression cleared, and she looked at April. "Why not?"

April sighed, picked up a small pebble on the dock and tossed it into the water, where it landed with a delicate splash, then disappeared into the darkness.

"You had it worse," she said. "Ramona had it worse, even. Her mother left when she was thirteen, so she really knows what it's like to deal with that kind of rejection, and she—"

"I don't want to talk about Ramona right now," Daphne said softly. She turned so she was facing April, one leg hanging off the dock and the other tucked under her as she leaned closer. "I want to talk about you."

April blinked at her. "I . . . We . . ."

"You sort of do that a lot," Daphne said. Her voice was so quiet. So close.

"Do what?" April whispered.

"Deflect," Daphne said, then smiled a little. "I think that's the right term. Put the focus on other people instead of yourself."

"Did you learn that in therapy?"

"I can't afford therapy," Daphne said. "Though god knows I need it. My parents were adamantly opposed to any kind of psychology that wasn't from a Christian point of view and provided by a pastor, and I—" Daphne froze and pursed her mouth, exhaling heavily through her nose. "You did it again."

"Did what?" April said, laughing nervously. "I have no clue what you're talking about."

"You change the subject, or you make things seem like less than what they are. Things that bother you or things that have hurt you. Or you make them not about you at all."

April scoffed. "That's not . . . I don't . . ."

But she trailed off. She shut up, because shit, Daphne was right. She wasn't sure when it happened, when she'd started making herself smaller, more palatable. Maybe it was when Elena left her, or maybe it went back even further than that, back to when she was a loud and strange little kid, begging her mother for a Rainbow Brite party and in love with the stars.

She didn't know.

Didn't matter, really.

All that mattered was that it was true, and she'd known it was true for a long time. But hearing Daphne say it, someone who had no reason to sugarcoat anything, who had only met April a few weeks ago. For *the* Daphne Love to see her so clearly, so completely—that was different. That was . . .

That was everything.

She reached out and twined her fingers with Daphne's. She didn't look at her. She just held her hand, and let Daphne hold her hand back, and looked out at the water under a waning moon.

After a while, she pulled Daphne's hand into her lap, held it there while she looked down at their fingers, watched as Daphne ran her thumb over one of her silver rings, a moonstone at its center.

"I don't really know what to do about it," April said. Daphne squeezed her hand tighter, and April finally looked at her. Her face was a blur in the dim light, but somehow, she could see her perfectly. "I'm a mess."

Daphne frowned, but her eyes were soft. "Everyone's a mess, April. You know *I* am."

"Tell me," April said.

"April," Daphne said. "We're not talking about—"

"Please," April said. "I hear what you're saying, but talking to you . . ." She shook her head, staring down at their fingers tangled together. "Talking to you helps. Sometimes I wonder if it's the only thing that does."

Daphne inhaled sharply, and April waited, running her thumb over a freckle on the back of Daphne's hand. Daphne's grip tightened.

"When I left home," she finally said quietly, "it didn't feel like a choice. It felt like life and death. Maybe not physically, but in every other way. And I'm still a mess over it. The more time that goes by, the farther I get from Crestwater, Tennessee, the more I know it's true. Since then, I've had one major relationship in my life, and not only was it built on lies, but I let her walk all over me. I let her own me."

"Why?" April asked.

Daphne sighed. "Because I wanted to be owned. I still do, in a lot of ways. When I lost my family, I felt completely untethered. I couldn't find my footing, I had no place to land, no place to return to on holidays. I took classes I couldn't afford just so I could stay on campus during the summer. I had Vivian, but I didn't know how to be a friend because I had no clue how to love myself. How to be *me*. I'd never been allowed to, and the sudden blast of freedom in college was overwhelming. And then . . ."

"And then Elena."

"And then Elena." Daphne wiped her eyes with her free hand. "I don't know. She was a *place*, if that makes sense. She made me feel safe. She made me feel like I belonged to someone."

April didn't say anything at first, but something glowed warm in the center of her chest. An understanding. A sharing.

"That makes sense," April said, and left it at that. Elena had come along in her life at a pretty similar time. She might not have been quite as unmoored as Daphne, but in every way that mattered, they'd been the same, secretly desperate for someone who would simply choose them over and over, come hell or high water. And Elena . . . she was good at making you feel like you were the only person in the world who mattered to her.

But really, it was all an illusion. Because Elena truly excelled at finding vulnerable women who needed her far more than she'd ever need them.

April swallowed, her mouth dry. "Do you think you'll ever talk to your family again?" she asked. "Make amends?"

Daphne was quiet for a bit, tapping her nail on one of April's rings.

"It would be a nice story, wouldn't it?" she finally said. "The queer kid runs away from an oppressive home, and years later the family realizes just how horrible they were to choose doctrine over their own daughter. They seek her out, write her letters, maybe even travel to wherever she is to profess their love, their regret. They all begin to heal, to become a family again."

"I think it's a sad story," April said. "But it has a nice ending."

Daphne nodded, then sniffed. "Unfortunately, not everyone

gets that ending. And after seven years, after the letters I wrote them when I first left, all the letters they never responded to, I don't think that's how my story concludes."

"I would travel to wherever you are."

Daphne's head popped up, her eyes wide.

April forced herself not to look away. She hadn't meant to say it, but it was out there now. And it was true. In some way, in some universe where Daphne and April were infinitely less complicated, April would travel to the moon to see Daphne Love smile. Or hear her laugh. Or just sit on a dock, holding her hand.

There.

She could admit it.

She had no clue what to do about it, but she could admit it.

"What do you want, April Evans?" Daphne asked, her voice a whisper.

And goddess, what a question.

The question, really.

She wanted so many things—she wanted a life full of art and beauty. She wanted a queer community with friends beyond Ramona, beyond Clover Lake. She wanted to travel and create, and she wanted the Devon. A chance, at least, to do something that felt big. That felt like stepping out of the tight circle she'd locked herself into for so many years.

But right now, on this dock with Daphne Love, of all people, she didn't want to talk about any of that. She only wanted one thing. A simple, beautiful, terrifying thing.

"I want to kiss you again," she said.

April expected Daphne to hesitate. To laugh shyly or shake her head as though April might be joking, but that wasn't what Daphne did at all.

Instead, she made a sound that nearly did April's head in—a

quick, almost relieved exhalation—before untangling her fingers and taking April's face in her hands.

Then Daphne kissed her.

She kissed her like she'd been waiting to kiss her every moment since Mirror Cove. For months, even. Maybe years. Her fingertips trailed down April's cheeks, and April's hand circled around Daphne's wrists, holding her in place. Their mouths teased for a second, then opened, Daphne's tongue sliding against April's so perfectly, April heard herself moan. It was quiet, but it was audible, and Daphne responded in kind, pressing deeper, licking into April's mouth and then tugging on her lower lip, desperation building between them. It was sweet and wild all at once, and April couldn't imagine anything better.

She couldn't even begin to think about anything she wanted more than this.

Except maybe her legs around Daphne's hips.

Her fingertips dancing along those elegant collarbones.

And goddammit, this was about what she wanted, wasn't it?

She broke contact just long enough to hook her arms around Daphne's neck and settle in her lap, her jean-clad legs circling Daphne's hips. Daphne held on to her waist, their mouths finding each other again. April sank her fingers into Daphne's hair, soft curls that smelled like her usual smoky vanilla mixed with the coconut from April's bodywash. She must've borrowed it in the shower, which made April feel suddenly wild with want. She imagined Daphne in their cabin's bathroom, naked, soap sliding between her breasts, down her stomach, even farther south where April wanted her mouth right now so badly, she nearly released a whine.

"Why are we at this party?" she asked against Daphne's mouth.

"I have no idea," Daphne said, then trailed her mouth to

April's neck, sucking harder than April expected, but fuck, she loved it. Still, the sting caused her to startle right when Daphne's hands were moving from her waist to her ass. The shift caused April's body to fall backward enough for them both to realize they were pretty damn close to the edge of the dock.

"Oh, holy shit," April said, clinging to Daphne's shoulders. She looked behind her, nothing but dark water below. "That was close."

"This should be a reality show," Daphne said, laughing, her chin resting on April's chest as she looked up at her. "*Extreme Making Out.*"

April laughed too, staring down at this beautiful person. She didn't want to make the same mistake that she had in the lake. Pulling away. Pulling back. Choosing something easy over what she truly wanted. She opened her mouth to say all of this, that she didn't care if it was complicated or fraught or if, at the end of the summer, one of them would be heading for the Devon while the other floundered in uncertainty.

"Daphne," she said, her thumb smoothing down a silky curl near Daphne's temple. "I—"

"April?"

April froze, recognizing Ramona's voice in the dark.

"Are you out here?" Ramona called.

Through the dim dock lights, April could see Ramona on the path from the house and heading toward them.

And she wasn't sure what happened then, but within half a second, both she and Daphne were on their feet, at least a foot of space between them. April didn't know who had moved first, or why, but here they were, breathing heavily and straightening their clothes just as Ramona came into clear view.

"Hey," Ramona said. "There you are."

"Here I am," April said brightly. Too damn brightly. Like the center of the sun bright. She cleared her throat.

Ramona tilted her head at her, eyes flicking to Daphne, who was standing impossibly straight, her hands clasped demurely in front of her. "You two okay?"

"Fine, fine, we're fine," April said. "We were just . . ."

But she trailed off, her hand waving vaguely in Daphne's direction. She felt sick, had no idea why she was acting like a high schooler caught making out in the janitor's closet, but she couldn't seem to act normally either.

Ramona didn't look convinced. "Okay. Well. Dinner's ready."

"Great," April said, shooting both of her thumbs into the air. "We'll be there in a—"

"You two go ahead," Daphne said, pulling her phone out of her dress pocket and frowning at the screen. "I need to take care of something."

April swallowed hard. "Are you sure?"

"I'm sure," Daphne said brightly, just as brightly as April had, smiling at her with all her teeth. But then she softened, met April's eyes. "It's okay. I promise."

April nodded, and Ramona looped her arm with April's as they turned down the pier and headed toward the house.

"What was that about?" Ramona asked.

April exhaled heavily, relief and regret swirling in her stomach. "Nothing. It wasn't about anything."

Chapter Twenty

DAPHNE HANDED OVER her ID to a person named Stone, along with thirty bucks she couldn't really afford to part with, but there was no way she was missing her first play party.

"You're all set," Stone said, offering their IDs back to Sasha, who tossed them over to April and Daphne, and not very respectively.

Daphne glanced down at April's smiling face on the New Hampshire ID, her hair a bit longer with crimson tips. She looked younger, slightly softer. Daphne wondered if she'd been with Elena then. Daphne held out the card to April, their fingers brushing, eyes meeting as Daphne felt her own ID slide into her palm.

They hadn't really talked since their moment on the dock last night. She couldn't imagine what April's best friend must think of her. It was such a weird situation, and Daphne didn't blame April for not knowing how to handle it. She herself felt so discombobulated after Ramona and April had gone back to the house for dinner that she'd answered a call from Elena without a second thought.

"Hi," she'd said, her eyes still on April and Ramona as they walked away.

"Hi, yourself," Elena said. Daphne exhaled as soon as she

heard her voice, muscle memory at work. Despite what had happened with April, despite the truth of who and what Elena was, she knew Daphne. Knew her through and through, and that settled around Daphne's heart like a hug.

"How are you?" Elena asked.

Daphne had lain down on the dock, staring up at the sky with the phone pressed to her ear.

"I don't know," she said.

"Bad night?"

"Just . . . weird. Confusing."

"Sounds like you need some cinnamon tea," Elena said softly. "And a bath with those bombs you like. The vetiver ones."

"Vetiver and wood sage," Daphne said.

"Yeah," Elena said. "I still have some."

"You didn't throw them out?"

Elena sighed. "I couldn't."

Daphne's eyes stung, and she hated it. She hated how Elena could still do this to her, melt her entire soul and heart with just a few stupid words about bath bombs.

"Why did you break up with me?" she asked. It was out of her mouth before she could stop it.

"Daphne," Elena said gently.

"Just tell me," Daphne said. "Please. Was there someone else?"

"No."

"Right," Daphne said, laughing mirthlessly. "And how am I supposed to believe you after what you did to April?"

"I never spoke to April again after we split up," Elena said sharply. "If there was someone else, we wouldn't be on the phone right now, Daphne."

Daphne sucked in a breath, a strange mix of disgust and horrible relief.

"Then tell me," she said, pushing through it.

Elena exhaled loudly. "Honestly?"

Daphne didn't answer, and Elena was quiet for a long time.

"I don't know," Elena said finally. "I felt stuck. *We* felt stuck. And I wasn't sure what to do about it except blow it all up."

Daphne let that settle between them, readied herself to say goodbye, but then Elena kept talking.

"I never should have done it. I never should have let you go," she said.

A whisper. A bomb exploding.

Daphne sat up quickly, her stomach undulating unpleasantly, and she had no idea how to respond.

How she felt.

What she thought.

The words blurred together, and she realized her eyes were filling with tears, and she didn't understand that either. Elena had put her through hell—her coldness during the last year of their relationship, always denying anything was wrong when Daphne asked, the constant gaslighting, all followed by an abrupt breakup after a beautiful date at Daphne's favorite restaurant, accompanied with the courtesy of calling Daphne a Lyft once she'd finished packing.

There'd been no conversation.

There'd been no transition period.

There was only *I think we both know it's time to end this*, followed by a gentle request for her apartment key.

And now, after all that, Elena wanted to take it back. There was a thrill in that, for sure. Daphne felt a sense of relief she wished didn't exist, the simple joy of being wanted.

But in the middle of everything, there was a *knowing*. Sudden and bright, like the first flash of lightning of a gathering summer storm.

She didn't love Elena Watson. In fact, she didn't think she'd loved her for a while, months before they'd even broken up. Daphne had needed her. Needed *someone*, and that was very different from want. From love and passion and desire.

"I have to go," Daphne had said, and then ended the call before Elena could respond. She stared at her phone's screen for a second, the lake lapping gently at the dock. And maybe it was the summer night, the swirl of feelings in her stomach about April, or maybe she was just tired of being stuck in a cycle she knew wasn't good for her.

Elena wasn't good for her.

She tapped on Elena's information, then selected *Block Caller*. She deleted Elena's number and email from her contacts and slipped her phone back into her pocket before standing up and walking back to the house.

And she felt . . . *good*.

She felt lighter and hopeful. There was a sadness there too, losing Elena all over again, but it was a cleansing sort of pain, like cutting an infection from her body. Later, on the drive back to Cloverwild, she and April were silent, but the atmosphere felt charged, a million things between them that Daphne wasn't sure how to talk about.

Now, nearly twenty-four hours later, she stood in a Victorian house with a literal sex dungeon in the basement, and she was determined to make the most of it.

"Oh, wow, those are boobs," she said as the three of them walked into the living room. She pressed close to Sasha, who laughed.

"And thank god for it," she said, arms folded. She was dressed in her usual tight white tee and tight black jeans.

Daphne tried not to stare at the person with soft brown skin on the puffy couch, who was wearing a sort of harness-like top comprised of black braided ropes, which knotted together between their two small breasts. Sparkly black discs covered their nipples, so it wasn't as though they were fully tits out, and they sat serenely talking to a person with curly red hair who was wearing a navy maxi dress. Still, the shock of all that skin made Daphne keenly aware that she'd never experienced anything like this before. She watched the couple for a second, both of them at ease and sipping on cans of sparkling water, until the person in the harness locked eyes with Daphne.

"Oh god, oh god," she whispered, looking down and grabbing Sasha's arm. She was giddy with nerves. Or maybe excitement. Horniness? God, probably all three at once.

"Okay, Pollyanna, you've got to relax," Sasha said. "We're not even to the good stuff yet."

"I know," Daphne said, forcing her eyes up. Granted, she didn't dare glance back at the couch. "I'm fine. This is fine."

"You don't have to do this if you're not comfortable," April said softly.

Daphne glanced at her and quickly found herself staring. April looked gorgeous tonight. Her iridescent hair was parted on the side and swooping over her forehead, the ends just brushing her shoulder. Her eye makeup was heavy, as usual, but it looked so good on her, and she'd paired it with a lilac-amber eye shadow and burgundy lips.

Also, she had on black leather pants.

Black leather pants and a lacy, Victorian-esque black top. Daphne wasn't even aware she was into leather pants, but as it turned out, she was.

Very into them.

She had to focus to keep from staring at April's ass every chance she got.

For herself, Daphne had struggled with a clothing choice, as her summer wardrobe consisted mostly of sundresses and solid-colored tees. She'd ended up choosing a plain black cocktail dress she used to wear to gallery functions—black seemed best for a play party, though she truly had no idea—with spaghetti straps, a squared neckline, and a simple skirt that hit mid-thigh.

"I want to be here," Daphne said, holding April's gaze. "I just need a second to adjust."

"Atta girl," Sasha said, nudging her arm. "Plus, there's no pressure to do anything. Some people just sit and talk. Some make out. Some play with sensation using feathers and thumpers."

"Thumpers?" Daphne asked.

"Other people just come here for a cuddle puddle," Sasha went on. "And some . . . well, some do more than all that." She shrugged, dark blue eyes glittering and shifting from Daphne to April and back to Daphne. "Just depends on what you want."

Daphne nodded, swallowed thickly. She didn't even understand some of the words Sasha used to describe the party, but that was okay. That was the point. She had no idea if she'd want to do anything at all—honestly, the idea of kissing a total stranger was both alluring and horrifying—but Sasha was right.

She had to relax.

"Let's go downstairs," Daphne said.

April lifted her lovely dark brows. "You don't want to ease into it?"

"I think she just did," Sasha said, winking at the person on the couch.

They grinned back, revealing very cute dimples and a charming gap between their teeth.

Sasha's wink escalated into that one-side-of-her-mouth grin, and Daphne had the distinct feeling she wouldn't be acting as tour guide for very long.

"I think I did too," Daphne said, pushing Sasha and April

toward the stairs that led to the basement. They both headed down them without hesitation, and Daphne forced herself to follow, despite her pounding heart and clammy palms.

Downstairs, the basement—or dungeon, rather—opened up into a large space that spanned the whole house. The lights were soft and golden, mostly salt lamps placed strategically on tiny tables, which also held baskets full of disposable gloves, condoms, a roll of paper towels, and a bottle of cleanser. Various equipment was placed around the room, including—according to Sasha as she pointed everything out—a St. Andrew's Cross, spanking benches, a curvy red sex chaise, a few wedges and pillows, and a cage. A swing dangled in the middle of the room, as yet unoccupied. Lo-fi music played from a Bluetooth speaker in one corner, the beat gentle and sexy.

There were only a few people down here right now, most of them investigating the furniture and toys as well. But as the three of them stood there taking in their surroundings, a couple made their way to the St. Andrew's Cross—two tall beams in the shape of an X, complete with hand and foot restraints at each end.

"Here we go," Sasha said quietly.

The two white women approached the cross with smiles, laughing as the woman with short dark hair helped the strawberry blonde woman lean her back against the cross. They were both dressed simply, but the respective shorts and skirt they wore left plenty of skin exposed. Short Hair secured Strawberry's wrists and ankles, and then they kissed.

They kissed deeply, Short Hair's entire body pressed against Strawberry, Short Hair's hands roaming and exploring. Strawberry released a moan, then they both giggled.

Daphne felt like a voyeur, and her cheeks were flaming hot, but she also couldn't look away as Short Hair picked up some sort of toy with long, rainbow-hued leather falls—a flogger, according to Sasha—and the couple started kissing again.

Daphne definitely felt . . . some kind of way.

Of course, she'd watched porn before. Good porn. The stuff with real people who make their own videos because they love sharing authentic sexual experiences. So it wasn't like she'd never seen people she didn't know making out. She'd seen them doing way more than what this couple was doing right now. But live and in person, in a sex dungeon full of people who were there to experience something pleasurable or empowering or beautiful—that was a very different thing than porn.

Daphne's breath felt short, and there was a very gentle but very distinct hum between her thighs.

Short Hair trailed the flogger's falls over Strawberry's thighs, then her arms, before stepping back and using the flogger like a whip. The toy *thwacked* gently, and Strawberry gasped sharply. Daphne made a sound not unlike a squeak.

"All right, lovers," Sasha said, turning away from the couple to face Daphne and April. "What do you want to try out first?"

"I thought you said there was no pressure for Daphne to do anything," April said drolly.

Sasha smirked. "I wasn't talking to her."

"Oh, oh, okay." April laughed and put her hands on her hips. "I'm game."

Sasha flourished her hand toward the nearest bench—it looked a little like a pommel horse, just without the handles, and had a place where a person could kneel and rest their upper body on the main component.

Which April did.

Daphne's mouth was suddenly very, very dry.

This wasn't even *sexy*.

At least, not in the traditional sense. Granted, yes, okay, Short Hair and Strawberry were making some very distinct noises that were definitely sexy, but that wasn't what Daphne was even focusing on right now.

Right now, April was fully clothed, yes, but she was kneeling on a spanking bench and sort of . . . wiggling her ass in the air.

Okay, so maybe this was very, very sexy.

And playful.

And funny.

Daphne was dizzy. She was severely dizzy and might have to sit down. She leaned against the wall on April's other side for a little support, while Sasha twitched her fingers over the table of toys, finally picking a thick, multicolored feather and what looked like a black leather riding crop.

Daphne didn't dare ask any questions. She didn't trust a thing that might come out of her mouth. Instead, she focused on taking in oxygen correctly and keeping her eyes off April's butt.

April, for her part, continued to shimmy her hips back and forth. "Show me whatcha got," she said as Sasha approached the table.

Sasha smirked for the twentieth time in the last hour, then locked gazes with Daphne.

Daphne blinked.

April looked back and forth between the two of them, her brow furrowed.

"What?" Daphne finally managed to ask.

Sasha didn't say anything. She simply held the crop and feather over the bench, offering them to Daphne.

"Madame," Sasha said with a flourish of her hand. "Or perhaps Ms. Love? Oh, that's got a certain ring to it, I have to admit."

"Wait, what?" Daphne said.

"Sasha," April said warningly.

"Remember when I said you two need to go ahead and fu—"

"Yes, Sasha, we remember," April said. Her butt wasn't wiggling now.

"Well," Sasha said, reaching over April to grab Daphne's hand. She smacked the toys into her palm, then closed her fingers around them. "Work it out. I'm going to get acquainted with some new friends."

And with that, Sasha turned and headed back upstairs, her boots stomping emphatically on every step.

Daphne stared after her for a second, her hand still held out over April, the feather and crop barely secured in her fist.

April was still on the bench and resting on her forearms. She turned her head toward Daphne, but didn't quite look at her. "We don't have to do anything," she said.

Daphne remained silent. She ran her fingers over the feather, feeling every individual barb, soft and silky. She needed a beat for her brain to catch up to her libido, if she was being honest. Sasha had said play wasn't always about sex—it was about sensation and communication and exploration too. It was about experimenting with certain roles, certain words, certain feelings.

Daphne set the crop on the floor, but kept hold of the feather.

"Daphne," April said. "We can just—"

"Shh," Daphne said, and pressed the very tip of the feather against April's cheek.

April's gaze flew to hers then, her eyes wide.

Daphne didn't look away this time as she trailed the feather down April's throat and around to the back of her neck.

"Okay?" Daphne asked.

April swallowed hard. Her eyes looked black in the dim light, completely pupilless, and her "Yes" was raspy and breathless.

Daphne stepped closer, her free hand resting on the bench while she flitted the feather down April's back. She had a top on, of course, but it was lacy, peeks of skin showing through, and April shivered, her eyes fluttering closed. She rested her forehead on her arms.

Daphne swirled the feather over her back, up and down, then side to side, her movements mostly languid, but she'd flick it quickly here and there, enjoying the control she had over this tiny little thing in her hands.

This woman on the bench.

She reached the small of April's back, the hem of her shirt riding up a little and revealing a strip of skin. She danced the feather over the sensitive spot, and April released a quiet sound. Half moan, half hum. Whatever it was, it made Daphne clench her legs together. She still felt a little dizzy, but she felt something else too—a steadiness she hadn't experienced in a long time.

A safety.

"Is this okay?" she asked softly, slipping a finger under April's shirt and lifting, just an inch before pausing.

"Yes," April said, her voice muffled in her arms.

Daphne pulled her top up slowly, letting each bit of lace scratch against April's skin as she did so. April sucked in a breath as the feather touched her bare back, as it swirled and circled. Daphne used her other hand too, drifting her short nails in opposition to the feather, like a kind of dance.

In the background, she vaguely registered Short Hair and Strawberry amping up a little, their noises a bit more breathy, more desperate, but Daphne didn't look over there. She was entranced by her own scene, by April's back arching and then curling like a cat's, her hips moving ever so slightly, her lungs working to regulate the feelings Daphne was causing.

It was intoxicating.

Ms. Love.

She smiled at the name, but didn't dare speak it. Didn't dare request it. She simply tucked it away, the feelings that it brought, and paused long enough to grab the riding crop from where she'd left it on the floor.

"This okay?" she asked, letting April feel the flat leather tip against the middle of her back.

April lifted her left thumb in acquiescence, and then Daphne watched as that same hand clenched into a fist as Daphne moved the crop lower. She was gentle, grazing the tool just like she had the feather. She passed it over the waistband of April's jeans, slowly traveling past her butt and toward the backs of her thighs.

There she paused.

Lifted the crop a few inches, then brought it back down. April inhaled sharply at the small snap. The impact hadn't been hard, just a shock, Daphne guessed. Still, she asked if April was good.

April looked over her shoulder this time, their eyes locking. They stared at each other for a second. More people came into the basement, more noises filled the room, more sighs and spanks and laughter. But Daphne felt as though she and April existed on some other plane, in an entirely different universe.

"I'm good, Ms. Love," April finally said. Her voice was soft, barely above a whisper, but to Daphne, it felt like a scream.

The very best kind.

She sucked in her own breath, lifted her chin, and nodded once, feeling more sexy and powerful and safe than she ever had in her entire life. She wasn't sure what it was, what was happening at all, but she knew she wanted more of it.

"Good," Daphne said firmly but softly, and April's eyes went completely black. "Keep looking at me."

"Yes, Ms. Love," April said, right before Daphne popped the crop against April's other thigh.

April's eyes fluttered closed, but she opened them again quickly and followed Daphne's directions. Daphne had the urge to say *Good girl*, but instead she simply moved the crop north to April's ass and snapped it swiftly through the air.

April smiled at that one.

A coy smile. An *Is that all you got* smile.

Daphne laughed, then popped it again on the other cheek, harder this time, and April's smile vanished, along with her breath.

"That's what I thought," Daphne whispered, then used the crop again, the hard *crack* echoing around them.

April's cheeks were flushed, her mouth open a little. They watched each other again for a few seconds, a sort of standoff. And then Daphne wasn't sure who even made the first move. But suddenly, April had gotten up, and Daphne was putting away the toys while April sprayed the bench with cleanser, wiping quickly before tossing the paper towel into the trash by the supply table.

Then they were moving, April leading the way, her fingers tangled with Daphne's. They went upstairs, through the living room, smiling and waving goodbye—Sasha simply saluted them with one finger from the couch—but never slowing down.

Not for one damn second.

THEY TUMBLED INTO April's car, and the thirty-minute drive back to Cloverwild felt interminable. They didn't speak. Daphne hardly dared to breathe as she clutched the handle over the passenger door, her entire body like a live wire. Music played through April's phone, something moody and gay, but Daphne didn't register much beyond the movement of the car, the way her own heart seemed to have left her chest, pumping everywhere else in her body except for beneath her ribs.

When they finally pulled into the Cloverwild staff lot, they both spilled out of the car, walking quickly to their cabin. The night was cool and cloudy, and Daphne felt a few raindrops on her arms as they climbed the stairs to their porch. April used her key card to unlock the door and then they were inside just as the rain started to fall a bit harder.

Daphne closed the door, pressed her back against the wood. She was breathing heavily. She had no idea why. They hadn't run. Had walked a bit briskly, maybe, but that didn't feel like the reason her lungs were suddenly having a hard time communicating with her brain. Bianca and Bob both mewed sleepily from April's bed, and Daphne had never been so glad the two cats hadn't gotten up to greet them.

April tossed her bag and keys onto her dresser, then turned around to face Daphne. The room was dimly lit, the small lamp on Daphne's bedside table the only light, coating the space and April's features in a golden glow.

The rain plinked onto the cabin's tin roof.

They still hadn't said a word since they'd left Stone's basement. And Daphne didn't want to change that. She didn't want words or questions. She didn't want soft and subtle and slow.

They moved at the same time, as though April had been thinking the exact same thing, colliding in the middle of the room in a blur of mouths and teeth and tongues. Daphne cupped April's face, then raked her nails through her hair, tugging at the roots a little. April moaned—the only sound Daphne did want to hear, over and over—and clutched at the waist of Daphne's black dress. Her hands felt perfect, like water in a desert, and Daphne wanted them everywhere all at once.

And April obliged.

She spread her fingers over Daphne's ribs, then up to her tits, squeezing and plucking at her nipples. Daphne had to rip her mouth from April's to cry out, to get some air in her lungs. April's lips were on her neck now, and she moved them toward the desk by the window as her hands climbed higher, scraping Daphne's spaghetti straps off her shoulders just as Daphne's butt hit the desk chair. April paused only to shove the chair out of the way, then climbed onto the desk and spread her legs, pulling Daphne between them.

Daphne went, her hands sliding up April's thighs, thumbs digging into the creases where her hips met her legs. She wanted more, deeper, wanted these leather pants in a puddle on the floor, but she couldn't think straight, couldn't even ask as April finished her work with Daphne's dress, pulling the bodice down until her tits were free.

Daphne gasped as April pushed her breasts together, her mouth finding her nipples, tongue swirling, teeth grazing. Daphne tilted her head back, her mouth open. She wanted to beg April to touch her, to make her come, but before she could even start to form a sentence, April's right hand trailed up her thigh and under her dress, April reading her mind again.

Not that it was hard.

Daphne's thoughts were very obvious, her hips pushing against April's hands, nothing but desperate whimpering sounds rolling out of her throat.

April didn't make her wait long. She pressed her thumb against Daphne's cotton underwear, circling up and then back down, spreading the mess Daphne's arousal had already made.

"Fuck," Daphne said, the first word between them. The right word though. The *only* word.

April took her nipple in her mouth again, sucking and licking as her fingers pushed aside Daphne's underwear and slid through her wet pussy. Daphne could hear how wet she was, completely soaked, and April groaned against her tits as she worked Daphne's clit.

"Fuck," Daphne said again, widening her legs. "Yes. Please."

April still didn't say a word. Instead, she slipped a finger inside Daphne, and then two, and Daphne nearly levitated off the floor. She humped April's hand, desperate and needy, gripping her shoulders for leverage. April pushed her away a little, but just long enough to close her own legs, then pull one of Daphne's over her own hip so that Daphne was balancing on one foot.

The angle though.

Daphne yelled another expletive at the ceiling as April's fingers slid even deeper into her cunt, curling and pumping, fucking her so good, Daphne felt dizzy.

She'd felt dizzy every day since she'd met April Evans, it was true, and god, she loved it. Every spin and twist, and right now, all she wanted was to come on April's fingers.

April adjusted her wrist, her thumb pressing perfectly on Daphne's clit, and Daphne came so hard, her vision went dark for a second. She'd felt it building, but then it exploded, a shock. She gripped April's shoulders, falling forward as the one leg she stood on gave out. April's other hand was tight around her waist, holding her up. Daphne kept waiting for the feeling to stop, for this to end and for April to pull away, but April kept fucking her, her fingers going even deeper, thumb circling right under her clit, and Daphne came again with her face buried in April's neck, her lavender hair a tangled mess in her eyes.

April held her for a few seconds while she caught her breath, while she came down. Finally, April slipped her fingers free, and Daphne pushed back to look at her.

April grinned, then opened her mouth to say something, but Daphne wasn't ready for that.

Not yet.

She put two fingers to April's mouth.

April's eyes went wide, but she obeyed.

"Good girl," Daphne whispered, and April released her own desperate whimper from deep in her chest.

And god, the sound of it made Daphne feel absolutely feral. She'd come hard twice, but she felt just as needy as she had before April had even touched her, just as desperate to make April feel the same way.

Maybe even more.

She removed her fingers from April's lips and placed one hand between her breasts, pushing her back until she was leaning against the window, then unbuttoned her leather pants. She unzipped them, then made April lift up so she could get them over her butt and down her legs. She ripped them off her ankles, threw them into a corner of the room, then spread April's legs wide.

She groaned at the sight—lacy black underwear.

April leaned back on her elbows, smirking. Daphne lifted a brow. In about ten seconds, she was going to make April eat that smirk.

Daphne walked to her bed and grabbed a pillow, then came back and flopped it on the floor in front of the desk before kneeling, her hands on April's knees.

"Oh, fuck," April said.

Daphne didn't respond.

Not with words anyway.

She'd waited too long for this, dreamed about it, touched herself multiple times by this point, imagining the way April smelled, how she tasted. She wasn't about to waste time talking.

She spread April's legs wider, her hands slicking down her thighs as she pressed close. She nosed April's center, that lacy material scratching at her skin. Daphne hooked her arms under April's thighs, her palms flat against the top of her ass, pulling her as close as Daphne could possibly get her. She inhaled, breathing in April's arousal, then licked right up her center, a hard press of her tongue.

"Oh my god," April said, her head falling back.

Daphne could taste April through the lace, feel how wet she was, and it was the hottest thing Daphne had maybe ever experienced. She and Elena had shared a pretty vibrant sex life, and Daphne, even in her limited experience, loved eating pussy and knew she was good at it.

But this.

April Evans.

Well, that was it, wasn't it?

This wasn't Elena. This wasn't anyone except April.

Daphne moaned against her, and April plunged her hand into Daphne's hair, pulling just enough to make Daphne feel even more feral. She lapped at April's cunt, swirling her tongue and using her teeth to pluck at the lace for more friction.

"Please," April said, her hips pumping against Daphne's mouth. "Fuck, Daphne, please."

Daphne wanted to give her everything. She wanted to rip that lace right off, bury her face skin to skin, but she was going to make April come like this first. There was something incredibly hot about April begging and Daphne acquiescing in slow, tortuous steps.

So when April tried to pull her underwear to the side, Daphne grabbed her hand and held it palm down on the desk, her tongue working even harder over that lace.

"Oh, god," April said. "Daphne, fuck."

Daphne hummed and licked, using her lips and teeth too, pulling April so tight against her she could barely breathe, but god, what a fucking way to go.

"I'm gonna come," April said, hips at a wild pace now. "Oh, fuck, Daph—"

She went silent for a second, her mouth open as her body shuddered under Daphne's mouth. She tossed her head back and screamed. That was the only word for it. She screamed, Daphne's name and *fuck, fuck, fuck* mixing together in the most perfect cocktail. It made Daphne feel so wild, she didn't even wait for April to come down. Instead, she shoved aside that underwear, literally ripping the left side in the process, and put her mouth directly on April's gorgeous pussy.

"God, fuck, Daphne," April said, bucking against her, but after that, there were no intelligible words. She leaned back farther on the desk, nearly lying down now, one hand still buried in Daphne's hair, and rutted against Daphne's face.

Daphne slid her tongue inside, pumping in and out of her with her nose bumping April's clit until she came again. April's legs locked up, closing around Daphne's ears, her cries nothing but a raspy moan this time.

She shuddered a few more times as Daphne slowed her touch, kissing gently now, grazing her hands softly down April's thighs to her knees. April still jolted, giggling this time. She was fully lying down on the desk now, her head resting against the window at an angle that couldn't be comfortable, but when Daphne looked up from between her legs, she was smiling.

"What the fuck was that, Love?" she asked, still out of breath. Her cheeks were flushed, her hair a mess, the back of it sticking to the window as the rain pelted the glass.

Daphne laughed, then pressed a kiss to the inside of April's thigh, which also resulted in a giggle. Then she stood up, her hands braced on April's knees.

"That?" She leaned between April's legs and slid her fingertips down April's thighs so that her thumbs rested right on either side of her pussy. "That was just a preview."

April's mouth dropped open, and god, Daphne loved this. She

didn't know who she was right now, where this domme energy came from, but she never wanted it to end.

She smiled, her own cheeks flaming hot as well, but she didn't care. She wasn't embarrassed. She wasn't shy. She was excited. Empowered.

She was *happy*.

She pulled back, then tilted her head as she smiled at April. "Do you have any toys?"

Chapter Twenty-One

DAPHNE'S VOICE WENT straight to April's clit. She'd already come twice, but fuck, she was pretty sure she could come thirty times, and it wouldn't be enough. Daphne made her feel completely unhinged and desperate. She could admit it now, after weeks of fighting it, convincing herself that the two of them in any capacity were a bad idea—they probably still were, but April didn't care.

She'd known she was in trouble the second she'd seen what Daphne was wearing for the play party earlier that evening. It was a simple black dress, but it was *short*, and April couldn't stop thinking of getting underneath that hem. The thought had plagued her all the way to Concord, as they'd paid Stone and listened to their rundown about the house rules, and as they'd descended into the basement.

But then.

God, and *then*.

Sasha, the little deviant, had totally set them up, but April wasn't even bothered about that right now. Because the second Daphne had taken that feather in her hand, April leaning on that bench with the smile wiped right off her face, April was a goner.

Annihilated.

She'd do anything.

Say anything.

Be anyone.

April had always considered herself a top-leaning switch in the bedroom. She'd bottom for a hookup occasionally if that was what they wanted, but she'd always enjoyed being in charge more. Controlling the scene, calling the shots, making sure she got what she needed, particularly if her hookup was a cis man. She tried to stick to men who were queer in some way, as they tended to be more aware of what people with vaginas and clits actually required in bed, but generally, she found things went smoother if she directed the show.

Elena, naturally, had been top leaning when it came to sex, though most of their escapades in bed were pretty neutral. Hot and exciting, but neither one of them dominated or submitted fully. Honestly, Elena was a bit of a pillow princess, which April had always loved.

She still loved that quality in a partner, but right now . . .

This.

She wasn't sure what the hell was happening to her brain or her body. She'd never experienced this before, not only being completely at another person's mercy, but *wanting* it.

Craving it.

And now, after that devilry Daphne had just performed with her tongue, she'd gone and mentioned *toys*.

"Toys?" April asked, because it was the only response she could get out at the moment, with Daphne's fingers mere inches from her cunt as she massaged the skin of April's upper thigh.

"You're going to play coy?" Daphne asked.

April swallowed. "If that's what you want."

Daphne's brows lifted, then she leaned closer, her body pressing between April's legs, the cotton of her dress brushing against

April's still-sensitive center. Daphne stopped a breath away from April's mouth.

"I want you to answer my question," Daphne said.

A whisper. Her words were like a knife, but her tone was like that fucking feather from Stone's house. April shivered, then lifted her chin so her lower lip grazed Daphne's. "Yes, Ms. Love. I have toys."

"Show me."

Daphne backed up then, let April close her legs and get off the desk. April still had her underwear on—granted, it was a little misshapen and more than a bit damp. Still, she was grateful for the coverage as she walked to her closet and took out a tote bag from a romance bookstore in Brooklyn, illustrated couples of all colors and genders mooning at one another printed on the ivory fabric. She placed it on her bed, the cats popping their heads up at the disturbance. April pulled the bag open, taking each toy out one at a time.

She had quite a few.

In the three years since Elena, she'd explored more with toys when she was not only by herself, but with people she hooked up with as well. Soon, several dildos of varying sizes, four different clitoral stimulators, a few insertable vibrators, two harnesses, and a bottle of April's favorite lube were splayed on the bed.

"Oh my god," Daphne said, stepping closer to the collection.

"See something you like?" April asked.

Daphne just stared, her eyes wide and her mouth open as she took everything in, looking like a kid in a candy store.

Or rather, like a horny lesbian in a sex toy shop.

She picked up a few things—a palm-sized pink clit stimulator, a wand whose battery April hoped wasn't dead—turning them over in her hands as though they might break, then putting them down again just as gingerly. April let her explore, rather enjoying the discovery, as well as the anticipation as to what Daphne would pick.

April shivered again, goose bumps breaking out all over her body.

Finally, Daphne picked up a dark purple double dildo. It had one long insertable shaft, but on the other end, there was a ridge and a slightly shorter bulb that went inside the wearer, no harness required.

Daphne slid her fingers down the long cock, then flicked her eyes to April. "I like this one."

April's mouth watered. "I do too."

Daphne smiled, her eyes liquid and dark, all that green drowning in her pupils. She stepped closer, drifting the fingers of her free hand over April's cheek, circling to the back of her head. She pulled her in for a kiss, slow and languid, and April felt as though she was flying, melting, disintegrating.

"You're really good at that," April said against her mouth, and Daphne responded by kissing her deeper, her tongue soft and wet and perfect. She set the double dildo back on the bed, then lifted April's shirt over her head, making quick work of her black bra as well. She palmed April's tits, plucking her nipples between her thumb and forefinger. April moaned against her neck, her own hands playing with the hem of Daphne's dress.

"Can I?" she asked. She wanted Daphne fully naked, more than she wanted air, but she knew who was in charge here. "Please," she said, running her mouth over the skin just below Daphne's ear. "Please, Ms. Love."

"God, I love that," Daphne said, her breath ragged. Her hands were less focused on April's chest, sliding down her ribs, thumbs pressing into her bones.

"What?" April asked.

"Hearing you beg."

"I'll do anything you want," April said, nails scraping gently at her shoulders. "Please, anything, I just need you naked."

"Get me naked, then," Daphne said.

April didn't waste any time. She dragged Daphne's dress down her torso, grabbing her underwear on the way down and pulling until everything was pooled at Daphne's feet. Daphne stepped out of it, and for a second, April just looked—smooth skin, random freckles and a few moles, supple breasts and dark pink nipples already hard.

God, she was gorgeous.

"Take yours off too, then lie down on my bed," Daphne said.

April nearly tripped in her haste, and Daphne laughed, following her to the bed and pressing down on top of her, legs straddling April's hips, setting the double dildo and lube next to her.

April moaned—just the sight of Daphne above her was quite possibly enough to make her come—and slid her hands up Daphne's stomach to her tits.

"Fuck," April said.

Daphne closed her eyes, let April touch her as much as she wanted, soft moans coming out of her mouth, her hips undulating so that April could feel how wet she was.

How wet they both were.

"God, Daphne, please," she said, hands on her ass now.

Daphne stopped. "Please, who?"

April grinned. Fuck, she loved this so much. "Please, Ms. Love."

"Please what?"

"Please fuck me."

Daphne leaned close, their stomachs, their tits, everything lining up, pressing together, damp and hot. She rolled her hips. "You want me to fuck you?"

"God, Da— Ms. Love. Yes. Please."

April felt lightheaded again, her cunt drenched and throbbing. She was at nearly crisis levels.

"How badly?" Daphne asked, those hips working again.

"So bad. Please."

"Tell me."

"Ms. Love, please put your cock in me, I need it so bad."

April was practically whining now, nearly crying, nearly laughing, she couldn't even tell anymore. She just needed. Wanted. That was all she was. Just hips moving toward Daphne, legs widening. She'd never felt this wild for someone before—never felt this desperate for someone to own her inside and out. She felt as though she was falling, but it wasn't terrifying. Wasn't dangerous. Instead, it was the softest she'd felt in a long time.

She felt safe.

She felt seen and fucking *safe*, and she wasn't sure she'd ever felt that combination of emotions in bed before. It was strange, this cocktail, and she never wanted to feel anything else.

Daphne kissed her again, softly at first, which was exactly what April needed for a second while she caught her breath. But then, the kiss turned rough, hard and dirty, tongues and teeth bumping, moans into each other's mouths.

And that was exactly what April needed too.

Everything. Every way. Every feeling, touch, hard and soft and perfect. April felt drunk on it, almost couldn't focus long enough to kiss Daphne back. She managed though, Daphne's own sounds fevered and ready. April slid her hands up Daphne's thighs and farther, thumbs meeting right at her clit. She circled slowly and Daphne moaned into her mouth.

"Wait," Daphne said, sitting up and pushing April's hands away as she got off her legs. She picked up the double dildo and the lube, then squeezed a pea-sized amount onto each end of the toy. April released a soft groan just watching her slick the moisture down the shaft.

"Ms. Love," she said.

That was it. Just Daphne's preferred name, all she could manage right now. April spread her legs, hips rolling toward the ceiling in anticipation. Daphne set one foot on the mattress, positioning the shorter bulb at her own entrance. Her breath hitched as she slid it inside, then released on a moan.

"You look so good," April said.

"You like watching me?" Daphne asked. Her voice was almost shy, which just about sent April over the edge.

"God, yeah," April said, reaching out to touch her thigh. She needed contact, anything to get closer. "You're so fucking sexy."

Daphne's cheeks were pink as she closed her eyes, a tiny smile on her mouth as she moved the toy in and out of her pussy, her breathing ragged and perfect.

April had never seen anything so gorgeous.

"Ms. Love," she said quietly.

Daphne opened her eyes, all pupil, and looked at April. Then without a word, she moved between April's legs, positioning the longer cock at April's entrance.

"Yes," April said, grabbing on to Daphne's hips.

"Put your hands over your head," Daphne said.

April obeyed, her fingers curling into the pillow, gripping it tightly.

"Good girl," Daphne said, her voice nearly a whisper. Her eyes roamed over April's body, drifting her hand down April's cheek, then to her throat. Her fingers closed around her neck, just for a second, but fuck if April didn't release a filthy moan. Daphne smiled, but kept up her journey, trailing over April's collarbones to her sternum, to each breast and nipple before traveling down her stomach until she reached her pussy. She slid her thumb through April's wetness, making April gasp and beg.

Then she did it again and again, lighter, then harder, dipping inside before circling her clit, never the same touch twice, and soon April was thrashing on the bed, writhing and begging to come.

"Ms. Love, please, please, Ms. Love" was all she could get out, sweat beading on her forehead and between her breasts.

Daphne slid the tip of the dildo inside April, and April nearly cried with relief, but then Daphne stopped.

"Ms. Love," April said, her voice barely recognizable.

"You need to come?" Daphne asked, her own breath irregular, her lavender hair a tangled mess around her face.

"Please, please, yes," April said.

Daphne leaned closer, one hand on her cock and the other braced next to April's head. Their noses bumped, but still Daphne held back. She looked April right in the eye, then kissed her once, keeping her mouth against April's.

"Then come," she said, and pushed the cock all the way into April, slow and deep and hard. April released a stream of words, *fuck*s and *Ms. Love*s and *oh my god*s mixed in as she came immediately and came hard. She didn't stop coming either, orgasms crashing through her like the sea in a storm as Daphne continued to fuck her, pumping her hips and telling April she was a good girl.

Soon Daphne's voice grew raspy too, and she buried her face in April's neck as she shuddered, her cries warm against April's skin. Even though she hadn't been instructed to, April slid her hands to Daphne's waist. She needed to hold on right now. She was in a free fall, couldn't get her breath, her voice, nothing. There was only Daphne and moans and sweat as they both came, trembling against each other.

It felt like it lasted forever, hard and fast, and then slowing, bit by bit, their bodies connected and moving in tandem. Daphne was lying fully on top of April by the time they both stilled, her hair splayed over the pillow and half of April's face, each other's sweat slicking their skin, but April didn't care. She loved it, in fact.

Daphne didn't move either. She stayed cocooned against April's neck, her warm breath slowing and tickling April's skin. She was shaking, and April kept her arms around her, holding her tightly. In a few seconds, they were breathing together, inhaling and exhaling in an identical rhythm.

Daphne laughed into April's neck, then finally lifted herself enough so April could see her face. And fuck, she was so beautiful—hair a mess, face flushed, eyes glassy. April couldn't help but tuck Daphne's hair behind her ears, then whisper, "There's my good girl."

She hadn't meant to say it—or say it quite so tenderly, but she didn't regret it either. It felt right, felt true.

Daphne's eyes widened a bit, but she smiled so sweetly, April had to pull her down for a kiss. A perfect kiss. Slow and languid, still sexy as hell, Daphne's tongue sliding against hers like a dance.

Jesus, April was completely addled by this girl in her arms, the soft sounds Daphne made as April held her face and kissed her. They kissed for what felt like forever until Daphne laughed into her mouth.

"My arms are about to give out," she said, collapsing with her face near April's ear again. "I think I just used muscles I didn't even know I had."

"Best workout in the world," April said, trailing her fingers along Daphne's back, and then they stayed like that for a while too, the rain still falling, ripples of thunder in the distance.

"Storm's coming," Daphne said, her voice muffled.

April said nothing, just held Daphne tighter.

Eventually, they shifted so they could remove the double dildo—April tossed it on a pile of her dirty clothes to deal with later—and then settled again side by side and facing each other, hands tucked under their chins, close but not touching. They stared at each other, skin still flushed. April had so much to say but wasn't sure she knew the right words. Wasn't sure the feeling had even translated into a known language yet. She felt full to overflowing—overwhelmed, even—and had the sudden urge to disappear into the bathroom for an hour just to get her breath back.

As though reading her mind, Daphne hooked one arm around April's waist, pulling her tighter.

"I'm not going anywhere," April said.

"Good," Daphne whispered, and April's throat tightened. Just this feeling of being known—and by the unlikeliest person—it was a drug she never wanted to stop taking.

"I'm sorry," April said after a few minutes, scooting a little closer so she could feel the warmth of Daphne's breath. "About what happened on the dock at Ramona's."

Daphne inhaled, let it out slowly. "I panicked too."

"It felt like a lot of different things happening all at once," April said.

"Were you embarrassed?" Daphne asked.

"God, no," April said, her hand going to Daphne's face. "Well, maybe a little, but not about you. About me."

"What about you?"

April sighed. "That's just it. I don't know. It's like what you said on the dock. I deflect. All the time. I think I've made a life out of deflecting."

Daphne's eyes went soft, and she pulled April even closer. They were breathing each other's air now, and April could feel herself shaking a little.

"I'm weird, I know," she went on. "I'm strange and moody and maybe a little silly sometimes, and I don't know how much of that is me, or how much of it is me trying to *find* me, if that makes sense."

"It does," Daphne said, fingers ghosting through her hair.

"My tattoos, my hair, my rings, my wardrobe—don't get me wrong, I do like it all. These are my choices, and I don't regret them, but sometimes, I just don't . . . I'm not sure who April Evans really is. I don't think I've ever known."

"I think everyone feels that from time to time," Daphne said. "But when you suddenly become aware of that feeling . . ."

"Yeah," April said. "I think I'm lost. Like . . . I know that's a thing that people say in movies and books, but I think I actually am. I have no fucking idea what I'm doing or what I want."

Daphne cupped her face and kissed her forehead. April gripped her wrist, holding Daphne in place as she said the next part.

"That moment on the dock," she said. "I think you scared me."

Daphne froze, shifting so she could look at April. "I scared you?"

April nodded. "Because right then, I knew exactly what I wanted."

Daphne's mouth parted, her eyes searching April's. But then her expression fell. "And we don't make sense."

April's smile was small. "I don't know. Probably not, honestly. We're . . . There's . . ."

"Elena."

April closed her eyes for a second, nodded. "And the Devon. And you're a lot younger than me."

"Eight years."

"That's a lot on this side of thirty."

"You're only saying that because you're on that side of thirty," Daphne said, propping herself up on her elbow. "From my perspective, those years are a blip. Elena was eleven years older than me."

"Yes, she was," April said, propping herself up as well so they were eye level. "And she treated you like shit and threw you away like an idiot."

Daphne's eyes went wide, and she closed her teeth over her bottom lip.

"Fuck," April said, hooking her hand behind Daphne's neck

and pulling until their foreheads met. "I didn't mean that to sound so harsh."

Daphne shook her head. "You're right."

"I added the whole *like an idiot* part because she's a fucking idiot."

"I know," Daphne said. "And I know she hurt you too. I know—"

"I'm going to deflect again here, but only because I want to make sure you hear me." April kept her hand in place, shifting so they could see each other clearly. "My point is that *I* don't want to be an idiot here. I don't want to hurt you. I don't want this to be some May-December romance that goes bad because I have no idea who I am."

"It's eight years, not eighteen," Daphne said. "Closer to seven, even. That's more May . . . July."

April cracked a smile. "Okay. I'll give you that one. But, Daphne—"

"I don't want to stop," Daphne said. She sat up all the way, naked and gorgeous, tangled in the sheet and crossing her legs before taking a deep breath. "I don't know what you're about to say, or what excuse you're about to make about how *this was fun, but*. I don't want the *but*."

"What do you want, then?" April asked. Her breath was shallow, heart beating quick and soft under her ribs, as though preparing for some unknown encounter.

"I want *this*," Daphne said, waving her hand between them. "And no, I don't know what this even is. Maybe it's just a fling. Maybe it's just mind-blowing sex and I don't want to give it up."

"Mind-blowing, huh?" April said, grinning.

"Maybe it's a big *fuck you* to Elena Watson," Daphne said, barreling onward.

"That would be satisfying, if a bit problematic," April said.

"Or maybe it's true love," Daphne said, and April had no quippy comeback for that one. "But that's the point. I don't know, and I want to find out. I've spent the last three years in a relationship where I thought I was safe, and look where that got me."

April swallowed hard. She'd felt safe with Elena too. Felt safe with hookups. Felt safe with coming home to Clover Lake, with staying in Clover Lake. And just as Daphne said, where had all of that gotten her? She wasn't sure if that safety was real. Those choices were easy. Logical, even. The illusion of safety.

"I want to *live* what I'm feeling," Daphne went on. "I want to be messy and stupid if that makes me happy right now, and I want that for you too. I choose me. And I want you to choose you. Whatever that means right now, in this very moment."

"Jesus, Sasha and I have created a monster," April said.

Daphne huffed a single laugh, but her eyebrows were lifted, her expression all seriousness as she waited for April to respond in kind.

And April knew she *would* wait. She wouldn't let April utter some pithy declarative sentence and move on, her brain creating some narrative that let her keep deflecting ad nauseam.

No.

Daphne would wait and wait and wait until April responded with her fucking *heart*. And April's heart already knew what it wanted. It wasn't easy. Wasn't logical at all. But it was the safest April had felt in a long time. A real, bone-deep kind of security she knew only came from choosing herself.

Choosing her own strange heart.

"Okay," she said.

"Okay?" Daphne asked, but a smile started to curve her mouth.

"You and me, Love," April said, her heart beating rapidly behind her ribs. "Whatever that means."

Daphne grinned, then grabbed April's arms and hauled her on

top of her, April's naked hips straddling her thighs. Daphne trailed her fingers over April's shoulders, across her collarbones to her neck until she was cradling April's face.

"That's *Ms.* Love," Daphne said, then pulled her down for a kiss that soon turned heated again.

And April let it.

She let herself fall, let herself want, let herself feel. And two hours later, when she and Daphne lay tangled together in the sheets, sated and sleepy, she never even considered sneaking away to her own bed.

She was safe and happy right where she was.

"By the way," April said, her eyelids growing heavier by the second, "my favorite color isn't actually black."

"No?" Daphne replied, her voice muzzy. She pressed her nose to April's neck. "What is it, then?"

"It's this," April said, tugging on the ends of Daphne's lavender hair.

She felt Daphne smile against her skin, her breath warm and her arms tightening around April's waist as they both drifted off to sleep.

Chapter Twenty-Two

THE NEXT SEVERAL weeks for Daphne passed in a blur of painting, teaching, and April Evans.

When they weren't working on their individual pieces for the Devon, she and April had spent every other moment together. They had slow and sleepy sex almost every morning, followed by wild and mind-altering sex nearly every night, and everything in between. April and Sasha had taken Daphne cliff diving (she'd screamed the entire way down), to a drag show in Concord (and she now needed to watch every single season of *RuPaul's Drag Race*), and they'd watched a dozen raunchy nineties movies Daphne had never been allowed to see growing up, like *Dazed and Confused*, *Empire Records*, and *Don't Tell Mom the Babysitter's Dead*.

They'd also talked late into the night.

Lying naked in one of their beds, sheets tangled around their waists, facing each other with their foreheads nearly touching. It was quiet and soft and intimate, and each night Daphne fell asleep absolutely positive she'd wake up in the morning to find it had all been a dream. But every day, she woke up with April by her side, her sleepy sounds as she stretched and yawned, her gorgeous, inked body under Daphne's fingertips.

Real.

And getting realer by the second.

Now, their Devon deadline was two days away—Nicola had requested a showing on the very morning of Ramona and Dylan's wedding, and with that showing came a decision, and with that decision came . . .

What?

Daphne sat on a stool in the art studio in the early evening of her twenty-sixth birthday, alone, blinking into space as she pictured it.

Pictured herself.

A whole life spreading out in London. She saw herself on the rain-soaked streets, soft clouds above. She could see herself rushing to a gallery opening, working on new pieces in some loft she rented, going to parties where Nicola treated her like *someone*, introducing her to other artists and critics.

It was all right there, a life she wanted. A life she could see. But then she thought of April, tried to see *where* and *how* and *when* beyond Nicola's decision in two days, and—

Her throat went thick, her mind a muddled wash of color, like looking at a painting that had been left in the rain.

This happened every time she tried to envision what came next with April, and she always ended up pushing it into a dusty corner of her brain, leaving a trail of question marks all the way there. So she didn't think too hard about it all. She didn't daydream, didn't dread. At least, she tried not to, but when she spent four hours a day painting her past—her own evolution—onto canvas, it was hard not to feel every emotion all at once.

She had three full paintings, bringing her to the point in her story when she left home. The first, of course, was her wildflower field piece. After this, she'd painted her vision for the chapel on her old church's property. The colors for this one were more muted, the sanctuary all gray-brown wooden pews and dried leaves on the dusty floor. The walls were whitewashed and dingy, the pulpit a rough rectangle with no embellishments and a simple wooden cross hanging on the wall above.

Next to the pulpit, Daphne stood as a young teenager, maybe fourteen or fifteen years old. She had on the same white dress she did in the wildflower painting, except this one was shorter on her growing legs and arms. Her hair was longer too, the curls more defined from puberty, and small breasts swelled underneath the cotton.

Her face was still a blur of paint.

But in this piece, the viewer could make out a few features, though undefined—the slightest green of her eyes, a shadow where her nostrils might be, a slash of pink below that.

The third piece was set at the small Crestwater bus station. The girl in this painting was eighteen, still in that white dress now far too small for her, her hair long and wild. She stood next to a green bench with a rugged brown suitcase in her hand, the ticket window just behind her. The sky was stormy, angry, and billowing with clouds. Rain poured down on the scene in sharp diagonal slashes and appeared to be pulling at the girl's blurry features, tugging them away.

Or rather, tugging *something* away to reveal what was underneath.

The viewer still couldn't see her face clearly, but Daphne could see herself emerging, a moth from a cocoon. The next piece, already in progress, was set in Boston—in Elena's art gallery, in fact—but she had no idea what to do for the fifth and final piece. Biographically, she could paint a thousand pieces, a thousand moments of becoming and unbecoming. The few she'd chosen felt right, but the conclusion . . .

She still wasn't sure what that looked like.

She still wasn't sure what *she* looked like.

So she sat on a stool in the art studio staring at her fourth painting and thinking about her last birthday.

Her birthdays had always been quiet affairs. Even when she lived with her family, her parents hadn't believed in making a big deal about them—too self-indulgent, her father had said. They'd celebrated stoically, with a simple cake and exactly one gift that was usually something like highlighters for studying or a new cover for her Bible, and absolutely zero parties.

Elena had known this.

So when Daphne had turned twenty-five, Elena had thrown her a party, filling their apartment with catered food and music and people who wore fancy cocktail dresses and sipped on sparkling glasses of Veuve Clicquot. Granted, they were mostly Elena's friends and colleagues, but Daphne hadn't cared, had barely noticed, reveling in the idea that someone had planned an elegant soiree for her.

Looking back, it wasn't Daphne's kind of party at all, but it was better than any other birthday she'd ever had. Today, her phone hadn't made a sound—she'd blocked the only person who might call or text—and no one else at Cloverwild even knew it was her birthday. It felt strange to tell them, to tell April, even. The mentality of making herself small—third after God and others—was a hell of a drug, one she knew she was still detoxing from, no matter how brave and bold she felt when kissing April Evans.

Her chest hitched, her eyes stinging as the light outside started diminishing, the sun sinking into the lake. She took out her phone and opened her call app, put in a Boston number she knew by heart. Didn't matter if she'd blocked it or not. She stared at the numbers, her thumb shaking over the green call button.

"Hey, there you are."

Daphne straightened on her stool at April's voice, wiped her eyes in case a rogue tear had escaped, and stuffed her phone into her pocket. She knew her face was probably blotchy anyway.

"Here I am," she said as April reached her side, cupping a cool hand on the back of Daphne's neck.

"You okay?" April asked.

Daphne nodded. They hadn't seen each other very much today. They'd woken up together, but Daphne had quickly gotten up and showered, claiming she needed to run some errands in town before their one o'clock class. Really, she'd taken the Cloverwild shuttle to Mirror Cove and watched the water for a while, feeling sorry for herself as the day of her birth ticked across the sky. After that, they'd had class. When it was over, Daphne had worked with a guest who was trying to perfect a watercolor portrait for her sister's birthday. They'd worked until April had eventually said goodbye to go work on her own project.

Daphne had spent the rest of the afternoon alone in the studio, staring at her latest painting of a girl in a too-small white dress with undefined features playing at being a woman in a Boston art gallery, about to meet the only person who had ever really loved her.

Except Daphne wasn't sure if Elena had ever loved anyone. April, Daphne herself, any other girlfriend she'd ever had. But it had felt like love, and something deep inside Daphne missed it so much.

Now, April looked at Daphne's fourth painting, head tilted. She wore black jeans and a teal racerback tank top, her favorite style. It was Daphne's favorite too—she loved the way April's tattooed shoulders looked in them, strong and a little butch.

"That's going to be gorgeous," April said.

"You think so?" Daphne asked, looking up at her. This was the first piece after the wildflower painting that April had seen.

April smiled, her thumb caressing the skin at the base of Daphne's neck. "I know so."

Daphne smiled too, then reached out and pulled April closer by her hips, resting her forehead against April's stomach.

"Hey," April said, her arms soft as she cradled Daphne's head. "I've barely seen you all day."

Daphne didn't move, just breathed April in. "I know. I'm sorry."

"Don't be sorry," April said. "Have you eaten?"

Daphne lifted her head. "Some toast this morning."

April tsked. "Well, that won't do, will it?"

Daphne shrugged.

April slid her hands to Daphne's face, thumbs swiping at her cheekbones. "Can you take a break? Come somewhere with me?"

Daphne lifted her brows. "Right now?"

April smiled. "Right now."

"I'll go anywhere with you, April Evans," Daphne said, and realized with a flutter in her belly that it was true.

True and terrifying.

She glanced at the woman in her fourth painting again, so lost and wandering, and she didn't even know it.

She didn't know anything.

And now, over three years later, Daphne wasn't sure what exactly had changed. She still felt small, desperate, and alone, and she was so, so tired of feeling like that. She wanted to be strong. Wanted to be *herself,* happy with her own company, brave enough to shout about her own damn birthday.

Still, she slipped her hand into April's, reveling in the warmth of her body next to hers, and followed her outside into the lavender twilight.

~

THEY ENDED UP driving into town, then walking down Lake Street hand in hand. The light was soft, the sun still hanging low in the sky, and the fresh air was already helping Daphne's mood. Suddenly, she was starving.

"I want a cheeseburger," she said. "And some fries. Oh, and some pie."

"Oh, yeah?" April said, slowing down as they approached Clover Moon Café. "Your timing couldn't be better."

She opened the door, ushering Daphne inside. The space smelled amazing—sugar and fried food and coffee all coalescing together—and Daphne's mouth watered. She was looking around the busy dining room for an open seat when she spotted Sasha at a booth in the back corner.

Along with Ramona and Dylan.

"Oh, she's here," Sasha said to the others.

Daphne frowned. "What is—"

"Happy birthday!" the group called in unison, smiling and waving.

Daphne blinked, those two words cresting over her slowly, like a phrase in a foreign language. As one, the group put on sparkly purple birthday hats and blew on those paper blowers, the honking sound echoing through the restaurant.

April squeezed her hand. "Happy birthday, Daphne."

She turned to look at April, mouth agape. "How did you . . ."

"Well, I knew you were a Cancer," April said, grinning. "And the night we dyed your hair, you confirmed it. July twenty-ninth."

"And you remembered that?" Daphne asked.

April tilted her head. "You're hard to forget, Love."

Daphne shook her head, then pulled April in for a kiss, prompting a loud whooping from a few random patrons in the dining room.

"Also," April said against her mouth. "You're an Aries rising."

Daphne blinked, laughing. "How could you possibly know that?"

April's smile dipped a little into something softer. "Because despite everything you fear about yourself, you're one badass bitch, Daphne Love."

Daphne's smile fell away too. "What?"

"Aries are bold and brave. I know you don't always feel like that, but the face you put out into the world, it's all fire and strength. Your paintings, your family, the way you grew up, the way you chose the life you wanted, even when you were only eighteen, even with everything that followed. It just makes sense."

Daphne stared at her, something deep inside aching, but not unpleasantly. The feeling was more akin to awe, even comfort at being seen like this, all her masks toppling to the ground.

April kissed her one more time before pulling her toward the group. Daphne swallowed down her swell of emotion, then caught Ramona's expression, a look that could only be described as concern on her face as she glanced between Daphne and April. Daphne didn't have time to think on it too much as Sasha pulled her into the booth next to her, April sliding in on the other side next to Ramona.

A whole honey whiskey pie sat in the center of the table, a single candle lit in the middle. April quickly called for attention, then led them all in a horrible rendition of the birthday song. Daphne laughed as she blew out the tiny flame, a thousand wishes flitting through her mind.

The Devon.

April.

A birthday just like this.

She had to hold back a few happy tears as everyone clapped, and then Owen, the owner of Clover Moon himself, came and took their food and drink order. The group fell into their own discussions, centered mostly around Dylan and Ramona's Cloverwild wedding, which was only two days away. Daphne knew April was helping, of course, but Olive was Ramona's maid of honor, and even right now, April's expression looked a bit glassy, a bit detached.

Daphne stretched her foot under the table, tapping April's ankle. April glanced across the table at her, then winked, and Daphne nearly melted into a puddle right there.

April cleared her throat, then started making a case for why she should be able to offer flash tattoos at the wedding.

"I'm still waiting to tattoo your ass, Dylan Monroe, as promised," April was saying.

"As promised?" Dylan said. "When was that promised?"

"It was implied when you walked into my shop for the first time," April said.

"Two years ago?"

"There's no statute of limitations on art."

Ramona laughed, and April smirked and folded her arms. She had that glint in her eye Daphne had quickly become obsessed with, mischievous and sexy and sassy all at once.

Owen set down a plate of golden fries, and Daphne stuffed a few into her mouth, grinning around the food as she hooked her feet around April's under the table. And in that one moment, she was happier than she'd ever been in her entire life.

Chapter Twenty-Three

APRIL LOVED WATCHING Daphne.

Her cheeks were a little flushed, her green eyes still bright with excitement and surprise. April hated that Daphne had been alone most of the day, but she was glad she was able to give her this tiny get-together, that April had planned something that made her smile this much. Her face was like a sunrise, and she—

"You're drooling," Sasha said, kicking her foot under the table.

"I am not," April said, clearing her throat and forcing the admittedly dopey smile off her face. Daphne was engrossed in a story Dylan was telling about her days on *Spellbound*, a show Daphne had watched obsessively in college, apparently.

Sasha lifted her brow in that knowing way she had. "Please. You're writing poetry in your head about her smile or her eyes or some shit."

April smiled without her teeth. She'd definitely keep just how true Sasha's assessment was to herself. "Or some shit? You're such a romantic."

"Speaking of romance," Sasha said, dragging a fry through some ranch and popping it in her mouth. "What are you going to do after Nicola pulls the trigger?"

"By all means, let's not dance around the issue," April said.

"Not my style," Sasha said.

"Oh, I've noticed," April said.

"Hey," Sasha said, presenting her hands, "I know what I'm doing next month."

"Ah yes, Airstreaming through the canyons."

"I already told you, Gertie is too feeble for an Airstream. She's in her golden years."

April blinked at her. "You're extremely weird."

"Takes one to know one."

"Fair enough," April said, laughing, but something deep in her chest fluttered. She looked around the café now, felt the warmth of Ramona's arm against hers as she joined in Dylan and Daphne's conversation, everything so familiar, but also strange somehow. Suddenly, everything in this setting looked odd, out of place, and she felt out of place inside of it.

"Where are you going again?" she asked Sasha.

Sasha shrugged. "West. Arizona, New Mexico, maybe Colorado. Trying to hit all fifty states. I'm somewhere in the thirties."

"That sounds incredible," April said, fiddling with the straw in her shake.

"Why, you interested?" Sasha asked.

"Me?" April asked, brows lifting. "I—"

But she caught sight of Daphne again then, laughing at something Dylan had said, all the uncertainty between them swelling in April's heart like a river in the rain.

"Here we go again," Sasha said, rolling her eyes. "You two are gross."

"You two who?" April asked, sipping her shake just for something else to focus on.

"Oh, please," Sasha said. "Ramona, back me up."

April stiffened a little as the conversation between the others halted abruptly.

"Back you up?" Ramona asked.

"Daphne and April," Sasha said. "Smiling like fools at each other all the time."

Ramona glanced at April, who kept her eyes on Sasha's clueless rat-fink face.

"I did notice something like that," Ramona said coolly.

"So what if we are?" April said quietly, calmly. Her heart was pounding though. She inhaled slowly. She hadn't told Ramona about anything that had happened in the last month after the engagement dinner. At least, not the specifics. She'd only seen Ramona with Dylan since that night, and they'd all been busy with wedding preparations. The only texts they'd exchanged had been wedding related as well, like how Ramona wanted the wedding party in blush-pink suits or dresses of their choice, while Dylan would don an ivory suit and Ramona would wear a gauzy ivory-and-floral dress she'd designed herself.

They also texted about how Blair Emmanuel, Dylan's best mate, was coming into town a few days before the wedding and renting the huge lake house where she and Dylan had filmed several scenes for their movie two years ago, *As If You Didn't Know*, for all their Hollywood friends to stay in, and no, Blair didn't need April's help planning the wedding shower, she and Olive had it covered, but thanks for asking. And there had been some communication about flowers (boho-inspired pale pink and ivory poppies, anemones, roses, and eucalyptus), the music (a queer band called Beach Glass that Dylan loved playing dreamy versions of queer pop songs), and how Dylan had decided to hire private security to deal with any paparazzi for the ceremony and reception, which would take place under a glowing silk tent in Ramona and Dylan's expansive backyard on the lake.

All of which resulted in April's staid responses of *Sounds lovely* and *I love a good violin*, because all of the information was simply relayed to April like a daily update feed.

There were no questions. No pleas for help. No stressful freak-outs on Ramona's part, no emotional venting. There weren't even any exclamations of happiness here and there. Other than an occasional *That will be so pretty*, April wasn't sure how to respond to any of it, particularly since her first instinct was *Blush pink, really?* She and Ramona still hadn't talked—really *talked*—since news of the engagement broke weeks ago. April knew they needed to, but didn't want to do anything to ruin this time for Ramona.

At least, that was what she told herself.

She was being selfless.

Swallowing any hurt or left-out feelings—and the fact that she *hated* wearing pink, how Ramona knew she only liked pink in her hair or in her favorite cocktail—for the sake of her best friend's happy day.

But deep down, she knew it was more than that, more sinister, even. She just didn't know how to address it, or even how to admit it to herself.

So she said nothing.

Kept it all inside, kept it to herself, including how she was having incredible sex with her ex's ex.

Now, Daphne laughed nervously, her cheeks rosy as she got up from the table. "I'm going to run to the restroom."

April nodded, then squeezed her outstretched hand.

"Okay, what exactly is going on between you two?" Ramona asked as soon as Daphne was out of sight.

Sasha tilted her head, frowning at April before mouthing, "Sorry."

April sighed and waved a hand.

"I mean," Ramona went on, "of course, I noticed when you came inside that the two of you . . . well . . . you—"

"Kissed," Dylan said bluntly.

"Yes," April said, "we kissed. We've *been* kissing."

"For how long?" Ramona asked, her brows dipping low.

April blew out a breath. "Um, the first time was the night you got into town? But it was a fluke."

"A fluke."

April shrugged. "Sort of like a dare on the solstice?" She told Ramona about Daphne's wildling escapades, and how Sasha and April had been helping her out.

"And you've kissed since then?" Ramona asked.

April opened her mouth. Closed it. When she'd held back all the details of her and Daphne's—Fling? Dalliance?—whatever they were doing, she hadn't thought about how awkward it would be when she eventually did tell Ramona. She'd never done this before, kept something from Ramona that felt this big, this affecting. Hell, one time a few years ago, she called Ramona from Leigh Reynolds's bed while Leigh showered, simply because she had to tell her best friend immediately about how Leigh had made her come four times in half an hour.

But the best friends sitting at this booth right now weren't the same April and Ramona of two years ago.

"Yeah." April rubbed her forehead. "We've kissed since then."

Ramona's frown deepened.

"And we've had sex," April said, fast and low.

"A lot," Sasha said under her breath. April kicked her under the table.

"You've . . . you what?" Ramona spluttered.

"They've had *sex*," Dylan whispered loudly, leaning close to Ramona's ear.

"Yes, I heard her," Ramona said, splaying her hands on the table. "I just don't . . . I'm not sure . . ."

April braced herself, waiting for Ramona to express hurt over this secret. She'd be justified in feeling that way—April would've felt the same. She *had* felt the same. April almost welcomed Ramona's reaction, because maybe this would open the door to talking about other things April didn't know how to bring up, all the reasons why, what the hell had happened to the April and Ramona they both knew and needed.

And how they were going to fix it.

But when Ramona finally got out a coherent sentence, she didn't express hurt. She didn't even express humor or shock. Instead, she winced and said, "I just don't know if it's a good idea."

She said the words softly. Gently. Lovingly. But they still landed heavily, a sudden downpour when it had been clear and sunny all day long.

"You . . . wait, you *what*?" April asked.

"Oh, boy," Dylan said, sipping on her water and looking straight ahead.

Ramona sighed. "Apes. Come on."

"Come *on*?"

Sasha's booted feet sandwiched April's under the table, the strangest hug she'd ever gotten, but she welcomed the pressure as her heart crawled up her throat.

"You know I'm right," Ramona said.

"You're *right*?"

Apparently, all April could do was repeat everything Ramona was saying right now, but for the life of her, she couldn't find a different reaction.

"I'm just worried," Ramona said, then quieted her voice even more. "She's *Daphne Love*. The woman whose Instagram you pored over for months when Elena left. The person you claimed ruined your life."

"That was heartbreak talking," April snapped. "Daphne had nothing to do with it."

"I know," Ramona said calmly. "But she's still that symbol in your mind. And what about the Devon? Also, she's *young*. Really young, and I just worry that you're not—"

"Stop," April said. Her voice was low and sharp, a knife slicing through Ramona's warnings.

No, her *insults*.

"Just stop," April said again.

Ramona closed her mouth, a pained expression on her face. And April knew she shouldn't say it. Knew she should just leave it alone, deal with this later, that this was Daphne's birthday and no place to air months—maybe even years—of friendship issues.

But April was never very good at *should*.

"You don't know anything about me," she said quietly, her eyes locked on Ramona's.

And that was all she needed to say.

Ramona's entire demeanor changed. She froze, then sort of deflated, her shoulders dropping, her throat working in a hard swallow.

"April," Dylan said, a questioning plea in her tone.

"It's okay," Ramona said, taking Dylan's hand and squeezing until her knuckles went white. She looked away, gripped her water glass with her free hand.

April felt a tinge of guilt, but there was no regret—what she'd said was true, at least right now at this point in their lives, and she'd needed to say it, needed to finally say *something*. Daphne slid back into the booth then, her hand on April's leg. Everyone was silent, though, and she must've picked up on the awkwardness, because she lifted her brows at April, mouthed, "Are you okay?"

April winked at her in response, even though she wasn't sure if she was okay or not. She felt numb, relieved, and sad all at once. One thing she did know, she wasn't about to let her own issues ruin this day for Daphne. They'd both had a shit year, and at least one of them was going to have a great fucking birthday.

Owen came back to check on them then, a welcome distraction, and they all ordered another round of fries and fresh shakes. After he left, April lobbed a question about Marlene Dietrich at Dylan to get the focus off herself and Ramona. Soon they were talking about bisexuals in Germany in the 1920s, and April had tangled her fingers with Daphne's under the table.

Ramona was mostly quiet, but April forced herself to focus on everyone else.

To focus on herself.

And after a few minutes and several bites of the best burger in New England, she didn't have to try.

She just did it.

Chapter Twenty-Four

AN HOUR LATER, April and Daphne were back on the sidewalk, meandering slowly through downtown. The night was warm, the air sugar scented and summery, a loamy breeze coming off the lake.

"Thank you for tonight," Daphne said, her arm looped through April's as they walked. "I didn't think anyone knew it was my birthday. And I was feeling . . ." She shook her head. "Anyway. I needed that. So thank you."

"You're very welcome," April said.

Daphne pulled April to a stop, swinging her around to face her and taking both of her hands. "Are *you* okay? Things looked a little tense with you and Ramona in the café."

April shrugged. "They were. It'll be okay though."

"You can talk to me," Daphne said. "About Ramona. The wedding. Anything." And suddenly Daphne was desperate for exactly that. She wanted to know April's thoughts, her fears, her sadness—she wanted to know everything.

April curled their hands together and held them against her chest, then kissed the top of Daphne's knuckles. "You're sweet. But tonight is not about me."

"But it can be."

"But it won't be," April said, smiling. "Because we're not done yet." She kissed Daphne's fingers one more time, then pulled her along the sidewalk.

"What do you mean?" Daphne asked.

April just laughed and kept walking until she stopped outside a darkened storefront. She took out a ring of keys from her bag, then selected one before sliding it into a turquoise-colored door.

"April, wait, what—"

But Daphne cut herself off when she saw the lettering in the window—WONDERLUST INK. "Oh my god. This is . . ."

"My failure of a shop, yes," April said, pushing the door open.

"I was going to say *yours*," Daphne said, nudging April's shoulder.

"I said it was *my* failure," April said, laughing as they walked inside the dark space. She clicked on a switch, and soft golden light spilled from the vintage-style fixtures set into the tin ceiling tiles.

Daphne gasped as the space came into focus. She couldn't help it. Art covered nearly every inch of the teal walls, a collection it had to have taken April years to amass, everything from images of Dolly Parton to Moira Rose from *Schitt's Creek* in her crow costume to landscapes done in funky colors. She had every queer identity flag represented, but painted in unique ways, like a humpback whale done in pansexual colors and the hues of the lesbian flag coloring an illustration of a Subaru Outback. Daphne guessed she'd done a lot of the art herself, and there were plenty of gothic touches, barren winter trees, old wells captured in black-and-white, as well as a few creepy nineteenth-century photographs of unsmiling and miserable-looking people. The space was moody and eclectic and strange.

It was perfect.

It was *April*.

"This is gorgeous," Daphne breathed.

April stuck her hands in her pockets, looking around as though with new eyes. "I guess it is."

"You guess?" Daphne asked, fingers trailing over a neon portrait of Elphaba from *Wicked*, the words *I don't cause commotions, I am one* swirling around her pointed black hat in elegant calligraphy. "It's magic."

April nodded, her eyes a little sad as she continued to survey the room. Finally, she picked up her bag and took out an iPad cocooned in a hunter-green case.

"I actually brought you here for a reason," she said, tucking the device under her arm. She gestured toward one of two client chairs, a pale pink pleather that had seen better days. Still, the station was clean, and there was plenty more art on the walls to capture Daphne's interest.

She sat down, still gazing around like a kid in a candy shop, when April sat on the rolling stool next to the chair and flipped open her iPad. Daphne's heart froze—she wanted to see April's Devon project so badly, but she knew that was hidden within the pages of a sketchbook.

April tapped around, then handed the iPad to Daphne. She took it, the case velvety under her paint-stained fingers. As she stared down at the screen, it took her a few seconds to realize what she was looking at.

And then, all at once, she knew exactly what it was.

"April," she said. "This is . . ." But she trailed off, taking in the colorful image on the screen. In the center, there was an old-fashioned lantern. It was shaded beautifully, grays and steel blues, and the top was slightly curled decoratively, the handle arching over the back.

And inside, a flame.

It was small but bright, all golds and pinks, glimmering on the tiny wick.

The real beauty of the piece surrounded the lanterns—wildflowers. Similar in color and style to the ones in Daphne's first painting, full blooming poppies and marigolds in apricot and coral and pumpkin, shy buds and green stems and leaves curling around them. And to the side, a single purple coneflower.

Daphne had never seen anything so perfect. It was simple and beautiful and—

"It's yours," April said.

"My tattoo," Daphne said, eyes still on the screen.

"You asked me to design one for you," April said. "So I did."

"You really did," Daphne said, glancing up at her. Her eyes felt damp.

April rolled the stool closer, rested her arms on Daphne's thighs. "I meant for this to make you smile."

Daphne laughed and wiped her eyes. "It does. It's perfect. I love it so much."

She stared at April, their eyes locked, and felt the sudden urge to finish that last sentence differently, insert a different pronoun after a very important word, but that was rash.

That was just emotions and art talking.

Wasn't it?

"Obviously, you don't have to *get* it," April said, tapping the screen. "But I wanted you to see it here just in case. And I wanted to show you Wonderlust."

"Oh," Daphne said, sitting up straighter. "You mean . . ." She waved her hand at the nearby counter and cabinets, complete with a sink and, she assumed, tattoo supplies.

"Whatever you want," April said, hands sliding up Daphne's thighs and squeezing reassuringly. "No pressure. A tattoo is a big deal, and I can make any changes to the drawing you want. Plus, this one will take a few hours, and we don't have to—"

"Yes," Daphne said firmly.

April's brows lifted. "Yes?"

"Yes. I want it now. Just like this," Daphne said, handing the iPad back to April. She'd honestly never been so sure of anything. Not leaving home, not art school. Not even Elena. But right now, this tattoo—this piece of art that April had created just for her—she knew beyond a doubt she wanted it inked onto her skin.

She kicked her feet up onto the chair, then lay back and closed her eyes, ready.

April laughed. "God, you're adorable."

Daphne flipped her eyes open, then reached out and grabbed the scooped neck of April's tank top, pulling her in for a kiss. She meant it to be quick, but once they'd started, she didn't want to stop.

Finally, she pulled back a little, April's mouth still close. "Ink me," she said.

April laughed again. "Yes, Ms. Love, but there are a few details to work out."

"Like what?"

"Like where you want it."

Daphne grinned. "Oh, that." She looked at the piece again on April's iPad. It was so lovely—so *her,* plucking at something deep inside her chest—she didn't want to hide it away. She wanted it visible.

Wanted to show the world.

Wild and soft.

A spark of light in the middle of chaos.

"Right here," she said, then tapped her right upper arm.

"You're sure?" April asked, sliding one hand to where Daphne had indicated. "This soft baby skin?"

Daphne laughed. "Mar the hell out of it."

"Yes, ma'am," April said softly, then kissed her one more time before she went to work.

It took some time to get everything set. April had to size the image for Daphne's arm, then print an outline that would transfer to Daphne's skin like a stencil. Soon, though, everything was ready, including a tattoo gun with new ink April said she'd just gotten from her distributor for the occasion.

"You bought new ink for me?" Daphne asked. She was sitting up on the chair, her legs out in front of her like she was at the dentist, her right arm propped on a paper-covered armrest stand next to her.

"Maybe," April said, grinning as she set the ink on her worktable, black latex gloves on her hands. She spread a bit of Vaseline over Daphne's arm. "You ready?"

Daphne swallowed. "Does it hurt?"

"Nah, feels like a massage."

"Really?"

"No, not really."

Daphne laughed but then stuck out her tongue.

"I'll be right here the whole time," April said, winking.

"I certainly hope so."

"Ready?" April asked again.

Daphne nodded, then added a "Yes" because a verbal confirmation seemed important when one was about to have a needle draw a design permanently into one's skin.

"Here we go," April said, and the tattoo gun started buzzing.

The needle came closer and closer and soon it was pressing into Daphne's skin, a dull sting. It felt like a needle scratching at a sunburn, but Daphne found she could handle it.

She sat back and tried to relax. April had turned on some chill music, and they talked off and on as April worked. Daphne was fascinated watching her draw, her hand steady and sure, the indelible art taking shape.

It took a while.

A few hours, in fact, during which Daphne alternated between being completely fine and even euphoric to wanting to punch April in the face, particularly during the shading.

"Pain endorphins," April said three hours in. "They come and go."

"Does this propensity toward violence also come and go?" Daphne asked, her teeth gritted as April colored in a stem near the inside of her elbow.

"Let's hope so," April said.

"You're lucky you're hot," Daphne said, and April laughed.

And actually, the entire process *was* kind of hot.

Intimate.

Daphne couldn't stop staring at April—the art she was creating, yes, but also her face as she did it, her warm breath on Daphne's arm, face pressed close.

Finally, after five hours and a few breaks for water and a little kissing, it was done. Daphne stood to look at it in the full-length mirror, gasping at what she saw. The colors, the shading, the design—it was everything she never knew she wanted on her skin.

April took a few pictures of it, then pressed a rectangle of clear Saniderm over the entire piece to protect it for several days. When she was finally done cleaning up, Daphne grabbed her by the hips and pulled her close.

"Oh, hey," April said, laughing, but Daphne didn't waste any time before kissing her.

She kissed her, and kissed her, and kissed her.

"Thank you," she said when they finally came up for air, her forehead pressed to April's. "This was the best birthday I've ever had."

April's smile was soft, a little vulnerable. "Really?"

"Really."

"That's all I wanted for you," April said.

Daphne took a deep breath, that urge to say some very big, very important words rising up in her again.

And they scared her, those words.

Because it was too soon.

Too much.

Too close to the last time Daphne had completely lost herself in someone else.

So she swallowed the emotion down, focused on the feel of April's skin, the way she smelled, the way she hummed a little when Daphne kissed her again. And Daphne's heart slowed, or maybe it sped up, she wasn't sure, but either way, she felt more settled, like there was nowhere else she belonged in this moment.

"I've got one more present for you," April whispered, and her fingers flipped the button free on Daphne's paint-stained jeans.

Daphne laughed. "Here?"

"Here," April said, walking Daphne backward toward the client chair, unzipping her pants and pulling them down as they went. Daphne's bare thighs hit the pleather, and she sat as April worked her jeans off, tossing them onto her rolling stool.

"Birthday surprise number three," April said as she slipped off Daphne's underwear.

Daphne leaned back and laughed again, a reaction that quickly fell away as April spread Daphne's thighs and settled between them, lying on the end of the chair on her stomach, her own legs bent at the knees and dangling in the air, her boots still on.

"I've always wanted to do this," April said, teeth grazing the inside of Daphne's thigh.

Daphne gasped, her hand sinking into April's hair. "Do what?" she managed to ask.

"This," April said, licking a slow stripe up Daphne's center.

"Oh my god."

"Right here on this pink chair," April went on, her tongue swirling lightly around Daphne's clit.

"Fuck."

"In my own shop." April used her fingers to spread Daphne's pussy, tongue sliding inside her for a second before she closed her mouth around her and sucked.

"April, fuck," Daphne said, her hips lifting off the chair.

"God, you taste good," April said, then hummed against Daphne's cunt.

"You . . . you've never done this here before?" Daphne asked, her words ragged, her breath labored.

"Never," April said, hooking her hands around Daphne's thighs and pulling her closer. "Just you."

Those words nearly sent Daphne over the edge. She could only make incoherent noises then. She spread her legs wider, scraped her nails through April's hair.

Just you.

Daphne rolled her hips, desperate for more. More of this feeling, more of April, more of anything she'd give her. April responded in kind, slipping two fingers inside Daphne, pumping them slow and deep, her tongue flicking and circling.

Just you.

Daphne cried out—April's name, *yes, please,* anything she could get out as April fucked her. Her legs started to tremble, her orgasm building from her toes upward.

Just you.

April's fingers did something devilish then. Daphne couldn't even tell what—curling or twisting, she didn't know, didn't care. She only knew that she came harder than she ever had in her life, her knees closing around April's ears, her nails digging into her scalp. It felt like it lasted forever, April's tongue continuing to work at her clit, and Daphne lost all sense of anything but April Evans between her legs.

Just you.

After she came down, she lay there for a second, eyes closed, trying to catch her breath. April kissed her softly on her thighs and hips, and Daphne giggled, jolting in the chair.

April laughed, then folded her hands on Daphne's lower belly, her chin resting on her knuckles. She looked up at Daphne with those eyes, all dark and mysterious. Daphne slid her fingers from April's hair to her face.

"Tell me what you're thinking," Daphne said.

April's expression shifted and she sighed, blinking slowly as though drugged. "I'm thinking you're the most perfect thing I've ever seen."

Daphne's already short breath vanished, and she swiped her thumb over April's soft cheek. April leaned into her, her eyes fluttering closed.

"What are we going to do?" Daphne asked quietly.

She hadn't really meant for the question to slip out. Six little words, but they held infinite weights of emotion, countless more questions about the future.

April's brows lowered and her mouth opened, but suddenly Daphne didn't want the answer. She didn't want to hear *I don't know* either, because that just made her feel as though there was something hard and heavy that they couldn't see, couldn't figure out, and she didn't want any of that right now.

She just wanted this.

Just you.

"I know what I want," Daphne said, sitting up a little and grinning.

April closed her mouth, blinking at Daphne's change in tone. "Oh yeah?"

Daphne nodded. "Two things. I want to get you back to the cabin and into a bed."

Their own world, just the two of them, reality and everything Daphne didn't know hours and hours away.

April smiled. "I think I can handle that."

Daphne took a deep breath. "But first, I want to see your Devon pieces."

April's expression slipped a little, her brows twitching low.

"Not because you're my competition," Daphne said.

"Aren't I?" April asked.

Daphne slid her hand through April's hair. "You are, I know. And in two days, we're going to show these pieces to Nicola as just that—competition for something life-changing. But that's not why I want to see them tonight."

"Why, then?"

"Because I want to see *you*."

If art reflected life, if April's pieces revealed her heart and soul even a fraction of the way Daphne felt her own paintings did, she didn't want to go another second without seeing what April had created, to see who April really was underneath all her starshine, her deflecting, her doubts that anyone could love her as she was.

"Okay," April said softly, then kissed the bare skin of Daphne's belly. "I'll show you anything you want."

Chapter Twenty-Five

CLOVERWILD'S MAIN LODGE was quiet this late at night.

As they walked through the lobby and toward the art studio, April's stomach swelled with butterflies. Of course, Daphne had seen her work, but it was mostly tattoos or a few slapdash drawings she had hanging on her walls in Wonderlust. There was her Instagram, and obviously, the piece now healing on Daphne's arm, but all of that was for other people.

Her pieces for the Devon were different. They didn't feel like the art she'd made to hang in her shop. They certainly didn't feel like a tattoo sketch, no matter how much she loved something she created to put on someone's body.

They felt like her.

Like *April Evans*, maybe for the first time in her life, and even her horoscope this morning had said as much.

> This week, you'll face a mirror, and you'll have to decide whether or not you like what you see. Is it time for a change? Or is it time to embrace and celebrate the reflection that has always been there?

Madame Andromeda's words flitted through April's mind as she and Daphne picked up their pace down the hall. Daphne squeezed her hand tighter, smiled at her, and then April realized all those butterflies weren't nerves. They were excitement. Because she wanted Daphne to see her too. See what April saw in the mirror. See the person becoming and unbecoming and then becoming again in the journey of the tarot.

Fool's Passage.

That was what April had decided to name her series, twenty-two illustrations on her favorite 9x12 vellum/medium-textured paper. From the Fool to Death to the World, April had poured the story of her life into every illustration, then used oil pastels to saturate the dreamy images, each piece with a different three-color theme.

She loved her pieces.

She loved them, *and* she observed them with a certain amount of longing, because the life she'd lived . . . well. It was beautiful, but she wanted more.

So much more.

As the studio came up on their right, April's heart picked up even more speed, but stuttered when she saw the door was already open, the light on inside. Only three people had a key to this room—her, Daphne, and Mia, and April couldn't imagine Cloverwild's owner hanging around the art studio at nearly midnight.

"Who—" April started to say, but cut herself off as they walked into the room, stopping short as though she'd been slapped.

A fountain of dark hair.

That was the first thing she saw, and that was all she needed. After three years, April still recognized her—the way she stood with her spine just past ninety degrees, the sharp angle of her shoulders. Even with her back to them, April could tell one arm was tucked across her chest, the other bent and resting atop it, her fingers barely touching her mouth.

Daphne gasped, a sound loud enough to grab the woman's attention. She turned to look at them, dressed in a white silk blouse tucked haphazardly into dark-wash jeans, but still in a way that looked couture and refined.

"Elena," Daphne said, pressing a hand to her stomach.

Elena lifted her chin, her dark eyes flicking to April only once before going back to Daphne.

"Hello, my love," she said.

And with those three words, April felt herself disintegrating, as though she was made of sugar and had been left out in the rain.

Hello, my love.

That was how she used to greet April, but she wasn't talking to April this time. April glanced at Daphne, who looked a little green, but who had also dropped April's hand and couldn't stop staring at their ex.

"Happy birthday," Elena said, then waved her hand at Daphne's first painting, set up on an easel at the front of the room. "I see you've been busy."

"How did you . . . What are you . . ." Daphne spluttered.

"You stopped answering my calls or texts," Elena said coolly. "And it's your birthday. I had to see you."

You stopped answering . . .

You stopped *answering . . .*

April blinked as the meaning of those words settled around her.

"I got in a few hours ago," Elena said, "but the owner didn't know where you were and wasn't comfortable letting me into your cabin. She said I could wait here. They're fully booked, apparently."

"And you found my painting?" Daphne asked. She still hadn't taken a step toward Elena. But neither had she glanced at April.

Not once since they walked into the room.

"I got bored," Elena said, then looked at the piece again. "It's really extraordinary. I knew you had it in you."

Daphne inhaled sharply.

April felt two feet tall.

Elena tilted her head at Daphne, eyes narrowing. "Did you get a tattoo?"

Daphne didn't answer, but April supposed the word *tattoo* stoked something in Elena's memory, or at least her manners, because she finally looked at April again and smiled.

"April," she said. "It's good to see you."

I can't say the same.

Is it really, you manipulative hag?

Fuck you, fuck you, and then fuck you again.

A myriad of retorts arranged themselves quickly in April's mind, coalescing on her tongue and ready for fire, but before April could figure out which was the most devastating—if a bit immature—Elena's attention shifted back to Daphne.

"Can we talk?" she asked. Her voice was softer now, her shoulders rounding a little in submission. "Alone? Please."

April waited for Daphne's response—*hell, no,* or even a polite *I don't think so,* because it was her birthday and April had taken her to dinner and given her a tattoo and then an orgasm, and she was about to share her art with Daphne, her whole fucking soul, so surely, *surely,* Daphne was not going to say yes to the woman who'd nearly wrecked both of their lives.

But then . . .

You stopped answering . . .

April squeezed her eyes shut. She could feel Daphne turning toward her, everything tumbling down around her.

"April," Daphne said softly, but April didn't wait to hear what she was going to say. The plea. The apologetic expression. She simply turned and walked out of the room, and she didn't slow down until she reached her car, started the engine, and peeled out of Cloverwild's parking lot, her tires spitting gravel.

APRIL DIDN'T REMEMBER turning onto certain roads or even getting out of her car. But half an hour later, she was standing on Ramona and Dylan's front porch, ringing the bell and shaking, despite the balmy breeze drifting off the lake.

It took a few minutes, but eventually the porch light flicked on, the lock slid back, and the large oak door swung open, revealing a bleary-looking Ramona with her hair piled on top of her head, sleep shorts adorned with cartoon illustrations of sushi, and a baby blue tank top that was on backward and inside out.

"Apes?" Ramona asked, blinking into the golden porch light. "What—"

"I saw Elena. She's here. With Daphne right now at Cloverwild."

Ramona's expression cleared quickly, eyes rounding and mouth dropping open a little. She said nothing, just opened the door wider, then led April into the kitchen. The stove light was on, but Ramona flipped the switch next to the sink as well. April sank onto a stool at the white-and-gray quartz island while Ramona filled a kettle with water, then set it on a burner before dropping two peppermint tea bags into dark blue mugs.

Still, neither of them said anything, not until they both had steaming cups of tea in front of them, April's hands curling around the warm ceramic. Even then, she wasn't sure what to say.

"So," Ramona finally said, leaning her elbows on the counter. "Elena?"

April nodded at her reflection in her tea. "Yeah."

"And Daphne . . ."

"I don't know. I think she's been talking to Elena on the phone, but I . . ." She set her mug down, dug the heels of her hands into her eyes. "Fuck, I just don't know."

And she didn't, but as she sat here, her heart beating fast as she thought about Daphne, about Elena, about the Devon, about everything that had happened this summer and still might happen, she realized she didn't want to talk about Daphne.

She couldn't.

Not until she talked about something else.

"What happened to us?" she asked, lifting her eyes to look at her best friend of nearly twenty-five years. Such a simple question, but as heavy as the sky pressing down on them.

Ramona sighed, a resigned expression on her face. "I don't know."

"I think we need to figure it out," April said. "Because I don't want to keep doing this. Feeling like this. It's not good for either of us."

Ramona nodded. "Let's start there, then. How *do* you feel?"

April took a sip of tea to order her thoughts, but they weren't so muddled after all. They were pretty damn clear, in fact.

"I feel lost," April said. Her voice cracked on the last word, but she forced herself steady. "And I feel left."

Ramona didn't look surprised or affronted. She just looked sad.

"How do you feel?" April asked.

Ramona's eyes were shiny in the dim light. "I feel guilty."

April frowned. She wished she could be as unsurprised as Ramona seemed to be at her own declaration, but she wasn't prepared for those words. "Guilty?"

Ramona nodded. "I know I left. I know I'm far away. I know I'm ha—"

She cut herself off, looked down at her tea.

"Happy," April said. "You know you're happy."

Ramona nodded again.

"I *want* you to be happy, Mona," April said.

Ramona tilted her head. "Do you?"

April's fingers tightened on her mug. "Yes. God. Of course."

"I know," Ramona said, shoulders drooping. "I know that, but lately, it hasn't felt like that. It feels like you're always annoyed with what I'm saying or how I'm saying it or what I'm not saying."

"I found out about your engagement through a tabloid."

"That wasn't my intention though."

"And I *know* that," April said. "But it still happened, and it wouldn't have if you'd just called me the night Dylan proposed. Texted. Anything. I want you to be happy. I'm glad you're in love and getting married and living in LA where you want to be, doing what you want to do, but I never thought I'd feel so outside of it all."

Ramona's brows dipped.

"I can be happy for you and *sad* that I don't feel like your best friend anymore," April said. "Two things can be true at once."

"You don't make it easy, April," Ramona said. "You tally everything I do, every missed text, every time I don't lead the conversation off with a question about your well-being. And then you take all that hurt and go silent. You didn't tell me about you and Daphne. You didn't tell me about closing your shop, renting out your house. God knows what else you're hiding away for a rainy day."

"A rainy day?"

"When it suits *you* to tell me."

They both went quiet then, and April knew Ramona was right. All of it. She held a grudge, she knew she did. She tucked hurt feelings away inside of her, taking them out every now and then to croon over them like Gollum and the Precious.

But April was right too, and she could tell Ramona knew it. And maybe neither one of them was really to blame. She trusted Ramona, and knew Ramona trusted her. They'd never do anything to intentionally hurt each other. For so long, they'd been Apes and Mona. Or Apes and Llama Face. Or Apes and Ra and Ram and all the nicknames April had called her over the years, a closeness that bordered on dependency, at least on April's part.

Maybe now, they needed to figure out how to be April and Ramona.

April took a breath and circled around the island to stand next to her best friend.

"Maybe we're just changing," she said. "And I think I've been really scared of that. Because *changing* felt like *losing*."

Ramona took her hand and squeezed it. "You could never lose me."

April nodded, squeezed back. "I know that. I do. I just . . . when I said I felt lost, I didn't just mean you."

"I know, honey."

"And I think, in the past, whenever I've felt unsure or things were unclear, *you* were always the constant."

Ramona pressed her mouth together, her eyes filling with tears.

"And that's not fair to you," April said. "I know that. You're allowed to change. I *wanted* you to change, to chase your dreams and get out of Clover Lake, and you did. I never want you to feel guilty for going after it. For being happy."

Ramona grabbed her other hand, curled them between them.

"But I also don't think I realized how much things would change," April said. "And how much I'd miss the way we'd always been."

"I didn't realize it either," Ramona said. "And I didn't think enough about how it would feel to be in your shoes, with both Olive and me gone. I've missed you so much, April. No one can replace you, but I also understand that I had Dylan and a new job and a new city, and you . . ."

"Had Bob and Bianca," April said, her voice deadpan.

Ramona laughed, a tear escaping down her cheek. "Don't forget Penny."

"I've avoided Penny as much as possible so I don't end up a headline."

Ramona laughed harder. "Been there."

April felt like an entire cavern had opened in her chest, her head, everywhere. She hadn't realized just how much her relationship with Ramona was weighing on her until this moment, until they'd acknowledged it all.

"I want to change with you," April said. "I want to figure out what you and I are *now*, not what we've always been."

Ramona smiled. "Me too. But I know you're my best friend. You always will be, no matter how much either of us has changed or will change in the future."

April nodded, then wrapped her arms around Ramona. "Agreed."

They held each other close, and for a while, April completely forgot about what had sent her flying to Ramona's in the first place. But then Ramona pulled back and sighed, setting her hands on April's shoulders.

"So," she said, lifting her brows.

April groaned. "Can we just forget what I said when you opened the door?"

"I don't think so."

"I mean, Elena who? Don't know her."

Ramona smiled, but in a way that told April she was not going to get away with deflecting quite so easily now.

"Unfortunately," Ramona said, "we both know her all too well."

April blew out a big breath, gazing at the coffered ceiling. She stared at the inset lights, counted the large squares created by the molding—nine in all, three across, three down—and thought about Daphne.

Because that was who this was really about. April didn't love Elena Watson. Elena was all wrong for her, and she'd known that for a long time. But the betrayal . . . that was still there, a fully intact layer around her heart. That feeling of not being good enough. Not being chosen. Never, ever being the *one*.

Elena had been April's partner.

Her almost-wife.

And she'd looked at April and said *never mind*. Walked away with someone new, someone better, someone sweeter.

Daphne fucking Love.

The tears came suddenly, a flash flood, filling her eyes and spilling out before she could even get her next breath.

"Oh, honey," Ramona said, sliding her hands down April's arms and squeezing.

But April wasn't crying over Elena, or even the fact that she'd left April for Daphne.

No, this was about Daphne herself. Independent from Elena, from April, even, from the Devon.

Just Daphne. Her smile, her laugh, the way she wanted to feel everything, do everything, no matter how long she'd spent afraid of those very same things. The way she kissed April like no one else in the world mattered or even existed. How she touched April's face and whispered against her mouth. How she talked to Bob in the cutest pet voice April had ever heard, calling him her perfect boy.

The way she painted.

The way she held April's hand, always tangling them together so two fingers rested between April's thumb and forefinger.

The way she snored a little when she'd had a drink.

The way it took her a full thirty minutes to wash her hair.

"I think . . ." April said, then couldn't get it out. She pressed her lips together, squeezed back the tears. Because she didn't want to say it. Didn't want to admit it. Not tonight, when Daphne was talking to their ex right this very second.

The ex who Daphne had only been away from for a little over two months.

The ex who was gorgeous and put together and wealthy and refined.

Still, the truth was the truth, and April knew she was safe here. No matter what Ramona had said about her and Daphne earlier that night, she was safe. Besides, Ramona was right—April and Daphne probably weren't the best idea. But none of that mattered, because despite how much April had tried to protect herself against this very feeling for the last three years, this kind of vulnerability, here she was.

"I think I might be in love with her," April finally said, pressing her hands to her warming cheeks.

And Ramona just rubbed April's arms and nodded. "I know, honey. I know."

Chapter Twenty-Six

DAPHNE FLINCHED AS the art studio door fell shut behind April. Her hands felt sweaty, her entire body trembling as though she were cold, even though it was stifling in here, the air-conditioning programmed to shut off at night.

Elena exhaled loudly. "Well, that was awkward."

Daphne frowned. "What did you expect?"

"I expected to come here and talk to you, not an ex from three years—"

"Just stop."

Elena's expression froze at Daphne's sharp tone, but then dropped, her features relaxing with realization. "You and April," she said.

It wasn't a question, and Daphne didn't plan on answering it. It was none of Elena's business, first of all. Secondly, Daphne had no idea what she'd say anyway.

She and April . . . what?

One thing she did know—April had been upset when she'd left here, and Daphne couldn't blame her. Daphne wanted to go after her, wanted to hold her and get mad with her.

How dare Elena show up like this and ask to speak to Daphne. How dare Elena do so many things, but still, Daphne's legs felt locked in place, her heart in her throat, her stomach somewhere near her feet.

Because Elena was here. Even after the hell she'd put Daphne through the last two months, she'd chased Daphne down on her birthday, traveled to Clover Lake, waited for hours in the art studio for her.

For *her.*

"Daphne," Elena said, a familiar sweet plea to her tone.

And god, Daphne tried to stop it, but her eyes fluttered closed at that voice, like a whispered declaration of love on a lazy Saturday morning.

"What do you want?" she forced herself to ask.

Elena smiled, that half-smirk curve to her mouth she employed when someone already knew the answer to their question.

"Elena," Daphne said, shaking her head. "I ca—"

"Hear me out, okay?" Elena asked. "Before you say no, just listen."

She held out her hand for Daphne to come closer and Daphne moved, bridging the gap between them before she was even aware that her brain had made the decision. A reflex.

Her fingers slid over Elena's, familiar short nails with their light pink manicure, perfect and shiny and soft. Elena tangled their fingers together, then walked them both over to the couch, making sure Daphne sat before she did. They stayed like that for a second, looking at each other, Elena's eyes roaming all over Daphne's face.

"I like your hair," Elena finally said.

Daphne laughed quietly. "You do not."

"I do too."

"You hate unconventional hair colors. You said it makes people seem desperate and sycophantic."

Elena laughed. "You do know me."

"I do."

"And I know you," Elena said, scooting a little closer. Their knees touched, and somehow, Daphne only just noticed that her hand was still in Elena's.

"I know you dyed your hair because you wanted to feel something after I broke up with you," Elena went on. "Wanted to experience something different. Wanted to *be* different."

Daphne's throat tightened, her eyes filling almost instantly. She looked down at her jeans, focused on the multicolored paint splatters over the cotton.

"But you don't need to change, baby," Elena said softly, pulling Daphne's hand into her lap, both hands cupping her fingers. "You're perfect the way you are. And it took me losing you to realize it."

Daphne shook her head as Elena pressed a kiss to the back of her hand, then ducked her head to try and capture Daphne's eyes. And she was successful, Daphne's own gaze latching on and following her like a baby duck imprinting on the first person she saw.

"You *do* know me," Elena said again. "And you know that sometimes I need space to understand how I'm feeling. I knew things between us were growing stagnant and we needed to either move forward or stop altogether. And I got scared."

Daphne closed her eyes, warm tears gathering at her lash line, then falling slowly, methodically, as her memory played back that horrible night Elena had told her it was all over.

The hurt.

The *shock*.

"I thought you were going to propose to me," she managed to say, her voice small and pathetic, but she couldn't help it. She'd felt small and pathetic then, and she felt small and pathetic now remembering it all over again.

"I know, baby," Elena said, kissing Daphne's hand again before releasing her.

Daphne kept her eyes closed, needing a minute to breathe, to gather herself. She heard Elena rustle next to her, then scoot closer and say her name.

So softly.

So gently.

Like a prayer, a song.

"Daphne," Elena said again. "Open your eyes for me."

Daphne did, the room coming into focus, Elena's face and her smell and her perfectly husky voice.

"I'm ready *now*," she said, then opened something in her hands.

A box.

A dark blue velvet box.

It creaked open elegantly, and there, nestled in more blue velvet, sat a ring.

A very big, very shiny ring.

It had a gold band, an oval-shaped bicolor Montana sapphire in the center. It was large, at least two carats if Daphne had to guess. The jewel's colors were incredible, a little gold and a little blue and a little green. Elena had always said it was the most beautiful gem she'd ever seen, that she wanted one of her own someday, maybe when she got married, a matching set with her wife.

And now she was offering that exact ring to Daphne, her eyes a little shiny, even though Daphne had never seen or heard the woman cry. Not once. Not even when Elena had accidentally bought ghost peppers for a charcuterie board and eaten one whole.

"Elena," Daphne breathed. Her eyes felt locked on the ring, mesmerized and stunned, like watching a total solar eclipse without glasses.

"I know," Elena said, her voice trembling. "It's a lot, but this is what I want. I want to marry you, Daphne Love. And I know it's what you want too." She plucked the ring from its cushioned home, then held it out to Daphne.

Daphne felt herself lean forward.

Saw herself reach out and take the ring between her thumb and forefinger, as though observing someone else's proposal, someone else's story.

"Please, Daphne," Elena said, her fingers still on the ring too so the two of them were frozen, the ring locking them together. "Say yes."

And god, that word—*yes*—was on the tip of her tongue.

She'd wanted this for so long. Maybe not engagement and marriage specifically, but a *person*.

A family.

Someone who was hers, and she was theirs, the first above all else. She suspected most kids felt that sense of priority with their parents or nuclear family, but she never had.

And now, Elena was offering her everything she'd ever wanted.

A real place to belong.

A real family.

Elena pulled the ring back, but only for a second as she took Daphne's left hand, slipped the ring on her fourth finger.

It fit perfectly.

Daphne held her hand in front of her and stared at the sparkle, the color, her heart pounding as the moment—what it really meant—washed over her again and again. She let it settle in her heart, settle in her bones and blood as she stared at that ring. And she stared and she stared and she stared.

"So?" Elena asked.

And when Daphne finally ripped her gaze from that beautiful stone, locking eyes with the person who wanted to spend their life with Daphne, meeting with that intense brown, that familiar sly smile, she knew exactly how to answer Elena's question.

Chapter Twenty-Seven

APRIL DIDN'T GO back to Cloverwild that night.

She didn't go back the next morning either. It was a Thursday, one day before the wedding, and she lay in bed staring at Daphne's name in her text messages. April hadn't heard from her at all—no text, no call, nothing—since she'd walked out of the art room nearly twelve hours ago, leaving Daphne with Elena.

April knew she should text her.

She should grow up, own her emotions, or at least regulate them a little, and find out what the hell happened, but she couldn't. In her mind, Daphne's lack of communication was loud and clear, sending a message April wasn't sure how to process, and she wasn't ready to have it all confirmed.

So instead, she tapped on Sasha's name, texting her to make sure Bob and Bianca got fed.

Why can't you feed them? Sasha texted back. Is everything ok?

April groaned. I'm at Ramona's.

And?

April groaned louder. AND I've got her wedding shower today.

Sasha: This wouldn't have anything to do with one Elena Watson showing up at Cloverwild yesterday, would it?

April: How did you even know about that?

She held her breath, wondering if maybe Daphne had reached out to Sasha to talk or for advice, or asked Sasha to make her a grilled cheese; hell, April didn't know. Anything to prove Daphne wasn't with Elena right now.

Sasha: Mia remembers her from back in your day

April: Back in my day? What am I, eighty-two?

Sasha: Also everyone is thriving on the gossip

April: It's a small town. It runs on gossip

Sasha: Do you want to know what I think?

April: I really don't

Sasha: Daphne wants YOU

April's teeth gritted together. She stared at the words, and a war broke out in her chest—hope and fear and doubt and certainty, and everything in between. She tapped on her previous text to Sasha, then emphasized it with two exclamation points.

Sasha: Fine. But I'm right

April: Can you check on Bob and Bianca please?

Sasha: On my way there now

April managed to type out a quick thank-you before burrowing under the feather duvet. It was nearly eleven, and April could hear activity throughout the house as Blair Emmanuel and a few more LA friends arrived for a brunch–slash–wedding shower that Blair and Olive had planned together, which started in exactly half an hour. Then later this evening, they'd all gather again for the rehearsal dinner, followed by the wedding tomorrow night.

Ramona's *wedding*.

April pulled the covers completely over her head.

She and Ramona were good—they were different, they were changing, but they'd be okay. She knew that. And she fully planned on pulling up her adulting panties and putting all of her enthusiasm and love into this wedding weekend, but god, she needed ten more minutes to get her shit together.

To push Daphne and Elena far, far, far from her mind.

Okay, maybe fifteen.

She pulled her phone under the covers with her and opened her music app, tapping on her favorite Paramore song to listen to when she was feeling particularly angsty. Then she opened the tarot app that she only used when she was too lazy to pull a physical card, tapped on the shuffle button, and asked *What the fuck* as the digital cards spun on the screen, finally stopping and revealing the Eight of Cups.

The card all about turning away from the past, from what's not working or serving anymore, and embracing the unknown.

"Oh, fuck you," she said, flung her phone onto the floor, and burrowed even deeper under the blankets. She wasn't sure how many of her designated minutes passed, but soon a knock sounded on the door.

"Yeah," she said as loudly as she could manage.

The door opened, the noises from downstairs burgeoning a little before muffling again as the door clicked shut.

"Uh-oh," Ramona said.

"What?" April asked, still completely cocooned.

"Well, you're *burrowing* and Paramore's '26' is playing on repeat, so I'd say things are grim."

"Well, Paramore feeds my brooding soul," April said. The mattress dipped as Ramona sat down and placed a hand on April's butt.

"That's my ass," April said.

"Good," Ramona said, then slapped it hard enough to make April yelp. "Can you come up for air for a second?"

Hayley Williams continued to croon sadly about reality and

heartbreak. April took a deep breath and slowly curled the blanket down to reveal her eyes only. Ramona smiled softly at her, dressed in a coral-colored sundress with a cinched bodice and tiny cherries printed all over the skirt. Her hair was down and cascading over her shoulders, and April realized how long it had gotten.

"You look so pretty," she said.

Ramona smiled wider. "Thank you."

"All of my clothes are at the cabin," April said, wincing. "Including the wide-legged pants I was going to wear to this shower."

Ramona waved a hand. "You can borrow something of Dylan's."

"Dylan is eight feet tall."

"I think I would've noticed if that were true."

April laughed. "My point stands."

"We'll find something that works," Ramona said.

"You're not worried your weird childhood BFF is going to embarrass you in front of your Hollywood friends?"

Ramona shrugged. "Actually, I'm counting on you to make me seem way cooler than I am."

"I can start talking about auras and the alignment of the planets if you want."

"Oh, please do. Then ask about everyone's moon sign and read their horoscopes while we eat the tiny food Blair is having catered."

"Only if the horoscopes are really dark."

Ramona laughed, then her expression grew serious. "Tomorrow's the big day, right?"

April's chest tightened. Tomorrow was Ramona and Dylan's wedding, but more relevant to April's future and entire existence, tomorrow was decision time. At nine a.m., April and Daphne would stand quietly while Nicola analyzed their pieces for the Devon in the art room, then decided who she was taking to London. April viewed the event as though she was underwater—it felt blurry and unformed, lacking oxygen and light.

And she wasn't sure what awaited her on the surface.

"It is," April said.

Ramona nodded, then tilted her head, eyes narrowing a little. "She hasn't called?"

April pressed her lips flat in answer.

Ramona sighed. "That doesn't mean anything. It just means—"

"That Daphne Love has now left *me* for Elena Watson, bringing us full fucking circle."

Ramona squeezed April's thigh. "I was going to say it *doesn't* mean that. At all. Daphne's been through a lot the past few months. She's probably just—"

"I don't want to talk about it," April said, sitting up and sending both of her hands through her hair. "Not because I don't want to talk to *you*. I just can't deal with this right now. And it's your day. *Your* weekend. I really want to be present."

Ramona nodded, then took April's hand. "I know all of this—the engagement, the wedding, everything—isn't exactly how you envisioned it. It's not even how *I* envisioned it."

April's throat felt a little achy. "But you're happy."

Ramona smiled. "I really am. And I want you *with* me in that happiness. Even if it's different from what we always dreamed or planned."

April squeezed her hand. "I'm with you," she said, and meant it. "Always. A hundred percent. Even with this stuffy wedding shower that Olive and Blair have been very bossy about."

Ramona laughed. "That's fair."

April pulled Ramona into her arms, and they held each other for a few seconds before April smacked a kiss to the top of her head.

"Now, before I submit fully," April said as she released Ramona, "I do require one thing."

"What's that?"

"You know."

Ramona's shoulders slumped. "Apes."

"Come on, come on. We need to commemorate your last single day with Llama Face. It's the proper thing to do."

Ramona groaned, but a smile played on her mouth, and April knew she had her. Ramona hooked her thumb under her top lip, her forefinger into her bottom, and then pulled them both outward, tongue rigid and sticking out as she made the funniest, most terrifying bleating sound in the history of all animal noises.

April cracked up, as she always did.

Ramona dropped her hands and wiggled her lips as though stretching them out.

"There," she said. "Did that ready you to face the day?"

"You know what?" April said, throwing the covers back and standing up, placing her fists on her hips like a superhero. She puffed out her chest and pushed Daphne and the Devon into the back of her mind so she could focus on her best friend. "It really, really did."

Chapter Twenty-Eight

THE NEXT MORNING, April thought she'd arrived early to the art studio. She wanted some time alone to set up her pieces for Nicola and focus on the task ahead of her, the prize.

The rehearsal dinner had gone smoothly yesterday—a short jaunt down the flower-bordered aisle in Ramona and Dylan's backyard, fifty white chairs already set up for guests, followed by a simple dinner with friends and family at Clover Moon, which Owen had closed to the public for the private event. April had managed to stay present and had even left her phone in Ramona's guest room so she wouldn't be checking for Daphne's text every five minutes. With Ramona's wedding at five o'clock tonight, she didn't need her own bullshit mucking everything up.

Considering she hadn't heard a peep out of Daphne, she wasn't sure there was any bullshit left to deal with anyway.

But fate—or the stars, the moon, the planets, or possibly just April's catastrophic luck—had other plans, because for the second time in forty-eight hours, she stopped cold as soon as she walked into the art room.

There, at the front of the room, perched on four different easels, were Daphne's paintings. Of course, April had seen the first piece—Daphne as a girl among the wildflowers—and she'd caught a glimpse of the fourth on Daphne's birthday, but this . . .

Seeing them all together, this story, even if it was unfinished—it ended thus far with Daphne meeting Elena in Boston, and the irony wasn't lost on April one bit—was an experience.

No, more than that. It was a commotion, a storm, an undoing.

The colors were incredible. Intricate and textured, with Daphne's ever-changing but omnipresent white dress like a blank space somehow, an absence of life, even while Daphne's face got a little clearer with each iteration.

April weaved through the student easels and chairs, coming to a stop in front of the display, eyes thirsty and drinking in the story. She kept going back to the second piece, the one with Daphne as a teen inside an old chapel, dead leaves on the floor, a cross soaring right above her head. The effect was haunting and melancholic, like a poem that hit somewhere deep inside April's gut in a way she couldn't put into words.

Didn't need to.

That was the beauty of art, the magic.

And right then, April knew—these pieces belonged in the Devon.

"Hi."

"Jesus," April said, clutching at her chest and whirling around to see Daphne sitting on the love seat.

"Nope," Daphne said with a soft smile. "Just me."

April managed to smile back as Daphne stood up, but her heart didn't slow its pace. Daphne was beautiful. Hair long and lavender, the curls glossy in the light. She wore a white dress, not unlike the one in her paintings, with spaghetti straps and a sweetheart bodice, and bright yellow heeled sandals on her feet.

She came closer, her eyes never leaving April's, and April felt the sudden need to run. Fuck the Devon, fuck London, fuck her future. She wasn't going to survive whatever Daphne Love had to say.

"Where's Elena?" April asked. She didn't really want to know the answer, but the question slipped out, the price of keeping her feet planted on the floor, a simple trade.

But Daphne shrugged, her slender shoulders glowing and lovely. "She left after we talked the other night."

April frowned, trying to process this information. "I don't understand. She *left*? Two days ago? Then why—"

"She asked me to marry her."

Those six words echoed through the room, loud and soft all at once, a declaration with thorns and explosives and barbed wire attached.

"She . . ." April stared but couldn't get anything out of her mouth. Her eyes flew to Daphne's left hand, but she had it tucked away, her arms folded over her chest as though she was cold.

Daphne looked down at the ground, shook her head. "I almost said yes." She took a deep, shuddering breath. "I was so close. The ring was on my finger."

April blinked. "Almost?" she said. Because it didn't seem real. None of it. The fact that Elena proposed, or the fact that Daphne said no—*did* she say no?—or the fact that April hadn't heard from her at all since this cataclysmic event.

"Almost," Daphne said again, then lifted her head to meet April's gaze. Her eyes were shiny, but no tears spilled over. She looked gorgeous—strong and sad all at once. "I couldn't do it."

April exhaled so heavily, a laugh mingled with her breath, relief overpowering every other emotion. She looped her hands behind Daphne's neck and pulled her closer, kissed her mouth once before holding her in a tight hug. Daphne held her too, arms around April's waist, and they stayed like that for a few seconds.

April could've lived there forever.

And she wanted to, she realized. Her relief was tangled with Daphne's rejection of Elena, she knew that. But underneath it all, the foundation, was the fact that she loved Daphne Love.

She *loved* her.

"Why didn't you call me?" April said, pulling back and kissing Daphne one more time. She kissed her cheeks then, one after the other, as she waited for Daphne to answer. She wasn't mad. Not anymore. There was too much of every other emotion to be mad about Daphne's silence, and she didn't care. She didn't fucking care about anything as long as it meant that Elena was gone and Daphne was here.

Here, and very much not engaged.

"I wanted to," Daphne said.

"I wanted to call you too," April said, her hands still roaming over Daphne's face, her mouth still pressing kisses anywhere she could get them.

"I was overwhelmed," Daphne said. "I needed some time to think, and when you didn't text or come back, I just—"

"I'm sorry," April said, holding Daphne's face between her hands, their foreheads pressed together. "I'm sorry, I didn't know what to do, and Ramona's shower was happening, and I think I freaked out a little."

"I get it," Daphne said. "I freaked out too."

"And that's okay," April said, thumbs swiping at Daphne's cheeks. "That's okay. What matters is right now. What matters is *us*."

She went in for another kiss, but Daphne circled her hands around April's wrists, pulling her back a little. She looked down again, teeth working at her lower lip.

"Daphne?" April asked. An alarm started deep in her belly, faint at first, hardly noticeable, but growing louder by the second.

Daphne lifted her eyes, her expression sorrowful.

Regretful.

"April, I—"

"Hello, you two."

At the sound of Nicola's voice, April felt her entire body lock up.

"I'm a little early," Nicola said from the doorway.

She was dressed professionally in wide-legged cream-colored pants, a brown silk blouse, and ivory heels. April looked down at her black jeans and black blazer, feeling suddenly unprepared.

"I'm sorry if I'm interrupting something," Nicola said.

"No, no," Daphne said, pulling April's hands from her face and then dropping them altogether. She straightened her shoulders, smiled. "You're fine."

April sucked in a breath as though coming up from the bottom of the lake for air, everything around her blurry for a split second. She glanced at Daphne once more, then managed a smile, which dimmed when she realized Nicola was indeed early, and she wasn't ready.

"I still need to set up my pieces," she said after clearing her throat. "I'm sorry, I'm a little behind this morning."

Nicola waved a hand. "You're perfect. Like I said, I'm early. I'll just pop over here and answer some emails." She motioned to the love seat, but April didn't miss how her eyes flitted first to Daphne's paintings, widening a little before looking away.

"Sure," April said, her voice quiet, but steady. "Thank you."

And then she went to work. She had to get this done, and if she thought about Daphne right now, the expression on her face right before Nicola walked in, the pained way she'd said April's name, she'd fall apart, or worse, she'd shut down or get defensive, her scorpion's tail lashing out in self-preservation.

So she worked.

She gathered the stack of her twenty-two pieces from a file box in the closet, each separated with a sheet of glassine paper to protect the pastels, then set them on eleven different easels just in front of Daphne's paintings. She placed them in order, from the Fool all the way to the World, making sure they were straight, unsmeared, perfect.

And they were.

She stepped back when she was finished, keenly aware that Daphne was close by, watching her.

"April," Daphne said, her tone so different now. Tender and proud. Full of love.

April squeezed her eyes closed, rolled her shoulders back.

"These are exquisite," Daphne said, stepping up to the Fool, then walking slowly down the line. "It's you. This is beautifully, perfectly you."

"Not so perfectly," April said.

Daphne turned to look at her, her fingers just grazing the corner of the Hanged One, April's favorite piece. In it, she'd placed herself upside down, of course, and her limbs were tangled with the trees surrounding her, all shades of green enveloping her. Below her, there was a small pond, but instead of her reflection, a tattooed hand reached up and out, fingertips nearly touching the crimson tips of her hair.

"That's what makes it perfect," Daphne said.

April smiled at her, then watched as Daphne moved along, finally making it to the World.

The end of the journey.

But this card felt more like a beginning.

It featured April standing in the middle of a road, the pavement dark and straight in front of her. It was a bit of a desert scene, mountains rising in the distance, the sun just peeking over a ridge, flooding the sky with pink and orange and lavender. April had a bag on her shoulder, and even though her back was to the viewer, it was clear she held one of her hands low on her forehead, a shade from the sun's rays as she looked ahead.

Looked forward.

To her, this piece felt like the partner to the Hanged One, even though many steps in the journey happened in between—from limbo to purpose, even if that purpose was still unformed, unseen, hiding down a long road.

She was upright, untangled, and ready for that road.

Daphne didn't say anything about the World, but she stared at it for what felt like hours. Finally, she simply glanced at April, a sort of understanding filling her eyes.

April inhaled sharply, then called to Nicola before either of them could say anything else. "We're ready for you."

"Wonderful." Nicola popped up from the couch, then took an iPad out of her bag before walking over to them. "I'm so excited to see what you have for me."

She started with April's project. She went slowly, methodically, scrutinizing each piece and scribbling some notes with her stylus every now and then. April stood by the Fool, waiting, while Daphne had moved to wait by her own pieces, giving the artist and the curator their time.

"Well," Nicola finally said after a good half hour. She tapped a few things on her iPad again before tucking it under her arm and looking at April. "A powerful series, April. You should be proud."

"I am," April said, her sweaty palms clasped together in front of her. "Thank you."

Nicola's smile was genuine, and as she walked toward Daphne, April felt a different kind of relief filling her, a golden light through her veins.

Nicola took longer on Daphne's pieces. Even though there were only four of them, she analyzed them like an art history student, nearly pressing her nose to the canvases, even touching the paint strokes here and there, with Daphne's permission. She wrote a lot of notes, made a lot of *hmm* noises, and by the time she was finished forty-five minutes later, April knew.

She knew, and her blood felt warm, her limbs languid, an excitement blooming in the center of chest like a firework in slow motion.

"I'm extremely impressed with both of you," Nicola said as she stood near Daphne's final piece. "Your work shows a true evolution, and what I love most is that both of your journeys are unfinished. As is true for all of us."

April swallowed, glancing at Daphne, who looked tense enough to snap, her shoulders rigid, her mouth held in a tight line. April wanted to hold her hand, to tell her it was all going to be fine, it was going to work out just like she dreamed, but she didn't move. Didn't dare breathe.

"Both of these projects deserve a place in the world," Nicola went on. "In fact, I demand that you find that place."

She glanced at April when she said this, and April let herself smile in acknowledgment.

"As for the Devon," Nicola said, then turned to face Daphne. "I'd like to feature your series, Daphne. If you're willing and able."

Daphne's mouth dropped open, true shock spilling over her face like a sunrise, spreading light until it reached her eyes.

"Really?" she asked, her voice a whisper.

"Really," Nicola said.

"Yes," Daphne said on a laugh. "Oh my god, yes, thank you so much."

Nicola smiled and held out her hand. "Welcome to the Devon family."

Daphne shook her hand, and April watched her while she chatted with Nicola for a second, setting up a time to meet on Monday to go over the details before Nicola flew back to London.

Finally, Nicola gathered her bag, tucking her iPad inside, and headed for the door. She paused at April's side, tilting her head as she glanced at the Fool again.

"Find a place," she said.

April smiled, a genuine bend of her mouth. "I will. I promise. Thank you."

"Good." Nicola winked at her, nudged her with an elbow in a sort of camaraderie that made April puff out her chest a little, then click-clacked out of the room, all class and grace.

April kept her eyes on the doorway for a second, the silence settling through the room.

"April," Daphne said.

April turned and her chest felt tight, her eyes aching, but not because of Nicola's decision. She'd known what the outcome was here, in her heart, maybe ever since the first time she saw Daphne's painting, before Nicola even sauntered into the art room and invited Daphne to be considered for the Devon.

That choice was right, it was perfect, and April knew it.

So right now, she wasn't shaking from losing out on something. She wasn't even thinking about what the hell she was going to do now.

Because she knew exactly what she wanted.

"Congratulations," she said, stepping toward Daphne, her voice trembling.

"Thank you," Daphne said, her voice quiet and trembling too. April wanted to tell her to shout it, to own it. But then Daphne cleared her throat, straightened her shoulders, and said it louder herself. Clearer.

"Good girl," April said.

Daphne laughed, then covered her mouth with her hands. "I can't believe it," she said through her fingers.

"I can. You belong in the Devon."

Daphne dropped her hands. "I don't think I could've gotten here without you."

"That's not true at all," April said.

She'd moved closer now, so close they were a breath apart. April took both of Daphne's hands in hers, held them to her chest.

"Thank you all the same," Daphne said, resting her forehead against April's.

"You're welcome all the same," April said.

"April," Daphne said, taking a deep breath and pulling back to look at her. She bit her lip again, just like she had before Nicola had arrived, as though she was bracing herself for something, some declaration.

But April needed to declare first.

"I want to come with you," she said.

Daphne's head popped up, her eyes round. "What?"

"Just hear me out," April said, her voice shaking a little. Her whole body was shaking, in fact, a dry leaf drinking up the first drops of rain.

"April," Daphne said. "I—"

"You belong in the Devon," April went on quickly, fingers tightening around Daphne's. "You do. No question. I'm so happy for you. And I'm going to do what Nicola said—I'm going to find a place for *Fool's Passage*."

"Good."

"But I want to do that with you."

Daphne's mouth opened a little, lower lip trembling.

"I want to go to London with you," April said. "It's the perfect time. I'll rework my pieces. I think it might make a great tarot deck, and I'll write the guidebook too. Get a job in a café or tattoo shop while I work on it, I don't care. We'll bash around London, you and me, while you become a star."

"A star," Daphne said, shaking her head.

"Or whatever you want to be. You can do anything, Daphne Love. You believe that now, don't you?"

Daphne's eyes fluttered closed for a second before opening again, tears brimming and then spilling over. April leaned forward and kissed them away, untangled their hands so she could hold Daphne's face in hers.

"You believe that?" April said again.

Daphne nodded. "I do. But—"

"Good, good," April said, laughing a little even as her own tears threatened to fall. "So we'll go together. We'll do this together. Figure this out, making it whatever we want—"

"April, I can't."

Everything stopped.

The tears, the laugh on April's mouth. The relief that had just started to burgeon in her chest. The excitement. Everything.

"What?" April asked. Because maybe she heard wrong, heard a *t* on the end of Daphne's own declaration when there wasn't one, her fears creating a scenario that didn't exist.

But when more tears streamed down Daphne's cheeks, when she removed April's hands from her face, clutching at her fingers and holding them to her own chest, a plea in her expression, April knew her hearing was just fine.

"April," Daphne said softly.

April wasn't sure what to say. Her instinct was to pull away, to run, to say *okay, never mind, that's fine.*

I'm fine.

But she wasn't.

And she had nowhere else to go.

Chapter Twenty-Nine

"APRIL," DAPHNE SAID again, holding April's hands tight to her chest.

So tight.

Because she had to make April understand. The expression on her face was breaking Daphne's heart.

But Daphne knew this was right.

She'd spent the last day and a half thinking about this, ever since she'd slipped that beautiful ring off her finger and handed it back to Elena. She'd said no then too, a word that somehow made her come alive, sparked a forever-dormant flame to life in her chest.

"When Elena asked me to marry her," she said to April now, "I almost said yes."

April's brows flickered a little in response, her eyes wide and dark and fathomless.

"I almost said *yes*," Daphne went on, "to a woman who threw me out of her apartment with next to nothing. Who'd spent three years breaking me down to a version of myself she preferred. Who went to bed with me in the first place when she was promised to someone else."

April's jaw tightened, her fingers twitching, but Daphne had to keep going.

"I almost said *yes*, because I have no idea who I am, April," she said, her words coming faster now. "I've wanted a family my entire life. Even before I left home. My parents spent my first eighteen years trying to break me into a version of myself *they* preferred. I spent three years in college breaking myself into a version other people preferred—the queer community, the art community, whoever. It didn't matter. If they showed me some attention, some love, I bent and twisted into something they liked."

April's lower lip shook, a tear spilling down her smooth cheek.

"And then Elena came along, and I thought I'd found it," Daphne said. "But I'd only found another way to change myself for someone else, and I wanted her love—anyone's love—so badly, I didn't see it. I never saw it. Not until I met you."

"Daphne," April said softly. A whisper.

"No, no, let me get this out," Daphne said. Her fingers were numb on April's, but she couldn't let go. Not yet. "I met you and I met Sasha, and for the first time in my life, I felt like me. But *me* was a stranger. Slowly, I started getting to know her."

"And?" April asked.

"I liked her," Daphne said, her smile small but sure. "I like her a lot. I think I fell in love with her."

April smiled back. "Good."

"It is," Daphne said, then took a deep breath. "But I fell in love with someone else too."

April tilted her head. "Sasha?"

Daphne laughed, and April laughed too, and that April could make a silly joke in this moment just made Daphne love her all the more.

She untangled their hands and held April's face close to her own. "You, you idiot."

April laughed, her fingers soft on Daphne's wrist. "Oh, good, because I think I fell in love with you too."

"Really?"

"Really," April said, and Daphne kissed her then. Soft and sweet, and in that moment, she wanted nothing more than to go deeper, harder, take April back to their cabin and undress her slowly.

But she couldn't.

She had to do this.

Had to choose herself first.

"But?" April asked when Daphne broke the kiss.

Daphne shook her head. "It's not a *but*. It's . . ." She exhaled, searching for the right way to say it. "It's timing."

April's brows lowered a little, but she stayed silent.

"I scared myself, April," Daphne said. "With how close I was to giving in to Elena. To settling for someone safe, someone who didn't care if I ever changed, ever grew."

"I'm not Elena."

"God, no, I know," Daphne said, kissing April's forehead. "Never."

"And if we love each other . . ." April trailed off, her eyes searching Daphne's now.

"I love you," Daphne said firmly. "I do. *And* I don't know what that means. I don't know what that looks like. I don't know how to love you without losing myself. I don't know how to find myself and love you at the same time. I've never experienced that balance. I've spent my entire life loving other people and ignoring myself. And that's not real love, is it?"

April's shoulders dropped a little, as though everything that Daphne was trying to say had just settled heavy and true.

"No," April said, "it's not."

"I want to love you well, April Evans," Daphne said. "That's the truest thing I know. And I can't do that right now. I can't do that until I figure out how to love myself first."

They were silent after that, standing close, Daphne's hands cupped around April's slender neck, her fingers playing in her hair. April held on to Daphne too, her eyes lowered as she processed everything.

And Daphne let her. She let this moody, beautiful, perfect little scorpion take everything in right now, because at least she was *here*. At least she wasn't running, wasn't deflecting.

April was choosing herself too. At least, that was what Daphne hoped. What she wanted more than anything.

"Okay," April finally said, lifting her eyes to Daphne. "Okay."

One simple word, so much more to talk about and plan, even, but right now, in this moment, *okay* was enough.

Okay was a start, and when April pushed up to her tiptoes and wound her arms around Daphne's shoulders, kissing her and whispering *okay* against her mouth, Daphne believed it was true.

It would all be okay.

They would be okay.

Chapter Thirty

EIGHT HOURS LATER, April walked down the aisle in Ramona's backyard wearing a blush-pink dress that fell to just below her knees, gossamer spaghetti straps showing off her tattoos. She held a small bouquet of pale pink poppies while the duo Beach Glass—a woman with silver-streaked hair who played the violin, and a thick-banged brunette on an acoustic guitar—played a dreamy rendition of a well-known queer pop song."

The evening was lovely.

The sun was low over the water, streaking the sky orange and pink and gold, and the small grassy area where the ceremony would take place was filled with familiar faces and movie stars, a strange amalgam of small town and Hollywood.

It was beautiful though.

Perfect.

When April reached the officiant—Dylan's agent, Laurel—and turned so she could watch Dylan walk down the aisle with her parents, decked out in a sleek ivory silk suit, she felt steady.

She felt full and happy for her best friend.

She even liked her pink dress, the color making her ink pop.

She loved the music, the lighting, and when Ramona appeared with Mr. Riley, she felt as though her heart might burst.

Ramona was resplendent in a gauzy A-line gown, sleeveless and V-necked, the ivory tulle flowing over appliqué peonies and poppies and anemones. Her bouquet, a larger version of April's, exploded with the colors featured in her dress, all shades of pink and the pop of minty green from the eucalyptus.

April caught Olive's eye next to her and winked. Olive was already crying happily, their sweet girl.

The ceremony was lovely and brief, Ramona and Dylan making tearful promises and holding hands. April was determined to focus on the moment, to not let her mind wander, not even let her eye shift to the guests, where her parents sat rigidly on Ramona's side in shades of beige. Aside from one painful phone call with her father to discuss the lease of her shop's space—which wasn't up until next March, and she'd already discussed a small fee for breaking the contract with Leland, the landlord, and how that would be cheaper than paying six more months of rent—she hadn't spoken to them much since the engagement dinner.

She also didn't let herself glance at Daphne, who was sitting with Sasha, dressed in a lacy lavender midi dress that fit her perfectly.

Well. She *tried* not to let herself look at Daphne.

She failed. Many times.

Because Daphne was beautiful.

Entrancing.

Glowing.

Since this morning, since Nicola's decision and everything April and Daphne had talked about, Daphne seemed to have come even more alive. She looked powerful and confident, her curls wild, her shoulders relaxed, her expression serene. April had never seen anyone so lovely, and her chest swelled as she caught Daphne's eye for the tenth time during the ceremony, Daphne smiling softly at her.

Her chest swelled . . . and then retracted, growing smaller, closing in around her heart. This sequence happened over and over and over. Happiness and pride and sadness, a dizzying mix of emotions.

Everything all at once.

And that was the way it would be for a while, April was sure of it. Because as much as her mind knew that everything Daphne had said in the art studio was right, was true, was *good*, her heart clung to a different story.

A tale of breaking and leaving and, once again, being the one who was left behind.

THE RECEPTION WAS under an amber-lit silk tent connected to Ramona's back patio.

April sat alone at a cloth-covered table after a lovely dinner of salmon and asparagus, her bouquet next to her, and snagged a tiny glass of chocolate mousse off the tray of one of the servers, who were ambulating around the space with patisserie-esque desserts. She sipped on her pink lady, freshly made at the open bar and served in a blush-pink glass, and tried to look entertained as Beach Glass, now joined by a full band, played through a collection of originals and classic love songs.

Ramona glided through the tent, gorgeous and smiling, Dylan by her side as though glued.

But, April supposed, that was the point, wasn't it?

She sighed, took a large gulp of her cocktail.

"My pink ladies are better," Sasha said, falling into a chair next to April, legs spread. She wore a black suit and a formfitting white shirt unbuttoned to her sternum, platinum hair tall and slicked back on the sides.

"How do you know?" April asked, nodding at the glass of club soda in Sasha's hand.

"I just do," Sasha said, winking.

April rolled her eyes but smiled before stuffing a spoonful of mousse into her mouth. She groaned. "Is your mousse better?"

"My everything is better."

"So confident."

"Only way to be, my darling."

April focused on her dessert, wishing she were as self-aggrandizing as Sasha.

"So," Sasha said pointedly, leaning forward and resting her elbows on her knees.

"Oh, god, here we go," April said, dropping her spoon.

"How are you holding up?" Sasha asked.

"I'm fine."

Sasha lifted a brow. "Are you?"

April sat back in her chair, eyes roaming the room of their own accord for Daphne. April had sat with the wedding party for dinner, so she hadn't really talked to Daphne much since this morning.

"I'm . . ." April searched for the right word, but she wasn't sure there was one. "I don't know. That's the truth."

Sasha nodded. "Makes sense. But I think it's the right decision."

"I know," April said. "That's what makes it confusing."

"You need to learn to love yourself too."

April scoffed. "Thank you, Doctor."

Sasha grinned. "Seriously though. What are you going to do? Daphne's leaving in two days. I'm taking off in a week. Are you going to stay here?"

Of course was on the tip of her tongue. Clover Lake was her home. The choice she'd always made. The steady surety in her life. She didn't get the Devon. She couldn't go to London with the woman she loved. She still owned a house, for the time being at least, though how she'd pay the mortgage after her renter moved out, she had no idea.

Maybe Mia would let her stay on full-time. Cloverwild was open year-round. Winter was a slower season, of course, but there was some skiing nearby, and surely there would be more rich people wanting to learn how to draw a fucking finch.

The thought, however, exhausted her.

No, more than that.

It terrified her. Bored her. Made her feel ashamed. Every negative emotion swirled in her chest when she thought of staying in Clover Lake.

But where else would she go? She couldn't afford LA, and while she knew Ramona would welcome her with open arms, she would not—would *not*—live with Dylan and Ramona like some pathetic hanger-on. She didn't like LA all that much anyway, but she truly had no other ideas.

She glanced at Sasha. "Where are you going again? Out west?"

Sasha nodded, sipped her club soda. "I'm heading to Europe after the new year, so why not? Plus, Jack and Carrie just invited me to their Halloween party in LA."

"Ah, right," April said. She'd heard many a tale of Jack and Carrie's infamous Halloween parties at their home in Laurel Canyon. She'd been invited to last year's, but Dylan had been in Germany, and Ramona was on set with Noelle Yang somewhere in the Midwest, so it hadn't seemed worth it. The theme this year was Masquerade, but in the past, they'd done everything from Disney Villains to the Zombie Apocalypse. Ramona had already mentioned the possibility of April coming out west for it this year, but April wasn't sure what she was doing tomorrow, much less in ninety days.

"You're just going to drive around for three months?" she asked Sasha.

Sasha shrugged. "Drive. Work. Wherever the wind takes me."

April sat up, leaned closer to Sasha, and narrowed her eyes. "Who the hell *are* you?"

Sasha laughed, sipped her drink.

"No, really," April said, softer this time. "What's the deal? Where's your family? Are they in LA? You grew up there, right?"

Sasha's expression fell. "Where's *yours*?"

"They already went home because they're the most boring people on the planet," April said, jutting her thumb toward the street.

Sasha huffed a laugh, gazing out at the crowd, her eyes far away. "They're not in LA anymore, no."

April waited for more, but for now, that seemed all that Sasha was willing to offer.

"Fine," April said. "Keep your secrets."

"I'm very good at that," Sasha said, tipping her glass toward April, but her eyes were still sad.

April lifted her glass as well, and they sat in an easy silence for a while, watching the dancers and the brides flutter through the room. Still, as April watched her town mingling with Hollywood, an idea formed.

More than an idea.

A longing.

Ever since Sasha had mentioned her road trip plans a few weeks ago, April had felt it, like an itch she couldn't quite reach. It wasn't a solid life plan. It wasn't even a yearlong plan. But it was something. And it made April *feel* something other than dread. It even made her feel excitement.

Passion and art and a wide-open road.

She wasn't sure how she'd feel in three months. What she'd

need or how much money would be left in her savings, but this was a start.

A stepping-off point to choosing herself. To *loving* herself, as much as she was loath to agree with Sasha's two cents.

"Can I come with you?" she asked Sasha.

Sasha's brows lifted. "Really?"

April nodded, a smile pulling at her mouth. "Yeah." She sat up straighter, her heart fluttering under her ribs. "I can pay my way. I'm clean. I'm a good driver. And I make fucking *great* playlists."

Sasha regarded her for a second, blue eyes narrowed slightly. Finally, she grinned. "A road trip buddy."

"A road trip buddy," April said. "All the way to LA."

"All right," Sasha said, nodding sagely. "All right, let's do it. But only if you agree to always, always call my car by her proper name."

April placed her hand on her heart. "Gertie, it would be a privilege."

Sasha laughed. "Damn right."

And just like that, April had a plan. She had *something*. Something she wanted, something that made her feel electric and alive.

She settled back in her chair and took another sip of her drink, tilting her head at her new travel companion. "What's your last name? I just realized I don't even know it. Or is that a secret too?"

Sasha cleared her throat, her smile small. "It's Sinclair."

"Nice to officially meet you, Sasha Sinclair," April said, holding out her free hand. Sasha laughed and they shook, then April set her glass on the table and sat on the edge of her chair, energy buzzing through her fingertips. "Okay, so, talk to me about packing for this trip."

"Well, you can't bring your cats, for one."

"Fuck, my cats," April said, freezing. "That's okay, I bet Mr. Riley will—"

"Hey," Daphne said, appearing next to April's chair, all lavender and curls and perfection.

April swallowed hard at the sight of her. "Hi."

"Do you want to dance?" Daphne asked as the music shifted to something slower, something languid and romantic.

"Oh," April said. "Um—"

"Yes, she does," Sasha said, standing up and stretching her lithe limbs.

"Bossy," April said. Sasha winked at her, then sauntered off into the crowd.

Daphne held out her hand, and when April took it, standing and following her to the small parquet dance floor, where Ramona and Dylan were also dancing, she couldn't keep her stomach from fluttering.

Daphne held her close, one arm around her waist, the other hand gripping April's, pressing it to Daphne's own heart. They didn't talk. April felt as though they barely even breathed.

They just held each other and danced.

And later, when Ramona hugged April tight in the driveway and whispered in her ear how much she loved her, a limo ready to whisk Dylan and Ramona off to the airport en route to Paris, Daphne was by her side then too.

She was by her side as Ramona disappeared down the street with her new wife.

She was by her side on the drive back to Cloverwild.

And she was by her side as they walked into their shared cabin, slowly undressed each other, mouths meeting without a word, hands tangling in each other's hair, and fell into bed one last time.

Chapter Thirty-One

DAPHNE HURRIED DOWN a London street, the September morning sun pouring vitamin D into her skin after a week of rain and gloom. Her heels clicked on the damp concrete, an almost jaunty rhythm as she crossed the road, the Devon looming above her like a cathedral.

The Devon was housed in a huge Victorian-era brick house, renovated to highlight contemporary art, with soaring ceilings, multistory windows, and stark white walls. Everything inside was bright and serene at the same time, from the blond wood floors to the arched interior walls for displays, a swirling maze through color and creation.

For the last month, Daphne had walked into this building every day. And every day, still, she paused in the foyer after pushing the ornate oak doors open, taking in the simple grandeur. Nicola had told her multiple times that she could come in through the employees' side entrance. She'd even given Daphne a key card, as the grant Nicola had procured for Daphne to work on her final piece for *Evolution* entitled her to a few perks as one of the Devon's artists-in-residence.

But she loved this moment in her day.

The moment when she opened a beautiful door and stepped into her literal dream. A paradise rivaling any version of Eden she'd ever imagined, heaven for the lonely queer girl she'd been in Tennessee.

Even today, as she stepped inside, a million thoughts in her head about her own art, she still caught her breath, eyes wide as she took in the architecture and regular pieces that called the Devon home. She shook her head, laughing softly to herself as she picked up her pace, heading to the back of the museum where all the offices were located, as well as the studio where she'd been working.

"Good morning, Daphne," Nicola said as Daphne entered the studio space.

"Oh, hi," Daphne said as she slipped off her dark gray bomber jacket. Underneath, she wore a tattered Evenflow T-shirt she'd found in a thrift shop in Chelsea and paint-splattered jeans. "You're here early."

Nicola stood near the windows of the large studio space, where Daphne's four completed pieces were currently set up on easels. Other works filled the room, but none of the artists were here yet. Even Nicola, who was dressed impeccably in a black pencil skirt and cobalt-blue silk blouse, didn't usually come in until ten.

It was currently seven thirty, as Daphne still hadn't shaken off the years of guilt-soaked early-rising training in the Love household.

"I am," Nicola said simply. Her arms were folded, brows slightly lowered, and though Daphne wasn't currently facing her pieces, she knew which one Nicola was scrutinizing.

Her fifth piece.

The final piece.

The one she hadn't had time to complete in Clover Lake but knew had to be a part of this series. A conclusion, of sorts, though she knew a person's evolution never really reached its final destination. Still, she couldn't end the series with meeting Elena Watson, and Nicola agreed. If she'd had the time, she could've painted five more pieces, and maybe one day she would. But for now, she needed one more to round out her story.

To end the journey—her own Fool's Passage—on a hopeful, empowering note.

Her stomach fluttered a little, thinking of the Fool.

April's Fool.

April.

She and April hadn't spoken very much since Daphne left Cloverwild two days after Ramona and Dylan's wedding. They'd texted here and there, and of course, Daphne knew April and Sasha were on a road trip together, but Daphne was determined to give April the space she needed.

And the space Daphne herself needed.

Even though, every time she thought of April, she wanted to text her. Cold-call her, just to hear her voice.

And she thought about April a lot. In fact, she was pretty sure all those thoughts were why she couldn't seem to figure out her fifth piece. She also suspected that Nicola was here an hour past sunrise for that very reason.

"I'm concerned," Nicola said.

Daphne sighed quietly, then joined Nicola at her fifth piece.

Her very unformed, very blank-canvas fifth piece.

"I'll figure it out," Daphne said. "I promise."

"I have no doubt about that," Nicola said, turning to look at her. "I'm concerned about timing. You have less than three weeks until the pieces for the show need to be matted and framed. October will be here before you know it."

Daphne pressed her hand to her stomach, which had knotted uncomfortably. "I know."

Nicola eyed her for a second before sighing. "I know this is very personal." She waved her hand toward Daphne's series. "But it's also professional. Do you understand?"

"I do. I promise," Daphne said, nodding vigorously. "I have a plan all worked out."

Nicola's brows lifted. "That's encouraging. I'll leave you to it, then."

"Thank you," Daphne said. "I won't let you down."

Nicola smiled. "I'm counting on it."

Then she left, her heels clicking across the wooden floors like tap shoes. Daphne stood for a few seconds in the silence, breathing heavily and glaring at her empty canvas. Finally, she took out her phone and tapped on her text thread with April. Her thumb hovered over the message window, her stomach even more of a mess now, but then she switched over to a different thread before she could think too much about it.

I'm panicking, she typed.

Three little bubbles popped up immediately, and she exhaled, glad Sasha wasn't in the middle of driving or sleeping, as Daphne had no idea what time zone Sasha was in right now.

Sasha: Still blank?

Daphne: Smooth brain, no wrinkles

Her phone vibrated as Sasha's profile picture—her face with her tongue poking through her first two fingers—popped up on her screen. Daphne slid her thumb over the phone to answer the video call.

"What are you doing?" she whisper-hissed.

"Calm down," Sasha said, clearly cocooned in the bed of some roadside motel. Her platinum hair was impossibly tall and messy, her short cut a little longer than the last time Daphne had seen her. "We got separate rooms tonight because April has a cold and this motel didn't have anything with two beds available."

Daphne frowned, her chest hitching a little. "Is she okay?"

"She's fine. No fever or anything, just sniffly."

Daphne's shoulders loosened, but she still hated the idea of April being sick and her not being there to help—

She squeezed her eyes closed, then shook her head and smiled.

"You're ridiculous," Sasha said.

"Gee, thanks," Daphne said.

Sasha just laughed. "You know what I'm talking about."

"Look," Daphne said, sighing heavily. "Am I in love with April?"

"Rhetorical question, I assume," said Sasha, "as the words *madly* and *deeply* come to mind."

"But am I going to do anything about it right now?" Daphne pressed on.

Sasha scowled, then put on an affected, high-pitched voice, fluttering her hand around in, honestly, an insulting impression. "No, I won't because I'm a strong, independent lady and I don't need anyone."

"Is that supposed to be me?"

"I call it like I see it."

"I need *you*, don't I?"

"You need me because I am, admittedly, brilliant and wise, but also because I'm April adjacent."

Daphne frowned. "Sasha. That's not true. I love you."

"How could you not? My point stands though."

Daphne rubbed her forehead. She *did* love Sasha, but dear god, she was exhausting.

And possibly right.

"Listen, I didn't text you to talk about April," Daphne said. "I need to bounce some ideas off someone for my fifth piece, and I can't do that with Nicola, who is pretty much my boss and probably freaking out that she's backing the wrong horse."

Sasha sat up, sending a hand through her charmingly disastrous hair. She wore a stretched-out white tank top. "One and the same."

"What?"

"April," Sasha said, "and your fifth piece."

Daphne wrinkled her nose, even as something bright started to burn underneath her ribs.

"You didn't get here by yourself," Sasha said, waving her hand at Daphne's face. "This brand-new you."

"I know that."

"So. Let her in. You keep trying to avoid her, give her space, give yourself space, and I get it. I even commend you for going to London alone. You're brave and capable and strong, and you know it now. You've proven it to yourself already, Daph."

Daphne's eyes started to sting a little. "Thanks, Sasha," she said softly.

"Don't thank me yet," Sasha said. "Remember how I called you ridiculous?"

"I recall."

"Well, it bears repeating. You know what that fifth piece is supposed to be. *I* know what that fifth piece is supposed to be. April even knows. Hell, I bet Nicola knows it too."

Daphne groaned, tangled a hand in her faded lavender hair. "This is *my* journey, Sasha. *My* evolution. No one else's."

Sasha's eyes softened. "Exactly."

Daphne went silent for a few seconds, processing, sifting, fighting. She changed the subject, asking where Sasha and April were headed next (Carlsbad Caverns), and if they were still on track to be in LA at the end of October for Jack and Carrie's party (they should roll into Tinseltown on the 31).

After she ended the call, Daphne stood in front of her blank canvas for a long time. She stood and stared and thought until an image formed in her mind. She'd seen the image before, had felt it, even, the warmth and peace and safety.

The love.

And she realized that in order to tell the kind of story she wanted, the story that was *hers*, the story that was true, she didn't need five pieces.

She needed six.

She picked up her pencil and started sketching.

Chapter Thirty-Two

THE END OF October in LA was summer hot. April stared out Gertie's passenger window, her iPad in her lap, stylus dangling loosely in her fingers, and took in the mountains in the distance, a heat haze settling over the city, so wildly different from the East Coast.

For the last three months, she'd actually missed Clover Lake. She hadn't expected to, but she felt a tenderness toward the quaint downtown in her memory, Clover Moon Café and Owen's perfect fries. She missed the lake and the watery sunsets, and she even missed Penny's boundary-crossing inquisitions about her life. She missed her house—though she'd found a renter through the end of the year who more than covered her mortgage—and of course, she missed her cats, who had been staying with Mr. Riley since she'd left. He texted regular pictures, and they'd even video chatted a few times, Bianca with her tail turned up at April, and Bob trying to butt against her face on the phone screen.

She missed Ramona. She knew she always would, but they talked on the phone at least once a week and texted nearly every day. And when a text went unanswered for a day or so, on either of their parts, April was okay.

She felt . . . *good*. She felt like herself.

Honestly, the independence of the last three months had been life-changing. Of course, Sasha had been with her, but Sasha was a bit of a lone wolf herself.

"It takes a lot of alone time to keep up this level of charm," Sasha had said about a week into their trip, sliding noise-canceling headphones over her head in their motel room just outside Chicago, then disappearing for the rest of the night.

And April found she didn't mind.

She needed the time to process . . . well, her entire life. And flying down highways with the wind in her hair and the sun spreading colors all over the western sky, sliding her hands over the smooth striped stone at the Wave, or standing inside a cavern lit with phosphorescence was the perfect environment for some good old-fashioned contemplation.

And goddess, did she contemplate.

She thought and dreamed and longed. She let herself cry when she needed to, let the future terrify her if that was what she felt in that moment.

She let herself miss Daphne.

She let herself text Daphne too, but only once a week, and she'd asked Sasha to hold her to it.

She and Daphne had parted on good terms. After their last night together—a night during which neither of them slept very much, too busy soaking each other in, hands roaming, mouths exploring—they'd stood on the front porch of their cabin and kissed goodbye. They'd made no promises, they'd devised no plan. And while April had spent the rest of that day in a gloomy haze, she knew it was the right thing.

But April knew something else too—she loved Daphne Love, and three months exploring the country with Sasha Sinclair hadn't changed that.

April looked down at her iPad. She'd worked a lot these past three months on her tarot deck, digitizing the twenty-two *Fool's Passage* pieces into Procreate so she could make changes easily, then making plans for fifty-six more pieces for the Minor Arcana. The Major Arcana she'd already created needed a few revisions. For one, she didn't want the person on each card to be *her*. She wanted a diverse cast, all races and genders and shapes. And the Minor Arcana would take some time, a theme for every suit—wands, cups, swords, and pentacles. She was already about halfway through the cups, her favorite suit, and her head was always working on ideas for the rest, ideas for the guidebook she'd write, ideas for a title for her deck.

Star Journey Tarot was her favorite name right now, but she hadn't settled on anything. She planned to run a Kickstarter campaign when the entire project was ready, but she'd also emailed a query letter and samples of her illustrations to several agents in the last month, a process that felt like the fiery depths of hell.

But a thrilling kind of hell.

She wanted to bring her deck to life, she knew that, but she also wanted to work on book covers, illustrate picture books, maybe even work on her own story or graphic novel. She already had a pretty solid Instagram following from her years as a tattooist, and she was excited to start posting different types of art on her page.

She was *excited*.

Period.

And she couldn't remember the last time she'd felt that way. About anything.

Anything other than Daphne Love.

April tucked her iPad back into her bag at her feet as Sasha turned onto Laurel Canyon Boulevard, also known as Love Street.

"Figures," April said, propping her leg up on the seat. Sasha said nothing, and April glanced at her. "You okay?"

Sasha blinked, as though she'd been deep in thought, then frowned. "Yeah, fine."

"Convincing."

Sasha sighed and shrugged. "I used to live around here."

April sat up straighter. In the last three months, Sasha had revealed very little about her past or her family. April had gleaned tiny tidbits, like that Sasha was an only child and her mother was Norwegian, but not much beyond that.

"When did your parents leave LA?"

Sasha pressed her mouth flat. "They didn't."

"I thought they didn't live here anymore."

"They don't."

April rubbed her forehead. "You know, for all your *put yourself first* advice, you're really bad at doing the same."

"I put myself first every day," Sasha said, turning onto a side road.

"And keep everyone else at arm's length," April said. "That's not putting yourself first. That's hiding."

Sasha scowled, but said nothing as they drove deeper into Laurel Canyon, the Maps app on Sasha's phone calling out directions to Jack and Carrie's house. April didn't say anything else as Sasha drove, but when they pulled up in front of a large modern white house surrounded by greenery, water bubbling from a fountain in the front yard, Sasha made no move to get out of the car.

April looked at her, looked at her phone. They still had a couple of hours until the party, but Dylan and Ramona were already here, and April couldn't wait to see Ramona.

"Sash?" April said.

"My parents died," Sasha said, leaning her head against the headrest. "In a car accident. Two years ago. They were documentary filmmakers, and that's all I want to say about it right now, okay?"

She didn't look at April, didn't show any obvious emotion on her face. But April noticed her jaw was tight, her nostrils flaring with the effort of holding back, holding in.

April let the news settle for a second. Suddenly, Sasha's constant refusal to let April drive Gertie over the last few months—even once on the safest, widest road—made a lot more sense. She reached out and took Sasha's hand.

"Okay," she said softly, then squeezed Sasha's fingers before letting her go.

Sasha glanced at her, blue eyes darker than usual, her smile small and grateful. "Do you think Jack and Carrie have any weed?"

April laughed. "From what I hear, they're pretty herbal these days, so it could go either way."

She opened her door to get out, but then her phone buzzed in the cupholder, and when she picked it up, she saw that Ramona had sent her a link. April's thumb hovered over the text, the article's headline already fully visible in the preview.

NEWCOMER SHINES AT THE DEVON

She sucked in a sharp breath.

"What is it?" Sasha asked, releasing the buckle on her seat belt.

It took April a few swallows to answer. "Daphne's show."

"That just closed a couple days ago, yeah?"

April shut herself back into the car and nodded, which was all she could manage at the moment. Of course, she knew the Devon's *Evolution* show had opened a few weeks ago. She and Daphne had texted a bit about it—how Daphne was nervous, how April knew she'd be amazing—but they'd barely talked since it started. April and Sasha had sent her some congratulatory flowers, the card very pointedly from both of them, but other than that, April hadn't wanted to press Daphne too much for details. This was Daphne's moment, Daphne's success, and April wanted her to experience it however she wanted.

Now, April clicked on the article, which led her to the site of a contemporary art magazine based in London. April's eyes had teeth, quickly devouring the words about the show's details, about Nicola, about other artists, chewing ravenously to get to Daphne.

Her heart nearly stopped when she saw Daphne's name in print.

> The shining star of the exhibition, however, is a newcomer from across the pond. Daphne Love hails from Crestwater, Tennessee, and her six-piece series, eerily entitled *Preacher's Daughter*, drew in viewers with her emotional use of texture, color, and theme. An autobiographical series, the paintings depict a young woman unbecoming and becoming, a true evolution of mind, body, and spirit.

April's eyes welled suddenly with tears, a huge smile on her face as she wiped them away.

"She did it," she said to Sasha, laughing. "She fucking did it."

"Of course she did."

April nodded, tears still streaming. The article went on to talk about some commissions Daphne had gotten as a result of the show, a couple of big names in the London art world, as well as invitations from a few reputable galleries and museums, including the Museum of Modern Art in New York City. April's heart felt full and electric, a new rhythm under her ribs. She kept scrolling to where the article featured photographs of Daphne's series. She took in the first four familiar paintings, still as resplendent and moving as they ever were.

Then she got to the fifth piece.

She'd never seen this one, of course. She assumed Daphne had created it, along with the sixth, once she got to London. In the painting, Daphne stood on a cobbled London street, rain falling from a gloomy gray sky. She wore the same white dress, the hem tattered and more than halfway up her thigh, and the sleeves were ripped, revealing her upper arms.

Revealing her tattoo.

Her hair was lavender, blond roots just starting to grow out, creating a lovely ombré effect, and the rain hadn't quite soaked it to her scalp yet.

Her eyes were cast upward toward the sky, and she had a smile on her face, her expression serene, but also anticipatory.

Her features though . . . they were just a hair shy of perfectly clear. April had to zoom in on the digital image, and she still wasn't completely sure, but it definitely looked like her face was still a little bit off, a little blurred.

She scrolled to the last piece, her heart in her throat, and when she saw it, she clapped a hand over her mouth. She couldn't help it.

"Holy shit," she said through her fingers.

"What?" Sasha asked, leaning over Gertie's center console to try and get a glimpse of April's phone. "What's happening?"

But April needed a second to process what she was seeing on her screen.

Daphne's sixth and final painting.

In it, Daphne's facial features were completely clear. It was a closer image of her, just the chest up, and she was smiling widely, showing all of her teeth, her eyes cast down, lavender hair beautiful and curling over her shoulders, the roots just a bit more grown out than the previous painting.

And the white dress was gone.

In this piece, she wore a sky blue dress with a sweetheart

bodice, thin straps over her lovely shoulders. It took April a second to place it, but this was the same dress Daphne had worn the night of the solstice party.

The first time she and April had kissed.

But that wasn't what had made April gasp, what had stolen her words and her breath.

A person stood behind Daphne, their arms circled around her shoulders, holding her back tight against their chest. Their face was mostly hidden, only below their nose visible at the tip of the canvas, their head turned to the side, iridescent hair hitting right at their neck. They wore a gauzy-looking off-the-shoulder top, dark blue and dotted with moons and stars.

And their arms.

Their arms were covered in tattoos. Scorpion girls and flowers and trees, the edge of a tiny pair of scissors visible just inside their elbow, ink curling over their collarbones and shoulders and down their wrists.

"Fuck," Sasha said when April finally angled her phone so Sasha could see. "Is that who I think it is?"

"Do you think it's me?" April finally managed to ask, her voice dazed, her brain whirling.

"Uh, yeah."

"Then I think you're right."

"Hey, you're here!"

April looked up to see Ramona running down the diamond-patterned driveway in a pair of cutoffs and a purple T-shirt with a black cat printed on the front. Dylan was behind her, smiling and waving.

April couldn't get out of the car fast enough. She stuffed her phone into her pocket, eyes welling with tears, and fell into her best friend's arms.

Chapter Thirty-Three

HALF AN HOUR later, April paced in one of Jack and Carrie's many guest rooms, chewing on her thumbnail. The room was calming and beachy with light blue walls, a queen-size bed framed by drapey silks from a custom headboard and covered in blue and cream linens, and a rattan swing chair secured to the ceiling.

"What are you going to do?" Ramona asked. She sat on the edge of the bed with April's phone, staring down at Daphne's paintings.

"I have no idea," April said, throwing herself into the swing chair and causing it to sway like a pendulum. "What the hell *can* I do?"

"You could call her," Ramona said.

"I can't call her," April said, launching herself out of the chair and ambulating the room again. Her heartbeat felt like it was everywhere, the reality of that sixth painting pressing heavier and heavier on her ribs with each second. "What would I say? 'Oh, hey, Daph, um, nice painting, do you like me, check yes or no.'"

Ramona grinned. "Well . . . yeah."

"I can't think about this right now," April said. She flopped onto the bed this time, sending a few throw pillows flying. She propped herself up on one elbow. "How's married life? How's work?"

Ramona laughed. "Oh, no, we FaceTimed for an hour two days ago, so you know exactly how those things are going."

"Blissful. Dream come true," April said drolly, but she was smiling.

"Yes," Ramona said, lifting her chin. "But we're not talking about me right now. We're talking about you and the fact that the woman you love put you in a painting that just made her career."

April groaned, letting her head fall onto the remaining pillows. She felt the mattress shift as Ramona scooted closer, lying down and wrapping her arm over April's stomach.

"I know you're being a moody little Scorpio right now," Ramona said, "but take a breath."

"Spoken like a true Libra," April deadpanned, but she did as Ramona instructed. She breathed. And then breathed a little more, deep inhales and exhales, and soon, she and Ramona were breathing together in tandem, then laughing when they both started to feel dizzy.

"Fine," April said when their lungs and brains had returned to normal functioning. She turned to look at her best friend. "Breathing done. Now what?"

Ramona smiled softly. "Anything you want."

Such a simple phrase—three words, five syllables, but April felt each and every one in the center of her chest.

"Anything I want," she said.

Ramona nodded, then kissed April on the cheek before getting off the bed. "I've got to go get dressed for this thing." She jutted her thumb toward the window, the light outside turning a blue-lavender as evening barreled toward them. April could hear the dull thrum of people setting up for the party in the large backyard.

"Please tell me you and Dylan have matching costumes," April said, remaining prone in the pillows.

"Naturally," Ramona said, then tossed April's phone next to her on the mattress. "You know what to do with that."

"Watch cat videos until I forget my own name?"

Ramona laughed, then closed the door after her as she left the room.

April blew out a breath and stared up at the rattan fan spinning in slow circles. Next to her, her phone felt warm and heavy, like an entire other person was pressed against her side.

Before she could think twice, she grabbed it and tapped on Daphne's name in her messages. She scanned their thread, three months of casual conversation, check-ins, dancing around how April still felt about her.

How Daphne still felt.

April tapped on the message window, a simple question swirling in her brain. Her heart picked up its pace, fingers shaking as excitement and fear coalesced in her chest.

Still, she wanted to say it.

To ask.

She had to know, so her thumbs flew, typing out her question.

Do you still love me? Check yes or no.

Then she hit send.

~

TWO HOURS LATER, the sun had set, and April wandered around alone at a party that could rival one of Gatsby's soirees, sipping on a glass of golden champagne. She hadn't seen Ramona or Dylan since they'd all walked outside together over an hour ago—Ramona dressed in an elaborate Mardi Gras–esque gown and Dylan in a complementing silk suit that Liberace would envy—but at least April looked incredible.

It had taken her nearly two months of sifting through racks in thrift stores all over the country, but she'd finally found the perfect costume for tonight in a tiny shop in Santa Fe. It was black, all lace and sharp shoulders, with lacy leggings underneath a mesh overlay, a lacy bodice that crawled up her neck, bulbed sleeves, and a matching lace mask that covered her entire face from the cheekbones up. It was a little itchy, but she felt like a Victorian femme fatale. All she needed was a whip and a glass of absinthe.

There had to be at least two hundred people here, all of them masked, and the entire back of Jack and Carrie's property was lit with golden lights and filled with partygoers, flowers, streamers, and music. April spotted Sasha by the buffet table—dressed in the fuchsia suit April had insisted she purchase at the same Santa Fe shop—and chatting with a woman with long red hair. Of course, *chatting* may have been a bit of an understatement, as Sasha leaned in close and the woman smiled, eyes glittering beneath her mask at Sasha's charm.

April laughed to herself and walked to the edge of the property to get a little quiet, a little perspective, stopping at a stone barrier that overlooked the deep cuts and ridges of Laurel Canyon. Far beyond, April knew the Pacific was probably visible, but it was too dark to see right now, the stars above sparkling softly.

She took her phone out of a tiny pocket hidden near her waist, glanced at the screen quickly before stuffing it out of sight again.

Nothing from Daphne.

Granted, April had sent the message at nearly one a.m. London time, so there was absolutely no reason to feel the need to fling herself into the canyon.

Metaphorically, of course.

And yet.

She sighed, knocking back the last of her champagne before

turning back toward the house to go fetch another, but stopped short when another person blocked her path.

They were about ten feet away, and wore an ornate grass green dress, all lace and silk, every part of their body hugged tightly and covered. Their mask was shaped like a butterfly, hair piled on top of their head in an elegant mess, the color indiscernible in the evening light.

"God," April said, startling and holding her stomach. "Warn a girl, will you?"

"Sorry," the person said, their green-painted lips curling into a smile, their head tilting.

And April's breath caught.

It caught, tangled, stopped, left her body altogether, because even with that two-syllable word, she knew that voice. She knew that head tilt too. Knew that mouth that was smiling slyly at her right now.

Her own mouth dropped open, and she stepped back a little from the shock of it all. The impossibility.

The person stepped closer though. Closer and closer, April moving backward on instinct until her butt hit the stone wall. The person's hands went to her waist, and April's fingers gripped their lace-covered elbows, faces leaning close, a breath apart.

"Yes," Daphne said. "I check yes."

April laughed, then ripped off her mask before taking Daphne's off a bit more gently. Her eyes were lovely, rimmed with a sparkly green paint and long black lashes.

And they were fixed on April.

"What the hell are you doing here?" April asked, her hands back on Daphne's arms, fingers tightening as though Daphne might vanish at any second, an apparition on the wind.

"I'm here for you," Daphne said.

April closed her eyes for a second, letting those words soak through her skin, her bones, straight to the center of her chest. "Really?"

"Really," Daphne said, her arms circling April's waist now, pulling her closer.

"Why?" April asked, even though she already felt like water in Daphne's hands. She still needed to know.

Daphne was silent for a beat, her eyes searching April's. Finally, she sighed, her arms even tighter around April. "Because I spent three months getting to know myself. Living by myself. Working by myself. Every single choice was my own, every single action was only what I wanted to do."

"Sounds like bliss."

Daphne smiled softly. "It was. And it wasn't."

April said nothing, but her lungs felt frozen, her heartbeats, even her blood flow.

"I needed that time," Daphne said. "I needed it for me, but I needed it for you too."

"For me?"

Daphne leaned her forehead against April's. "I needed the time alone to realize I don't want to be alone. But more than that, I needed the time alone to realize that it wasn't even about being alone. I like myself. I'm strong and capable, even when I'm scared."

April pulled back to look her in the eyes. "You are. You're a wildling. You're a fucking *Leo*."

Daphne laughed but nodded. "I know that now. And part of being strong even when I'm scared is admitting that I want to be with you. I want *you*."

"Me," April said. It wasn't a question, but it wasn't declarative either. More like a whispered word to the stars, some language that hadn't been defined yet.

"You," Daphne said, cupping April's hands in her face. "If you'll have me."

"I'll have you," April said, tears swelling and overflowing quickly. She laughed, took Daphne's face in her hands too. "I'll have you, Daphne Love. For as long as you want me."

She kissed Daphne then, their tears mixing together, both of them laughing as they cried, hands tangling in hair and then roaming down backs to waists and back to each other's faces.

"I love you," April said against her mouth. "I'm so proud of you."

"I'm proud of *you*," Daphne said. "I want to hear everything. How the trip has been, if you've heard from any agents, how your deck is—"

"Wait," April said, tilting her head and smiling. "I didn't tell you about the agents and querying."

Daphne fought her own smile. "Well. I might have . . ."

"You've been talking to Sasha about me."

"Guilty." Daphne grinned.

"You could've asked."

"I didn't want you to feel like you had to tell me things. If you . . ." She took a deep breath. "If you didn't feel the way you had at Cloverwild."

"Well, I do."

Daphne tucked a piece of hair behind April's ear. "I know that now."

"I might have plied Sasha for information too," April said. "Just a little."

Daphne laughed. "Oh, did you?"

"She didn't tell me about painting number six though," April said, growing serious.

Daphne's smile vanished too, but her eyes were shining and soft. "She didn't know. No one did except Nicola."

"It's incredible," April said. "*You're* incredible." Then she kissed Daphne hard, whispering "I can't believe you're here" against her mouth.

"I'm here," Daphne said, and deepened the kiss, their limbs entwining again, tongues exploring. April grew warm, desperate to be out of this ridiculous costume, desperate to peel Daphne's dress from her body, desperate for a bed they didn't have to leave for days or weeks or months.

They came up for air, and April sighed, resting her forehead against Daphne's as they held each other. She knew Daphne had gotten a ton of commissions from the Devon's show. She also knew her own savings were running low, that she wanted to start some freelance work, maybe get a job in a tattoo shop somewhere while she worked on her deck and built up her illustration portfolio. She knew Daphne was here by her side right now. And she knew this was exactly where they both wanted to be.

And she knew she loved Daphne Love.

But that was all. There was so much else she didn't know. Wasn't sure about. But somehow, none of that scared her. And even if it did a little, deep in her bones at her most vulnerable moments, she knew she had Daphne. She had Ramona and she had Dylan. She had Sasha. She had her people.

"What do we do now?" she asked, her hands in Daphne's faded lavender hair.

Daphne pulled her closer, tighter. "Anything we want."

Chapter Thirty-Four

TWO MONTHS LATER

THIRTEEN HOURS BEFORE they boarded a plane bound for London, April led Daphne deep into the snowy Clover Lake woods.

It was late, nearly midnight, and a fresh layer of snow crunched under their boots. In addition to her mint-green peacoat and matching hat, a lavender scarf Ramona had knitted her for Christmas, and a pair of vegan leather mittens, Daphne also wore a blindfold.

"Don't let me fall," she said.

"I promise," April said, her arm looped through Daphne's, her own puffy black coat and dark purple knit hat keeping her moderately warm. Her teeth chattered a little, but she felt a giddiness in her chest as they walked, the light of the silvery full moon so bright on the path that she hadn't even needed to use her phone to see.

She knew this trail like the back of her hand.

Daphne's feet tangled with a root, and she and April broke into laughter as April struggled to hold them both upright.

"Are we in the woods?" Daphne asked.

"Nah," April said as she guided Daphne over a log that had

fallen across the trail, probably during the last heavier snow. "We're in the middle of downtown."

"Very funny," Daphne said.

April laughed, loving every minute of this.

Since LA, she and Daphne had been traveling between Chicago and New York City and even Boston, all cities where Daphne's new agent had set up meetings for her with galleries to discuss showings and commissions. As a result, Daphne had at least a year's worth of work ahead of her, as well as a contract with the Devon as their artist-in-residence.

Tomorrow, she'd be heading back to London, and April was going with her, along with Bob and Bianca.

Permanently.

She and Daphne had signed a lease on a tiny, pet-friendly flat in Soho that Nicola had helped them find. April already had an interview set up next week with a queer-owned tattoo shop called Medusa, and she'd just sent a fresh batch of query emails to agents who represented illustrators.

April couldn't wait to get settled in London. The transient nature of her life for the last five months had ignited in her a passion for travel and discovering new places, but it had also cemented her desire for a home.

A new home.

She loved Clover Lake. She always would, and she'd probably miss it more than she could imagine right now, but she was ready for something new.

She was ready for a life she chose with her whole heart.

Despite her readiness, she and Daphne had spent the last two weeks staying with Ramona and Dylan in Clover Lake. The time had been bittersweet, soul filling and heart healing, but tinged with the weight of the extra miles April and Ramona were about to put between them.

But it was right.

They both knew it, and they could celebrate that.

Earlier that day, April and Daphne had had a perfectly civil lunch with April's parents, followed by a much more raucous dinner at Mr. Riley's house, which included Olive and her girlfriend, Marley. It had felt like old times, but better with Ramona's wife and April's partner by their sides, as well as Bob and Bianca. Bob, of course, attached himself to Daphne the moment he saw her and threw a fit if she so much as went to the bathroom.

April smiled to herself now, squeezing Daphne closer and glancing up at the starry night as they approached their destination.

"You're looking at the sky, aren't you?" Daphne asked.

April laughed. "How did you know?"

"You went all quiet and contemplative."

"You know me too well."

"Okay, that's sweet and all, but I'd rather you look straight ahead when I can't see a damn thing."

April laughed harder. "That's fair, but we're almost there and I don't see a single obstacle in our path."

"And where might that be?"

April grinned, even though Daphne couldn't see her. After dinner, April had asked Daphne to go for a walk and had promptly slipped a blindfold over her eyes the second they were outside. Daphne, very much used to April's quirks by this point, had simply laughed and let herself be led into the woods, though they could be walking down the side of I-93 for all she knew.

Finally, the path broadened and opened into a small circular clearing, a spot April always thought of as a kind of fairy ring when she was small. Over the years, through hopes and heartbreaks, the clearing had lost its magic for her, this spot in particular, and she was ready to change that.

She was ready to believe in magic again.

"Okay, we're here," she said, pulling Daphne to a stop in front of her. She lifted the blindfold gently, and Daphne blinked even though the light was already dim, nothing but a purple-white glow from the moon.

Daphne looked around, and it took her a second or two, but realization finally broke over her expression.

"Moon Lovers Trail," she said, her voice soft and whispered. Her eyes snapped back to April's. "You brought me back to Moon Lovers Trail."

"I did," April said, sliding her gloved hands around Daphne's waist. "Before we left, I wanted a do-over."

"A do-over?"

April nodded. "This is the first place we kissed, and I feel so different now. I feel softer and braver and more like myself, and I wanted to kiss you on this trail under a full moon on purpose. Just as we are right now."

Daphne looped her arms over April's shoulders. "I'd really like that."

"Yeah?" April asked, pressing closer so that their noses bumped. "Even though it means we might live happily ever after?"

"Especially because it means we might live happily ever after."

April smiled, and their mouths were a breath apart when she pulled back a fraction. "First, we should draw a tarot card."

She reached into her coat and pulled out her favorite tarot deck, which she'd slipped into her pocket after dinner, the wheels of her plan already spinning in her head. She held out the deck between them carefully, and in the middle of the stack of cards, she'd placed a folded piece of paper. The edges stuck out of the deck, clearly torn from a sketchbook or notebook.

Daphne frowned at her, but April said nothing, simply lifted her brows, hoping Daphne would go for the obvious choice. Just as she hoped, Daphne wiggled the piece of paper carefully from the deck in April's hands, then held it up between them.

"Is this my card?" she asked.

"You pulled it," April said, shrugging. "It must be."

Daphne grinned as she unfolded the paper carefully, as though it might turn to ash in her hand. Once it was fully unfurled, her eyes roamed the image on the paper, her mouth dropping open a little when she realized what she was looking at.

It was the tarot card sketch of the two of them in the lake at Mirror Cove that April had drawn back in the summer. Their hair was wet, April's tattoos on full display, Daphne's fingertips just grazing April's face, their lips close in a near kiss.

The Lovers.

April had torn the drawing out of her sketchbook that night, but she'd found it tucked in the back pocket a few weeks ago, and she knew this was the exact image she wanted to use for the Lovers card in her tarot deck. She'd reworked every other Major Arcana so that she wasn't the main character, but this one . . . this was hers and Daphne's.

Their journey.

And she wanted to share it with the world.

But first, she wanted to share it with Daphne.

"It's us," Daphne said, her voice trembling with emotion.

"It's us," April said, then explained how she wanted this card to be a part of her deck.

"I think it's perfect," Daphne said. "I think you're perfect."

April laughed. "Perfect for you, maybe."

"Exactly," Daphne said, then took April's face in her hand, the paper crinkling between her fingers. "Kiss me, April Evans."

And so, April did.

Acknowledgments

Every book is different, each one an adventure with its own challenges and triumphs. April's story, much like April herself, is my recalcitrant child. She went through many iterations before I finally found her story, but once I did, I fell in love with her. Daphne's own journey into queerness and with her past is very close to my heart. While not a mirror of my experience, it's certainly a window, and I'm grateful to be able to put a bit of that experience into words.

Thank you to my agent, as always, my literary ride or die, Rebecca Podos.

Thank you to my editor, Angela Kim, for your patience and trust while I found April's story—and changed everything thirty thousand words in. This was not an easy story, but you believed I'd find it and, even more, allowed me the space to find it. Thank you for your editorial insights along the way, brilliant as always. And thank you, Elizabeth Vinson, for your keen editorial thoughts as well.

I have an amazing team at Berkley, so thank you, Kristin Cipolla, Elisha Katz, Kim-Salina I, and Tara O'Connor, for supporting this book through publication and beyond.

Thank you, Katie Anderson, for the stunning cover design. Thank you, Leni Kauffman, for the breathtaking cover illustration. You both capture the spirit and emotions of my characters so perfectly—you're a dream come true!

Thank you, Brooke Wilsner, for being my first reader, as always, and a great friend. Your faith in me and enthusiasm mean the world.

Thank you, Kathryn Johnson, for being my Tuesday work date, for listening, and for being a friend. Thank you to my Night Coven—Julia, Natalie, Kathryn, and Sarah—for all the spicy cherry margaritas and laughs. I'm ready for the coffee cup tattoo when you are.

Thank you, Christina, Zabe, Emma, and Crash, for your friendship, encouragement, and memes.

Thank you, Meryl, for your friendship, humor, and love. Each day is a gift, and I'm grateful for all of ours.

Thank you, Craig, Benjamin, William, Luna, and Hazel. You are my home and always will be.

Keep reading for an excerpt of

Take a Chance, Sasha Sinclair

The next contemporary romance by Ashley Herring Blake

AS SOON AS Sasha Sinclair drove over the town line, she felt it.

Granted, she wasn't sure what *it* was. Not exactly.

A puff of frigid air.

A shiver lifting the hairs on the back of her neck.

Or, much more likely, *it* was simply a cool day in early October and had nothing at all to do with the fact that Blair Mountain, North Carolina, was considered one of the most haunted towns in America.

She drove Gertie—her well-loved Subaru Outback, naturally named for the iconic butch lesbian Gertrude Stein—into the city center. The trees rose up like sentinels guarding the mountain pass, maples and yellowwoods and sweet gums just starting to shift their colors from green to gold and crimson. Decorative banners hung from lampposts and fluttered in the breeze—a deep purple background with an ombré red-orange rose in the middle—and round pumpkins already dotted the sidewalks, fall-leafed wreaths placed on shop doors like town seals.

Sasha pulled into a parking spot near a café called Roseleaf and stepped outside. The air was certainly cool, bordering on cold. She pulled her olive-green bomber jacket closer around her thin frame, ran a hand through her short white-blond hair so that it stuck up even taller than normal, and looked around.

She'd never been to Blair Mountain.

And yet, everything around her looked slightly familiar, tinged with a blurry glow of childhood memories and nostalgia.

Stories.

And the smell . . . She inhaled deeply, trying to place it. It took her a second, but when she did, her heart fluttered under her ribs. There, just beneath that dying-leaf smell of autumn and a bit of sugar, was the subtle scent of roses.

Even in the dead of winter, Sash, her father had told her more than once. *Roses, like tiny miracles. Tiny stories that need to be told.*

Sasha shook her head, then rubbed furiously at her nose as though she could clear out the scent.

Clear out the memory.

She turned and leaned her butt against Gertie's driver door, then closed her eyes. Breathed in deep, trying to get her thickening throat to unclench.

In the last three years, she'd lived in over fifty American cities, as well as Paris, Prague, and Lisbon. She'd driven from coast to coast in her gay car and worked as a line cook, a bartender, a ski-school instructor, and a farmhand mucking out stalls and feeding chickens. She'd shot the proverbial shit at countless small-town watering holes, made easy friends wherever she went—no matter how fleeting those friendships might be—and engaged with a bevy of enthusiastic local shes and theys for a night or two of stringless fun.

So, no, she would not be brought down by a tiny Southern town she'd never even been to before at the sheer whiff of a ghost rose.

Absolutely fucking not.

This was work.

This was a job.

The job, granted, the one she'd been waiting three years for, the one her parents had only dreamed about, but still. She had too much on the line to blow it with sticky emotions and memories.

She glanced at her phone—10:53 a.m. She still had seven minutes before she was supposed to meet Adeline Bishop in Roseleaf, and she might need all four hundred and twenty seconds to get her shit together. She hadn't expected this feeling—a tight pull in the center of her chest, an amalgamation of dread and excitement, her fingertips tingling like she couldn't get enough oxygen—but maybe she should have. *Feelings*, however, weren't exactly her strong suit lately.

Not for three years now.

And that was exactly how she liked it.

She tucked her phone into her back pocket, then bounced up and down on her booted toes, stretching her neck from side to side like she was a boxer heading into the ring. She should review one of the myriad files she had packed in her bag, all filled with her parents' research about Blair Mountain and the Bishops and the Rose Witch. That would be the smart thing to do, prepare as much as possible, but by now she'd heard every bullet point in those folders a million times as a bedtime story, read through the news clippings and articles and book excerpts herself on countless nights in one nameless town after another. She knew it all, could probably recite it in her sleep. And right now, she needed to get her heart rate under control, not amp it up again with more awareness about how important this meeting was.

How much she wanted this.

And how much she dreaded it.

Fucking *emotions*, she swore to god.

So instead of digging into her files, she gave herself a pep talk, trying to fill her brain with . . . she didn't know. Wrinkly pugs and leather jackets. Pumpkin-spiced doughnuts. The strong cortado she was craving, and hoping against hope that this small-town café could make a decent version of, which then reminded her of her stint in Lisbon this past summer and that barista she'd met on her last night there, how Sasha had wrapped her long auburn hair around her fist and—

Okay, no, that was definitely not helping. The last thing Sasha needed was to show up for a meeting with the matriarch of the infamous Bishop family all *charged.*

She cleared her throat, did some more neck stretching and toe bouncing, garnering strange looks from a few passersby on the sidewalk. With four minutes still left to fill, she was glad when her phone buzzed against her butt. She fished the device from her pocket, then tapped on a text from April on the screen.

Met the Sanderson Sisters yet?

Sasha smirked. Wrong town.

Send me a picture of a witch flying a vacuum cleaner through the starry night, I beg you.

This was followed up with three praying hands emojis, and Sasha couldn't help but laugh. She'd just seen April and her girlfriend, Daphne, in London a few months ago, but she had to admit, she felt this strange ache in her chest when she thought of her little Goth friend. She was pretty sure the sensation was akin to *missing,* which was not something she often let herself feel for anyone she encountered along her travels. April, however, was proving harder to shake than most. She'd met April and her partner, Daphne, a little over a year ago in Clover Lake, New Hampshire, while she worked as a bartender at a lakeside lodge, and April had accompanied her on a three month-long road trip across the country last September. Since then, April texted every few days, and

Sasha, despite her usual operating procedure once she'd moved on from a place or person, always answered.

If I see someone airborne and straddling a vacuum cleaner, I'm getting a CAT scan, she texted. Sending you a pic will be the least of my concerns.

Killjoy, April texted back.

I think you mean logical.

April sent a rolling eyes emoji, then texted, Good luck! And go easy on yourself. Your horoscope says you're being too self-critical.

Sasha sent back her own rolling eyes emoji, along with a middle finger emoji. April simply cackled. Literally, she texted the word *cackles* set in between two asterisks.

Oh and Daphne says hey.

Sasha texted back her own greeting, then clicked her phone's screen dark. April knew about this job, about the film. Firstly, it was hard to keep secrets from the woman. Regardless of the fact that she was barely five foot two, she was slightly scary. Secondly, the story of the Rose Witch was nationally famous, as was the town of Blair Mountain, and despite Sasha's desire to keep things on the surface, she also didn't lie to people who had been good to her.

April and Daphne were the only two people in Sasha's life who knew about her parents, and even then, when she'd told them both this past spring about Blair Mountain and her parents' dream, she'd kept it brief. Sasha hadn't shared her story with anyone else she'd met in the last three years. It only made things awkward and uncomfortable, their expressions morphing from interest to horror to pity, *I'm so sorry*s falling out of their mouths automatically, as though words could change one goddamn thing. Even after she'd gotten to know April, spent hours on the road with her, laughed with her and watched her moon over Daphne during their time apart last fall, Sasha had a hard time sharing her baggage. It was *hers*, after all, and she'd carried it just fine for the last three years.

She checked her phone one more time—one minute to go—then opened Gertie's back door and grabbed her father's worn messenger bag. It was the color of caramel and still smelled of leather, despite its age. She tucked her phone into a side pocket, then slung the bag over her shoulder before locking the car and heading toward the café.

She walked quickly. Confidently. Boots clomping heavily on the cobbled sidewalks. More than once, she'd been told she had Big Dyke Energy, and honestly, she agreed. She was five foot ten, knew exactly how to wear a plain white tee and tight-fitting jeans, and had worn her naturally platinum blonde hair very short and very gay since she was fifteen. She had the walk—a bit of a saunter, bit of a stomp—she had the crooked grin, and she knew how to sit with her legs spread on an airplane without pissing off her seatmate.

Right now though, she could feel her shoulders trying to squeeze themselves around her neck, like an animal curling up for a nap. She pulled open Roseleaf's heavy oak door, hinges squeaking, and stepped into what felt like another world. The space was small and cozy and warm. Mismatched chairs and tables filled the space, with a teal-colored tufted love seat by the window. The walls were either exposed brick or a shabby chic–style floral wallpaper, and almost completely covered with framed vintage art and photographs, everything from images of herbs and cauldrons to nameless people with liquid eyes and sad mouths. The oak bar featured mismatched stools as well, with countless colorful bottles and jars lining the wall behind. Plants were everywhere, greenery spilling over shelves and drooping across tables, as well as a few pops of orange from tiny pumpkins here and there.

Sasha blinked, trying to take in the full effect, but there was so much to look at, so much to process, she ended up just staring open-mouthed while every patron inside stared back.

Big Dyke Energy, indeed.

She snapped her mouth shut and straightened her posture. She wasn't sure what Adeline Bishop looked like, as the Bishop family didn't exactly post selfies online. They owned two businesses in Blair Mountain—Thornrose Apothecary, a tea shop that Alice Bishop, aka, the Rose Witch, opened when she moved to town in 1901; and Ghostlight, a small, occult-themed amusement park featuring palm readings and haunted mountain coasters, which Georgianna Bishop began in 1955 with nothing more than a striped tent where she put on strange and spooky shows for the townsfolk. Each business had a social media presence, but Sasha had yet to see a single photograph of any Bishop—they were all women, all unmarried, all living under the same roof, if Sasha's research held up—and she was prone to believe that was intentional.

If she were a member of the infamous Bishop family, she wasn't sure she'd splash her face all over the internet either.

Still, when she locked eyes with the amber gaze of the woman in her late fifties sitting on the love seat, alone, with long salt-and-pepper hair and an appraising slant to her full mouth, Sasha felt something flicker in her gut.

Adeline Bishop.

Had to be.

She was dressed plainly, medium-wash jeans and a drapey green sweater, brown boots that laced halfway up her calves with an ironically witchy heel. Her nails were painted dark purple. Sasha approached her with more confidence than she felt, knuckles going white around her bag's strap.

"Ms. Bishop?" she asked as soon as she was close enough. The hum of the café had started up again, but Sasha still felt as though every eye in the place was stuck to her back.

The woman smiled without her teeth. "How did you know?" Her voice was like butter, smooth and calm and devastating. "Do I look like a witch?"

Sasha opened her mouth. Closed it. No clue what the hell to say to that.

Luckily, Ms. Bishop revealed her teeth then—straight and white, definitely not filed down to sharp points like some idiots on the internet suggested of the Bishop women—and laughed.

"Please, call me Adeline," she said, then motioned to the space next to her on the love seat. "Do you need a drink?"

Sasha unhooked her bag from around her shoulder and sat on the edge of the sofa. "Thank you, yes, I was going to get a cor—"

"I have tea," Adeline said, then picked up a pink milk-glass teapot from the circular coffee table and poured a stream of shimmering liquid into a matching teacup. She added a dollop of golden honey before handing the beverage over to Sasha.

Sasha took the delicate cup, a thick, sweet scent rising with the steam. Adeline lifted a brow, clearly waiting for Sasha to drink. Sasha sipped, expecting to hate it—she hated tea, all of which tasted like barely flavored bathwater, in her opinion—but her eyes fluttered closed as the liquid hit her tongue.

It was warm, of course, and a little sweet. Something floral played underneath, almost perfume-like, though it wasn't overpowering. And instead of smiling politely and setting the cup down, Sasha took another sip.

"Good?" Adeline said.

Sasha nodded, her eyelids languid, her limbs a bit heavy. She wasn't sleepy, exactly, just relaxed.

"It's our Peace Tea blend," Adeline said. "A little passionflower, violet blossoms, a sprig of thyme." She glanced down Sasha's form. "Two sprigs, actually. Calms the nerves."

Sasha set the dainty cup on the table and rested her elbows on her knees, leaning forward in a way that usually charmed strangers. "Does it seem like my nerves need calming?"

Adeline simply smiled again, wholly uncharmed, it would seem. She plucked a familiar navy blue envelope from the pocket of her jeans and set it on the table. "Now. About your letter."

Sasha sat up straight and inhaled sharply, her cheeks flooding with heat and color. Sasha Sinclair didn't often blush, but that letter certainly did the trick. She'd written it two months ago, soon after her visit with April and Daphne, then dropped it into a red cylindrical public mailbox in the middle of the night in Lisbon, the business address from Thornrose's website scribbled across the paper.

She'd also been slightly high when she penned the missive, a detail she planned to leave out of this conversation altogether. Sasha never drank, but she did enjoy a preroll or a gummy from time to time, even though weed tended to make her a bit more emotional than her usual methods of operation, a bit more pensive. Still, she meant every word in that letter, and she was pretty sure the contents had helped land her this meeting, when every other effort to make contact with the Bishop family before now had failed.

Her parents had tried for years, since before Sasha was born and for as long as she could remember after. They'd never gotten a positive response. Her parents had even visited Blair Mountain a few times, always meeting with a door slammed in his face, or the professional runaround.

The Bishop family has no interest in being the subject of a documentary. Thank you very much for your inquiry, now kindly fuck off.

Essentially.

Two months ago, after an admittedly lonely night in Lisbon, Sasha had popped not one but two sour-apple-flavored gummies, and had planned to sit out on her balcony in her rented loft, stare at the stars, and listen to sad music, when she found herself pouring her emotional baggage onto a piece of creamy paper she'd found in the vintage desk by the window. She'd forgone titles and pretense, scribbling messily and quickly.

Dear Adeline . . .

"Intriguing," Adeline said now, tapping a nail against the paper.

"Is it?" Sasha asked.

"You're sitting here, aren't you?" Adeline said.

Sasha let herself smile. "I am."

Six weeks after Sasha had mailed the letter, she'd received an email from Adeline inviting her to come to Blair Mountain for a chat. No details other than a time and place, no explanation as to what the hell *a chat* actually meant.

And here Sasha was, details be damned.

"The only daughter of two reputable documentary filmmakers," Adeline said, pulling the letter free from the envelope. "Wandering the globe and looking for a purpose after their untimely deaths."

Sasha swallowed hard, felt her jaw clench a little. Of course, she was well aware what she'd written in that letter.

Dear Adeline, my name is Sasha Sinclair, and my parents have been dead for three years . . .

But hearing it summed up so succinctly and spoken out loud—and by Adeline Bishop of all people, the current matriarch of the Bishop family, whose story had been Sasha's parents' dream project for decades—hit a bit differently than it had when she was dreamily high and spilling her guts in the middle of the night four thousand miles away in a rare moment of desperation.

Honestly, she hadn't expected a response. And she certainly hadn't expected to be sitting here with Adeline herself.

"I remember your parents," Adeline said now, tilting her head.

Sasha's eyes widened. "You do?"

Adeline nodded, waving the opened letter through the air. "They wrote to me often, and to my mother before I took over operations ten years ago. Visited once or twice, as I recall. They were passionate, I'll give them that. Julian and Freya Sinclair."

Sasha's heart did something at the sound of their names, a flutter or skip or crack.

Adeline's amber eyes narrowed softly. "You look like her."

Sasha had to glance down then, clench her teeth together to keep something inside—what, exactly, she wasn't sure. Sadness, elation, pride. It was all there, bubbling like a witch's brew. She inhaled slowly, remembering standing with her mother in front of her bathroom mirror on the day of her high school graduation, robed in royal blue, colorful tassels and ribbons looped around her neck. Her mom had smiled at her, dressed in a breezy green maxi dress, then made a joke about her doppelganger heading out into the world with an unfair lack of crow's feet. They'd both laughed, their matching sapphire-blue eyes glittering in the glass, matching pale Norwegian skin, matching blond hair the color of whipped butter, only the length betraying any difference.

Sasha forced herself to look up, but only when she was sure she could speak without her voice trembling did she say, "I do."

Adeline went silent then, watching Sasha intently, comfortably. "How did it happen?" she finally asked.

Sasha's throat went tight again. "Car accident." She said it fast, a common phrase, too common in her world now. She prayed to April's stars Adeline wouldn't ask for more details. It was on the internet anyway, a tragedy laid out under a few words tapped into a search engine.

Adeline simply nodded, her expression grave but free from pity. "I've seen a few of their films. They were talented."

Sasha's smile was quick. Small, but definitely genuine. "Really? Do you have a favorite?"

Adeline thought for a second, sipped her tea, clearly in no hurry whatsoever. Sasha was happy to wait though, happy to hear something about her parents' artistic legacy.

"What can I say," Adeline said, "I'm a sucker for a good missing persons story."

"*Fae and Foe*," Sasha said, nodding vigorously, recalling the penultimate film her parents had ever made about Margaret Winder, an iconic fantasy author who had faked her own disappearance in the thirties to run off with the woman she loved. It had been nominated for an Oscar that year—Best Documentary Feature Film—though it had lost out to a film about an underground music movement in Chicago.

"One of my favorites too," Sasha finally said.

"I read all of Margaret Winder's books to my daughters when they were little," Adeline said. "She was a legend."

"My parents did the same."

Adeline tipped her chin in acknowledgment. "And you worked with them?"

"I did. I studied film at USC, then joined their company after I graduated." Sasha had worked on all her parents' films in her twenties, doing everything from taking lunch orders and making coffee runs, to revising scripts, blocking scenes, and thinking through things like lighting and music for the most emotional impact.

On the last couple of films, however—*Fae and Foe* included—Sasha had worked mostly on the human relations side of things. She loved being behind a camera, loved setting up shots and thinking through the visuals, and she was good at it. But she was *great* at talking to people. And more importantly, getting them to talk back. There were eighteen-hour days followed by sleepless nights when she should've been resting but was thinking about how to get a recalcitrant subject to open up. There was irritation and elation, shadowing someone for days for just ten minutes of life-changing recollection. Bringing true stories to a screen, figuring out how to fit an entire life, entire legends and tragedies and triumphs, into two hours on a strip of film was hard work. It was thankless and grueling, even painful at times, requiring tough decisions and sacrifices, constantly walking that delicate line between truth telling and intrusion, but Sasha's parents had loved it.

Sasha had loved it.

"And since they died?" Adeline asked.

Sasha folded her hands in her lap. She knew this question was coming. "Aurora Films is mine."

"But you haven't made any films since."

Sasha lifted her brows. It wasn't a question.

"I do my homework, Sasha," Adeline said.

Sasha sighed. "No. I haven't. I've been finding my way for the last few years."

"And your way is here? In Blair Mountain with a witch's family?"

"*Are* you a witch's family?"

Adeline just laughed.

Sasha laughed too, though her stomach was in knots. Adeline Bishop was incredibly intriguing and simultaneously incredibly hard to read, but that just made Sasha want to dig deeper, try harder. She knew what her father would say—Adeline was putting up a defense mechanism, a survival tactic born from decades of family myth and discrimination, an entire town that both feared the Bishops and used their infamy to put money in their own pockets. Sasha could picture exactly how her mother would create a scene with the Bishop family, sketching it all out in words, beautiful and tragic and compelling.

What this scene was, exactly, Sasha couldn't say. She was the wrong Sinclair altogether to be finally drinking tea with a Bishop. But here she was, chasing a dream she wasn't sure she could make come true. Even if Adeline agreed to the film, Sasha certainly wasn't the award-winning Julian and Freya Sinclair.

Still, she had to try. The ongoing story of Alice Bishop and her descendants was the golden goose of the documentary film world, not only for Julian and Freya, but for most of their peers as well. Sasha wasn't sure she'd even be in Blair Mountain this time tomorrow, but she was here today. She had a chance, a moment. A purpose.

"Why meet with me now?" Sasha asked.

Adeline only lifted a single devastating brow.

"My parents reached out countless times," Sasha went on. "They wrote, they knocked on your door, they emailed, they called. You always said no. I'm sure you've had other offers as well, other filmmakers clamoring for your story. So why me?"

Adeline leaned forward, her strange eyes like tiny circles of fire. "Because no one, not your parents, not anyone else, ever told me *why*."

Sasha's eyes flicked down to the letter still on the table—that humiliating, vulnerable, heart-on-her-sleeve letter. "And my *why* is enough?"

"For now," Adeline said, picking up Sasha's letter and folding it into her pocket again.

Sasha's already erratic heart stopped beating altogether. "What does that mean?"

Adeline sighed. "I understand something about family expectations. The Bishops have a complicated relationship with that word—

legacy. We hold it too close, or we don't hold it close enough. We're proud of it, we resent it, we fear it."

Sasha forced herself to keep eye contact, her palms sweating. "And what's your relationship to your legacy right now?"

Adeline's smile was small as she sipped her tea, eyeing Sasha over the pink rim of her cup. "That's the question, isn't it? And that's why I'm saying yes."

It took a few seconds for the word—simple, three letters—to really sink into Sasha's consciousness.

"Yes?" she asked.

"That's what I said," Adeline said.

"You're saying yes."

Adeline laughed. "Careful, I might change my mind."

"No, no, god," Sasha said. "Sorry. I just . . ." She exhaled. "I'm surprised. I didn't think I had a chance in hell."

Adeline shrugged. "You still might not. Whatever paperwork you're going to make me sign, I have a few conditions. Actually, just one."

Sasha said nothing. She waited while Adeline set her tea down and looked around the room—a room full of townsfolk where no one had said hello to her, no one had waved. A room full of glances and whispers.

"I get final approval," Adeline said. "My entire family, in fact. We all have to agree on the final product."

"Of course," Sasha said automatically. She wasn't sure if that was the right answer, to be honest. She'd never dealt with the contracts for Aurora Films, nor had she ever consulted with their lawyer about the wording. One thing she knew for sure—she wanted to make a film that the Bishop family would love.

"You're sure?" Adeline said. "Think about it for a second. You make an entire film about my family, pour your heart and soul and mind and money into it, something to make your own parents proud, and then I pull the plug."

Sasha inhaled slowly and tried not to let the sudden swell of panic show on her face.

"Or more likely," Adeline said, "my daughter pulls it."

"Your daughter."

"My eldest," Adeline said, then smiled fondly, almost mischievously. "She's going to hate this project. She's going to hate *you*."

Sasha sat back and set an ankle on her knee. Now *this* was familiar territory. This was where Sasha Sinclair shined. "Is that a challenge?"

Adeline laughed. "My dear, it's a gauntlet."

Sasha laughed too, feeling completely at ease. She linked her hands and placed them behind her head. "Gauntlet accepted."

Photo provided by the author

ASHLEY HERRING BLAKE is an award-winning author. She loves coffee, cats, melancholy songs, and happy books. She is the author of the adult romance novels *Delilah Green Doesn't Care*, *Astrid Parker Doesn't Fail*, *Iris Kelly Doesn't Date*, *Make the Season Bright*, and *Dream On, Ramona Riley*, the young adult novels *Suffer Love*, *How to Make a Wish*, and *Girl Made of Stars*, and the middle-grade novels *Ivy Aberdeen's Letter to the World*, *The Mighty Heart of Sunny St. James*, and *Hazel Bly and the Deep Blue Sea*. She's also a coeditor of the young adult romance anthology *Fools in Love*. She lives on a very tiny island off the coast of Georgia with her family.

VISIT ASHLEY HERRING BLAKE ONLINE

AshleyHerringBlake.com

AshleyHBlake

AEHBlake